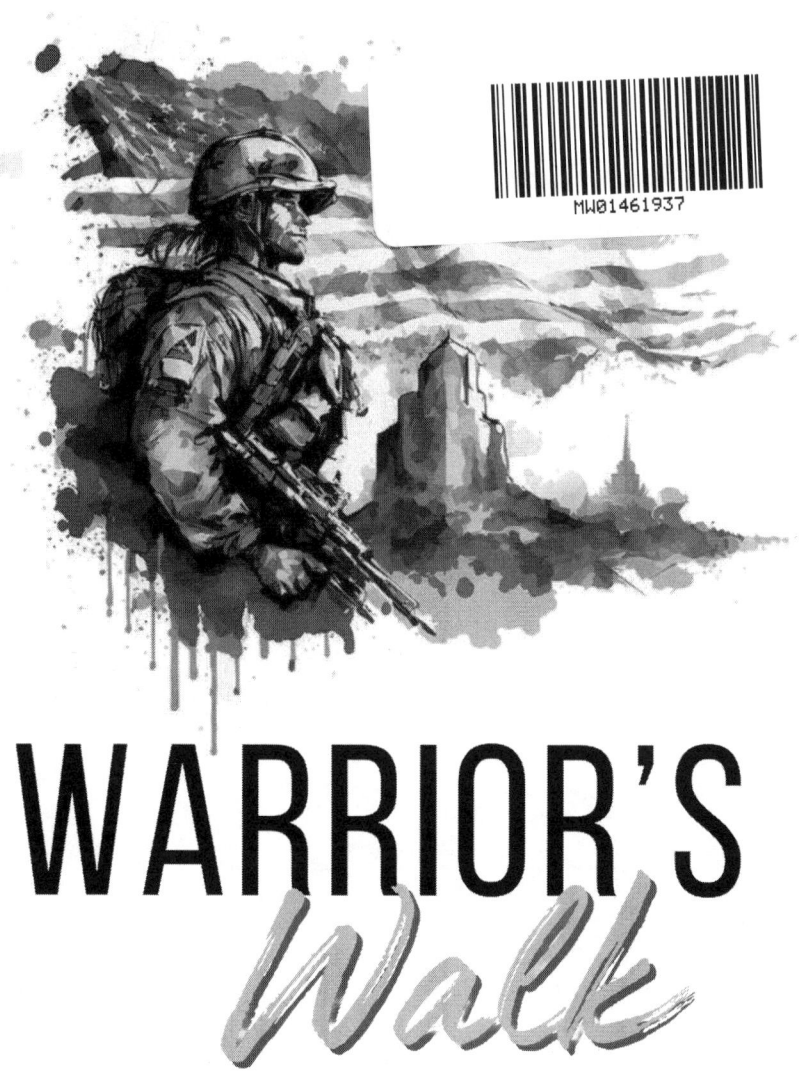

WARRIOR'S
Walk

SCARS AND STRIPES TRILOGY THREE

RAQUEL RILEY

THE COMBAT MEDIC'S CREED

My task is to provide to the utmost limits of my capability the best possible care to those in need of my aid and assistance.

To this end I will aid all those who are needful, paying no heed to my own desires and wants; treating friend, foe and stranger alike, placing their needs above my own.

To no man will I cause or permit harm to befall, nor will I refuse aid to any who seek it.

I will willingly share my knowledge and skills with all those who seek it.

I seek neither reward nor honor for my efforts for the satisfaction of accomplishment is sufficient.

These obligations I willingly and freely take upon myself in the tradition of those that have come before me.

These Things I Do So That Others May Live.

Combat Medics never stand taller than when they kneel to treat the wounded!

Saving Lives in the midst of utter chaos!

Airborne Creed

I am an Airborne trooper!

I jump by parachute from any plane in flight. I volunteered to do it, knowing full well the hazards of my choice.

I serve in a mighty Airborne Force – famed for deeds in War – renowned for readiness in peace.
It is my pledge to uphold its honor and prestige in all that I am – in all I do.

I am an elite trooper – a sky trooper – a spearhead trooper.

I blaze the way to far flung goals – behind, before, above my country's enemy's front lines.

I know that someday I may have to fight without support for days on end. Therefore, I keep my mind and body always fit to do my part in any Airborne mission. I am self reliant and unafraid. I shoot true, and march fast and far.
I fight hard and will excel in everything I do just in case of war.

I will never fail a fellow paratrooper. I cherish the sacred trust and the lives of men with whom I serve.
Leaders have my fullest loyalty, and those who I lead will never, never find me lacking.

I have pride in being Airborne! I will never let it down! In peace, I do not shrink from the dullest duty nor
protest the toughest training. My weapon and equipment will always be combat ready.
I will be neatly dressed, show courtesy and watch my behavior in a proper Airborne military manner.

In battle, I fear no enemy's ability, nor underestimate his ability, power or threats. I will fight him with all my might and skills – staying
alert to avoid traps and try to escape if I should ever be captured.
I will never surrender while I still have the means to fight, though I may be the last paratrooper.

My goal in peace and war is to succeed in any mission of the day or night, even though I may die doing so.
For I belong to a proud and glorious team…

The AIRBORNE, the ARMY, my Country – the UNITED STATES OF AMERICA. I am its chosen few,
I volunteer to fight where others may not want to go or serve.

I am a trooper of the sky! I am my Nation's best! In peace and war I will never fail, Anytime, Anyplace, Anywhere…I am Airborne!
I volunteered as a parachutist, fully realizing the hazard of my chosen service and by my thoughts and
actions will always uphold the prestige, honor and high esprit-de-corps of parachute troops.

I realize that a parachutist is not merely a Soldier who arrives by parachute to fight, but is an elite shock trooper and that his country
expects him to march farther and faster, to fight harder, and to be more self-reliant than any other Soldier.
Parachutists of all allied armies belong to this great brotherhood.

I shall never fail my fellow comrades by shirking any duty or training, but will always keep myself
mentally and physically fit and shoulder my full share of the task, whatever it may be.

I shall always accord my superiors fullest loyalty and I will always bear in mind the sacred trust I
have in the lives of the men I will accompany into battle.

I shall show other Soldiers by my military courtesy, neatness of dress and care of my weapons and
equipment that I am a picked and well trained Soldier.

I shall endeavor always to reflect the high standards of training and morale of parachute troops.

I shall respect the abilities of my enemies, I will fight fairly and with all my might, surrender is not in my creed.

I shall display a high degree of initiative and will fight on to my objective and mission, though I be the lone survivor.

I shall prove my ability as a fighting man against the enemy on the field of battle, not by quarreling with
my comrades in arms or by bragging about my deeds.

I shall always realize that battles are won by an army fighting as a team, that I fight first and blaze the
path into battle for others to follow and to carry the battle on.

I belong to the finest unit in the world. By my actions and deeds alone, I speak for my fighting ability. I will strive to uphold the honor and
prestige of my outfit, making my country proud of me and of the unit to which I belong.

Copyright © 2024 by Raquel Riley

www.raquelriley.com

All rights reserved.

No part of this book may be used, reproduced, or transmitted in any form or by any electronic or mechanical means, including information storage and retrieval systems, without written permission from the author, except for the use of brief quotations in a book review.

This is a work of fiction. Names, characters, places, and incidents either are the product of the author's imagination or are used fictitiously. Any resemblance to actual persons, living or dead, businesses, companies, events, or locales is entirely coincidental. The use of any real company and/or product names is for literary effect only. All products and brand names are registered trademarks of their respective holders/companies.

This book contains sexually explicit material which is only suitable for mature audiences.

Cover design by Raquel Riley

Editing by Christy Ragle and by Jenn Reads Books

For Riggs,
You've always been the strong one, looking after the Bitches and the vets and soldiers everywhere. I'm glad you finally found someone who can look after YOU.

For Rhett,
You are stronger and braver than you give yourself credit for. Even after suffering incredible losses, you're always smiling and loving. You are an amazing and unforgettable man, and I'm honored to tell your story. Keep your fuckin' boots on and keep marching.

CONTENT WARNING

This book deals with heavy sensitive topics like mental health and depression, low self-esteem, and healing after loss.

On-page gory death of side characters and a parent, vulgar language, disfigurement and amputation, anger, and self-hatred.

Alcohol and pill use.

FOREWORD

I spent hours researching for this book, but I'm no expert on military life and law. There may be inconsistencies mentioned.

Mention of military bases with retired names, like Ft. Bragg, are referred to as such as this story takes place during the Obama administration before the names were changed. Ft. Bragg is now Ft. Liberty, and the FOB or Forward Operating Base in Afghanistan, Arian, is now defunct.

Careful research and sensitivity screening was done for survivors of war and survivors of trauma. Any derogatory words mentioned by the main character are his own feelings about himself, not others, due to his grief process.

Extensive research was done on Polycystic Kidney Disease, stroke, and aneurysm, but I am not a doctor with a medical background.

Some parts of this book may be hard to read, but it only makes the hard-earned HEA that much sweeter.

Please read with an open heart and heed the trigger warnings. I hope Riggs and Rhett hold a special place in your heart like they do mine.

With Love,

Raquel Riley

GLOSSARY OF TERMS

POG- POG stands for "Person Other than Grunt," referring to literally anyone who is not a boots-on-the-ground soldier. Used as a derogatory remark.

SFC- Sergeant First Class rank

C-17 Globemaster- A large military transport aircraft used to carry troops and cargo.

Civvies- Civilian clothing, (not uniforms).

DD- Designated driver. A person not consuming alcohol.

DEFAC- Dining Facility Amenity Center. A place to eat on base.

Big Voice- The loud speaker system on base.

CHU- Containerized Housing Unit. Usually made of metal shipping containers.

Dustoff- emergency patient evacuation of casualties from a combat zone.

Bird- Helicopter

Moon Dust- Fine sand in the desert.

Helo- Helicopter

Backboard- A stretcher used to transport injured patients.

FOB- Temporary Forward Operating Base on foreign land.

Paracord- Parachute cord made of nylon.

HIPAA- Health Insurance Portability and Accountability Act. Patient's rights.

Rear D- Rear Detachment Unit. These soldiers are responsible for keeping the unit running at the duty station as well as providing a link between the deployed unit and the FRG (Family Readiness Group). Typically, there is an officer who is appointed as the commander. This is rarely the unit's normal commander.

ASVAB- The Armed Services Vocational Aptitude Battery tests your knowledge of basic concepts and skills to date, and it determines what branch and rank in the military you are eligible for.

C-4- A common variety of the plastic explosive family known as Composition C, which uses RDX as its explosive agent.

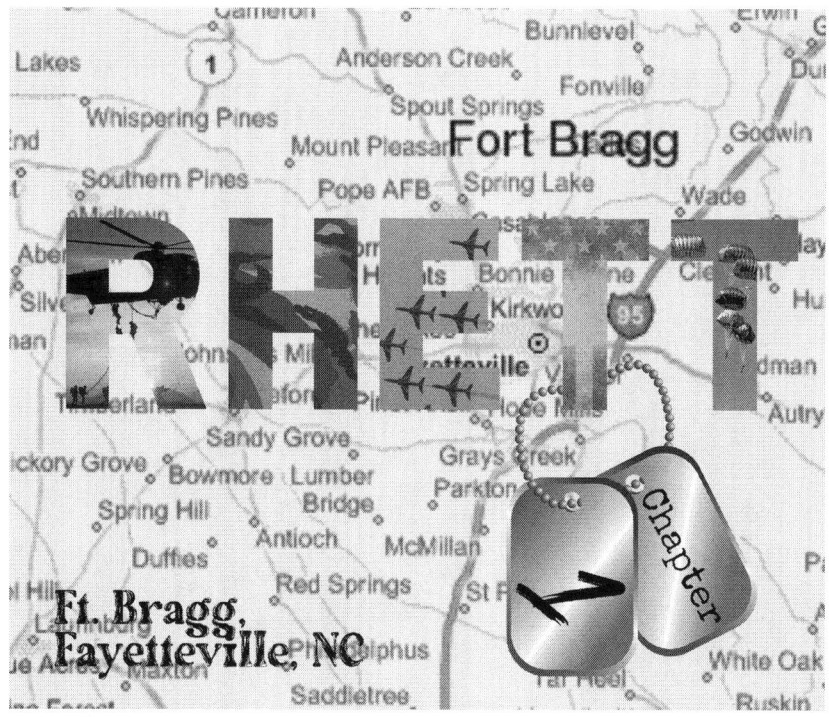

RHETT
Ft. Bragg, Fayetteville, NC
Chapter 1

AIN'T no feeling in the world like free falling.

Nothing compares to the thrill of flying through the air, hundreds of feet above the world, watching the ground rush up to meet you. It's like tempting fate, like daring God. Every time we jump, we're gambling with our lives. So far, I've had a flush hand—knock on wood. I'm addicted to the gamble—like an addict with a wad of cash and no morals—I live for my next fix. To feel the wind burn my face, to feel the force of gravity peel my skin and lips back from my bones. To feel weightless; like I can fly, like I can drift away on the wind. Not many people get to see Earth from this angle. They don't get to fall through a cloud or soar higher than an eagle.

Only the lucky few, and the 82nd Airborne.

My chute opens, and my body snaps back violently as the drag kicks in, slowing my descent. Six more minutes till impact.

I glance to my right and see my buddy Biddell shooting me his pinky and forefinger—the universal hand signal for 'rock on.'

I return it with another one—my middle finger.

From this height, I can practically see the entire state of North Carolina. The smoky peaks of the Blue Ridge mountains, the tops of towering pine trees, and the tallest buildings in Charlotte, Greensboro, and Durham. But the view fades fast the further I fall.

Two minutes till impact.

Every time I jump, I feel that familiar thrill—the rolling in my stomach, adrenaline igniting in my blood. Realistically, I know I can't jump forever, not with the toll it's taking on my ankles and knees. I'm going to miss the shit out of this when it finally comes to an end.

But for the next nine months, I'm gonna enjoy every minute I spend free falling, knowing they might be my last.

I'm out of time. The ground is less than fifty feet beneath me, and I prepare for impact. It's impossible to land gracefully. Even with a chute, you're basically crashing into the Earth at twenty-six miles per hour. Tomorrow, I'm gonna be sore *everywhere*, but today, today I'm fucking living.

My feet hit first, and I try to duck and roll with the momentum. My chute collapses around me, and the wind catches it, dragging my body across the rocky ground. Just as I come to a halt, a body lands on top of me, his boots digging into my back.

"Ow, fuck!" The initial impact my body absorbs is enough

to rattle my fucking teeth, but the force of Biddell's hulking body crashing into me squeezes the air from my lungs.

I wheeze, coughing up the dust I kicked up on impact, and try to roll away from him. "Get the fuck off me, POG."

He struggles to roll to his knees, coughing up dust. "Like I can control... Where I fucking land."

"To some degree, yeah, you fuckin' can."

He spits to clear his mouth. "Stop your bitching and help me up."

"Help your fuckin' self, cockwomble." Rolling to my knees, I push to my feet, making my way to Biddell. He grabs the hand I offer, and I haul him to his feet, grinning along with him.

"Nice landing," Warren jokes, backslapping the both of us.

I can already hear the endless reel of jokes that will surely follow from now until forever. Fucking knuckleheads. The guys in my unit may not be the sharpest bullets in the magazine, but they're the best guys I know. My brothers and sisters. I would literally die to protect them.

The Sergeant First Class's voice rings out across the field. "Let's go, ladies! This ain't fucking playtime! Get your chutes and line the fuck up!"

"Keep your fuckin' boots on, Jesus Christ," I mumble under my breath. I hadn't seen his ass jump thirty thousand feet.

We scramble into formation, still coughing, waiting for our hearts to stop racing. The SFC paces the line. "That was mediocre. You know what happens when you have a mediocre jump in combat?"

He stops pacing right in front of me. "You die, sir!"

"That's right, Marsh. You fucking die. Do you want to die, Marsh?"

"Not today, sir!"

"Get back to the landing strip and do it again!"

Exhausted, thirsty, and sweating, we hike seven miles in full gear back to the airfield and board the C-17. Last week, we received our orders to deploy. Since then, it's been training, training, and more training from the ass-crack of dawn till sundown. Scratch that... we did two night jumps this week.

Eight more days till we deploy. I'd boxed up a few things I couldn't take with me—my gaming console, civvies, a box of photos, and paperwork, and stashed it in Army storage on base along with my car.

"Man, when this shit's over, we're going drinking tonight," Biddell calls. "Warren's the DD!"

"Bullshit," Warren coughs. "I designate Ormen."

"I designate your mother," Ormen shouts.

I chuff, shaking my head. It's always like this. Someone was dumber than dirt, someone's mother was knocked up by the entire battalion, and someone drew the short straw and life sucked extra hard for them.

Luckily, today it's not me or my mother.

———

The Footlocker is far from the nicest bar in town, but it's close to the base and has good drink specials after nine PM. We gathered a group of six guys, including myself, in two cars.

Our waitress places a platter of chicken wings and loaded

nachos on the table, and you would think we were rabid pigs, the way we tear into the food. My buddies aren't the kind of guys that use a napkin to wipe their greasy fingers. No, their jeans suffice just fine.

I tip back my bottle, squeezing my eyes shut as the lager burns the back of my throat. "Damn, that tastes good after a long day in the field!"

"Shit, horse piss tastes good after a long day in the field," Ormen argues.

"He's not wrong," Biddell seconds.

"What do you think it's gonna be like over there?" Warren asks.

Villaro snorts. "Shit, my buddy came back, told me it's hot as donkey balls, and all you do is choke on the fucking sand."

"To donkey balls!" Mandell toasts.

I tune them out after that, scrolling through my phone. The less I think about what it's going to be like, the better chance I've got at keeping my cool and not freaking the fuck out. Am I nervous? Hell yeah. But I'm also excited. No doubt, I'll live to regret that sentiment—if I'm lucky.

A text from my mother makes my phone vibrate.

> Mama:
> Call me before you leave. Love you always, xoxo

She's the fucking best. If I ever meet a woman half as good as my mama, I'll marry her in a heartbeat, but it's not gonna happen. My mama has them all beat.

My buddies are usually a rowdy bunch, but they get louder suddenly, and it catches my attention, my head snapping up. Warren is flirting with a girl across the room. She's seated at the bar with her girlfriend, making come-fuck-me eyes at him.

Warren slaps a twenty on the table to cover his bill and pushes out his chair. "Shit, I don't know about all you losers, but this is my last chance to get laid before we deploy. I'm out. I'll catch you back at base."

Cue the peanut gallery and all their stale jokes.

Biddell smacks my arm. "She's got a friend, Marsh, and she's looking at you. What're you gonna do about it, my man?"

I glance over my shoulder to check her out, and sure enough, the cute blonde is staring back at me. "She ain't lookin' at me, man."

Truth be told, I'm more interested in the man sitting beside her, but he's obviously straight, talking to a woman. Not that I can show any interest in him in front of my buddies. The chick is cute, but she don't look like she's gonna offer much resistance, and I'm the type of guy who loves the thrill of the chase. Usually, men tend to put up more of a fight. They make you work for it, and that gets my dick hard.

"Hell yeah, she is," Biddell insists. "Look at you. Black hair, green eyes. Dimples."

"They're hazel."

"What the fuck ever. You gonna go talk to her? Or are you passing your sloppy seconds on to us?"

My mama would slap the taste right outta my mouth if she heard us talking about a girl like this. Thank God Mama isn't here. Like Warren had, I drop a twenty on the table and approach the bar.

"Evenin' doll. How's your night goin'?"

"Better now that I've got you to talk to." Her coy smile is framed by glossy peach lips. Damn, I want to know what that gloss tastes like.

"Is that right? I'm Rhett, by the way."

"Tamara. Let me guess, you're Army, aren't you?"

"What gave me away?" I ask, looking sheepish. It's all an act. Of course, I'm Army. The base is less than ten minutes down the road. Every man and woman in a fifteen-mile radius is Army.

"You've just got that look," she says, teasing her bottom lip with her teeth. "Is that your unit or squad?" Tamara looks over my shoulder at the guys.

"Yes ma'am, my battalion."

"Oh, does that mean you're Airborne?"

Tamara knows a thing or two about the Army herself, it seems. "That's right, eighty-second, at your service."

She does this little giggle thing that all girls do when they want to look cute. "Let me ask you a question," she starts. "What would make you want to go and jump out of a perfectly good airplane? Are you a daredevil?"

Tamara's got this twinkle in her pretty brown eyes, like she gets off on the fact that I might be a bad boy. I'm not. I hate to disappoint her, but I'm not the bad boy she's hoping for. Thrill seeker? Yes. Adrenaline junkie? Most definitely. But a bad boy?

Nope. I'm as easygoing and rule-abiding as they come. My mama raised a good boy.

I lean in closer, catching a whiff of her sweet perfume. "You know that feelin' you get when you ride a roller coaster and your stomach flips over?" She nods, tossing her hair over her shoulder. "Or when you meet a cute guy at the bar, and you can't help but stare at his mouth as he talks because you just want that first kiss so damn bad?" Her eyes grow round and she licks her lips. Tamara is definitely staring at my mouth now, just like I'd hoped. "And when you finally taste his kiss for the first time, all those butterflies take off in your stomach, making you feel all tingly and electric?"

"Yeah," she breathes, leaning closer.

"Well, that's why I jump out of airplanes. To chase that feeling." Smirking, I pull back, not giving her the kiss she's seeking. Gotta keep 'em on the hook a little longer. Tamara sports a pretty little pout. "So, tell me, darlin', what feelin' are you chasin'?"

She doesn't answer, just wraps her manicured hand around the back of my head and pulls me in, planting her lips on mine, bold as can be.

"Do you want to get out of here?" She sounds all breathy, clearly turned on from the kiss. "My apartment isn't far from here."

"Well, what kind of gentleman would I be if I didn't escort you home?"

"I've got my car," she points out.

"That's all right. You lead and I'll follow, just to make sure you get home safe." Total fucking lie. If she doesn't invite me in, I'll be pissed. Well, disappointed, for sure.

True to her word, she doesn't live far, and I pull into the lot and park beside her. I hurry to grab her door for her, and she leans against the side of her car, snagging the belt loops on my jeans to pull me in close for a sweet kiss.

"Listen, just so we're clear, there're no strings attached here. No expectations. I don't want to be that kind of guy," I lie. "But in less than a week, I leave for the other side of the world."

"Well, in that case," she smiles, "let me give you a proper sendoff."

Hell yeah. Tamara definitely didn't disappoint.

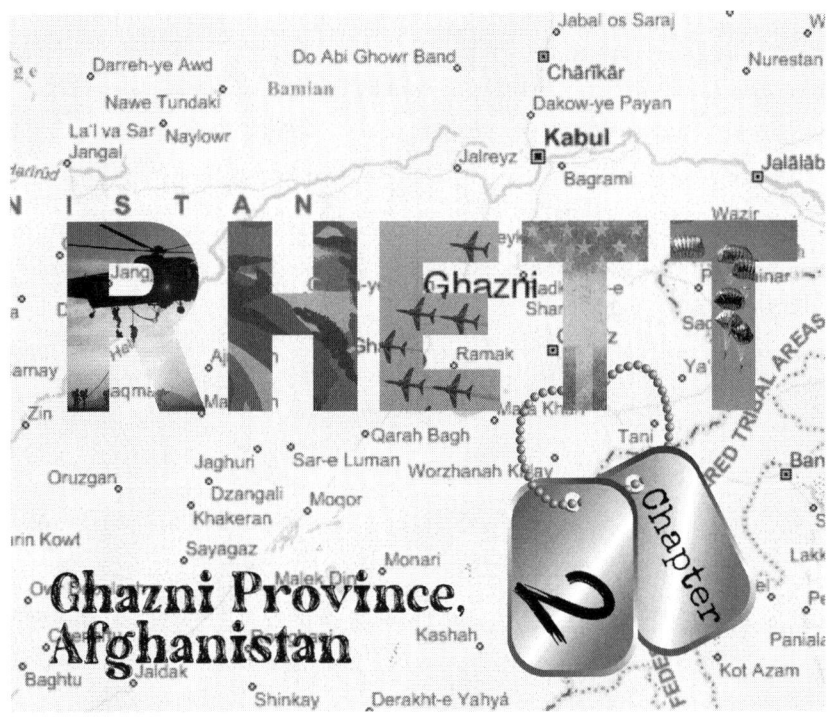

"DOROTHY, I don't think we're in Kansas anymore," Biddell had joked with all seriousness when we stepped off the plane in Kandahar.

That was six months ago, and it still rings true. The desert is no joke. Everything out here is trying to kill me. The sun, the sand, the wind, and the fucking insurgents. Did I mention the snakes and scorpions? Even on base, I have to watch my step. The food and the stench will kill you faster than a Russian assault rifle.

This place...it's kinda bleak. I've felt a heavy fog of depression creep over me slowly these past few months. It's not just the weather and the landscape, either; it's the mood. There's no morale here, and everyone seems subdued, washed out. There's no color, no joy, no break. Every week I cross off another block on my calendar, counting the days until my deployment is over. Sometimes, there are moments where I can forget, even for a handful of minutes—like when we play hacky sack using someone's sock filled with dry rice, or just hanging out with the guys during our downtime, joking with each other like we used to back at home.

I miss going to the bar with my buddies. I miss shopping at the PX for food I actually want to eat. Hell, I miss my mama. I used to think Ft. Bragg was a suckhole, but I'd give just about anything to go back right now. On the weekends, we used to play a pickup game of softball. The other day I caught myself thinking about trees. I miss seeing green trees and grass. I miss the seasons of North Carolina, watching the leaves turn orange and red and gold, and feeling the air turn crisp and thin.

"What the fuck even is this shit?" Ormen asks, stabbing the brown, puck-shaped lump on his plate.

We're gathered around a folding table in the mess tent. "The meat identifier is brown gravy, so it must be Salisbury steak?" I guess.

"You call that gravy? It's gelatinous," Warren complains, scrunching his nose.

"Shit, I'm starving. You gonna eat that or not?" Biddell asks.

To think, we used to complain about the food at the DFAC. I'd gladly eat that dog food again. Compared to the crap they serve here? That shit was gourmet.

I've actually lost weight. I can tell from the way my pants fit.

"Eighty-Second, all soldiers report to general command in full gear, ASAP. Eighty-second, all soldiers report to general command in full gear, ASAP." The announcement blares over the *big voice*, the loudspeaker.

"Shit, what do you think it is?" Ormen asks.

"I don't know, but let's hurry the fuck up," I urge, scooting my chair back.

"Shit, I can't jump on a full stomach. I'll puke my guts out," Biddell complains.

We duck into our CHU, a metal shipping container that houses four bunks each, and grab our gear and guns.

By the time we reach the General Command room, an office constructed of thin plywood, there's already a group forming outside. I recognize my lieutenant colonel.

He addresses us when the last guy joins us, kicking up dust as he runs to catch up. "New orders. A reconnaissance team fell under heavy fire. They're pinned down in a valley surrounded by mountains. The terrain is too rough for backup on foot to reach them anytime soon. Air strike isn't a viable option because they're practically on top of each other. You're dropping into a hot zone. It's gonna get hairy, so heads up. This is what you trained for. You ready?"

That last part is rhetorical because it doesn't matter if we're ready or not. We're going either way.

"Oohrah!"

"Death from above!" They shout the 82's motto.

Shouts of, "All the way!" our other motto, ring out.

We shuffle through the front gate and circle around the parking lot. One by one, we file onto the mammoth C-17. My nerves are frayed and adrenaline replaces any fear I might and should be feeling. I'm not thinking about enemy fire and loss of life; I'm thinking about my training, recalling everything I learned in Jump School, and the wisdom passed on to us by our colonel.

My skin flushes with heat. It's the adrenaline. I'm sweating through my damn undershirt. Ormen elbows me, grinning like a loon.

"You ready, Marsh?"

"Fuck yeah. All the way, baby."

He high-fives me, and the guys around us whoop. This is it. This is our moment to show the rest of the fuckers in the military we're not just sheep with guns. We're fucking warriors. On my left, Biddell hangs his head, hand over his heart.

"You good, man?" I don't have to ask. I already know he's not. Brian's been my best friend for most of the last four years, and I can read him like a book. He's shitting his fucking pants.

He nods, and when he looks up, his dark eyes seem grave. "Tell my ma I love her. My shit in storage? Check through it before she gets it."

A sliver of fear stabs through me. "Don't you fuckin' jinx me, man. Cut that shit right now, Brian!" I don't even wanna pretend he's serious. A world without Brian Biddell? Yeah, no, that's not a world I want to live in.

He nods again, lowering his head. He's scared, and unlike the rest of us, he's not afraid to show it. The powerful engine and boosters of the C-17 are loud as fuck, making the din inside the aircraft noisy enough that we have to shout. I focus on the sound for the next twenty minutes as we reach the altitude necessary to jump. They throw the doors open and we line up.

My heart pounds loudly in my ears. I feel juiced up, ready

for anything. I stare down at my boots as I shuffle along behind the guy in front of me. The closer we get to the door, the louder the pounding in my head becomes. Sweat covers my forehead. My scalp feels hot and itchy. I can feel the wind on my face as it roars loudly past the Globemaster.

Death from above. I recite the words over and over in my head. If it's me or them, it's gonna fucking be them. I've never taken a life, but today I just might. I'm fully prepared to defend myself and my brothers. No matter what it takes.

I step up to the open door and plant my boots on the yellow safety tape on the floor. "Geronimo!" I shout, leaping into thin air, and I plunge myself into a free fall. My stomach flips over. The familiar feeling is a small comfort. I know what comes next and I focus on that. My chute deploys and my body snaps back as the thin nylon catches air. My stomach settles somewhat. Every time I jump, I sigh with relief when my chute opens properly.

From this height, all I can see are mountaintops. The sound of gunfire and shouting doesn't reach this high up. It's peaceful and quiet, at least for another three minutes.

With a minute left, the men on the ground come into focus. I can hear the popping of gunfire, and I can faintly smell the acrid smoke from grenade blasts.

I search the ground to make sure I'm not landing in a bad spot and the sharp whiz of bullets fire past my head. They sound like buzzing bees. Panic seizes my heart. My body jerks as my chute gets nailed, and I watch in horror as it loses its shape. My stomach roils and I know I'm fucked royally.

A body crashes into me, throwing me off course.

"Fuck, Biddell!"

His blood splatters on my face. A coppery tang fills my mouth. He's been shot. A dark red stain blooms over his chest. I'm falling faster, too fast. My chute is busted and performing at half-function. Biddell's body falls away. I swallow hard and take a deep gulp of air into my lungs, knowing it might be my last breath.

Holy Mary, mother of God, pray for us sinners now and at the hour of our death, Amen.

My body hits the ground hard, jarring every bone in my body, and before I can think to tuck and roll and grab my gun, blinding white-hot pain rips through my legs, dulling every other sense and thought. The sound of my bones breaking echoes through my ears and head. It's a sound I can *feel*, and I know it's a sound I'll never forget. When I come to a halt, I can't see shit as my chute drapes over me, blanketing me in darkness.

Someone scrambles to uncover me. They unclip my ruined chute.

There's only one thought on my mind. "Biddell! Where's Biddell?"

"Fuck man, look at your leg!" It's Ormen. He shouts at me, crouching down over my prone body.

I can't think straight from the pain, but I muster the strength to look. It hurts a whole lot worse after seeing the extent of the damage. Through the gash in my pants exposing my lower leg, jagged shards of white bone poke from my torn flesh. The bottom half of my leg twists at an odd angle, and blood pours from the wound.

Ormen rifles through his ruck, grabs a tourniquet, and ties it off around my thigh.

"Holy fuckin' fuck!" Bile bubbles in the back of my throat and spills from my mouth as I lose the contents of my stomach. The pain robs me of breath, and I can feel a heaviness in my chest from the lack of oxygen in my frozen lungs.

"Breathe, Rhett," Ormen barks, frantically looking around. "Help!"

Swallowing the bitter saliva left in my mouth, I drop my head and clench my eyes shut, focusing on breathing through the pain. In through my nose, out through my mouth.

"Biddell landed. Go check him!" Ormen shouts at someone.

"We've got to rendezvous," someone yells back. Warren—I barely recognize his panicked voice.

The buzzing is back in my ears, and the fight around me fades into a dull roar. My body burns hot with pain and I feel weak and a little woozy from the loss of blood. Ormen wrestles my ruck from my shoulders and uses it to prop up my leg, strapping it tightly to the two broken halves for support. Pain pulses in my stomach like a heartbeat as he jostles me.

"We gotta move, man." He grabs me under the arms and drags me over the rocky ground at least twenty feet. Every bump and rock feel like massive boulders. The edges of my vision turn dark and I have to fight to stay conscious. Ormen drops me on a pile of bodies, some writhing in pain, some still, most likely dead or close to it.

He crouches down in my line of sight. "Dustoff inbound. Just gotta hang on, buddy."

He places his hand in mine, and I squeeze back, lifting it so

I can see it. But the skin is black—not Ormen's—and I turn my head to see a still body lying beside me. *Biddell*. I squeeze his hand, shouting at him, although I know he's already gone.

My voice is hoarse and shaky with tears and pain. "Hold on, Biddell! Help's comin'."

The shouting around me grows louder, punctuated by the staccato popping of gunshots. They're closing in on us, and I'm lying here like dead fucking weight, unable to fight or help my unit. Gritting my teeth against the pain about to rob me of consciousness, I grab my gun slung around my neck, and hold it up, ready to blow any motherfucker who walks into my line of sight into kingdom fucking come. My strength comes from adrenaline and fear, which helps numb some of the pain to keep me conscious.

The gunfire never stops. How big is the pile of bodies around me going to grow before it's all over? My pant leg is sopping wet with my blood and I wonder how long I can hang on before help arrives. Will I even make it that long? The soldiers protecting us are standing out in the open, easy targets, refusing to take cover. I'm putting them at risk. Ormen, Warren, and the others... I'm jeopardizing their lives, lives that I can't even help defend at the moment.

It could have been seven minutes or seventeen, I'm not really sure because time stops tracking, but I can hear the whirring of rotor blades get louder as the bird comes closer. The cloud of moon dust it kicks up as it lands chokes me, blinding my eyes. Ormen tries to drag me to the helo, but I reach out for Biddell.

"You gotta let go, Marsh! Let him go!" he yells over the roar of the blades.

Like fuck I will.

Ormen pries my fingers from Biddell's lifeless hand and drags me as I scream—from pain, from loss, from fear—and hoists me onto a stretcher and onto the helo. My throat's sore from screaming. I don't stop until he drops Biddell beside me. I reach out for him again, squeezing my pain into him like I'm trying to use it to revive him.

"I'll see you back at base, brother. Hang tight. Look after him for me," Ormen shouts, squeezing my shoulder. Then he grabs his gun and charges into the fight, yelling out a primal war cry. "All the way, motherfuckers! All the fucking way!"

Chapter 3

Ghazni Province, Afghanistan

HE DOESN'T SO MUCH as flinch as I slide the needle beneath his skin to start his IV. "Hold that bag above your head," I order, shoving the pouch of blood at him. I can see from the amount of blood covering his uniform that he's lost too much.

"Isn't that your job?" he grumbles as he lifts his arm above his head.

"I'll gladly hold the bag while you stabilize your leg."

He squeezes his eyes shut and drops his head back down on the backboard. There isn't much I can do for his leg mid-flight. It needs to be cleaned, disinfected, and pieced back together with painstaking care by a surgeon. I'm mostly trying to stem the loss of blood.

"Fuck my leg! Help him. Help my buddy."

His hand that isn't holding the bag of blood is gripping the hand of the man next to him.

I have to shout above the roar of the blades. "There's nothing I can do for him! He's gone. And if I don't work on your leg, you will be too."

Untying the ruck sack from beneath his knee, I strap a plastic splint to his leg and tighten the tourniquet. Fragments of bone stick out in every direction, and his torn skin hangs like a tattered rag. The other leg is most likely broken, or at least fractured, but there's no blood. Running my hands over his shin, I check for obvious breaks, but come up short.

I douse his leg with saline solution, and his scream pierces through the chaos surrounding us.

"Hand me that saline," another medic insists, and I pass it to him. He's working on another soldier with a gunshot wound to his shoulder.

"Give me something for the pain," my patient begs. His voice is shredded from the agony wracking his body.

"Can't give you much more than one shot of morphine. Your blood pressure is tanked."

"Fuck that," he pants. "Don't care if I die, just don't want to die hurting this bad."

My protective instincts fire up. "You're not going to die. Not on my watch." I stab the top of his thigh—the only part of his leg left intact—with an injection of morphine. His face is ravaged from pain and grief, and I lean over him, looking directly at him. "You know, all this blood really brings out the color of your eyes."

He cracks his eyes open and squints at me. They're hazel.

Muddy green with flecks of gold. I was only making a joke to take his mind off the pain, but his eyes really are beautiful.

"They're my best feature." He tries to smirk, but his mouth pulls into a tight, straight line.

His grimace makes my chest flood with sympathy and concern. He's a soldier, a warrior, and I know that for every ounce of agony he's feeling, his face is only showing a tenth of it.

"Are you flirting with me, soldier?"

His laugh morphs into a wet cough that makes his body shake, increasing his misery tenfold.

The blood seeping from his leg in multiple places is lessening. Maybe he won't bleed out before we get back to the base.

"That was a hell of a jump." It takes enormous balls to jump thirty-five thousand feet into a hot zone under enemy fire.

"Looks like it was my last one," he wheezes.

"I hope not. I bet you're a hell of a soldier."

I can see the FOB coming into view as our helo descends. There's already a team of soldiers rushing toward the tiny airstrip in anticipation of our landing.

"We're about to touch down. Keep that bag raised above your head unless someone takes it from you."

"Yes sir," he rasps.

I wrap my fingers around his wrist, the one holding onto his buddy's lifeless hand. "You're gonna have to let go, soldier." He gives me one small nod, and I take it as permission, tugging his hand from his friend's and taking possession of it. "You can hold mine instead," I offer.

I'm surprised by the strength of his grip in his condition.

"Don't... Don't let me go."

He licks his bottom lip and his tongue sticks. I realize how dry his mouth must be and how much care he needs right now beyond life-saving measures. There are currently eighteen hundred soldiers stationed at this base, and I'm responsible for keeping each and every one of them healthy, but right now, *this guy*, *this* hand gripped so tightly in mine, is the only life I care about. If I let go, he may not make it. I don't think I can live with that on my conscience.

This is my fourth deployment in thirteen years. I've saved many lives, and I've lost many lives, but I absolutely refuse to gamble with *this* man's life.

"I'm right here, soldier. I won't leave your side."

Things move quickly after that. We rush the patient into the medical bay where I assist a doctor and a team of nurses as we try in vain to piece his leg back together again. After an hour, the doctor raises his head, catching my eyes across my patient's body. The look on his face says it all. He shakes his head minutely. There's nothing more we can do for him. He backs away, peeling off his gloves. The place looks like a battlefield, littered with bloody gauze, latex gloves, and the detritus of plastic packaging.

The infusion of blood I gave him in the helo stabilized his blood pressure enough that he could sustain another injection of morphine. It was enough to partially knock him out so we could work on his leg, but it's beginning to wear off now. The nurses move around me, cleaning up and checking on the other patients. He opens his eyes, looking high as fuck. They're glassy and the whites are now tinged red. The first thing he does is grab my hand and squeeze.

"Did you fix me?"

Sometimes, I hate my fucking job. My heart pounds as I wonder how to tell him. I've delivered bad news to hundreds of patients, maybe more, so why is it so hard *this* time with *this* man?

I don't even know him.

"There's nothing we can do here. You have a ride back to the States in a few hours, at first light. There're two other soldiers going back with you that need more help than we can give them here."

"Back to Bragg?"

"That's right. Womack Army Medical Center will take good care of you." If anyone would know, I would. When I'm not deployed, I work there.

"Where'd they take my buddy?"

"He'll be riding back with you to the States."

"Yeah, in a box."

His voice breaks on the last word, and tears gather in his eyes. He glances down at his leg. It's bandaged and splinted as best we could.

"Look, I know it hurts. I've been there. I lost a buddy." My throat feels swollen with emotion and it's hard to swallow. "It hurts so fucking much, and... there's nowhere to put all that pain; it can't even fit inside of you. You gotta let it out."

He looks away, scrunching his eyes shut to stem his tears. "Just go. Leave me alone."

That I can't do, even if I was inclined to. He's shaking off the morphine and the shock, and I've got to monitor him to make sure there are no side effects or that his blood pressure doesn't crash.

"I told you I wouldn't leave you alone. I'm staying."

"Go, I said!"

His scream is broken as he falls apart, his shoulders shaking with silent sobs. I pull the curtain around us, which is all the privacy I can offer him. Pulling up a chair to the side of his gurney, I take a seat and grab his hand again. His sobs become louder, and he gives in to his heart-wrenching agony, finally falling apart. It sounds messy as he wails miserably for the friend he lost, for his leg and his career, for the drop in adrenaline and fear that kept him going for the past two hours. His raw emotion brings mine to the surface, and I fight back my own tears.

It's impossible for me to remain unaffected by the sound of his bawling. His pain is so palpable I can almost feel it. The nurse in me wants to take away his suffering and heal his wounds. I want to soothe his broken heart and give him back everything he's lost. But the soldier in me knows none of that is possible.

"Tell me about your friend. What was his name?"

"Brian Biddell. After boot camp, we were stationed at Bragg in the same barracks. God, he was fuckin' annoying. Showed up everywhere I went. Figured it would be easier to just make friends with him than to keep avoidin' him."

There was a note of humor in his voice that underscored his sadness. "Sometimes those turn out to be the best ones." A thin line of white foam had gathered in the corners of his mouth. I push to my feet, trying to untangle my fingers from his.

"Don't go," he says, sounding panicked.

"Just gonna grab you some water. Your mouth is dry."

The roar of the C-17 thunders overhead. I move over to the supply cabinet to grab the water as medics usher in two more soldiers, fresh from the fight. Voices outside grow louder, and I duck my head out the door to see that the sun has set. The sky is a painted canvas of dark purples and blues. The two new patients are sorted by the nurses, so I grab the bottle and return to my patient.

Uncapping the lid, I slide my arm beneath his head to prop him up and tilt the bottle to his chapped lips. "Take a sip."

He manages to take a tiny sip, but most of it dribbles down his dirty chin. Setting it aside, I resume my seat, and he grabs for my hand again. The bar patch sewn onto the breast of his uniform says Marsh. With the hand he's not holding, I dig his dog tags out from under his shirt and read the name engraved in the metal.

Rhett B Marsh. He's twenty-three, and his blood type is A-positive.

"Rhett, huh? Nice to meet you. I bet there's gonna be some people back home happy to see you return."

"My mama is gonna kick my ass. She made me promise not to get hurt."

I crack a smile, imagining this tough-as-nails soldier being dressed down by his mother. "I'm Riggs."

"Riggs? Hell, that's even worse than Rhett. Did your mother not like you?"

His sarcasm makes me chuff. "That's my last name. First name is Navarro."

He barely manages to nod. "What do they call you for short?"

"Riggs," I crack, trying to keep a straight face.

The corner of his mouth pulls up into a semblance of a smile. "My mama, she's a real southern belle. Her favorite movie is *Gone With The Wind*."

I recall the B on his dog tag. "Let me guess, your middle name is Butler? Like Rhett Butler?" I'm just cracking dumb jokes because I want to see him smile again. A full one this time.

"You guessed it. But don't tell anyone. That's my darkest secret."

"Get the fuck out of here," I choke. "For real?"

This time, both corners of his mouth curve. "Cross my heart."

"By God," I breathe. "A real southern gentleman."

I think he tries to laugh, but coughs instead. "Never said I was a gentleman."

"Yo, Marsh! You in here?" The voices come from the door, and I guess it must be his buddies coming to check on him.

"Sounds like you've got company, soldier." Why am I still calling him that now that I know his name?

I slip my hand from his grip and push to my feet to give them the chair.

Rhett turns his pleading eyes on me. "You'll be back, right?"

"Yeah, I'll be back." His transport doesn't leave for eight more hours, and I plan to spend them with him. I'm on shift all night anyway, with nothing but time on my hands. But even if I weren't, walking away from him just feels... I just can't do it.

I busy myself with paperwork, updating his chart while he visits with his friends. They're loud, and I can hear their voices drift across the med bay as they try to rally his spirits. They're juiced on adrenaline, high from the fight, and even though they all just lost a good friend, they're choosing to focus on the one they've still got left instead of bringing him down with the pain of Biddell's loss.

I've got to respect that about them.

Reading over his stats, I realize how close I'd come to losing him. His blood pressure hadn't just tanked, it'd been in the damn toilet. He lost a lot of blood. Thankfully, no arteries were severed.

I hadn't met Rhett Butler Marsh until today. He's a stranger to me. So why can't I walk away? Why am I committed to sitting by his side, holding his hand, and bearing witness to his tears, until I board him on the transport?

He has a beautiful face; harsh, rugged angles softened by plush lips and thick, dark lashes. It's a face I never want to haunt me in my dreams. But if I'd lost him today, he surely would. Every night of my life. Just like Mark Grainger.

Leaning against the counter, I watch him with his buddies. His arms are down by his sides, not gripping them for dear life. His mouth is pulled into a tight line, grimacing through his pain as he tries to put on a good face for them. Totally opposite of how he was with me. He fell apart in front of me, not afraid to show me his pain. I think that was the moment that solidified my need to protect him. My chest feels heavy, and I rub the heel of my hand over my heart as it begins to burn.

Why am I so afraid of losing you when you're not even mine?

When his buddies clear out, I drift back over to his side, and he automatically reaches for my hand. He grits his teeth, talking through them.

"Am I gonna lose my leg?"

"I'm no surgeon, but... I've seen a lot of bad breaks, and this one is—"

"You're also not a fuckin' recruiter, so don't blow sunshine up my ass. Give it to me straight, doc."

"Most likely, they'll be able to fix it, but afterwards...that's when the danger sets in. Infection, gangrene..." *Please God, don't let him lose his leg.*

Rhett turns his head away. "I'd rather fuckin' die."

Red-hot anger surges through me. I grab his chin, forcing him to meet my eyes. "Don't you fucking dare! I busted my ass to keep you alive, and you're gonna fucking live, dammit. Don't cry like a pussy over a broken leg, soldier. The rest of you works just fine. I know plenty of guys who live a full, happy life with just one leg. Be grateful you're still alive!"

Tears stream from his bloodshot eyes and I feel like a world-class prick.

"I'm..." he coughs and then winces from the way it shakes his body. "I'm scared."

I can see it in his eyes—stark, naked fear. "The worst of it is over, soldier. It's all downhill from here." A total fucking lie, but it's what he needs to hear right now.

His lids grow heavy, drooping to half-mast, and he maintains eye contact with me until his lids close slowly. Once he's fully knocked out, I check his vitals again and swap out the bandage on his leg. Rhett sleeps fitfully, jerking and mumbling, his face drawn tight. I want to ease his pain, to smooth his features and comfort him. If we were just two guys in a bar, I would love to see him laugh, to watch his eyes shine with life and mirth, to experience the full assault of his personality. Rhett looks like he would be a real charmer. If only we cou—but no, we're not just two guys in a bar. He's my patient who's fighting for his life, who just lost his friend, and in seven hours, he'll be gone, and I'll never see him again.

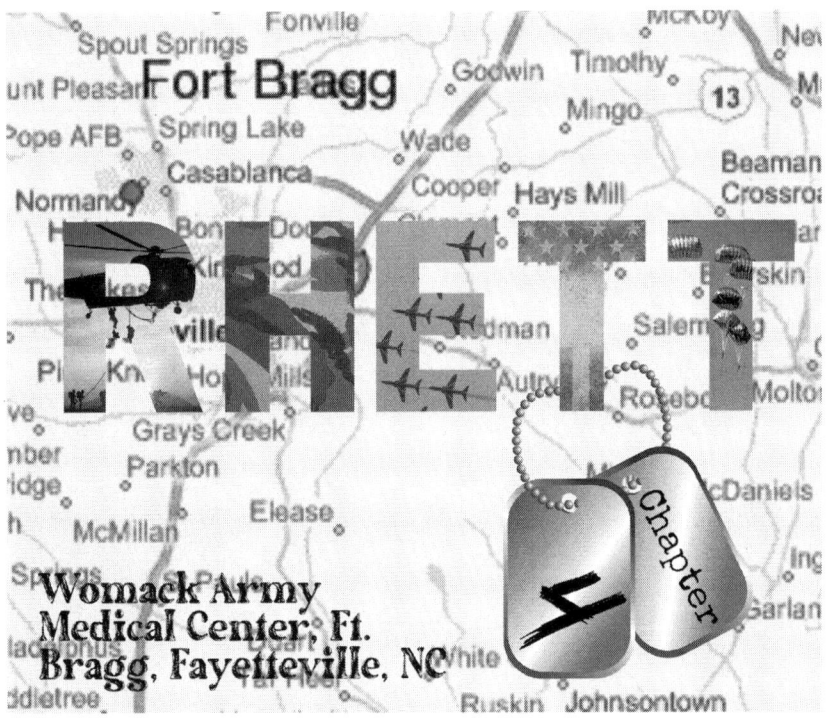

Womack Army Medical Center, Ft. Bragg, Fayetteville, NC

Chapter 4

I WOKE several times during the flight but was never more than half-conscious. I dreamt of Riggs. Hazy thoughts of his whiskey eyes and scruffy face smiling at me. His deep, smooth voice talking me through my grief. I'll never see him again and that thought makes me feel kinda empty inside. He's a total stranger to me, but for a few short hours, he was everything I needed—my angel of mercy. A strong hand to hold in the darkness, a comforting smile through the misery. I'll never forget him. Of course, it was just my luck that my nurse was hot as fuck when I was at my absolute worst. There's no better way to make a lasting impression on a guy than to bleed all over him and then cry like a snot-nosed baby.

They kept the morphine flowing steadily, thank God. But

once we land? All the transporting and jostling? Yeah, not even the morphine can cushion this blow. The jagged breaks in my bones are grating against nerves that make pain dance up my spine and radiate into every nerve ending in my broken body. It's a pain that goes beyond screaming, beyond crying, even. It's breath-robbing, heart-seizing, dizziness-inducing pain. I'm rushed from the plane to Womack Army Medical Center and sent straight into surgery. The last thing I see is the nurse's face leaning over me, smiling as she tells me to close my eyes.

When I open them again, I'm in a hospital room. The sun shining through my window is too bright for my sensitive eyes, but I can't move to close the blinds. Ironic, really. I'm a soldier, I fight for freedom, yet here I am, a prisoner. I'm imprisoned in this hospital bed—I've lost all freedom and autonomy over my will and my body. My future is uncertain, and so is whether I'll ever walk again.

"Hey!" I shout futilely. My voice sounds hoarse from disuse. "Help!"

Ten minutes pass before a pretty nurse walks in, pushing a rolling med cart. "Specialist Marsh, you're awake!" She smiles, walking over to my bedside to read my monitor. She records my vitals in her chart. "I'm Liza, your nurse. How are you feeling? Can you rate your pain for me on a scale from one to ten?"

"Uh, seven?"

"Is the pain in your legs?"

"Everywhere. I hurt all over." The impact of the fall affected my entire body. "My leg feels like a five, maybe?"

"That's great," she beams. That makes me snicker. Level five pain is great? I'm totally screwed, then. "I'll give you another dose. We transitioned you off morphine. So, you're going to feel some pain, but hopefully, level five is manageable. At least, for now. Every couple of days, you should feel a bit better."

"Can I see it? My leg?"

"Of course." She moves to my bedside, turning down my blanket. "You're all wrapped and bandaged, but when I change your dressing tomorrow, you'll get a clearer picture. Basically, your leg looks a little bit like *Frankenstein's Monster*," she grins. "Two rods, seven pins, two plates, staples, sutures, and a partridge in a pear tree. Oh, and a skin graft. The torn flesh over your shin couldn't be saved. You waited too long, or rather, the Army waited too long to transport you here. So we took a graft from your thigh."

"Is that all?" I ask, managing half a smile.

"Actually, no. Your other leg has a fractured femur and tibia, but not a clean break. I guess you could say you got into a fight with the ground and you lost."

"I guess you could say that," I agreed.

"The doctor will round on you in a couple of hours to discuss it with you. In the meantime, I can't offer you anything more delicious than *Jell-O* or soup for dinner. You're on a liquid diet for twenty-four hours after surgery in case there are complications and you have to go back in."

"I'm not hungry anyway, but thanks. In fact, I feel a little sick."

"It's all the pain meds and antibiotics, and you have an empty stomach, not to mention your pain and everything you've been through. I can give you something to settle your stomach."

Nodding, I smile gratefully. Liza's a doll. When she leaves, I turn my head to stare out the window. *Alone again*. Less than forty-eight hours ago, I was in the middle of a war zone, living my worst nightmare. Surrounded by bullets and shouting men and women and the roar of the helo blades and jet engines. Now, there's nothing but the eternal solitude and silence that surrounds me. I'm not used to sitting on my ass doing nothing, and now I have all the time in the world to do just that. *Nothing*.

I can't shut my brain off. Thoughts of Brian and the rest of my team play on an endless loop in my head, like a movie reel.

Brian's gone. Gone forever.

Hot tears burn my eyes, and I don't even try to keep them inside. What would the point be? I'm all alone. There's no one to see me fall apart. The view beyond my window becomes distorted and wavy as my tears fall harder, soaking my cheeks and dripping onto the blanket covering my lap. Our barrack rooms were connected by a shared bathroom. Brian always left the doors open so he could shout to me without having to get up from his bed. We used to shop together at the PX and split everything in half to save on groceries. A large pack of pork chops—two for me, and two for him. The family-size box of cereal that we split into *Ziploc* bags. A twelve-pack of soda that we shared. He was the other half of me, and now that half was missing.

A loud broken sob wrenches from my chest. His loss hurts so badly it feels like a physical injury. There's so much anguish and emotion squeezing my heart that it's hard to breathe.

"Brian," I choke, squeezing my eyes shut. "I...miss you."

I hear a quiet knock on my door before it's pushed open,

and a doctor dressed in a white coat walks in. Grabbing the hem of my blanket, I wipe my eyes and nose and struggle to draw a ragged breath into my lungs to calm myself.

"Specialist Marsh?"

"Yeah," I rasp, my voice unsteady.

"I'm Doctor Silman. I'm the one who did the surgery on your leg. You made a real mess of things," he tells me with a smile. I don't answer because, what can I say to that? It was probably meant to be rhetorical and I'm not in a joking mood. "We were able to piece you back together like Humpty Dumpty. Thankfully, your knee didn't shatter, so we managed to save it, but with the damage done to it, you'll likely need a replacement somewhere down the line."

"Will I—" My voice sounds so strangled that it's not even coming across clearly, and I have to cough twice to clear it before speaking. "Will I be able to walk again?"

"Not right away, of course," he smiles. "But you'll get there. It's going to be a long road."

Why does everyone keep saying that? I'm already tired of hearing it.

"It'll be six to eight weeks before your fractures heal on your left leg. By that time, you should be able to bear weight on your right leg. But you're looking at six months before you can even consider resuming normal activity. We're going to start you on some light physical therapy that you can do right there in the bed, and after you're discharged, when you can bear weight on your right leg, you can begin more intensive therapy."

"So, I'll be here for what, eight weeks?"

The doc nods. "This is our LTAC unit."

"Am I supposed to know what that means?"

He chuckles. "Long-term acute care. Any patient that is with us for longer than twenty-eight days is moved to long-term care." He places a stack of paperwork on my tray table and I have to fight not to roll my eyes. I've read books that aren't as thick as this stack. "If you get bored, you can start on this file." One thing about the Army, they love their paperwork. "I'll be back to round on you tomorrow. Take care."

And then I'm alone again. Alone with my thoughts, my grief, and my fears. I have nothing but time on my hands to sit and think and worry and remember, and I'm pretty sure I'm going to drive myself mad watching this movie over and over again in my head. I need a distraction. I need to feel less alone, connected to someone, anyone, in some way. Palming my cell phone on the bedside table, I dial the only number I have memorized by heart.

"Mama? It's me, Rhett. I'm... I'm back...Home." She sounds joyous, but her happiness brings tears to my eyes. Somehow, just hearing her comforting voice makes me feel safe enough to tap into my grief, and it flows through me like an open tap, making my chest feel heavy and tight. Hot tears burn my eyes and roll down my cheeks. "Yeah, Mama, I'm safe. But...Mama? I got hurt."

Day three of sitting on my ass and trying not to go insane isn't going so well. I build a long stick made from connected straws that extends about twelve feet before it gets too heavy-ended and bends in half.

Day four - I make a splatter paint masterpiece on the wall using red *Jell-O*. Liza is not amused.

Day five - I sleep mostly, catch a show on the making of the transatlantic railway, and sleep some more.

Day seven - I'm fucking cranky beyond reason. My leg itches but I can't scratch it. Liza says it's the skin graft and stitches healing. She changed my dressings and wrapped it in a soft cast. She was right; it looks just like *Frankenstein's Monster's* leg, pieced and patched together with jagged scars and stitches. It's a fucking mess.

Day nine - I doodle on a sketch pad, contemplating the sleeve of tats I'm gonna get to disguise my scars. My psychological state is deteriorating rapidly. I feel restless and jittery, but empty. So empty. What I wouldn't give to get the fuck outta here and attend Brian's funeral. Grabbing my phone, I google his mom's name, hoping to find her number. There are only two Sandra Biddell's in the Fort Worth area, and I call both, reaching her on the second try.

"Yes, ma'am, this is Rhett Marsh, Brian's buddy." She has to know me; we shared a barracks unit for two years. I met her briefly when she visited the base.

"Rhett?" Emotion thickens her voice, distorting it, and I can tell she's crying from just hearing my name.

"Yes ma'am. It's me. How—" My voice fails me and I clear my throat before continuing. "How are you?"

"I'm trying, Rhett, but I'm not okay. How are you?"

"I'm so sorry, ma'am. He was my best friend. I—I miss him."

My fucking voice cracks and I cough again. "I'm in the hospital. Got injured on the same jump as he did." I'm not telling her about his body crashing into mine after he got shot, about tasting his blood on my tongue, or how I clung to him afterward.

"Oh, I'm so sorry to hear that, Rhett. Are you going to be all right?"

"Yes ma'am, eventually." I feel guilty for admitting I'm gonna live when Brian didn't. "Ma'am? I was with him... after we lost him, I held onto him. He wasn't alone, ma'am." Shit, I said I wasn't gonna mention that, but I did leave out the unnecessary details, at least. Maybe it would bring her comfort to know he wasn't alone. It brought me comfort.

Sandra breaks down again, and I remain silent as she pours out her tears. "I'm glad he had you, Rhett. Thank you, honey. They're going to ship his belongings home. If there's something you want, please call back and let me know. I wish you a speedy recovery."

"Actually, if you could send me a copy of the obituary or somethin', I'd really appreciate that."

"Done. Anything else?"

"Not that I can think of, ma'am. I just want you to know you and your family are in my thoughts and prayers. Brian's a hero. He's *my* hero."

"Thank you," she cries, and I know I need to let her go before I join her over the edge. As soon as I hang up, it hits me. He asked me to go through his things before his mother saw them. I snort, the first sign of a laugh in over a week. He probably had a porn collection or something. Lube and a cock ring, maybe. But there was no way I could manage to go through his stuff before they ship it to her. I'm stuck in this goddamn bed for five more weeks, at least!

Fuck, I made him a promise. My best friend's last request, and there's no way I ain't gonna fulfill it. I just have to figure out how.

I grab the bed remote and press the red button, and a moment later, Liza's sweet voice fills the speaker. "Do you need something?" she asks.

"Yeah, I need a favor."

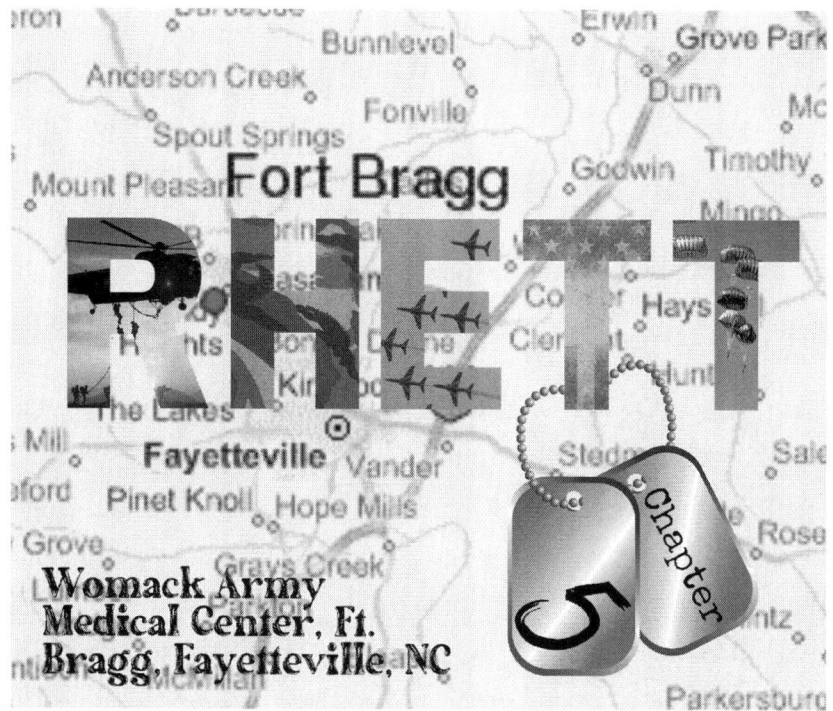

Chapter 5

Womack Army Medical Center, Ft. Bragg, Fayetteville, NC

LIZA BANGS her hip into the door frame as she hustles into my room, balancing a large heavy box in her arms. "I can't see where I'm going. If I trip over something, you're in trouble," she threatens with a laugh. She dumps it on my bed beside my feet, huffing as she stretches her arms. "How many favors did you have to call in to get this box?"

"All of 'em." Which is the truth. Four days ago, I called a buddy on base whose wife has a cousin who works in the office responsible for keeping track of the personal items stored by deployed soldiers. He explained to her about my promise to Brian to make sure his mom never saw what was in his stuff before they shipped it to her. Overriding policy, she allowed

Liza to pick up the box for me, with strict orders that I return it the next day, just like it never happened.

"It's a good thing I had an extra uniform in my locker. I was covered in dust. Do you know how many boxes I had to sift through to find his?" Liza complains.

"Thank you. Seriously," I stress. "This means… everythin' to me."

She sighs loudly. "I'm happy to do it. I mean, how can my need to eat lunch compare to breaking your deathbed promise to your bestie?"

I give her a grateful smile and reach for the box, but I can only bend so far before I tighten muscles that make pain shoot through my leg.

"Sit back and let me help you," she insists, pulling out her surgical scissors from her pocket to cut through the tape on the box.

She opens the flaps, but I stop her. "Liza, I can't let you look through this box."

She huffs. "Seriously, Marsh? Do you know what I went through to get this? And now you won't even let me see the goods?"

She has a point, but I just can't. I have no idea what I'm about to discover, but whatever it is, it's private. It's Brian's secret, and I don't have the right to share it with anyone, at least not until I know what it is.

"Sorry, not sorry. You gotta go, but thank you for all you've done."

"And all I still have to do to return it," she points out,

pushing to her feet. "I guess I'm gonna go chart. I wish you would have saved me from it."

"I'll make it up to you," I call out as she slips through the door. How the hell am I gonna make it up to her? Unless she wants a cup of red Jell-O, or a lemon *ICEE*, I'm shit out of luck in the gift department.

Using my metal grabber stick, gifted to me by the PT department, I stick it in the box and pull out whatever's on top—a file folder full of paperwork. I sift through the pages, but it's all useless. Just a bunch of bullshit forms and contracts. Next, I pull out a black velvet pouch full of challenge coins he'd earned over the years. A stack of old photos from his junior high years and a *Dallas Cowboys* jersey. Reaching into the box again, I come out empty. Whatever it is, it's too heavy for the grabber to pick it up. I take a deep breath and hold it in my lungs, grunting against the pain in my leg as I reach forward to pull it out. It's a bright blue plastic box, and when I open it, my eyes go round with shock as I spy the head of a silicone cock, bigger than mine, which is saying something. It's the same bright blue as the discreet packaging, complete with a set of balls and a suction cup base. I'm reluctant to touch it because I know where it's been, or I can guess, so I close it back up.

Is that what he didn't want his mother to find? Why would he even have a dildo? It's not something straight guys typically use, although they're missing out. I tip the corner of the box toward me and spy an old cigar box at the bottom. Again, I hold my breath and grunt as I reach for it.

"Fuck, that hurts!" I breathe out as a sharp pain stabs my leg.

The cigar box isn't heavy, but the once-colorful label is worn with age. Did it hold sentimental value to him? I've never seen him smoke one. I open the lid and immediately freeze. Naked pics of some dude's ass. My heart spikes with adrenaline. I feel wary, almost as if I'm about to uncover a hidden truth I might not want to discover. But Brian trusted me with this secret, whatever it is, so I take a deep breath and sift through the rest of the contents. There are at least a dozen *Polaroids* of this guy—all naked shots showing off his dick and his ass. It's a really nice ass, if I'm being honest.

With my heart in my throat, I replace the pictures and pick up the stack of letters. I have a feeling I already know what they're gonna say, but I unfold the wrinkled paper, anyway.

Dear Bri,

I miss you, baby. Bad. Our last visit was too short. But I'll never forget it. Hopefully, these pics will keep me on your mind until we're together again. Let me know when you get another leave, we'll plan something unforgettable.

Yours always,
Drake

Bri? Drake? Something unforgettable?! What in the ever-loving fuck have I uncovered? The rest of the letters are more of the same—basically love letters describing their 'good times' and secret trysts. And I know for a fact they were secret, 'cause Brian never mentioned a guy to me. I would have remembered that. The last two times he had leave, he told me he went home to Fort Worth, Texas, to visit his mother. So, either he lied to me, or this Drake dude lives in his hometown.

I drop the letters in the box and rub my chest where my heart is starting to burn hot. I feel like I've been gut-punched. Who the fuck was Brian Biddell? Because the guy I thought I knew doesn't match up to the man I'm uncovering in this box. He's been my best friend for three and a half years. I know all his secrets, or at least I thought I did.

You're a fucking hypocrite.

I knew him about as well as I let him know me. I never told him I like guys just as much, if not a little more than I like girls. I kept that to myself. So why am I blaming him for having secrets? The same exact fucking secrets I have?

Shit! All that time wasted. I could have been honest with him and he with me. Why did I think I couldn't trust him with the truth? Why did he think he couldn't trust me? We're so fucking dumb. I snort, thinking how he would laugh with me about this if he knew the truth.

I wonder if this Drake dude knows Brian died. Damn, is that supposed to be my job as his best friend to inform this guy? Do I have to write him a letter or call him up and tell him that Brian is never coming home again?

I set the box aside and fall back against my pillow with a sigh, letting my head roll toward the window. Suddenly, I feel exhausted and empty, just like every time I think of Brian. Will it ever stop hurting this much?

Liza comes to take the box, and for the next two days, I sleep pretty much nonstop. The sadness of my grief has given way to depression, and I just feel numb. Tired and heavy and totally uninterested in participating in my life. She tries to cheer me up by sitting on the end of my bed and talking to me about the mundane aspects of her day, a funny incident with a patient, her best friend's drama, how she had to chuck the blue dildo into the biohazard bin and hope no one figured out it came from her, but I couldn't care about a word of it.

That's her life, not mine. I don't have a life anymore. I have nothing but the pain in my leg and the hole in my heart where my best friend used to live. My friends are on the other side of the world, my mother lives three states away and isn't able to visit, and I've lost the ability to fend for myself. I feel like a useless fucking leech, like a boil on the ass of humanity. I have nothing left to contribute. I'm just a resource suck and a depressing one at that.

Liza pushes her way into my room, banging her med cart noisily against the door frame. She dumps a handful of glossy brochures on my tray table. "I brought you riveting literature to keep you awake."

I scan the titles, snorting. *'Help the VA help you.' 'Physical therapy unlocks the door to your future.' 'Be your best self - a guide to avoiding opioid addiction.'* And my favorite, *'TriCare cares.'*

"Absolutely riveting," I mock in a deadpan voice.

"You know, I've got a whole bookshelf at home. I could lend you some titles that are actually riveting," she suggests.

"Like?" I've never been a big reader. There just wasn't time for it. I prefer more physical hobbies. But now that I'm stuck upside down on my ass, why the fuck not? I haven't got anything better to do.

Liza shrugs. "I read mostly romance, but I'll see what I've got."

Great, my life has been reduced to reading medical brochures and *Harlequin* romances. Shoot me now. If only I had my paracord, I could hang myself and end my suffering.

"Don't give me that look, marshmallow," she chastises. "I'm trying to do you a favor. Reading spicy sex scenes has got to be better than educating yourself about the opioid trap."

There's that nickname again, *marshmallow*. She's been using it for the last few days, trying to cheer me up. It's fewer syllables than Specialist Marsh, and she swears that I'm soft and gooey on the inside, despite my misery.

"Fine, bring me your trashy smut. Now get out. I'm taking a nap," I grump.

"When aren't you?" she snaps, placing my pill cup on the tray table.

I glare at the stack of books on my tray table. Some are worn and some look brand new. *Loving Emma* by Raquel Riley, *A Fair Warning* by Dianna Roman, *Fighting the Lure* by Katherine McIntyre, and a book on origami. Leafing through the back covers, I skim the blurbs. Fighting the Lure is an MMA book about two chicks, a sister's best friend trope. *Kinky*. Actually, that explains a lot about Liza. Loving Emma says it's about a taboo relationship between an older man and the young girl he adopts. *What the fuck is she into?* I return it to the stack and grab the book on origami, the safest bet.

I pass two hours learning the ancient Japanese art of folding paper until a man enters my room holding a medical file. I assume it's mine.

"Specialist Marsh, I'm Tony Soliel, the physical therapist assigned to you." He glances at my chart. "I see you've been with us for almost four weeks now. Time to start getting back in shape."

I'd laugh if I found it even remotely funny. But it's just sad. "I don't know what you're expectin' of me, doc, but there ain't much I can do laid up in bed with two broken legs."

"I understand that," he laughs. "But there's still plenty we can do. You know, patients on bedrest lose up to five percent muscle mass each day, and you can lose up to forty percent of your strength in the first week. I've got a list of simple exercises we can start with to strengthen your core and your back and arms. You can do them right from the bed."

Fuck. Not only am I an invalid with two broken legs, but now he's telling me I'm gonna get fat and flabby while I'm waiting to recover. Can my life suck any harder?

Embrace it. That's what we say in the Army—embrace the suck.

"Whatever, just tell me what you want me to do." Then I can get back to my nap and folding my little fucking papers.

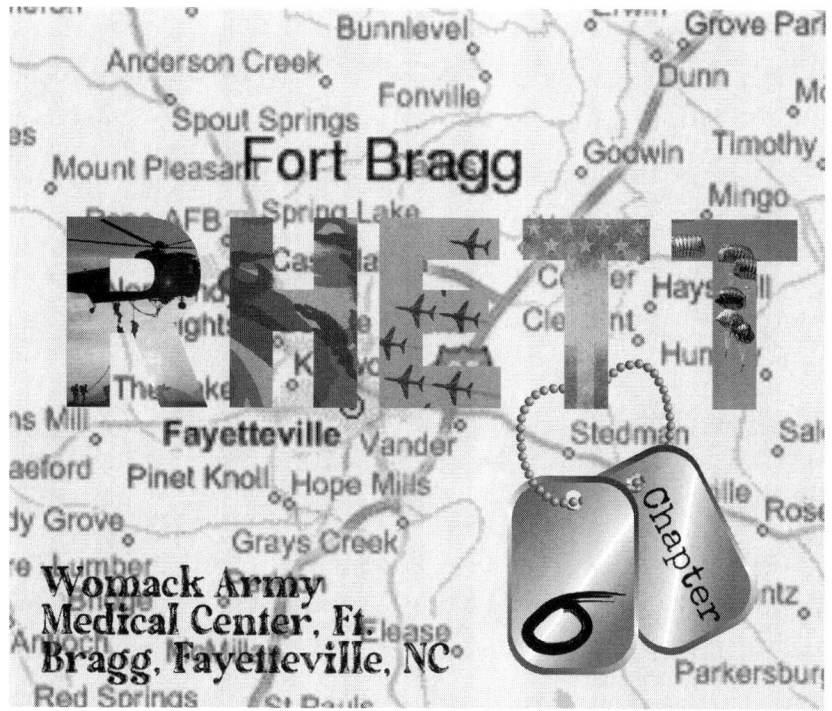

IT TAKES me nearly a week to work up the courage to track down Drake's info. Using the address on the envelope, I found him online. He lives in Fort Worth, went to school with Brian, and they're the same age. Were they sweethearts in high school? Had they been hiding their relationship that long?

Taking a deep breath, I dial his number, almost hoping he doesn't answer, or that I have the wrong number. But I don't. He answers on the third ring.

"Hello?" He sounds curious, or suspicious, and I wonder what the caller ID shows.

"Is this—" I have to clear my throat and try again. "Is this Drake Wahl?"

"Yeah. Who's this?"

"My name's Rhett Marsh. I'm Brian's buddy."

"How'd you get this number?" He's definitely suspicious now, but then he asks, "Is Brian okay?"

"Uh, so, we were, um…" What the fuck am I supposed to say? "We served together. He was my best friend."

"Yeah, he's mentioned you." Drake doesn't notice my use of past tense, which only makes this harder 'cause I'm gonna have to spell it out for him.

"He…he's never mentioned you before."

"I'll ask you again, Rhett. How'd you get this number?"

"I looked it up. Listen, about Brian, he… we… he's gone, Drake. We were deployed, and we had to make a dangerous jump, and he…" My throat closes up and I have to swallow hard to push down the lump of emotion blocking it. "He got shot. He died." Clearing my throat again, I repeat, "He's gone, Drake."

He's silent, and then I hear an anguished sob. "No. No, he's coming home. Two more months left of his deployment and he's coming home. We… we had plans."

I don't know what to say. He's working it out, coming to terms with it, and I just remain silent throughout his denial. I can relate to his feelings.

"He can't be gone. He's…"

"I'm sorry, Drake."

He falls apart, a high-pitched keen, and the sound of his tears squeezes my already broken heart until it can't beat anymore. Why is fate so fucking cruel?

"How'd you find out about me?" he asks brokenly.

"Your letters were in a box of Brian's stuff in storage. He asked me to go through it before it was mailed home. I gotta admit, man, I've never heard your name on his lips before, and I thought I knew everything about him. This was a surprise."

"Yeah, maybe that's why he never said anything. You just wouldn't get it."

"You're wrong. I do get it. He should've told me." And I should've told him my secret. "I'll mail your stuff back to you. Maybe...maybe you could call his mom and see if she's planning a memorial service or something."

"Yeah, maybe. Can I ask you something?"

"I guess so."

"Did he die quickly?"

Fucking tears, damn! They're running down my cheeks. "Yeah, he never knew what hit him." I swipe them away. "And he wasn't alone. I was with him the whole time."

He chokes up again. "I loved him. Someday, when he got out, we were gonna make plans. He was... he was mine."

I swallow hard. "I know how bad it hurts, man. I'm sure he loved you, too."

It feels so bizarre to say that to a guy about my best friend, but I know deep down in my heart it's the truth. Brian would never have kept those letters and pictures if he hadn't been in love. He just wouldn't have risked it.

"I'm gonna hang up now. Call his mom. Take care, Drake."

"Thanks, Rhett. I'm sure it wasn't easy for you to call me. I appreciate it."

Harder than you'll ever know.

As soon as I hang up, a wave of sadness swamps me. I feel empty and sad and just... tired. Same as always lately. My mission is complete. My promise fulfilled. Now what? What the fuck do I do now? What's my purpose?

My lids droop closed and I sigh heavily. Settling Brian's affairs drove me all week to keep going and keep living, but with that behind me now, I've got nothing. I don't have a purpose anymore. I'm fucking useless.

When I open my eyes again, Liza is sitting on the end of my bed eating a mini cup of ice cream. It's plain vanilla from the cafeteria. "Hey, sleepy. I brought you ice cream, too." She motions to my tray table where my cup sits with a plastic spoon sticking out of it. "Nice menagerie. I think I might take the swan home with me."

She's pointing to the little petting zoo I have lined up on my tray table of origami animals I made using the stack of brochures she gave me.

"Thanks, but I'm not hungry."

My appetite is half of what it used to be. Maybe because I'm not as active as I once was, or maybe it's my depression. I'm losing weight, and I feel kinda weak, like every little movement is exhausting, despite feeling restless.

To emphasize my point, Tony walks in smiling like he's excited about PT. I'm glad one of us is.

"You ready to sweat?" he jokes, like we're doing hardcore exercises. My grandmama used to watch this exercise show on television geared toward older folks or people with physical limitations called Sit and Be Fit, where they did exercises while seated in a chair. Nothing strenuous whatsoever. I used to think she was real cute doing those chair workouts. Now I have to laugh at myself 'cause they were tougher than what I'm capable of doing now.

Fucking pathetic.

"I'll just get out of your way," Liza insists, grabbing my uneaten cup of ice cream. She chucks it in the can on her way out.

"Just two more weeks until the real fun begins," Tony says, sounding way too positive.

Two more weeks until I can bear weight on my leg. Then maybe I can regain some of my mobility, move to a step-down unit, and work on being discharged. So I can return to... to I don't fucking know what. I need to talk to my chain of command about my reenlistment status. I'd been all set to sign up for another four years of jumping out of planes, or however long my knees and ankles would allow me to continue, but now that that's off the table, I'll have to choose something else.

My cell phone rings and I grab it from my tray table and answer, "Hello?"

"Are you there, baby?" my mama asks. She always sounds worried and concerned. It's hard for her, knowing I'm so far away and hurting and there's nothing she can do for me.

"Yeah, Mama, I'm here." Where else would I be?

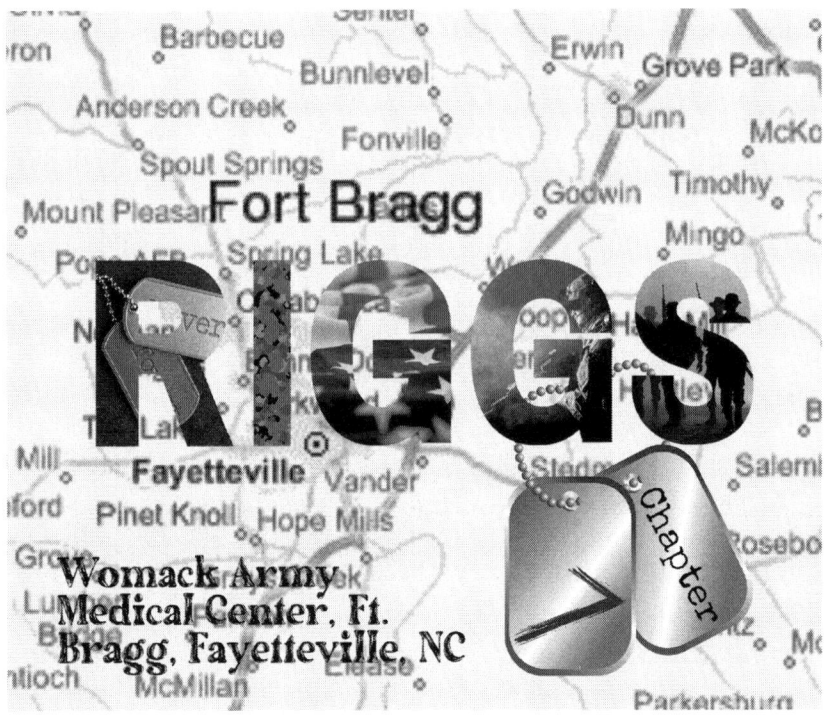

Womack Army Medical Center, Ft. Bragg, Fayetteville, NC

Chapter 7 — RIGGS

I STAND OUTSIDE his door for the umpteenth time, and as soon as Liza walks out, I grab her clipboard from her med cart.

"Hey," she barks, trying to take it back. "That's private information."

"I work here. Don't give me that HIPAA bullshit."

"You know, you could just go in and ask him how he's doing. You don't have to stalk him."

That word makes my body heat with awareness. "I'm not stalking him," I insist.

Her raised eyebrow says she thinks I'm full of shit. I *am* full of shit. I'm totally stalking him. I've already seen his x-rays and Tony's patient notes on his progress. Basically, he hasn't done jack shit in the way of therapy yet. But what I want to know isn't in his chart. I want to know how he's doing—mentally, emotionally. How he's holding up.

The last leg of my deployment felt like the longest I've ever served. There wasn't a single night I fell asleep without him on my mind, wondering how he was adjusting, how his leg had healed. I even wondered whether he ever thought of me.

No, I squashed those thoughts immediately. I had no business thinking thoughts like that. Rhett was my patient, however briefly, and I did my best to save his life. That's it. That's all there was to it. The fact he stayed with me, that I can't shake him from my mind? That's all on me, not him.

Liza glares at me with her hand on her hip. "Did you find what you're looking for?"

"No."

"That's because it's not in the file."

With a huff, I drop the chart on her cart and meet her accusing eyes. "How's he holding up?"

"He's not," she says bluntly. "He's miserable and depressed and he passes his time making animals out of brochures." Liza plucks a crane from her med cart and drops it in my hand.

Rhett made this? This is what he's been reduced to? A brave warrior who now folds paper to keep his mind from imploding? My heart bleeds for him. I know how much he's lost. Not just his career or his mobility, but his best friend. His entire life as he knew it is over. The problem is that he has nothing to replace it with. Not yet, at least.

"Go in there, talk to him," she urges for the hundredth time.

"He's not my patient."

"But is he your friend?" she asks.

No, he's not even my friend. Not really. He's just... someone I can't stop thinking about. Someone I connected with instantly. Someone I have no business asking after.

Instead, I say, "If you order from that Greek place for lunch, let me know. I'm in." And then I leave her standing there, staring after me as I walk away. Because that's all she's going to get from me, my lunch order. I know she's burning with curiosity about how I know Rhett and why I care so much. I certainly don't show that level of interest in any of my other patients beyond the progress they're making in my gym. So why Rhett?

Liza hasn't asked me outright yet, but she will eventually, and when she does? I have no idea what I'll say.

"That's it, push a little harder. Just a little more. You're almost there."

Rhett's grunts echo loudly in the silent room. They filter through the partially open door out into the hall where I'm standing, stalking him *again*.

"You can do it. Don't give up," Tony encourages.

His positivity and soft touch make my teeth grind together, and I can only imagine how it must make Rhett feel. I respect my colleague, but right now, I feel like his methods are shit. Rhett is a soldier. He's not used to being treated with kid gloves. Tony is doing him a disservice with his cheerleader act. If he were my patient, I'd... *He's not your patient. You don't get to have an opinion about his recovery.*

"Tomorrow, you start the hard work in the gym. We'll stand you up and see how much weight you can bear on your leg. Are you excited?" Tony asks.

"Fuckin' thrilled," Rhett deadpans, and I cover my snicker with my hand.

I love his thinly veiled sarcasm. If I can't get a patient to be excited about their recovery, I'll take anger as a close second favorite emotion. Anger means they still feel something, and I can turn it and twist it to motivate them, but I worry Rhett is becoming passive and disinterested, which scares me because that means he's given up. Disinterested means that you have to motivate them or make them angry to get them to start cooperating and caring again, and I just don't think Tony has the capability to do that with Rhett.

But *I* do. I can make him feel again. I can get him to care.

He's not your patient.

I'm sick and fucking tired of having to remind myself of that. With a deep sigh, I make myself step away from his door and get back to work.

―――

The following day, when Tony rolls Rhett's wheelchair into the gym, I busy myself in the back corner, folding a stack of towels. With my ball cap pulled low over my eyes and my newly grown scruffy beard, Rhett doesn't recognize me. In fact, he never even looks my way.

Tony wheels him to the parallel bars, and Rhett grabs on with both hands, his face screwed tight with pain as he hoists himself to his feet. The cast on his left leg is gone. His x-rays show that his fractures have healed. His right leg is a fucking mess, but they did the best they could. It was a miracle they saved it at all. Today he wears a soft cast around it to allow for movement of his knee.

I peek sideways at him, stealing glances. His face is mottled red and dotted with a sheen of sweat. His mouth pulls into a tight line before he bites his bottom lip.

"I can't," he huffs, dropping into his chair.

"That's all right; you're doing great," Tony cheers.

My hands ball into fists.

"Let's try it again," he urges brightly.

Every muscle in my body tenses as I watch Rhett struggle to pull himself up again. This time, he hangs on for about a minute before collapsing in his chair.

Better.

Tony claps Rhett's shoulder. "You're doing fantastic!"

His voice has never bothered me before, so why does it sound like nails scraping across a chalkboard now?

"Let's try some leg extensions before we add some weight to it," Tony suggests.

It's not what I would choose. I would make him take a step or two before giving up. I would make him walk to me.

He's not your patient.

I've seen all I can take for today. I shelve the stack of folded towels in the linen closet and slip out of the gym without drawing his attention.

———

The following day, he's at it again, struggling to hold his weight as he grips the parallel bars for dear life. Rhett is dressed in gray sweats and a T-shirt with the army logo, but he's a mess. His hair has grown out long, and it's greasy. His face is covered in scruff, a lot like mine. Apparently, we've both given up.

Tony positions himself behind Rhett, and he grips his hips to hold him steady. "Take a step forward," he urges. Rhett struggles but moves his right leg forward, bearing weight on it. Tony closes the distance between them, his body brushing against Rhett's back. "Good, take another one. I believe in you, Marsh. You can do this."

A red haze clouds my vision, or maybe it's green. I'm fucking pissed that he has his hands on Rhett. Tony's just doing his job, but I don't like it. Not one fucking bit. I've never held him like that. I've never brought my body into close contact with his, close enough to feel the heat of his skin, close enough to smell him. I held his hand for hours in the darkness. I listened to the sound of his grief spill from his eyes, but I've never held *him*.

Tony helps him back to his chair, clapping him on the back with pride. "You did amazing! I'm so proud of you."

The clipboard slips from my hand, dropping to the ground with a clatter, and Rhett's head snaps up. His eyes focus on me. His jaw gapes in shock.

"Riggs?" I meet his wild-eyed gaze. "Fuck, Riggs!"

Fuck is right.

Rhett rolls his chair over to me, and then he engages the brake and braces his hands on the armrests, struggling to push to his feet.

You said you wanted a chance to put your hands on him. Well, here it is.

My hands rest on his waist, keeping him steady as he stands. And then his arms are around me, his slightly sour yet musky scent fills my nose, and I can feel the heat from his body, *finally*. He squeezes me tight, the stubble of his cheek abrasive against mine.

"How? Why are you... How?" Chuckling, I pull back to look at his shocked face. "You were over there and now..."

"And now I'm here."

"How?" he asks again, and I know I've blown his mind. He never thought he'd see me again. Did he care? Did he even spare me a passing thought?

Unlike him, I knew I would see him again. I knew he was a patient here at Womack, and that he still would be by the time I returned home. The anticipation of seeing him again gnawed at my gut for weeks. Worry, sympathy, and excitement —his reaction to seeing me now validated the ulcer I gave myself.

"Finished my deployment. Came home. I work as a physical therapist here."

"But in Afghanistan, you were my medic."

"I'm a combat medic in the Army reserves."

"No shit?" he says with an impressed smile.

Again, I snicker. I can't see his dimples beneath the layer of scruff covering his cheeks, which disappoints me to no end. I thought about them many nights as I lay in bed praying for sleep. Even with his unkempt hair and beard, he looks young, healthy, and gorgeous... when he smiles, at least. And I know for a fact, from Liza's reports, and my own stalking, this is the first time he's smiled in weeks.

Knowing that makes my heart beat faster. It shouldn't, but it does.

It's obvious that I have an effect on him, and I'm only slightly ashamed that I love it so much.

His leg starts to buckle, and he grabs on tighter around my neck. I tighten my hold on his waist, and my jaw tenses when I feel the sharp protrusion of his hip bones. He's lost so much weight.

I try to untangle his arms from my neck, although I'm loath to let him go. "Let's get you seated," I suggest.

"Wait," he insists, tightening his hold. The fingers of his left hand dig into my neck, but I don't mind. He holds on tight and salutes me with his right hand, standing as straight and stiff as his spine will allow.

"You don't have to salute me, soldier."

"Yeah, I do. You saved my life."

There's that lump again in my throat, making it difficult to swallow. "It was my honor."

He allows me to help him down into his chair, but he stares up at me with this ridiculous smile that reaches his eyes. He's looking at me like I'm the second coming of Christ or something, and I feel totally self-conscious because we're drawing the attention of others.

Tony saunters over. "Riggs, you didn't tell me you knew my patient. You've been home for weeks and haven't said a word."

I watch as the light dims from Rhett's bright eyes. *Fucking motherfucker.*

"You've been back for weeks?" Rhett asks.

He isn't smiling any longer. "Just over two weeks now."

"Did you... Did you know I was a patient here?"

Of course I knew. I signed off on his medical transport. I knew full well he was headed back to Womack. He can read my answer from the look on my face.

"How come you didn't come see me?"

"I—" clearing my throat, I try again, "I was busy settling back into my routine and I didn't want to take your focus from your recovery." All lies and empty excuses, which I know he sees right through.

"Well, I'm a multitasker. I can manage both you and my recovery. So don't be a stranger."

The wounded pride on his face tears at my heart. I can feel his disappointment in me, and I worry that he's going to turn it around on himself and take it personally. But of course it's fucking personal.

I stayed away because it felt *too* personal.

"Whatever you want, soldier. Maybe I'll stop by your room tomorrow, and we can fold paper together."

Fuck, as soon as the words are out of my mouth, I know I've given myself away. A satisfied smile spreads slowly over Rhett's face, and the look in his eyes changes to one of understanding. He knows I've been stalking him. Or at the very least, checking in on him.

"Sounds good. Bring a handful of brochures with you. I'll save you a cup of ice cream."

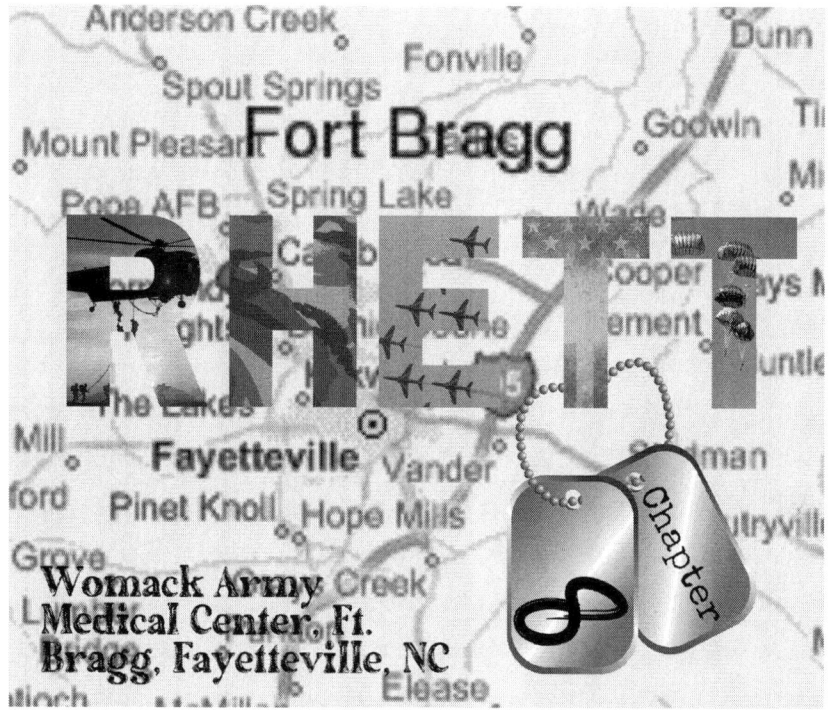

JUST OVER TWO WEEKS NOW.

I can't stop replaying the words in my head. He knew I was here; he obviously checked on me, or at least asked Liza about me. Otherwise, how would he know I'm folding fucking paper to keep from going nuts? But had he come to see me himself? No. No, he hadn't. The question is, is it because he couldn't be bothered? Or was there some other reason he stayed away?

I didn't expect that he'd lain awake thinking of me at night like I had him, but come on! Didn't he feel like we had a special connection? I did. I mean, he saved my life. I cried tears on his shoulder while he held my fucking hand. He stayed with me long after he could've walked away, and I'd bet my next cup of Jell-O it hadn't been because he felt it was his duty.

Maybe I'm crazy. Maybe I imagined the connection between us because I had just lost my best friend and I was desperate to feel... something, anything. Maybe Navarro Riggs is just one of those good guys that stands above the rest, with his bleeding heart and his endless sympathy for his patients. Maybe I was just another face in the crowd.

My memory of that night is hazy. I was suffering from blinding pain in both my legs; the morphine and loss of blood made my brain feel soft, but some things stayed with me. His strong grip. His sweet, pungent musk—cinnamon and vanilla and oranges—like *Old Spice*. A totally old-school scent, which somehow fits him perfectly. I remember the look in his dark eyes and the teasing half smirk on his rugged face as he joked with me about how the blood on my uniform brought out the color of my eyes. I have a feeling Riggs is the only man on Earth who could make a joke like that on a helicopter under gunfire in the middle of a fucking battlefield.

I thought no one ever looked sexier than he had in my memory. Sometimes it's the small things that take up such a large part of your brain and stay with you forever. Just a look, a scent, one teasing sentence you can't get out of your head.

That's Riggs. He's stuck in my head. But apparently, he forgot all about me.

Riggs breezes into my room, catching me off guard while Liza is changing my bandages.

She looks up from her task with a curl of her glossy lips. "It's about time."

Riggs comes closer, and his face tightens when he sees the maze of scars and stitches that cover my leg from ankle to thigh.

"Pretty, ain't it?"

He catches my self-pitying look and snorts. "I've seen worse. At least you got to keep it."

Liza fastens the soft cast around my leg and smiles at me. "All right, Marshmallow, all done. I'll be back with your dinner tray shortly."

He waits until she leaves before taking a seat on the edge of my bed. "Marshmallow?"

I give him my best never-fail, flirty smile. "'Cause I'm sweet and soft on the inside."

Riggs laughs. "I bet."

The last time he saw me—the only time, really—I was suffering from so much pain and grief, that I wasn't myself. He never got to see the real me, the irresistible side of Rhett Butler Marsh. Riggs has no idea how much fun I can be. And although that version of me has been drowned in an ocean of grief lately, and just... numb, I can muster a trace of my former self for him.

For Riggs.

"You came," I murmur softly.

"I told you I would."

Fuck, he looks good. Even with the beard, I can't get enough of looking at his face. His brown eyes are the color of aged whiskey. His jaw and chin have squared angles that make him look tough and hard. I wouldn't say his peach lips are generous, but they're definitely kissable, especially now that they're framed by all that dark scruff. I've always been attracted to men like him, men who could clearly dominate me and kick my ass but would never because their granite exterior hides a heart of gold. I would bet anything that Riggs's heart is gold plated. Fourteen fucking karats.

When he looks away and clears his throat, I realize I'm staring at him, and I can feel the tension becoming thicker, pushing all the air out of the room. It's a strange feeling to feel so connected to someone, but not have any clue what to say to them. Like, I know him on a soul-deep level, but we're total strangers. At his core, I know the kind of man that he is, but I don't know anything about him other than his name.

I guess that's the awkward beauty of trauma bonding with someone.

"My contract is up in five weeks, and I have no idea what I'm gonna do."

His eyes fall back on me again. "Did you have plans to reenlist?"

Nodding, I swallow. "Me and Brian, we were gonna re-up. Four more years of Airborne. But now—"

Riggs chuffs. "Your days of jumping out of planes are behind you, soldier. You're going to have to think of something else to do with the rest of your life."

Thanks for the reminder. "My heart just ain't in it no more." Without my best friend, without the opportunity to do the only job I've ever dreamed of, I just can't think about what comes next.

He leans forward intently. "Have you thought about taking a sabbatical?"

"What do you mean?"

"Don't reenlist," he shrugs. "Take some time off, heal, and hit your therapy hard. Maybe go to school and put your G.I. Bill to use. Then, in a year or two, you can decide whether you want to go back. Maybe you'll have a clearer picture of what you want to do by then. If you can pass the fitness test, the Army will take you back in a heartbeat."

A sabbatical. School. I can't see myself in either role. I become restless easily, and I'm not the book-smart type.

"What am I supposed to do for work? While I'm recovering and going to school?"

"I don't know. Find a job."

I look away, out the window. My room is on the second floor, overlooking the parking lot. All day long, I see people come and go, and wish I could be among them, and now that I'm going to have the chance, I'm scared shitless. Probably because I don't have any direction.

"My unit comes back next month. It'll be good to see them again. I don't know, I guess I can apply at The Footlocker or somethin'."

Riggs shakes his head. "I guess you could. You could spend your weekends drinking with your buddies and reliving your glory days while you serve them shots. But I can tell you, you're just going to become bitter and resentful, and every time they tell a story you aren't a part of, it'll just dig into your heart that much deeper."

"Then what the fuck am I supposed to do?" I snap. Why does he think he has all the answers when I have none? He doesn't even know me.

Riggs's face hardens in the wake of my anger. He reaches into his back pocket and pulls out a glossy brochure that he throws down on my tray table.

"No, thanks. I'm not in the mood to make fuckin' origami."

"Neither am I," he counters.

"Then what's that?" I ask, glaring at the brochure.

"*That* is your ticket out of here. *That* is your next step."

Reluctantly, I pick it up. "BALLS?" I ask. "BALLS are the answer to my future?"

He chuckles, his expression losing some of its attitude. "Beyond the Army: Legion of Love Soldiers. It's a not-for-profit organization that helps guys like you."

"Guys like me? What, losers with no future? Former soldiers with two bum legs and no prospects?"

"Exactly," he replies smugly.

I squint, reading the fine print beneath the logo. "Black Mountain? Isn't that like four hours from here?"

"Three and a half."

"What's this ball legion gonna do for me?"

"Give you back your life. Or help you find a new one, one that you can live with, maybe even one that you can fall in love with."

I snort. "Sure. Are they magically gonna heal my legs so I can jump again?"

"No, smart ass. I told you, your days of jumping out of planes are over. It's time to find a new dream."

I can feel anger bubbling inside me like a pot boiling over. He says it like it's nothing because it costs him nothing to say. Get a new dream. Get over the fact that you spent your entire adult life training to be something you can no longer be. Get a new life, and a new best friend, and forget the old one that died. Move four hours away to Hicktown and forget about the team you've lived with for four years. My fist comes down hard on the plastic tray table, startling Riggs.

"Just like that, huh? Just walk away and get a new life."

His dark eyes narrow to slits, but other than that, his face smooths out in a mask of calm serenity. "Or you can kick around Fayetteville and hope that your buddies throw you a bone now and then when you're not too busy with work and school. And every time you pass an Army vehicle on the road or hear a plane or jet fly overhead, your heart can burn with nostalgia for the good old days."

His words are meant to paint a grim picture of what my life will be like if I stay, and as much as I want to deny it, I know he's right. Without the 82nd, I'd hate my life here. Like a pathetic ex-lover, hanging onto a life they're no longer a part of.

"And how do you know this place isn't just a bunch of propaganda bullshit?"

"Because I volunteer there."

I laugh again. "Really? Is there anything you don't do? You save lives in the desert and rehabilitate broken soldiers here at Womack, and now you're gonna tell me you're collectin' homeless veterans like stray dogs in Black Mountain, North Carolina? Do you even have time for a personal life?"

"Too busy saving the world," he smirks.

I'm not gonna acknowledge the rush of relief I feel at hearing he doesn't have a private life outside of work. The only downside is that I fall into that same category. I'm *work*.

"You drive four hours away to volunteer on your days off? Are you a glutton for punishment or a candidate for martyrdom?"

"Actually, you're not the only one considering a change of scenery. I've been thinking about spending more time out there and less time here."

"Why? Why would you do that?"

Riggs shrugs. "Because it makes me feel good, and lately, I just want to chase that good feeling. I'm ready for less sacrifice and more reward."

I'm not sure what that means, but the idea of following him out there is appealing, not gonna lie.

"What am I supposed to do for money out there? Can't be many job opportunities in a small town like Black Mountain."

"Like you said, slinging shots at the local bar."

"So really, the only difference between Fayetteville and Black Mountain is that I won't be runnin' into the ghosts of my past 'round every corner? I'll still be workin' in some hole-in-the-wall beer joint?"

"Oh, I don't know about that. The Black Mountain Tavern is a step up from a beer joint. They've got live music on Friday nights." He smiles because he knows he's being an ass. "But seriously, I guarantee you won't be sorry. BALLS can help you live a better life. They can help you figure out what you're meant to do next, and I promise you'll fit right in with those guys. You're already making ball jokes."

"I'll think about it," I concede.

Riggs stands. He reaches into his back pocket and pulls out

another pamphlet, highlighting the importance of educating yourself on the risks and management of hepatitis.

"Make me an eagle."

He tosses it on my tray table and throws me a smile before gifting me with a view of his perfect ass, swaying side to side in his fitted black scrub pants as he walks away.

The man is seriously fucking fine. But fine enough to move four hours away to the middle of Nowhere-ville? That remains to be seen.

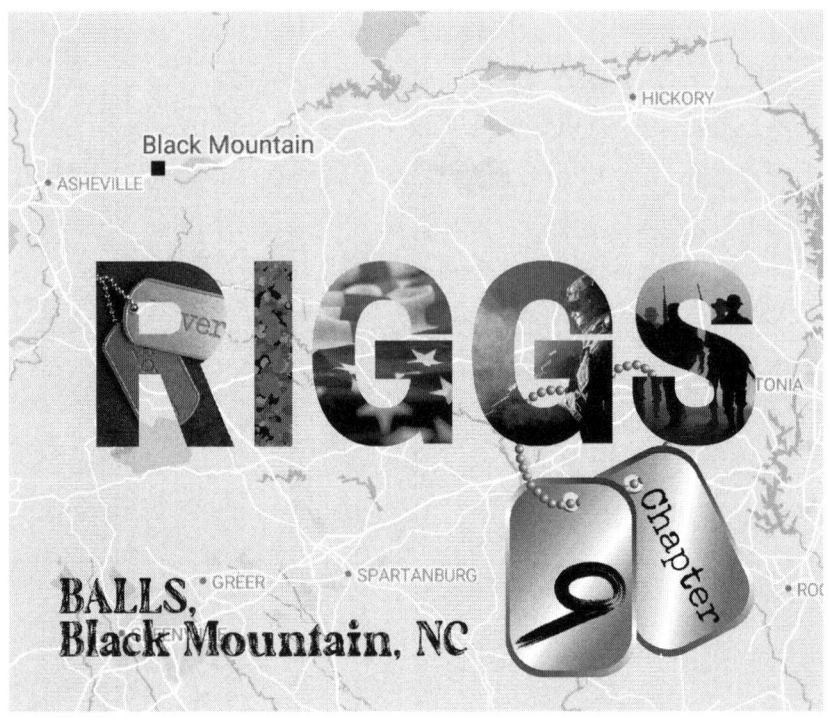

THE DRIVE from Fayetteville to Black Mountain is breathtaking and unforgettable. Usually, I put my nineties rock and alternative soundtrack on and roll down the windows. Even in the summer, the breeze feels amazing, especially the higher in elevation you get. The views of the Uwharrie National Forest in the fall are spectacular, although its gorgeous anytime of year. But when I pass the South Mountains and enter the Pisgah National Forest, I know I'm home.

That's what Black Mountain feels like to me—home.

I can breathe up here. My heart slows down and my head evens out. My heart and soul are in these mountains.

Years ago, I bought a little house up here. Nothing special, just a two-bedroom, one-bath place on five acres. It was the view that sold me. The backyard overlooks a valley below with the prettiest little stream. When the leaves on the trees turn colors, it looks like God himself painted an unimaginable canvas of fiery and golden hues that are to die for.

Not only that, but the people are friendlier, there's no traffic, and time just seems to slow down up here. It's the kind of place where you stop taking things for granted and start enjoying living.

I park my truck in front of the house, grab my duffel from the backseat, and check my mail. The first thing I always do when I get here is fire up the hot tub, strip down, and soak away my stress. The steamy bubbles and breathtaking view are the most effective elixirs. After my mail is sorted and my bag is squared away, I climb into the hot tub and sigh with pleasure as the hot water bubbles over my shoulders, loosening every tight knot beneath my skin. The sun is setting over the ridge, a rusty blazing ball of fire in a pastel sky.

If only I could stay forever.

Maybe... maybe I can.

My eyes drift closed and I focus on the hum of the jets and bubbles, on the steam bathing my face, opening up my lungs with each inhaled breath. The effervescent bubbles tickle my soft cock, and I brush my hand over it. Mindlessly, I tug at it a few times, and it feels good, good enough that I consider playing with it. I don't have my phone with me, so watching a video is out of the question. Instead, I try to recall a face or body to focus on, but the only one that comes to mind is his.

Rhett's.

I let go of my dick and open my eyes to clear my head. I

refuse to jack off to him. His gorgeous face, those playful hazel eyes, and lickable dimples are not going to get airtime in my head. But no matter how many faces I run through, I keep coming back to his.

Fuck it. There's no one here to know I got off to him, and it certainly won't be the first time.

I close my eyes and reach again for my cock, recalling the strength and warmth of his hand in mine, the vulnerability in his eyes, and the intimate connection between us that was forged in the most unlikely circumstances. Those memories are replaced by newer ones—the electric light in his eyes when I walked into his hospital room. His smiling face and unadulterated joy when he discovered me in the therapy room. The fire sparking in his hazel eyes when he challenged me about moving on and starting over.

I imagine Rhett in new scenarios, instances where I make him laugh. His rugged, smiling face, shining with happiness. What if I touched him? Would I see fire in his eyes? Would they burn for me? What does his mouth taste like? I'd bet his tongue feels like warm velvet. In my fantasy, his nipples are tight and brown, and his chest is barely furry, just enough to remind me he's all male.

My dick is rock hard now, and my fist moves up and down in lazy strokes as I stoke the fire slowly building in my groin. I tip my head back, resting it against the edge of the tub, and draw another humid breath deep into my lungs.

I fantasize about an intense dialogue between us, where our verbal sparring has a flirty edge. Rhett seems like he could go toe-to-toe with me and hold his own, which I find incredibly hot. When he's not depressed and grieving, or in unimaginable pain, I bet he's a hell raiser. I have no idea if he's into guys or not, but in my dream, he's totally into me. Fucking me with his eyes, teasing his bottom lip to make me want to suck on it. If I ever got him beneath me, I would fucking wreck him. Rhett looks like he's built sturdy enough to take a good pounding.

The combination of the warm water and teasing bubbles and my strong grip brings me to the edge quickly. I imagine sinking my teeth into his lip, sucking his tongue into my mouth, and drinking up his sweet flavor. The muscles in my stomach contract and roll in a wave of pleasure. My tight fist milks the thick seed from my shaft as I shoot into the warm water with a satisfied grunt.

My body sags like an empty sack.

I feel loose. I feel satisfied.

Fuck, that was great. Rhett Marsh would be an incredible lay. I carefully tuck that fantasy away with the others and pretend that my mind never went there.

I pull my truck into the parking lot of the NC Mountain Region branch of BALLS and hustle inside. Margaret Anne is always ready with a smile and a warm cup of coffee. She heads the volunteer services department, but you can't pull her away from the front desk. She wouldn't dream of not being there, front and center, to greet someone when they came through the front doors.

"Afternoon, MA," I greet, taking the proffered cup of coffee.

Her sleek gray bob bounces as she smiles. "Afternoon, Riggs. Welcome back."

Sipping on the coffee as I make my way down the long corridor to Brewer Marx's office, I pass several veterans and staff I recognize and wave hello. His door is open and I slip inside, tossing my empty paper cup in his trashcan.

"You ready for lunch?"

He's seated at his desk going through patient files. Brewer looks up, removing his reading glasses, and smiles. "Back so soon? Feels like you just left," he teases.

"That's what I want to talk to you about. Come on, lunch is on me."

He chuckles, pushing to his feet. "You realize they serve free lunch here, don't you?"

Of course, which is why I offered to treat. "What can I say? I'm a big spender."

BALLS serves a hot meal every afternoon to vets and their families free of charge. On the menu today is a hot, open-faced roast beef sandwich with a side of mashed potatoes, gravy, and steamed vegetables. I snag an extra slice of bread so I can make a proper sandwich out of it. We take a seat, and I dig into my sandwich with both hands when I notice a man and his son seated two tables away. The boy smiles at me and waves.

"Hey, Dylan," I mumble around a mouthful of roast beef. Shyly, he waves back, his big grin showing off his two missing front teeth. He comes in here just about every day to eat with his dad, who attends physical and occupational therapy. "I'll be right back," I tell Brewer. The east wall of the cafeteria is lined with vending machines. I slip a dollar in the slot and press the buttons for a chocolate chip granola bar. It drops into the bin and I retrieve it and make my way back to Dylan. "Here ya go, kiddo," I offer, messing up his hair. He grabs for it happily. "Not until after you finish your sandwich," I insist. Dylan's father salutes me and I return the gesture.

I'm not a big fan of standing on ceremony, especially when I'm away from base, but I recognize the gesture as his way of saying thank you while still maintaining his dignity.

When I sit down, Brewer snickers. "What?" I ask. He just shakes his head. The downside of having a best friend who's a shrink is knowing he always sees right through you.

"You're such a Daddy," he whispers. His grin is decidedly mischievous.

"I'm going to take that as a compliment, and hope that you meant I'll make a great father someday." Brewer is aware of my sexuality, despite the fact I never date.

His snicker turns into a deep, shoulder-shaking laugh. "Take it however you want."

I spare him a glare before picking up my sandwich. "Just because I'm a hard ass with a soft heart doesn't mean that I..." I can't even finish defending myself because he's laughing so hard tears come to his eyes, and I'm just becoming more pissed watching him. "Fuck off, Brewer." Taking a huge bite of beef, I ignore him as I take my time chewing, and it isn't until I swallow minutes later that I continue. "I had a reason for asking you to lunch."

Brewer sobers, taking a sip of his tea. "What's going on?"

I take a deep breath and put my sandwich down, wiping my fingers on my napkin. "I think I'm really leaving Womack this time. I've written a resignation letter to hand in next week."

He looks as surprised as if I had told him I was getting married tomorrow. "Wow, didn't see that coming. Ever since you got back from this last deployment, I've noticed a change in you. Is everything okay?"

I breathe out a heavy sigh and lean back in my chair. "You're right. I guess I've come to a crossroads and my deployment made things very clear to me. I don't know… I feel like I'm chasing my tail trying to treat the problem and not the solution. Placing bandages on cuts so they can go back out and blow off their whole fucking leg. I'm just feeding the war machine."

"Riggs, being a combat medic and an Army nurse is important work. Someone has to be there to save them and patch them up so they can return home to their families."

"I'm not saying it isn't important work. I get the purpose of the role and the good it does. I'm saving lives, but at the end of the day, they're still putting their lives at risk. I'm a healer more than I'll ever be a soldier. I'm tired of just stemming the flow of blood and stitching cuts. I want to heal. I want to change lives instead of saving them."

"That's… powerful. I know you didn't come to this decision lightly. Did something happen over there?"

I can tell Brewer anything, but the truth is, meeting Rhett did something to me. It shook something loose inside my head and my heart about the kind of soldier and the kind of healer I want to be. It just feels private, though, like something I'm not ready to share, even with my best friend.

"When I'm at BALLS, I feel like I'm finally making a difference. Being out in the field feels like filling a hole with water and watching the sand fill it back in. It's futile. The Army docs and the VA just treat the symptoms, not the solution to the problem. That's all we're trained to do. When I was over there, that truth was never more glaringly obvious to me, and when I came home, everything I saw just reiterated the idea that I wasn't really doing anything to make a dent in the problem. I want to be the solution. I'm tired of seeing soldiers get hooked on drugs to manage the pain instead of receiving the therapy they need. It would be so easy to help them if we could just offer them the right resources."

Nobody understands that better than Brewer. He's a recovering addict who never would have gotten hooked on drugs, if not for his old war injury. In the same vein, he'd fallen in love with Nash Sommers, another vet turned addict because of the war. Brewer ran the addiction support group here at BALLS, while I tried my damnedest to make a difference running the Bitches with Stitches, a trauma support group for veterans.

My gaze drifts over to the table where Dylan sits with his dad. Robert was a soldier serving his country proudly until he suffered an injury during training that they deemed his fault. He wasn't eligible for disability benefits and became hooked on drugs to manage his pain, which earned him a dishonorable discharge and disqualified him from receiving veterans' benefits. I'm proud to serve an organization like BALLS that doesn't turn guys like him away.

Thanks to Brewer, Robert is getting the help he needs so that he and Dylan can live a better life.

"Sounds like you've got a solid plan worked out," Brewer

says. "Does this have anything to do with the job you applied for here?"

Weeks ago, a full-time position became available in the physical therapy department, and I put my hat into the ring immediately. "Should find out today."

"You'll get it," he says confidently. "Then *I* can take *you* to lunch to celebrate."

"Let me guess, you're treating me to a hot lunch here in the BALLS cafeteria?"

Brewer laughs. "I'm a big spender, like you."

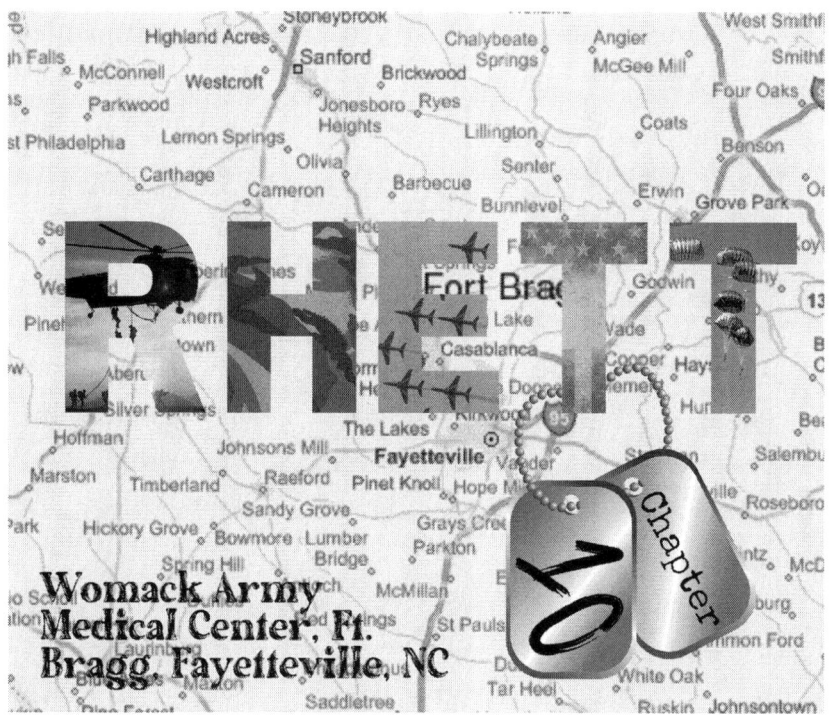

Chapter 10

RHETT

Womack Army Medical Center, Ft. Bragg, Fayetteville, NC

LIZA IS CHANGING MY BANDAGES, going over my wound care instructions for what feels like the fiftieth time when I hear heavy, booted feet coming down the hallway. They slow as they approach my door, and I snap my head up, feeling hopeful. To my everlasting disappointment, Tony ducks his head in my room and my face falls, which doesn't go unnoticed by Liza.

"Just checking in to see if you're all ready for discharge tomorrow," Tony chirps.

"I guess so," I say unenthusiastically.

"So, you're going to continue with therapy?" he asks.

"That's the plan." I slide the BALLS brochure toward him.

Tony picks it up and scans the front cover. "I've heard good things about this place. I'm sure they'll get you back on your feet again, pun intended," he jokes with a laugh.

My face remains passive, and Liza nudges me. "Good one," I add, humoring him.

"All right, then, Specialist Marsh. It's been a pleasure, sir." He holds his hand out to shake mine, and I follow through with the gesture. I may not be crazy about him, but he's a good guy.

When he disappears through the door, and his bootsteps fade down the hall, I turn to Liza, who's looking at me with a raised brow.

"Sorry to disappoint you, but he's not here today or tomorrow."

We both know who *he* is. "You gonna make me ask where he is?"

A little smile plays around her lips like she loves lording the minuscule morsel of power over me. "On his days off, he heads up to Black Mountain."

To BALLS. I close my eyes and breathe out a heavy sigh. That means I won't see him again before I'm discharged.

Liza finishes wrapping up my leg and throws the empty packaging in the trash. Then she snaps off her gloves and chucks them in the trash, too. "Listen, I get it. Riggs is a likable guy. Honorable, charismatic, that face... but you're walking down a dead-end street. First of all, he's married to his job, and nothing comes before that. In fact, in the six years I've known him, I don't think I've ever seen him date. He works seven days a week, between here and volunteering. If you feel like you have some special connection with him, it's a testament to how good he is at his job. He tries to make all his patients feel that way."

I refuse to open my eyes and show her how deeply her words wound my pride. We do have a special connection; I felt it from the first night. And as much as he tries to maintain his cool distance from me, I know Riggs feels it too. I felt it when he touched me and I saw it in his eyes. Some things you just can't fake or hide.

"Come to think of it," she continues, "I'm not even sure of his orientation." She's saying she's not sure if he's into men or women. Both maybe? Just like me. Even if he's never admitted to anyone that he's attracted to men, I know he's attracted to me. I felt the spark between us.

Even still, I might be heading down a dead-end street, like she said. I've been hiding my sexuality for years because I felt it was a necessity, or maybe it was just easier. Who's to say Riggs isn't doing the same thing? Liza said he doesn't date, but maybe that's because he doesn't want to admit who he's attracted to.

In two weeks, I'll no longer be a soldier in the United States Army, which means I don't have to hide anymore. I still have no idea how to come out to my buddies after I've hidden myself away from them for so long, but to everyone else I meet from here on out, I can be myself. My true self. After reading Drake's letters to Brian and seeing how much time they wasted by lying, I've made up my mind. I don't ever want to be in that situation. I don't want to be the guy who lives half a life because he doesn't have the balls to face judgment from others. From the people he loves.

Fuck that.

Rhett Marsh is a bisexual man.

Rhett Marsh was a soldier in the 82nd Airborne.

Rhett Marsh is...

I don't know how to answer that last one, but I'm gonna fucking find out.

"Look at me, Marshmallow," Liza demands. "Haven't you suffered enough? Don't set yourself up for failure. Find someone who is available and willing. Focus on your health and recovery. Get your life back."

Everything she's saying sounds wise and logical, but I don't hear a fucking word because when I want something, I go get it, and what I want is Navarro Riggs.

"Enough about him," I evade, changing the subject. "I need to focus on my next steps. I've got two weeks left before my contract runs out. My Staff Sergeant is still deployed with my unit, but the Staff Sergeant I'm reporting to in my rear D unit came by to see me this morning."

Liza looks grim. "What'd he say?"

"Basically, I'm fucked. The Army is fuckin' me, deep and without lube."

"Well, that's how they like it, rough and dry."

I blow out an irritated breath. "With only two weeks left, they can't find temporary housing for me, so they're insisting I use my accrued paid leave to cover the few remaining days of my contract, essentially forcing me out. So when I leave tomorrow, I'm done. I'm out. On my own. The problem is, I've got nowhere to go. I never filled out my paperwork to transfer my belongings because I thought I was reenlisting. I've got two days to pick up my stuff and my car and get my ass off base. Also, I qualify for VA benefits, but not disability pay."

"What?" Liza shrieks. "You shattered your legs! You got shot down in combat."

"I did, but I healed." My overly bright smile is meant to be sarcastic. I give Liza two thumbs up and she snorts. "If I develop complications from here on out, I can file a new claim with the VA, but I don't have a standing one. I've got some combat pay saved up from when I was overseas, but it's not much."

"Well, fuck that," she swears, rounding the bed and taking a seat by my feet. "The day you're discharged is my day off, and I'll help you pick up your stuff and your car."

"And go where?" I ask, feeling hopeless and overwhelmed. Lately, everything feels like a series of unfortunate events compounding my sanity. It would be so easy to just give up and hide my head between my legs and cry like a little bitch, but where would that get me?

"Lucky for you, my best friend has a condo in Black Mountain. She's living with her boyfriend right now, so she's willing to sublet it. The building is safe, and I can vouch for your next-door neighbor. He's a great guy. Fair warning, though, she's going to collect the security deposit. The last tenant I recommended to her threw a shovel through the wall and splintered the front door."

"Jesus. What kind of company do you keep?"

Liza laughs. "Nash is a good guy. He's just got some dark demons haunting him."

"So, you think she'll rent to me?"

"Of course she will. Who could turn down a cute marshmallow like you?"

"God, would you quit with that shit? No self-respectin' man wants to be described as a cute marshmallow."

Liza leans forward to pinch my cheeks, and I kick her playfully with my good leg... well, half-decent leg. She laughs so hard she snorts like a little piggy, and then we're both laughing. It's got to be the first time I've heard the sound of my own laughter in weeks. Instead of making me feel better, it just makes me feel sad. I have to fight back tears as I recall my life before the fall. I used to laugh all the time, with Brian, Warren, and Ormen. My life was full of laughter. I used to take it for granted. I hope I never take happiness for granted again. It's a precious commodity that I'm in short supply of.

"I don't mean to sound ungrateful, but what am I gonna do with a whole apartment? I've got, like, two boxes full of stuff in storage. Some clothes, paperwork, and medals, my gaming console, and some games. I don't have shit to furnish an apartment with. I've lived in barracks housing for four years."

Liza's face pulls tight in concentration. "Let me make some calls," she suggests, patting my leg before pushing to her feet.

―――――

"Jesus, Mary, and Joseph! Can we not listen to somethin' other than... than whatever the hell this is?" I bitch. Liza just laughs and turns the music up louder, singing along to the pop song on the radio. "There, that's the turnoff," I say, pointing to the exit sign over the highway.

Two days ago, I felt overwhelmed lying in my hospital bed, feeling a total loss of control over my life. Today, I feel slightly hopeful, but also afraid to hope. After all I've been through, I can't take another letdown. Not getting this apartment would be a crushing defeat.

When the song ends, Liza turns the volume down. "So, my friend is going to meet us there. You can walk through the apartment, and if you like it, you can sign the lease. Then I'll leave your car with you and she can take me back home."

"Thanks for driving." My leg isn't solid enough to put the kind of pressure on it I would need to make the four-hour drive.

"Anytime, Marshmallow. You want to stop for lunch?"

"Sure, just drive through somewhere." Then I start thinking about how I have to buy groceries, but I'll need a ride to the grocery store. That segues into worrying about how I don't have pots and pans to cook in or plates to eat on. And then my good mood spirals right out the open window.

Fucking fuck, I'm a damn mess. I'm a soldier trained to survive under the harshest conditions, and yet here I am, not able to even fend for myself to cover my basic needs. What a joke.

Liza pulls through a fast food place, and we order spicy chicken sandwiches, onion rings, and shakes to go. The greasy goodness tastes transformative, much better than hospital food, and I can't disguise my moan of pure pleasure.

"Mmm, this tastes like gourmet cuisine after eating Womack's cafeteria food."

Liza laughs. "Okay, let's play best and worst," she mumbles around a mouthful of chicken.

"What's best and worst?"

"You have to tell me your best and worst of whatever topic

we choose." She merges back onto the highway, managing the steering wheel and her sandwich at the same time. "Let's start with you. Best thing you ever ate."

This sounds easy. I can do this. I pop an onion ring into my mouth and chew as I think. "My mama's gumbo."

"Aw, that's sweet. Worst?"

"Anything I've cooked," I say jokingly.

"At least you're honest," she laughs. "Best thing I ever ate was last year for my birthday. A bunch of the girls at the hospital took me out to dinner at this hot pot place. I tried so many new things and, oh my gosh, everything was so delicious. They had to roll me out of there."

I watch her with a smile on my lips. Liza is so animated when she talks, using her expressions and her hands; she just sucks you right in. "Worst thing?"

"Anything they serve at Womack." We bust out laughing together. "Okay, best movie. Go."

Taking a sip of my shake, I try to think. "Uh, *An Officer And A Gentleman.*"

"Really? Nothing from after you were born?" She smirks, and I return it.

"My mama used to watch all the classics on repeat. We had the complete VHS library. I don't know why, but that movie stuck with me."

"Is that why you wanted to be a soldier?"

"I don't know. I don't think just one movie did it for me, but I had a healthy admiration and respect for the military. My mama had a thing for World War II movies that romanticized war."

She clutches her heart and says in a false southern belle voice, "How romantic. I do declare." I swat her arm. "What's the worst movie?"

Giving her a sideways glance, I admit, "*Gone With The Wind*."

Liza gasps dramatically. "Rhett Butler Marsh, don't you speak blasphemy in my presence!" She catches my eye roll and adds, "I'm calling your mama and telling on you."

"Don't you dare! You know that's her favorite movie, obviously."

"So, what do you have against Scarlett and Rhett?"

"Nothing really, but after my fifty-seventh viewing, every fuckin' word they utter grates my nerves."

Liza straight up cackles. "Don't think I won't leverage this blackmail against you," she threatens.

"You break my mama's heart, I break both your legs. Then we'll be twins." I grab another onion ring. "What about you?"

"Best has to be *13 Going On 30*."

"You can't be serious," I tease.

Liza shrugs. "I love a good romance. Worst movie is anything scary or gory. I can't watch them."

"Talk about leverage and blackmail," I hint.

She swats me back, giggling. Honest to God, I've never heard Liza giggle. Didn't know she was capable of making that sound.

"All right, what's your best day?"

My chest pulls tight and I swallow. The questions are getting a little deeper now. "I'm hoping it's this one," I admit. I'm nervous as hell that something is gonna go wrong and blow my fresh start out of the water. Liza covers my hand with hers.

"It's gonna be fine, Marshmallow. Just trust in me."

With a deep sigh, I blow out my reservations. "My best day was the day I joined the 82nd."

She smiles softly. "And your worst?"

I hesitate, thinking back over the years filled with both good and bad memories, all of them unforgettable. "The same day." I can't look at her. I don't want to see sorrow or pity on her face, so I look out the window instead, counting the pine trees whizzing by.

"I'm sorry. I shouldn't even have asked. Obviously, your worst day was… Anyway, I'm done with this game. Let's sing." She turns up the radio loud and absolutely desecrates *'Party In The USA'* by Miley Cyrus.

I'm not in a singing, playful mood, but I join in just to try to force the bad thoughts from my mind. They're like bad juju, putting a hex on my good day, and I won't allow anything to jinx me today.

RHETT

Chapter 22

Black Mountain, NC

I DON'T KNOW what I was expecting, but it wasn't this. This place is... *nice*. Countless towering pines camouflage the two-story brick façade. A colorful garden of flowers compliments a courtyard with benches and a birdbath. My favorite feature is the walking trail that loops the building, or at least, it would have been my favorite feature before I broke both of my legs.

We follow Liza's best friend into the condo, which I'm grateful is on the first floor. It would be a bitch to navigate those stairs every day, especially with groceries in my arms. Right away, the smell of cinnamon assaults my nose, but it's pleasant, homey; like fresh baked pies have been baking in the oven.

"I didn't realize the place came furnished. Will I have to pay extra for that?"

Marcy laughs. "This isn't my stuff, hon. It's yours."

"Mine? You must be mistaken. I don't have stuff."

Liza squeezes my shoulder and smiles. "Come on, let's take a look around."

The front door opens into the living room with the kitchen off to the right. The two rooms are separated by a breakfast bar. I follow the girls down the long hallway, passing a coat closet and a linen closet before we come up to the bedroom. It's spacious and bright, with a big window and a walk-in closet. There's a connected bathroom with a walk-in shower, and another bathroom with a bathtub down the hall for guests.

"So, what do you think?" Marcy asks.

"It's nice. Real nice." The hallways are wide enough to not squash my shoulders and bump my elbows as I clumsily make my way on my crutches, and the shower stall is big enough for my plastic chair.

But it doesn't feel like home. I'm not sure it ever will.

I remind myself that everything is temporary, and this is just another phase of my life I have to squeeze through. All this stuff, it's not me. It's too fancy to be me. Growing up in my mama's house, I was surrounded by antiques and mismatched furniture. Even still to this day, my childhood bedroom remains untouched, exactly as I left it with my old twin bed with cartoon sheets and second-hand furniture. Then I moved into the barracks where everything smelled like mildew and sweaty socks. Nothing issued by the Army can be described as high-quality. I had a twin bed with a squeaky metal frame, a desk made of pressboard that was as sturdy as cardboard, and a thin mattress that I'm pretty sure at least fifty other guys had slept on before me. And now, this...

Whoever decorated this place has a hard-on for IKEA. Everything looks new, every piece matches, and everything smells and looks modern and clean. I feel like a fish out of water, swimming in someone else's pond.

Marcy slaps a packet of lease papers on the breakfast bar and offers me a pen. "All you have to do is sign on the dotted line and it's yours for the next six months."

I'm out of options, and I would be a fool to pass this place up. It's in my budget, but nicer than I can afford, so I eagerly sign my name.

"Welcome home. I'll make a copy and mail it to you," she tells me on her way to the door. "Am I giving you a ride back, Liza?"

I was hoping she'd stick around and help me settle in, but she drove me here in my car, so I understand she can't stay.

Liza squeezes me in a perfumed hug. "Take care, Marshmallow. Don't think I won't be checking in," she warns with a smile.

I hold the door open as the girls leave, and just as I'm about to shut it, I jump, startled at Liza's squeal. It's one of those high-pitched girly sounds akin to nails scraping a chalkboard.

"Mandy! I was hoping to run into you," she gushes excitedly.

I don't know whether to slam the door shut on them or grab her by the arm and haul her back inside. This guy Mandy looks like a hulking beast of a man, whose only job is to kick ass and take names. Half his face is burned, the angry puckered skin crawling down his neck into his collar. He has white scars criss-crossing his forearms and hands that are mostly covered by tattoos, and even scars on his other cheek, the one that's not burned. The guy looks like he could deadlift a *Mack* truck without breaking a sweat.

"Come meet Marshmallow," Liza squeals.

Fucking wonderful. Compare me to a goddamn mushy sweet treat in the presence of this badass alpha male who's probably related to a pro wrestler, from the looks of him. That doesn't fuck with my masculinity at all.

He ambles into my living room, his wide shoulders effectively blocking my exit. "Hey, I'm Mandy. Are you Rhett?"

"Who wants to know?" I ask.

He chuffs like he's amused I'm trying to hide my identity from him. "I live next door. Also, I'm your ball buddy."

Fucking ball buddy? Suddenly, I'm less worried about my life and more worried about my dick. No, not my dick, my *ass*. "Is that some sort of euphemism for being down to fuck?"

For a big guy, he sure does scare easily. His face blanches white and his eyes become huge. "What? No! No, no, man. I'm your BALLS buddy."

"Yeah, you keep sayin' that like I'm supposed to know what it means."

Laughing, Mandy runs a hand through his short hair. "You know, Beyond the Army: Legion of Love Soldiers. I volunteer there, and they've got this program where they pair up buddies with other vets in need."

What the fuck? "They just hand out friends?" In preschool, we followed the buddy system when we went to the bathroom, or on field trips, and in the Army, we were assigned battle buddies, but I don't think either of those things apply here.

Mandy smiles. "No, not like that. But when you need a ride to the store or just someone to talk to, you call your buddy. I've got a buddy myself. He comes with me to doctor visits."

"So, you want to be my Ball Buddy?" I'm trying to keep a straight face.

"I know. It sounds fucking stupid, but it is what it is. BALLS saved my life, so now I'm giving back, trying to save someone else's."

"So, you're trying to save me?" The ladies at my mama's church tried to save me. They haven't succeeded yet.

Mandy snorts. "Something like that, smartass." He shakes his head. "Here, give me your phone. I'll put my number in it."

Reluctantly, I hand it over and he punches his number in and then hands it back and walks over to the kitchen, pulling open the door on my fridge. Mandy looks inside like a nosy biddy.

"Shit, I should eat here," he mumbles, then shuts the door and straightens. "You've got plenty of food for now, but when you get low, I'll take you to the store."

What the fuck? Who just goes through someone's fridge like that? "I sure as fuck didn't pay for any of it. I don't know where it came from."

"Knock, knock," a voice calls out from the front door as they rap on it.

I know that voice.

From the kitchen, Mandy calls, "Riggs?"

"Hey, Mandy." They exchange a one-armed hug.

"What are you doing here?" I'm stunned that Riggs is standing in my living room. "How'd you find me?"

They laugh and Mandy says, "He'll catch on soon." He claps my shoulder. "It's a small town and an even smaller circle. News travels fast."

"Are you settling in?" Riggs asks. His eyes travel up and down my body, almost like he's drinking me in, and it makes my heart skip a beat.

"I don't know. I feel like Dorothy plucked out of Kansas and dropped flat on my ass in Oz."

Riggs chuckles. "Mandy, are you keeping an eye on my patient?"

His patient? No two words could sound sweeter.

"Trying to. He thinks I'm trying to get into his pants."

I'm so busy gawking at Riggs that it takes a moment for me to realize he just threw me under the bus. "What? No! I mean, that's what you made it sound like when you said you wanted to be my ball buddy. You know, like buddies who sit around feeling up each other's balls. What was I supposed to think?"

He chokes on his laugh, trying to hide it. "Don't worry, the ball jokes will grow on you," Riggs assures me.

"Well, I'm gonna take off," Mandy mumbles. "You know where to find me."

He shuts the door behind him, and I'm left standing in my living room with Riggs. *Alone.* He's staring at me and a delicious curl of heat licks through my body. Fuck, the sexual tension with this guy is ridiculous.

"Why don't we sit so you can take some weight off your leg?" he suggests.

I wait for him to take a seat first so I can sit as close to him as possible. The soft gray microfiber gives way beneath my ass, and I sink into the plush cushion. "Damn, this couch is nice."

"Yeah, I got lucky."

"Wait, you did this? All of this? You're the one that furnished my apartment?"

Color blooms above the scruff on his cheeks. "I made a few calls, cashed in a few favors. It's no big deal."

"Are you serious? Of course, it's a big deal! I have nothing. Literally just two boxes downstairs in the trunk of my car. That's it. I can't believe you did all of this for me. And the food..."

"You were in need, and I was able to help. It's that simple, Rhett."

It's not simple at all. He went out of his way to make my life easier. To make sure that I have what I need. He's looking after me, caretaking my ass. I fucking love it.

"This is just part of what BALLS does. Helping vets in need."

I doubt this has BALLS written all over it. More like Riggs. This isn't what the *organization* does, this is what *Riggs* does.

"Well, I really like everything you chose for me. I've never had nice things like this. Feels kind of weird, actually, but I'm sure it'll grow on me."

"Wait until you see the sheets," he says with a wicked smirk.

Just thinking about Riggs touching my bed, or being anywhere near it, makes my dick kick in my pants. "Maybe we should go to my bedroom, and you can show me what you chose for me to sleep on yourself."

His eyes narrow as he realizes I'm hitting on him. "I'm gonna go downstairs and grab your boxes from your trunk." Before I can even relax, he's back, juggling two stacked boxes in his arms. "Where do you want these?"

"Um, here, I guess," I decide, pointing to the coffee table. "I need to go through them. I haven't seen this stuff in almost a year. I can't even remember what's in there."

Riggs looks sympathetic. "I remember that feeling. After coming back from my second deployment, when I received possession of my stuff, I just felt so detached from it all. I crossed an ocean and a desert and fought in the same war twice, and all I had to my name fit inside two boxes. I couldn't understand how those few unimportant things defined me. It was all I had. Then I started thinking of all I sacrificed and how I had nothing to show for it." Riggs shakes his head. "That's not true, you know. I had plenty to show for my sacrifice, but none of it was in that box, nor could I understand it at the time. I had such a tough time adjusting." My heart sinks down to the pit of my stomach. He's seen some shit, like me. I can hear it in his voice, his sadness. "How are you adjusting?"

I breathe out a heavy sigh. "Some days are easier than others, and I don't mean the pain in my legs."

"I know exactly what you mean," Riggs empathizes.

"It's sorta like I got up and went to take a piss before the credits rolled on the movie; like it switched off mid-production. Everything over there was so loud and busy and... and... brown." Riggs chuckles softly. "Life here is slower, quieter, and so much more colorful. Sometimes... sometimes I just feel lost."

He reaches over to cover my hand with his. The warmth

from his skin bleeds through mine, and I suddenly realize I'm cold. Or maybe I'm just lonely, and that feels like being cold. I flip my hand over, my fingers grasping his, and my heart jolts when he doesn't let go.

"You're not lost, soldier. You're right where you're supposed to be. I promise it gets easier with time."

"And in the meantime, if I feel lost, I can reach out and hold your hand?" I ask hopefully, a playful smile on my face.

Riggs barks out a laugh. "You never quit, do you?" he says fondly. "It's getting late. I'm going to leave you to settle in." He pushes to his feet and walks over to the breakfast bar, grabbing my phone. Riggs tosses it to me and thankfully, I catch it before it hits me in the face, which would be totally awkward. "Open it for me."

I punch in my passcode and toss it back. Riggs enters his number and places it back down on the bar. He rocks back on his heels, taking a last glance around. "You've got Mandy's number, and if he doesn't answer, you can call me."

"Can I—"

"Call him first," he emphasizes, cutting me off.

Too bad Riggs can't be my ball buddy. I'd totally let him in my pants.

"I'll see you tomorrow at the gym. I hope you sleep well tonight because you're going to need your rest for tomorrow," he says with an evil grin, shutting the door behind him.

Fuck, he's gonna work my ass to the bone, and not in a sexy way, unfortunately.

After sitting for a few minutes, I get stiff when I try to move again, so it's a struggle for me to get up so I can lock the door behind him. I grab my phone and dial the only number I know by heart.

"Hey, Mama. It's me, Rhett."

"Hey, my little pecan. Are you settled in?"

"Yeah, the new place is real nice, Mama. You should see it. I have all new furniture and before you ask, I have a whole fridge full of food."

"How nice. If only you knew how to cook it," she teases.

The truth is, I do know how to cook because I grew up watching her and I learned from the best. But I've never needed to practice because my mama always beat me to the stove. She loved to cook for me.

"I'll be fine, I promise. How do you feel?" The last couple times we've talked, she sounded tired… off somehow. I haven't seen her in more than a year, so I have no idea what's wrong, and it's just like her to keep things from me so she doesn't *worry me*.

"Oh, you know, tired as a tick but blessed as a bluebird."

"Are bluebirds particularly blessed?" I tease.

"Don't you sass me, pecan. You're never too old to get a lickin'."

My smile stretches from ear to ear. "Yes, ma'am." Despite my unfamiliar surroundings and slight feeling of detachment, hearing my mama's warm voice feels like a comfort, reminding me that no matter where I am, I'm never far from home.

We talk for nearly twenty minutes and when we hang up, I shuffle into my bedroom, intending to pass the fuck out, but when I pull back the khaki green comforter on my bed, a sharp bark of laughter echoes off the walls.

That fucker Riggs put kids' sheets on my bed!

The beige background sets off the Army-green paratroopers jumping from helos. Shaking my head, I don't even try to hide my smile. Why should I? I fucking love them, and there's no one here but me. From the way things just went down, I'll be the only one sleeping on them for a long time.

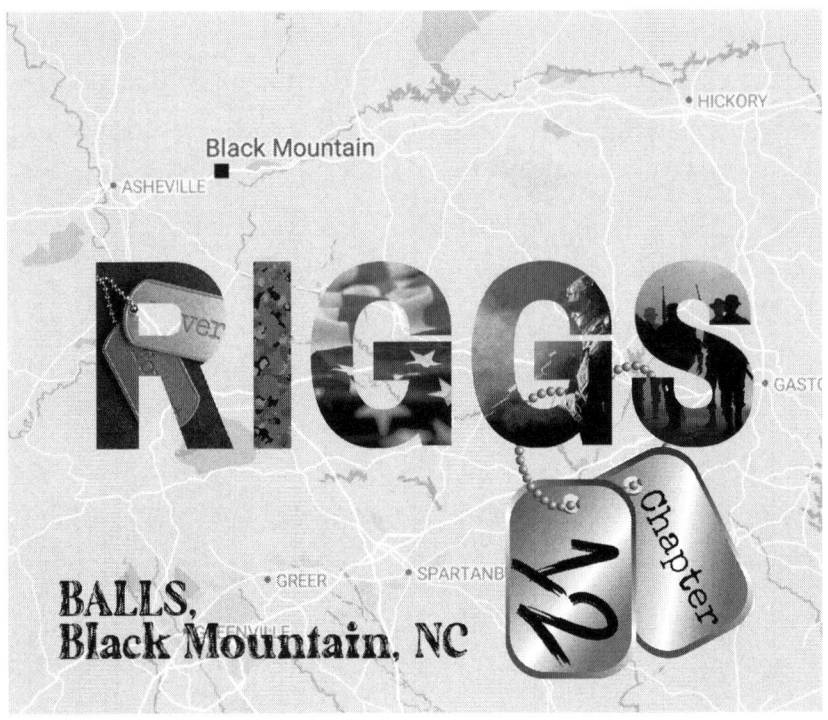

Chapter 12
BALLS, Black Mountain, NC

"SO," Brewer says, wiping his mouth with his napkin. A teasing smirk plays around his lips. "The word around the water cooler is that you put your notice in at Womack."

"I wasn't aware that BALLS had a water cooler," I reply, evading his question. Let him dangle for a minute.

"Okay, not the water cooler, the reception desk," Brewer clarifies.

"Margaret Anne is a nosy gossip, but she's got a good heart."

"She's over the moon that you'll be around every day now."

I can't hide my smile. I've been at Womack for six years now, and so many of them have become friends, especially Liza, but these people, this place, they feel like home. This is where

I'm supposed to be, and I'm probably almost as thrilled as Margaret Anne.

"I told you I was going to put my notice in weeks ago. Why are you acting like this is the first you've heard of it?"

Brewer snorts. "Do you know how many times I've heard you swear you were going to quit? Speaking of gossip, the word around the knitting circle is that there's a new Bitch in town, and you have a mysterious, secret past with him. So, what gives? Why do you make me beg for the juicy stuff?"

I chuff. Fucking Brewer. As a therapist, it's his job to work his way into people's heads, to get to the root of their trauma. But as my best friend, it's his job to just be a nosy pain in my ass. He excels at both.

"His name is Rhett. Rhett Marsh." I realize I'm smiling, and quickly school my features so as not to give myself away.

"So they were right! There *is* someone." Brewer looks overjoyed. He thinks he's got leverage on me, and he's waited years for it.

"He's exactly what they said—new in town. That's it." I never should have encouraged him to date a Bitch. They're the nosiest, most meddlesome group of men I've ever encountered. They're also my brothers, so I put up with them gladly.

"What about the mysterious past part? Don't skip that."

I shake my head, my eyes narrowing. "You're as bad as they are." Brewer chuckles. "I met him on my last deployment. He was my patient."

"Juicy," he baits me, wanting more.

"Nope, not juicy. It's dry. There's nothing more to tell."

Brewer snorts. "You're so full of shit. But that's fine, keep your secrets. If there's one thing I've learned, it's that they spill themselves if you just give them time."

I regard him with a raised brow. "And you've got plenty of time, huh?"

"Loads," he teases, eyes sparkling with mischief.

I don't really care if they know I worked on Rhett's leg, or, according to him, saved his life. As long as nobody, including Rhett, uncovers the feelings he sparked in me that night. The feelings he stokes like hot embers every time we meet. That's a secret I won't be spilling—ever.

"Finish your sandwich. I've got to hit the gym before my group session starts."

As soon as I walk into the gym, Rhett is already hard at work with weights strapped to his ankles. He struggles through a set of leg lifts, and when he begins to scissor his legs open and closed, a fine sheen of sweat breaks out across his brow.

His dark hair is longer than when I first met him, and carefully mussed. His dark stubble isn't too thick to hide his dimples. He looks incredibly young—and delicious—in black nylon shorts and a T-shirt with the sleeves cut off. Even after loafing in the hospital for weeks recuperating, his biceps are defined and thick. I catch a hint of black ink trailing down his arm that disappears inside his shirt.

What I wouldn't give to peel his shirt off and get a closer look at his sweaty, tatted skin.

Fucking get a grip. Ain't gonna happen.

When he spots me, his hazel eyes light with interest. "Riggs!" He flags me from across the gym, drawing everyone's attention, and my body heats with awareness. I don't mind having all eyes on me when I'm barking orders, but curious eyes? Yeah, no. Not a fan.

I really have no choice but to approach him.

"This gym is sick! It's nothing like the one at Womack," he gushes.

"That's the beauty of private donations," I tease.

"So," he asks, looking up at me from under that thick, dark fringe of lashes that caught and held my attention for hours that first night. "Am I finally going to have you to myself?" Like a practiced flirt, he waits for his innuendo to hit its mark before amending, "I mean, as my physical therapist?"

He doesn't look even remotely bashful about the slip, and I'm convinced it was deliberate.

That would be a terrible idea. Absolutely disastrous. "We'll see. Right now I'm just on volunteer status, but if I get the position I applied for, it might be a conflict of interest."

"Why? We're not sleeping together." His expression and his eyes say '*yet*,' but he doesn't voice it out loud.

He's right; it's not a conflict of interest because we're not sleeping together. Yet or ever. That's just me pushing him away for my own peace of mind.

No, that's just you leaving the door open so he can slip into your bed in the future, my mind screams. *Fuck you,* I tell it. My conscience is a nosy motherfucker.

Boldly, he repositions himself so that when he extends his leg for his next leg lift, his foot rises between my thighs. I catch his foot before it connects with my nuts, wrapping my fingers around his ankle in a vise-like grip, my expression severe.

"*You're* not sleeping with anyone because your legs don't work. And if *I* were sleeping with someone, it wouldn't be any of your business. Focus on what's important, soldier. Your recovery, not your sex life."

Damn, that almost sounded believable. I'm fucking good when I want to be. The disappointment on his face only stings a little.

He bends to remove the weights, but I stop him. "Don't even try it. You've got fifteen more reps to do before you quit."

"Sounds like a fuckin' party," he quips with a huff.

"You can't spell party without PT."

Rhett looks up at me like he's disappointed and shakes his head. "Please tell me you don't have any more of those saved up somewhere."

"I've got a fuck-ton more," I say with a deadpan expression. "And when you finish those leg lifts, head over to the mats and do some stretching. Your goal is to get where you can extend your leg completely and touch your toes."

Rhett frowns. "You're a fuckin' sadist. I bet you don't have a lotta friends."

This time, my laugh is genuine. "You wouldn't be the first person to say that, but you're wrong; people love me. I think it's my can-do attitude." Now I'm just fucking with him, and it works because Rhett smiles. I thought he was hot as fuck before, with tears in his eyes or with his face drawn tight with pain, or with his blank, thousand-yard stare. But Rhett smiling? He's fucking gorgeous.

He finishes his exercises and then heads to the mats to stretch. I cringe, hearing the bones in his leg snap, crackle, and pop like breakfast cereal. He hides his pain well behind a mild grimace, but I know how much the façade costs him. He's hurting, evident by his sweat and his pale coloring. He's nearly finished when Mandy strolls in looking for him.

"Yo, Rhett. You ready?"

He brightens visibly. "Do we get to leave now?"

I bite back my smile, knowing Mandy is dragging him to the support group next.

"The gym, yeah. But we're not finished milking BALLS dry. The fun's just getting started."

Rhett's expression falls. "I'm up for whatever, as long as you quit the lame-ass ball jokes."

Mandy chuckles and extends a hand, helping Rhett up.

"Shit, I can't. I'm stuck," he huffs, sounding irritated.

Mandy looks to me for assistance, and I set my clipboard down and walk over to them. Squatting down, I explain to Rhett, "When your leg locks up like this, roll to your left hip, get your left knee under you, and push yourself to a kneeling position. Then you can slowly manipulate your right knee until you can bend it; like you're lunging."

Rhett tries it and flails around as he rolls, face-planting on the mat. "A little help, please?" he grates, frustrated with himself.

I stay Mandy's shoulder with my hand. "Try again."

This time he succeeds, glaring as he pushes to his knees. "Thanks," he says with zero gratitude.

Rhett may not appreciate my approach now, but when he's

alone and stuck like this, he'll thank me. Well, probably not, at least not out loud.

Thinking of his spitfire personality makes me smile to myself. It's crazy that I can predict his reaction so accurately after only knowing him for such a short time, but I know I'm spot-on.

When he's on his feet, Mandy leads him towards the doors. He nods at me, and I wink. I can't wait to see Rhett's reaction to the Bitches. I have absolutely no idea how to predict that one.

I busy myself in the gym for a few more minutes so that I'm the last to arrive, and when I push through the doors of the classroom, the Bitches are all present and seated in a circle, some of them already pulling colorful balls of yarn from their bags.

"Riggs, how ya hanging, man?" McCormick asks.

"High and tight, unlike yours," I tease. Of course, Stiles laughs.

Any dig at McCormick is hilarious to him. McCormick is an easy target with his loud mouth and burnt-orange hair and beard. He's easy-going, good-natured, and even-tempered... until he's not. Once, a while back, he had a bad time and called me in the middle of the night. His voice sounded spooked, haunted, and scared, and I had goosebumps all over as I drove to his apartment in the dark, wee hours of the night. We sat on the floor of his kitchen for hours as he rocked back-and-forth, reliving some of his worst days. I hope it's a long-ass time before he has another episode like that, for his sake and mine.

Stiles, his sidekick, basically, is a lot like him in the personality department, which is probably why they get along so well.

Where McCormick is red, Stiles is dark. They're both tatted and scarred, with McCormick missing a leg, and are proud vets, Bitches, and members of the ALR—the American Legion of Riders, a veteran motorcycle club.

They're all eyeing Rhett, and I know from Brewer's comments earlier that the Bitches already had a heads up about him, probably from Mandy. Armando Cahill looks like a beast of a man, but he's a big softie inside. It would be just like him to call the guys and let them know Rhett moved into the neighborhood and to be on their best behavior with him until he settles in.

I take my usual seat and call the meeting to attention. "Listen up, gentlemen. This is Rhett Marsh. Let's give him a proper Bitchin' welcome."

They go around the circle round-Robin style, starting with Mandy. "You already know me, but I'll say it again, anyway. I'm Mandy, retired Army, your neighbor, and proud to be your ball buddy."

I notice West Wardell glaring. He's not happy about sharing his ball buddy with Rhett.

"Dude, I told you to quit with the ball jokes. I'm fuckin' serious," Rhett complains, making Jax snicker.

McCormick goes next. "McCormick, retired Army, ALR member, and proud Bitch. Here's our phone tree. You find yourself in a jam, a flashback, or just feeling down, start at the top and call each number until someone answers." He crosses the circle to hand Rhett the paper.

Stiles follows. "Stiles, retired Army and ALR member. Call me anytime."

"Jax. Retired Army and ALR. Give me a call if you need me." I smile and nod at Jax. His anger issues and faux mohawk —faux hawk?—might give the impression that he's an asshole, and he is, mostly, but I know for a fact he's a good guy. They all are.

I'm supposed to be next but I look to Brandt Aguilar instead. "What about you?" he asks me.

"Rhett already knows all about me. Your turn."

I might as well have handed them gasoline and lit a match because I can feel their curiosity burning hotter than hellfire.

Brandt shrugs. "I'm Brandt. Retired Army. Glad to have you join us. I've got a hearing problem, so speak up. If I don't answer, it's 'cause I didn't hear you, not 'cause I'm a dick."

West snorts. "Says who? You're totally a dick." He shakes his head and turns his attention to Rhett. "West Wardell, retired Army. This is my partner, boyfriend, whatever you call it," he taps Brandt's shoulder. "I hope you stick around. This place is good for you."

Sommers grins. "I'm Nash. Retired Army and recovering addict. I don't ride, I don't drink, and I don't knit well, but I can bitch like a pro, apparently."

Pharo is absent today, and I'm pretty sure he's deployed, so it's back to Rhett again. "Nice to meet you all. I just got one question. What the fuck is this group and why am I here?"

My snicker draws several more. "Welcome to the Bitches With Stitches. We're a support group for vets with trauma. And... we knit. It's therapeutic."

Rhett looks around the circle at the huge battle-scarred and inked vets, some of them missing limbs, all of them holding knitting needles and yarn. He shrugs. "Cool. I'm into origami, so why not knitting too? but I gotta be honest, I'm not much of a sharer. I'm just followin' Mandy around 'cause he's my ride home."

He handles his introduction better than some have, and I'm glad he's giving it a chance instead of running for the door. He'll come around in time and become a regular old Bitch like the rest of us.

If anyone needs to share with the group, it's Rhett. He's got fresh trauma and I'm sure he intends to bottle it up and stuff it down deep until it shreds him apart from the inside like cut glass shards.

As the guys take turns sharing about their week, I can feel his eyes on me, but I dare not look. Not until it's his turn again.

"I don't have much to say, just that I'm grateful to Riggs for —well, everythin'. Everythin' I have, even my life, is because of him. I only wish there was some way I could return the favor."

His stare lingers, burning hot through me, and I have no doubt he wants to return the favor. Preferably while we're both naked.

Fuck, if I had a chance to get my dick inside him, hell, it would probably be physically impossible for me to pull out. It'd be too good, too tight and hot and perfect. I'd fuck him up so damn good.

A wave of heat rolls through my belly and I swallow hard, feeling slightly uncomfortable with his eyes still pegging me so intensely.

Why, God? Why him? Why Rhett Butler Marsh, the gorgeous flirt with the silly name, the vet with too much fresh trauma, both physically and mentally? Of all the guys to break my dry spell, why can't it be someone easy? Someone I'd allow myself to have? Why does it have to be him?

Rhett is like my kryptonite. He's poison in my blood. He weakens me, brings forth all my fears and insecurities, and makes me doubt my instincts. He's the bad choice you make when you're drunk and your inhibitions are low. The one that you regret in the morning. The guy you don't bring home to meet your mother. The guy's not made for promises and plans and declarations, which is ironic considering his mother named him after an icon of romance.

Rhett Marsh is a one-night stand, a bad boy good for only one night. He's dangerous to me, and I plan to stay far away and heed all the red flags.

RHETT
Chapter 13
Black Mountain, NC

USING MY CRUTCHES, I hop into the bathroom, set my phone on the counter, and reach into the stall to turn on the water. It takes a minute to warm up and I wait so I can adjust it to scalding; just how I like it, melting the skin off my bones. There are times now when I can hobble along without the crutches, like from my bedroom to the kitchen, or when I'm sitting on the couch and I need to run to the bathroom. But after the intense workout I had today, there's no way I can manage.

My knee throbs, punctuated by white-hot daggers of pain, with each step I take. My hip aches from my uneven gait and the twinge of pain in my lower back reminds me it's time for my meds. I'll wait until after my shower so I can take them with food.

When the glass stall fills with steam, I strip out of my clothes, lean my crutches against the wall, and step under the scorching spray. I'm cheating, leaning heavily on the back of my safety chair instead of sitting, but I can't wash my ass if I'm sitting on it.

I slide my soapy hand between my cheeks, brushing my fingers through the fuzz surrounding my hole. Bearing down, the tip of my finger breaches my rim and I sigh with pleasure.

Been too long since I fingered my ass.

My workouts at BALLS leave me feeling exhausted by the end of the day, and once I plop down on my cushy new couch and relax, it's lights out. I've fallen asleep there the past two nights.

Fuck it, I need this.

Sitting down in my chair, I spread my knees and glide my soapy hand up and down my shaft, getting it sudsy and slippery before cupping my balls. The weight of them feels good in my palm and I give them a couple of satisfying tugs before returning to my shaft.

With the aid of the soap, I can feel every engorged vein squish under my fingers. My wrist twists over the crown and I sigh again, tilting my head back under the hot spray. Say what you want about medical equipment, but this shit right here is the fucking pinnacle of life. A warm head massage from the shower spray while jacking off and my skin enveloped in a steamy kiss? Fuck yeah, I'll take this all day long.

When my leg heals, I'm keeping this chair.

My eyes slide shut and his face fills my head—*Riggs*—because who else would I fantasize about? Seriously, I've dreamt of him every time I've touched myself since meeting him. You could say I'm obsessed, but I wouldn't because it sounds, well, obsessive. I don't want to be *that* guy, the guy that can't take a hint. But I refuse to give up yet. Riggs and I are just getting started.

I've pushed myself hard all week, past the point of pain and well into excruciating territory, all just to prove to him I'm taking my rehab seriously. At this point, I'm doing it more for him than me, but I'm not sure it even matters why, as long as I show up and get it done. Results are what matter, not the whys and how-tos.

Hell, that even sounds like something Riggs would say. I'm starting to channel him, apparently.

Taking two lungfuls of thick steam into my chest, I breathe deep and imagine it's Rigg's rough-skinned hand wrapped around my dick, pumping me until I gasp. My heart beats faster, the pressure in my chest building, until I feel almost lightheaded, and I squeeze the tip of my sensitive cock. It's too much, too good, and I groan, the sound rumbling like a lion's roar in the tiny stall. With my other hand, I tug my balls, and I'm there... so close I can taste it. I love this part—teetering on the verge of ecstasy. If I continue to pump, I'll come, but if I slow my strokes, I can crest again before I finish. It's been so long since I've come that I decide to drag it out.

Releasing my sac, I stroke up and down my shaft until I become impatient and speed up again, eager to feel the rush of release. God, what I wouldn't give to ride him, to feel him grip my hips, slamming me down hard on his cock. His deep voice urging me to ride him faster, harder, to take his load. My orgasm comes fast and hard, and I shout as I spray my chest.

I turn my chair toward the water so the cum rinses away under the hard spray and push to my feet, leaning on the back of the chair for support. To be honest, slipping in the shower scares the fuck outta me. Not only would I further damage my leg and set back my recovery, but who the fuck would help me up?

Of course, my phone starts ringing before I'm even out of the stall. I lunge for it, dripping wet and wobbly. "Hello?"

"Hey, ball buddy," Mandy's deep voice rumbles.

"I told you not to call me that, especially when I'm naked and wet."

"Huh? Why are you answering the phone when you're naked? I won't even ask about the wet part."

"Cause it was ringin', dickcheese!"

"Whatever. You wanna come with? Me and the guys are heading to the Black Mountain Tavern."

"Uh, I think that's the place Liza told me to apply to. So, yeah, I'll come. I gotta find a job."

"Great! Leaving in twenty."

Exactly twenty minutes later, Mandy knocks on my front door. I'm not in a great hurry to answer it considering I've got my leg propped up on my bed trying to refasten my soft cast around my jeans. It has so many moving parts and *Velcro* straps; you need a degree in rocket science to figure it out. He pounds again, this time much louder.

"Alright, damn! Keep your fuckin' boots on. I'm comin'." Slowly, I make my way to the door and there's Mandy, casually leaning against the door frame as if he hadn't just tried to beat the damn thing down.

He grins. "You ready?"

My eyes roll. "You're annoyin', you know that?"

Mandy chuckles, unaffected, and steps past me. "What do we need? Crutches? Keys? Did you take your meds? You know, there're some meds that don't react well with alcohol. Are you taking any of those?"

"What are you, my mama? Don't worry about what I'm takin'."

He flushes deep red. "Just trying to look after you."

This guy takes his job as my ball buddy deadly seriously, which is kinda sweet—*kinda*—except that it's annoying.

Mandy drives and I fidget the entire way. I've met the guys, and they seemed alright or whatever, but this is different than sitting beside them in group and listening to them bitch. This is hanging out one-on-one, this is intimate. They'll ask questions, try to get to know me, and the last thing I want is to make new friends.

I have friends... well, had. Who knows if they'll still keep in touch now that I'm gone. *Biddell's gone.*

Friends *leave.*

Friends *hurt.*

Friends aren't always *forever.*

New friends just means new grief. God knows I've got plenty, I don't need more.

Mandy glances over. "Quit biting your nails. You'll make them bleed."

It's a metaphor for my life. Fate keeps picking at the scab on my grief until it bleeds and bleeds. Until it stains everything.

The Black Mountain Tavern has a good vibe—with a stone and wood façade. The theme carries inside with rustic wood beams overhead, a wood floor, and brick walls. The long bartop extends the entire length of the right side and the left has groupings of tables and chairs. Booths line the back wall, and there's a dance floor in the middle. The live band sets up on the small stage beside the front door.

We're the last to arrive. The guys wave us over to a long table. It looks like they shoved three together to fit us all.

I spot the lineup of usual suspects I remember from group. West and Brandt, Stiles and McCormick, Jax and Nash, with the addition of two guys I don't recognize. One of them is with Nash and the other has wavy dark hair pulled into a ponytail, his amber highlights glinting under the bar lights. His golden eyes say, 'don't fuck with me,' and because his shoulders are three times the width of mine, I don't.

The one face I don't see is Riggs's.

The disappointment stings.

The guys order a round of drinks, and I can't help but notice that the table is split in two, with one half sharing a pitcher of beer, and the other half, our half—with Nash and his partner, Mandy, and me—drinking soda. I remember Nash saying he was a recovering addict when he introduced himself in group, and I guess his partner is either supporting him, or also a recovering addict.

I lean into Mandy. "I hope you aren't not drinkin' on my account."

He shakes his head. "I'm not a big drinker. Makes me feel depressed and anxious." Mandy snorts. "Like I need more of that."

I love to drink, but Mandy was spot-on about my meds not reacting well with alcohol.

"That's funny for a guy who hangs out in a bar every weekend," West snipes.

"Hooters isn't a bar; it's a family-friendly restaurant," Mandy defends.

West rolls his eyes. "Yeah, sure, Mandy. Those tiny orange shorts are fun for the whole family."

"Hey, Rhett. This is Brewer," Nash introduces.

I nod at him. "Is Nash your ball buddy?" I tease, having already guessed they're a couple.

Brewer snorts. "Be careful. That's how it starts. Then, before you know it, bam! You fall asleep together every night and you're watering his plant and feeding his cat. It's a slippery slope," Brewer warns.

The guys in hearing distance snicker, and Brandt adds, "I don't think that's how it works, Brewer. Mandy has two nuts in his sack and he's not dating either one of them, far as I know," he says to me with a smirk.

I like him. These guys are as ridiculous as my buddies.

Slowly, I start to relax and listen in. The conversation flows easily with lots of snark and banter. Seems they love to rib each other.

"I'll be right back," I say to Mandy.

Gathering up my courage and my crutches, I make my way to the bar.

"What can I get you?" the bartender asks.

"Wonderin' if y'all are hirin'?"

"Maybe. What kind of work are you looking for?"

I take a deep breath and look him straight in the eye. "Look man, I'm willin' to do whatever y'all need. I just really need to get back to work." I've never applied for a job in my life. I graduated from high school and joined the Army.

"I get it. Do you have a resume?"

Heat creeps up the back of my neck and I feel a bit nauseous. "Uh, no." What the fuck am I supposed to put on a resume? I jumped out of planes? Once, my sergeant made me mop the entire first floor of my barracks after tracking mud inside. Would that count as janitorial experience? I can pack a chute quicker than anyone in my unit, but that means fuck-all in a bar. "I've been deployed for the past nine months. Before that, I spent three years at Bragg. I'm 82nd Airborne."

The bartender looks me over. "That how you broke your leg?"

I nod before answering. "Yes sir. I'm healin' up. Got rehab all day, every day, but my nights are free to work."

"You got ID?"

I reach into my back pocket and pull out my wallet, fishing

out my military ID. He looks it over and smiles. "That's good enough for me. If you can take orders from Uncle Sam for four years, you can take them from me. I'm Brian."

The name stabs me in the heart, but I can't fault him; it's a common name. "Rhett Marsh," I offer, shaking his hand.

"I need help tending bar and stocking liquor. Might ask you to push a mop now and then."

"That sounds great. I'll do whatever needs doin'."

McCormick comes up behind me and claps my shoulder. "Hey, Brian, you give my brother a job?"

"Well, hell, Rhett. Why didn't you say you knew McCormick? That's the only resume you need 'round here, man," Brian laughs.

I laugh with him, shaking my head. Mandy wasn't lying when he said Black Mountain was a small town.

The microphone makes a screeching sound and McCormick yells, "Fuck yeah! Karaoke, Bitches!"

A feeling like a heavy stone sinks in the pit of my stomach. "This is gonna get ugly real fast," I say to Brian.

Laughing, he clasps my hand in a shake. "You'll do just fine 'round here. I'll see you tomorrow night at seven."

Feeling lighter than I did when I walked in, I rejoin the guys who are looking over the song list like they're studying for the ASVAB.

"Whatchu singing, Rhett?"

I glance at Stiles and shake my head. "Not singin', man."

"We'll see about that," he laughs.

When I raise my head again, scanning the crowd for Riggs,

my eyes settle on a cute blonde. She's a curvy little thing with a big bright smile. And she's fixed it on me. Fuck, I've got no game in a damn cast and with a broken heart to boot. I haven't even thought about getting laid since the shit-show in Afghanistan.

Not true, liar. You think about getting banged by Riggs every fuckin' night.

That don't count, though, 'cause that's Riggs. Who wouldn't fantasize about him? That scruff, those dark eyes, and big rough hands and domineering attitude. Yeah, it's a given.

This cutie wants my attention, like now. She gets up and walks over to our table, and I pull out an empty chair for her. Her little blue dress hints at plenty of cleavage, and she leans forward to tease me.

"Hi, I'm Brandi, with an i."

"Yes you are," I say dumbly. Her tits are hypnotizing me. "I'm Rhett."

"Ohh, I love that name," she gushes. "What are you drinking?"

"Uh, *Coke?*" Mandy elbows me in the ribs without even looking my way. "Oh, um, can I buy you a drink?"

I don't even wanna buy her a drink. I'm fucking broke, and with my broken leg, I can't even fuck her. At least, not like I used to. Maybe I can lie on my back while she rides me—very carefully.

Hell, nothing about that even sounds remotely appealing. My dick likes her tits, but not enough to get hard for her.

"A margarita. I just love the taste. It comes in so many flavors!"

Jesus Christ, she's a bright one. If my buddies were here,

they'd be fucking me over by buying a margarita in every flavor and charging it to my card. A pang of sadness hits me square in the chest. Fuck, I miss them. I glance down the long table of laughing faces and feel a little lost among the crowd of my *new* buddies.

Starting life over just feels... exhausting.

Brandi with-an-i polishes off her margarita and takes me by the hand, dragging me from my chair.

"Come on, my song is up. Sing with me."

"Yeah, Rhett, sing with her," McCormick urges, laughing at me.

"Let me grab my crutches," I plead as she practically topples me over. "You're next," I threaten McCormick.

"Bet your sweet ass I am! I can sing real good," he boasts.

Almost every man at the table snickers.

To my everlasting horror and the amusement of my buddies, the song Brandi chose is *'Genie In A Bottle'* by Christina Aguilera. "I can't..." but she tugs me back onstage, winding her arm around my waist to squish me against her lush boobs, and I'm trapped, like a fucking genie in a bottle, ironically. Thankfully, the guys are whooping and laughing so loudly that it mostly drowns out my singing. If only West wasn't recording me on his phone, I might've been able to make everyone forget... eventually.

Every time she says I've gotta rub her the right way, she shimmies her ass against my hip. I glance across the bar and fucking fuck... Riggs is staring at me, jaw slightly agape.

The song dies down and Brandi ends with a big finish—she fists my shirt and pulls me down to plant a big, wet, sticky lipstick smooch on my lips. The bar cheers wildly; well, mostly just the Bitches, and when I look back at Riggs, he's no longer gaping.

    He's glaring.

    I fucking *hate* karaoke.

RHETT

Black Mountain, NC
Chapter 14

I SUFFER through McCormick's rendition of a Beach Boys' song, and every time he tries for that high note, my stomach threatens to regurgitate my burger. It's fucking painful to listen to. My ears aren't the only ones hurting. Most of the guys are sporting a grimace, except Stiles. He must be tone deaf because he's tapping his foot and bopping his head. For all of his bickering with McCormick, they sure do seem like two peas in a pod. I can't figure them out.

Brandt follows him with a song from the *Top Gun* soundtrack. The Bitches groan collectively, and I can't understand what they've got against *Top Gun*, 'cause it's a kick-ass movie, and the soundtrack is even better.

I glance at Riggs for what seems like the three hundred and

ninety-seventh time, and he turns his head away quickly, which means he was watching me. *Again.* Every time I glance in his direction, I realize he's been watching me. The idea should excite me, but instead, it feels like I'm sitting in the timeout chair, like I've done something wrong.

For the life of me, I can't figure out what.

Brandi orders another margarita, chocolate this time, and I've got to put my foot down. "Slow down there, girl. You can't be drinkin' all that and drivin' home."

She giggles, and the sound grates my nerves. "I thought I'd come home with you."

Like hell. "Well, you thought wrong," I say point blank.

Mandy pats my shoulder discreetly, and I realize he's been paying attention the whole time, watching my back. I should feel grateful, but I only feel defensive. Slightly bitter. It's not his job to watch my back; it's Brian's, Warren's, and Ormen's. My crew. But none of them are here, and these guys are. I've got to let go of that bitterness and just be thankful someone's watching it at all.

Brandi takes offense at the coldness of my words and pouts her pretty stained lips at me. "Girl, that ain't gonna work on me. You can sit and hang with us, but I'm cuttin' you off on the alcohol."

She grabs her drink, blows me a kiss, and vacates her seat.

"Thank fuck," Mandy mumbles. "Is that the kind of girl you attract? Desperate and greedy? Just give me a heads up, so I know next time we hang."

Chuckling, I shake my head. "I usually have better luck than that. Must be gettin' rusty." His phone vibrates on the table and he checks the screen, his face stretching into a frown. "Who's that?"

He shakes his head. "No one." My snort says I don't believe him. Mandy sighs. "A friend. I invited him to join us, but he says he can't make it."

"Maybe he hates karaoke as much as I do."

He gives me a sardonic look. "He loves being the center of attention. Probably has a date or something."

"Why wouldn't he just say so?" Mandy shrugs, but I don't believe him. "You like this guy?"

Honest to God, his cheeks pink. This big, scarred guy blushes.

"He's..." Mandy lowers his head, and the hint of a smile teases his lips. "He's like C-4; small and explosive. He's got this pretty face, with blond hair, and the way he dresses..." he chuffs. "His clothes don't make no sense, but he loves to show off his body. He pretends to be empty-headed, but he's damn smart. And... he cares, you know? He doesn't stare at my scars when he talks to me, he looks me in my eyes."

Smirking, I shake my head. "Shit, you've got it bad. Did he friend-zone you?"

He finishes off his soda, slamming down his empty glass.

The truth dawns on me. "You've never tried to shoot your shot?" I ask incredulously. "Why the fuck not?"

His head snaps up, and the look in his eyes is as cold and hard as forged steel. "Look at me. Why would I saddle someone I like with this face?"

"Get the fuck outta here. Don't give me that shit, Mandy. He obviously doesn't mind. You just said he sees past them."

"It's easy for a friend to see past them, less so for someone who has to sleep with me."

I scoff at his bullshit logic. "You're fuckin' bent."

Mandy's gaze lands on Riggs. "When you follow your own advice, you can give it to me."

"Let's drink. I know you said you don't often, but tonight seems like a good exception." Fuck my meds. I need a drink, bad, and so does Mandy.

He glances at his phone again before slipping it back into his pocket. "Yeah, it does sound like a good idea. First pitcher's on me."

Three pitchers and two rounds of whiskey shots later, Pharo offers to drive us home. That's the big shouldered guy with the blond highlights in his dark hair. The guy with the golden eyes and the mysterious name. What's even more mysterious is the fact that he deploys several times a month. He says he's in the reserves, but that don't make no sense to me.

"Man, you killed that Garth Brooks song, *'Friends In Low Places,'*" Mandy gushes.

"Yeah, *killed* is the appropriate word," Pharo mumbles. "If either of you knuckleheads throw up in my truck, I'm gonna make you lick it up," he warns.

Mandy finds that funny and busts out laughing, and when he snorts like a pig, he makes me laugh along with him. We've got tears in our eyes by the time Pharo pulls up in front of our building.

"You need help getting inside?" he asks.

"Nah, we'll manner… manage," Mandy assures him.

Pharo pinches the bridge of his nose. "Christ."

Not gonna lie, managing my crutches while sloppy drunk is difficult, and even more so with Mandy hanging on me like he's helping. It takes two full minutes to get the key in my lock, but once we're inside, we collapse on my couch.

"It looks really good in here," Mandy observes, taking stock of my apartment. "You should've seen it when the last guy lived here."

"Was he a slob?"

Mandy laughs. "Hell no, the place was bare-bones. He owned a mattress on the floor."

I wait for him to finish, but he doesn't say more. "That's it?"

"That's it," he swears.

"Was he a crack addict?" I joke.

This time, his laugh is more sarcasm than humor. "Close, but no. He was addicted to pills and alcohol."

"Damn, sounds like a real head case." I put my hand over my stomach, trying to slow the sloshing waves of alcohol roiling in my gut.

"It was Nash."

"Yeah, Nash said he's an addict."

"No," Mandy clarifies. "The addict *was* Nash." He says it slowly, enunciating each word.

"Nash was your neighbor?"

"Yup," he says, popping in the p.

"You make ball buddies of all your neighbors?"

"Yup," he repeats in the same tone.

"Damn, I thought I was special."

His hand finds mine, and he squeezes. "You are; just don't tell the other two. I tell them the same thing."

Fucker is laughing at me. "I feel a little sick."

He turns his head toward me. "Maybe you need another drink? Hair of the Dog!"

"I think I should switch to water." I reach for my crutches, intending to get a bottle of water from the fridge. Hobbling to the kitchen is a struggle, and I'm nearly breaking a sweat as I pass the breakfast bar. A wave of nausea and dizziness hits me hard, and my legs buckle beneath me. My ass hits the ground, hard enough to knock the wind from me.

"You okay?" Mandy calls.

I make a miserable groaning sound. "I think I broke myself."

"That doesn't sound good."

No shit. I try to roll my weight to my left side, but that just makes me dizzier. "I'm stuck."

"You mean you've fallen and you can't get up?" he asks before dissolving into a fit of laughter.

"I'm serious, help me."

With a loud groan, Mandy rises to his feet and shuffles into the kitchen, but he's not the savior I thought he was. He fucking trips over my leg and falls flat on his face—on top of my body. Mandy is a big fucker, and I feel his weight crushing me like a building collapsing on its foundation.

In this metaphor, I'm the foundation.

"Ow! My leg!" It's throbbing and feels like I've been stabbed through the knee by a sharp needle. That can't be good. "Get off me."

"I can't," he laughs.

"It's not funny. Get off me. I can't breathe. You weigh a fuck-ton."

"I know," he laughs harder. "I seriously can't get up. I think I might piss myself in a minute."

"Motherfucker, if you piss on me after nearly breakin' my leg again, I'll kill you."

"Looking forward to it," Mandy wheezes through tears of hilarity.

I don't know why it seems funny, because it's not *at all*, but his laughter is contagious, and now I'm laughing. Tears seep from my eyes and roll down into my ears.

"What the fuck do we do now?" I ask.

"Don't know," he sighs.

Mandy shifts his weight, and the stabbing pain in my knee subsides. We lay like this for a minute or two, neither of us speaking, and I realize we're not going anywhere, anytime soon.

"I think the reason that guy didn't tell you he had a date was because he didn't want to hurt your feelings or upset you. Maybe he didn't want to blow his chance with you."

"I doubt it."

"No, really. If he friend-zoned you, he'd be very clear that he was goin' on a date, so you'd understand the rules."

"What rules?"

"You know, not to cross the line. He didn't tell you 'cause he wants you to cross it."

"That sounds like terrible advice. I think you're trying to fuck me over."

"Why would I do that? You're my ball buddy." I reach up to pat his back in a friendly gesture.

"Do you think?" He sounds hopeful.

The last thing I want to do is take that from him, even if he did crush me under the weight of his body. "I really do. You should call him."

"No! Drunk dialing is a terrible idea."

"Yeah, usually," I laugh.

"You gonna tell Riggs you like him?"

I lead with a snort. "He'd have to be stupid not to know. I think I've been pretty obvious."

"Did he friend-zone you?" he asks.

"Worse; he patient-zoned me."

Mandy sighs and I realize his fingers are playing with the strands of my hair. "Love stinks."

"Damn! We should have sung that at karaoke instead of the friend song."

"I could never out sing Adam Sandler," he jokes.

Eventually, Mandy rolls his weight off my body, and I can breathe again. "What happened to your face?"

"Same thing that happened to your legs. War."

"I hate war."

He turns on his side to face me, and there's no laughter in his eyes anymore, just sadness and pain. "Me too."

I think about Brian, his face flashing through my mind, and my lids grow heavy. The mental snapshot turns fuzzy around the edges until it fades to black.

When they open again, I'm face-planted in a puddle of my drool. Bright sunlight streams through the kitchen and living room windows, burning my retinas. Everything hurts. Cold, hard linoleum is no substitute for a soft bed. Beside me, Mandy groans and raises his head.

"Tell me we didn't fall asleep on the floor."

"We fell asleep on the floor."

"I told you not to tell me," he curses.

"I'm too tired to take orders." It takes all my strength to roll to my back so I'm not breathing my drool. "Help me up."

"Shit, I need help myself." He struggles to sit up, his back popping in several places. "Damn, I pissed myself." Mandy gives a tired laugh, but can't execute it fully.

"You're moppin' that shit."

"Whatever," he mumbles, huffing and puffing as he rolls to his knees to get his feet beneath him.

When he's standing straight and tall, he offers me a hand. "Come on, let's get you to the couch."

"Fuck it. I'll just crawl there. It's easier than standin'." I crawl on my belly like a wounded soldier, pulling my weight with my arms across the carpet. When I reach the coffee table, I brace one hand on it and one on the couch cushion and pull myself up. "The fuck did we drink?"

"I don't remember," he says, shaking his head. "This is why drinking is bad." He wags his finger at me.

"No shit. That was a terrible idea you had. You're a bad influence on me."

"It was your idea!" Mandy argues.

"I don't think you can prove that, so I can blame you if I want."

Mandy huffs. "I'm going home to shower. Are you gonna be okay?"

"I guess. But you're comin' back later to mop my kitchen."

Before he leaves, he shuffles to the kitchen, opening the cabinet where I keep my meds, and takes out a handful for me.

Then he grabs a cold bottle of water from the fridge and places everything on the coffee table. "Here, this should help. You want coffee?"

"Nah. Maybe after my shower." He nods and moves to the door. "Hey." When he glances back over his shoulder, I add, "Thanks for bein' my buddy when I needed it."

"Don't mention it." He opens the door and turns back. "Seriously, don't mention it. Especially the part about the piss."

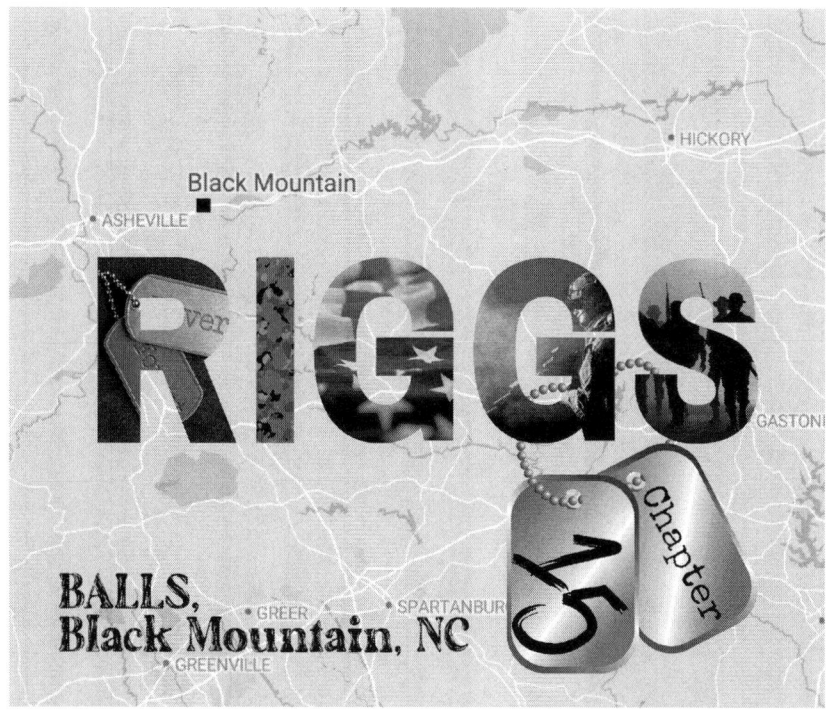

RIGGS

BALLS, Black Mountain, NC

Chapter 25

THIS DAY STARTED OFF GREAT, with news that I got the full-time position at BALLS. I even received a bump in salary. Then I had breakfast with Brewer, and things went to shit after that. It's been one problem after another, and I'm losing patience. It's not even three o'clock and I've got a headache starting to pound at the base of my skull.

When I walk into the classroom where I hold the Bitches with Stitches support group, I'm the last to arrive. Nine men fill the circle.

"All right, everybody listen up. I want to know who is responsible for the incident in the pool." Their shared looks of confusion don't produce any confessions. "Despite your nicknames, you're not bitches. You've got balls. So speak up."

Nothing but snickers from around the group. Losing my struggle, holding onto the last thin thread of my remaining patience, I glare at each and every one of them with narrowed eyes. "I'm listening. I want to know who was responsible for turning the pool water brown." The snickers turn into outright laughter, with Jax being the loudest. I fix my glare on him. "I wouldn't have pegged you for it, but if you did it, come clean."

"I didn't," he wheezes through his laughter. "Honest to God."

"Then why are you laughing?"

"Because whoever did it is a genius."

"I highly doubt that."

"It was a mistake," McCormick swears. More laughter ensues.

"Did you shit in the pool?" I ask, regretting that I need an answer, and regretting even more that I'm going to have to write an incident report about this.

"No! Tell them," he says to Stiles, smacking his arm.

Stiles is laughing too hard to spit out the words, clutching his belly like it aches. "We were trying to pay homage to pride month by kicking it off with a surprise for everyone."

McCormick continues for him since he's now laughing so hard, he's incapable of speech. "We only meant to dye the pool rainbow colors, but then it all sort of mixed together and turned brown." He shrugs, and all hell breaks loose. Pharo laughs quietest, but tears stream down his cheeks. West and Brandt have doubled over on top of each other.

"So you didn't shit in the pool? That's really all I need to know."

"Come on, Riggs, do I look like the kind of guy that would shit in the pool?"

I give up. Jax slips out of his chair, falling to his haunches. I can't see his face behind his hands, but I wouldn't be surprised if he had tears in his eyes like Pharo.

"Do you really want me to answer that, McCormick? Really?"

"No, sir," he answers, trying to keep a straight face, although it's as red as his hair.

"You owe me two volunteer hours in the gym. That's how long it took me to clean up your mess. You too, Stiles. In the meantime, get a hold of yourselves," I bark. "Let's get on with this meeting."

I might as well have walked out right then because the rest of the hour was just as unproductive as the first ten minutes. Every time someone began to share, someone else would start laughing again, and it was as contagious as a STI.

I'm actually relieved when group is over, which is something I never say. Most of the Bitches head out for wings and beer like they always do after group, but not Rhett, or West. They come back to the gym with me. Rhett has two more hours of physical therapy today, and West is training for the Warrior's Walk. Nash and West are competing this quarter to see who can finish the obstacle course in the shortest time.

These vets spend weeks, months, and even years rehabilitating after serious injuries, and the Warrior's Walk is their chance to prove themselves. Not just proving their fitness to others, but to themselves as well. I know from experience, no one is harsher when it comes to judging a soldier's ability than themselves. We are our toughest critics. Always comparing ourselves to what we used to be capable of before we were injured.

Completing the Warrior's Walk may seem like a cakewalk to someone with two good legs, someone who hasn't blown out a kidney or a lung, or isn't suffering from a broken back or shattered knee, but to the injured vets who almost lost everything, including their own lives, and have had to battle every day to come back from that, completing the obstacle course feels like a thousand-mile victory.

But instead of getting started on the treadmill, West is yakking it up with Rhett, as if they didn't just spend an hour together, bitching. I would call him to attention, but honestly, I'm just glad to see him settling in and making friends. I've noticed some resistance in him and I'm pretty sure it's because of his grief.

After all, who could blame him? He lost his best friend, his unit, his buddies, his career, hell, his whole fucking life. It all went down the drain, along with his mobility and his confidence.

He's starting over from scratch with nothing but a shred of hope.

Just another reason not to let him in your bed.

I hate how I constantly need to remind myself of the reasons why Rhett is a bad idea. But God, there are so many of them.

He's only twenty-three years old. I didn't know my elbow from my ass at twenty-three, not that I've learned a whole lot in the last nine years.

He's at the lowest point of his life and I would just be one more complication he doesn't need.

His primary focus should be his recovery, not his dick—*or mine*.

He's a bisexual flirt who gives any passing ass a second look. I can't blame him because I was much the same at his age, but I'm not going to make a fool of myself over a guy like him. Way too high risk for failure.

Unfortunately, my heart and my brain aren't on the same page, and my cock is in a whole other library. Every time my brain reminds me of the red flags, my heart tries to convince me of Rhett's numerous good qualities... like I need reminding.

"Wardell," I bark. "You gonna train for the Warrior's Walk, or just talk about it?"

He laughs and shakes his head. I used to intimidate him, so I must be losing my edge.

West gives Rhett a fist bump and then fires up the treadmill. He's got his hydraulic prosthetic on, which is best for quick, repetitive movement of his knee. It also absorbs impact well and causes less strain on his hip and back than his blade leg.

Rhett takes a seat on the weight bench beside me and bends at the waist to strap on his ankle weights. "What's that Warrior's Walk he's talking about? He's training for something?"

"Like an obstacle course for PT patients. It's an endurance test."

"Sort of like graduating from PT?"

I snort. "You never graduate from PT, soldier. With a leg like yours, you'll be seeing the inside of this gym every day for a long, long time."

He straightens and looks up at me, his lethal dimpled smile on full display. "I like the sound of that."

Everything with him is innuendo, and though I've come to expect it by now, it never fails to charm me.

"You're gonna like it a lot less when you find out what I have planned for you today."

Rhett groans. "When am I gonna compete in the Warrior's Walk?"

"Are you kidding? You're a long way from completing an obstacle course like that. You can barely walk in a straight line. Focus on putting one foot in front of the other, literally, before you start dreaming that big."

Nodding, he asks, "When I'm ready, will you train me?"

He looks so sincere, and I feel like he's asking because he truly believes I can motivate him to get there, and not because he's trying to spend more time with me one-on-one. "Yeah, soldier. When the time comes, I'll train you."

That seems to give him the motivation he needs to power through his leg exercises. By the time I move him to the parallel bars, he's sweating, and I know he's starting to feel the burn in his leg.

West slaps the stop button on the treadmill and wipes his face and neck down with a towel. He positions himself on the other end of the parallel bars, waiting for Rhett. A heaviness settles in my chest and I take a deep breath to push past it, feeling my lungs expand with air. It's moments like these that remind me how much I love my job. This is why I made the switch from nursing to PT.

There's nothing more powerful than watching a community

of vets rally around the new guy, lending their strength to help him get back on his feet. It's the kind of shit that makes my eyes water.

"These are the bitch bars," West snipes, "because it makes you feel like one when you realize how much of a struggle it is to walk ten fucking feet to the end, but I'm gonna stand right here and wait on your ass until you get here." He checks the black sports watch on his wrist. "I've got shit to do today, namely Brandt," he smirks, "so don't make me wait too long."

Rhett chuckles and grabs hold of the metal bars. His first four steps are strong, but then his leg starts to wobble, and his knuckles turn white as he grips the bars tighter.

"Move that right leg forward. Don't think about it, just do it. The longer you think about it, the heavier your leg feels." He glances at me, looking determined, and moves his right leg forward.

He takes another two wobbly steps before he's looking around in a panic for his crutches. "Don't even think about it," I bark.

"I gotta sit," Rhett pleads.

"What you need to do is keep walking."

"Riggs, I gotta sit."

"The only seat you're gonna find is when you fall on your ass and hit the floor, soldier. You're not going backward and you're not quitting. Even if it takes all day, you're going to get to the end of those bars."

Rhett is a passive guy, genial, fun. He's not an angry guy, so when his face pulls tight, the prelude to his hissy fit is unexpected, but totally understandable.

"I can't fuckin' make it to the end!"

"Eventually, you can. You just might need to sit down first," I insist calmly.

"That's what I fuckin' said!" he screams.

"No, you want to sit in a chair. I told you that's not available. If you sit on the floor, you'll have to get yourself back up again."

His hazel eyes turn the palest shade of green I've ever seen them as he glares angrily at me. I know he's dying to tell me to go fuck off, but he wouldn't dare.

"Are you angry? Anger is nothing but an outward expression of fear, hurt, and frustration." His nostrils flare, and he breathes harder as he struggles to maintain his stance. But he manages one more step forward. A step in the right direction. "That's it, keep moving. Don't give up."

His leg buckles, but he catches himself halfway down. West gives me a hesitant look, and I can tell he's worried, but he should know better. I wouldn't push Rhett this hard if I didn't think he could take it. I did the same exact thing to him, and it was exactly what he needed.

Rhett groans, a primal sound of pain and effort as he works to pull himself back up. His next step is wider, and I recognize the move. He's trying to cheat, to cover more distance in less time. At least, that's what he's thinking, but as a therapist, I know better. The move is going to cost him dearly. It takes more effort and puts more strain on his muscles to lunge than it does to take an extra step.

With a cry of relief, he stumbles over his feet the last three steps, crashing against West's solid chest as he threatens to knock them both over. West catches him in his arms and sets him on his feet as I hurry over with his crutches.

"I did it!" He's practically sobbing—a combination of pain, adrenaline, exhaustion, and relief.

"You fucking did it," West agrees.

"Which means you can do it again tomorrow." The look West gives me warns me I'm pushing my luck, and the look Rhett gives me confirms it. Fuck it, that's my job, and I'm damn good at it. This is what it takes to get back on your feet again. Neither of them have to like it, but they're both walking, so my methods speak for themselves. "The next time you feel like quitting on me, just remember this; you're not quitting on *me*, soldier, you're quitting on yourself."

"I'm going to take off," West says. "But I'll be back tomorrow if you need a cheerleader."

"Are you gonna wear a fuckin' skirt?" Rhett teases.

West chuckles and claps Rhett on the back. "I only wear that for Brandt. Sorry."

He walks off with a backward glance at me, probably warning me to take it easy on Rhett. When I turn back to Rhett, I'm facing the full force of his anger, a look I've never seen on his face before. It's fucking magnificent.

His eyes are burning shards of jade. Long strands of sweaty hair tease his forehead, and my fingers itch to swipe them aside. His lips are pulled into a tight line, and I can tell he's about to hand me my ass.

Go for it, soldier. I'm just going to hand it right back to you.

"I can't figure you out," he snarls.

"Good luck. I wouldn't even bother if I were you."

"No, you were different. Back there, in Afghanistan, you cared. You were kind. We had a co—"

"A connection?" I scoff, making light of the feelings I know for a fact we both felt. It's the only way I can maintain a safe distance between us. Especially after seeing him walk today. He needs me, but not as a lover. He needs me as his therapist, and I can't do that if I'm fucking him. "Don't kid yourself. I was just doing my job. Showing concern and compassion for my patient. It wasn't a connection, it was professionalism."

Rhett searches my face, looking deep into my eyes. I know what he's looking for, a trace of the man he thought he recognized. "No, I'm not buying that," he says disbelievingly. "I know what I felt."

I laugh cruelly. "What you felt was someone being nice to you after months alone in the desert. What you felt was in your pants, not your head."

His face hardens into a defensive mask. Whatever he's thinking about me right now, I can bet none of them are good thoughts. This is the only way I can shut him down for good. This has to happen.

"You think you're a badass?" I continue, adding insult to injury. "You're not. You're just another soldier who got hurt. My gym is full of them; look around. Most of them wear a bigger chip on their shoulder than you do. You'll have to try harder than that, kid, if you want to be a badass, and if all you want to do is write my name next to the notches carved into your headboard, it's not going to happen. Go get your dick wet somewhere else, and when you're done, you can come back here and show me what you've got. Don't step foot in my gym again unless you're ready to get your ass kicked and you're ready to work."

My heart burns like I was stung by a hornet when I see moisture gather in his eyes. His throat works like he's having trouble swallowing.

"That's fine. If that's what you want, that's what you'll get." Rhett turns away. "Married to your job, you miserable fucker," he mumbles under his breath as he hobbles off.

The glacier of ice left in his wake chills me to the bone. My words hit their intended target with deadly accuracy, killing two birds with one stone—both his heart and mine.

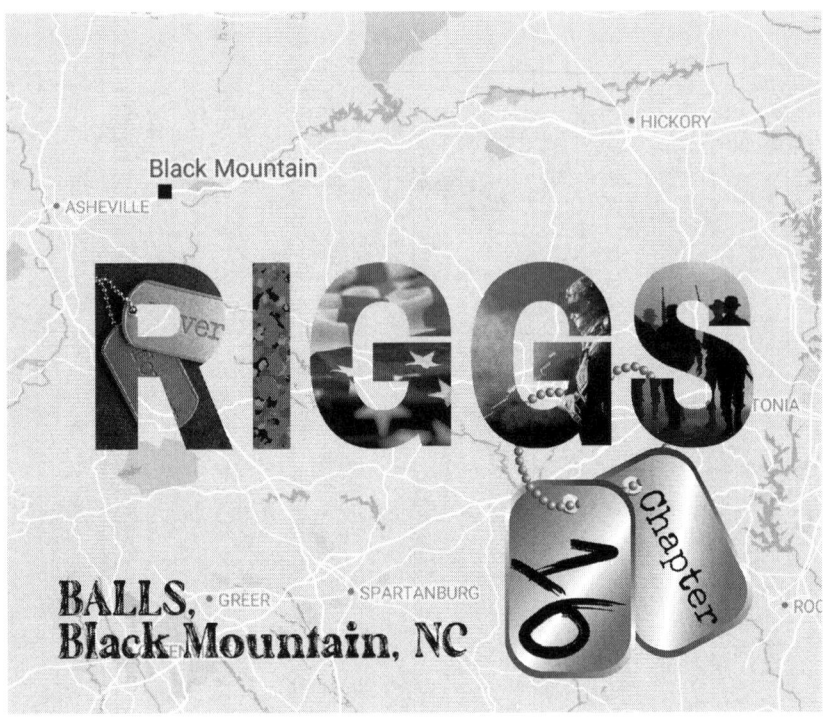

RIGGS

BALLS, Black Mountain, NC
Chapter 26

HE'S IGNORED me all week long. Well, maybe ignoring is wishful thinking. More like froze me out. Straight up hostile.

In group, he sits with his arms crossed, glaring at me, refusing to share. In the gym, he ignores every suggestion I make, choosing to follow the advice of the other trainers on hand instead. When I pass him in the hallway, he ignores me and looks the other way. My friendly greetings fall on deaf ears, and when I ask him how he's feeling, or to describe his pain level during his workouts, he stares right through me.

It's juvenile as fuck, but also... it's lonely. I wouldn't have thought Rhett ignoring me could make me feel that way, but that's exactly what it feels like. Like I've lost a good friend, someone important to me. Someone I needed.

I need Rhett?

I don't know, do I? Do I *need* him? Fuck, I don't even want to know the answer to that.

When I enter the gym, the first thing I see are Nash and West occupying side-by-side treadmills, tearing up the black rubber. They're both pushing themselves way too hard. I jog over to their machines and hit the reset buttons.

"Slow down, knuckleheads. You're both going to be limping tomorrow." Jesus, they act like this competition between them has a cash prize or something.

I turn to find Rhett, stabbing me with metaphorical daggers shooting from his eyes, and I breathe out a deep sigh, struggling for patience. Before I can inhale a calming breath, Brandon, another therapist, flags me from across the gym. He's headed in my direction.

"Riggs, we're all excited you're here full time now, but we've got to have a word about these new ideas you have for redecorating the gym."

He's smiling at me, looking at me like I'm supposed to know what he means, but I'm clueless. I've never had ideas about redecorating the gym. I look around, searching for anything different, new, out of place, but it's the same old equipment...

"Son of a bitch." With my head on a swivel, I search out the culprit, knowing exactly who I'm looking for—a Bitch. Like clockwork, every one of their ugly mugs appear in the doorway of the gym at once, laughing like a gaggle of—

"Congrats on your new job, Riggs!"

"Mazel Tov!"

"Break a leg!" McCormick ducks as another vet, who has a

leg in a full fiberglass cast, throws a sweaty towel at his head. "Sorry, it was a joke. I meant good luck."

These fuckheads. I finally take that calming breath deep into my lungs and find the first smile I've expressed today. I take in the changes around the gym, new posters hanging on the wall in place of the old ones with serene backgrounds and cliché motivational quotes. These are printed on neon poster board and the quotes are decidedly *un*motivating. Actually…

My laughter starts slowly and silently, picking up volume as I read more of them. They're my own words, my own quotes, things I say to my patients when they're struggling.

"It's going tibia okay," is written boldly on neon pink paper.

"PT stands for pain and torture."

"If it doesn't hurt, you're not doing it right," is printed on a bright orange backdrop.

"According to my stopwatch, you're far from finished."

On and on they go, circling the walls of the gym. My gaze finally comes to a stop on Rhett. He's struggling not to laugh, to maintain that stoic, pissed-off expression he's carried all week long. His frown slips when he sees me smiling openly at him.

"Did you have a hand in this?"

"And if I did?" he asks.

The challenge makes my heart kick. It's the way he looks at me, with a hint of his dimples peeking through and his hazel eyes daring me to threaten him.

My gaze travels to the rowing machine.

"Fuck me," he murmurs.

I can't help but laugh as my smile turns wicked. "No, thanks. What I have in mind is going to hurt a whole lot worse."

As soon as the front door shuts behind me, I strip off my shirt and my shorts and head straight for the back deck. Lifting the cover off of the hot tub, I test the water—still warm from last night. I fire up the jets and climb in. The hot water bubbles over my shoulders, caressing my neck and washing away my stress. The sun is just beginning to set over the horizon. It'll be dark in thirty minutes, and I'll be able to see the canvas of stars painted in the night sky glittering brightly. The setting sun reminds me of a giant orange beach ball set on fire, illuminating the valley in rusty light as it kisses the day goodbye.

My phone rings and I realize it's in the back pocket of my shorts, which I left on the deck as I stripped.

Damn, I gotta get that.

I climb out of the tub, water dripping from my cock as I scurry across the deck to grab it.

It's Liza, and I feel a little annoyed that I was in such a hurry. But no matter what I'm doing, whether I'm sleeping, soaking, or screwing, I can't *not* answer the phone. What if it's one of my brothers? I can't recall how many times I've answered their calls in the middle of the night, whether they were scared or in crisis.

I *always* have to answer the phone every time it rings.

"Hello?"

"Hello yourself. I see how it is. You quit and leave me behind in the dust and don't even call to update me. How are you settling in?"

"I'm settled. It took me five minutes," I joke, though it's true.

I was so ready for this life full time, there was no adjustment period.

"I miss you."

"Miss you too, girl. How's Womack?"

"Same old, same old, different day. You're not missing anything."

"I know," I laugh, convinced she's telling the truth. "Right now, I'm soaking in the hot tub, watching the sunset over the valley. In ten minutes, it'll be dark enough for me to count a hundred stars over my head."

"I kind of hate you," Liza teases with a sigh.

"You love me."

"So, how's Marshmallow doing?"

"Who?"

"Rhett," she says impatiently.

Of course, I knew who she was talking about, but I'm not going to let her know that, like I'm eager for the sound of his name.

"He's settling in, slowly making friends. *Very* slowly."

"He's lost a lot in a short amount of time. It doesn't surprise me he's cautious about letting new people in. How's his pain management?"

"I guess he's managing. Not gonna lie, PT is no party, no matter what I tell the guys."

"He should have about fifteen days left of his script, and he has another refill scheduled, but after that, I don't know."

"What is he taking?"

"Percocet."

Great, opioids. "I'll keep an eye on him. Don't worry about it."

"Of course I worry. I worry about all my boys. Speaking of, how are West and Nash?"

"Driving me crazy, competing for the Warrior's Walk."

"Is that some PT thing?"

"Yeah, Liza, it's a PT thing," I deadpan.

"So, are you dating anyone?"

"What in the hell would make you say that?" I ask, practically choking on the words.

"Because you've got all this time on your hands now that you're not running between two jobs."

"No, I'm not dating anyone."

"Well, it wouldn't kill you. Keep your eyes open."

"Good night, Liza."

"Fine," she huffs. "Good night."

A smile teases my lips as I lay the phone down on the edge of the tub, breathing in a lungful of steam. The first few stars shine through the dark purple sky above, and I tip my head back to stare up at them. The water bubbles around my shoulders, a soothing soundtrack that accompanies the cicadas and crickets. Just as I close my eyes, the phone rings again, and I reach for it blindly.

Damn, Liza, let me relax. "Did you forget something?"

"Riggs, I need you."

Definitely not Liza's voice. "Rhett?"

"I need help. Please, hurry."

Every muscle in my body tightens. "Where are you? What happened?"

"I fell," he pants, sounding out of breath. "In my bathroom. I can't get up. My leg is locked."

"Are you bleeding? Did you break something?" I'm already climbing out of the tub, scrambling for my discarded clothes.

"No, I don't know. I don't think so."

"I'm on my way. Hang tight."

"Riggs." I can hear him swallow. "The front door is locked."

"Well, how am I supposed to get in?"

"I think my bedroom window is unlocked. I had it open the other day to air the place out."

"You want me to break in?"

"It's not breaking in if I invite you. Hurry," he moans. I can hear the pain in his voice.

"I'll be right there. Hang on."

My heart is in my throat as I race to my truck. My clothes are damp and sticking to my skin. *He's okay. He's fine.* Despite my self-assurances, I'm driving twenty miles over the speed limit, running stop signs like they don't exist. I park beside his car and hop out, rushing around to the back of his building. I have to count in my head the number of windows I pass until I think I'm standing below the right one.

It *better* be the right one or I'm going to jail.

The window slides open easily, and I breathe a sigh of relief, hoisting myself up and over the edge. My landing is a mess, and I face-plant on his bed, getting tangled in his unmade sheets. I scramble to the foot of the bed and right myself before dashing into the bathroom. "Rhett," I call out.

"In here." His voice echoes off the tiled walls.

His body is sprawled across the floor and he's lying in a

puddle of water that dripped from his body—his still wet and glistening, *naked* body.

Stop, I scream in my head.

"Are you hurt?" I ask, crouching down beside him.

"I don't know. Everything hurts."

From the sound of his voice, he's telling the truth. "What were you doing?"

"Uh, showering?"

"Why didn't you call Mandy? He's right next door."

"'Cause I'm fuckin' naked. I'd rather you see my junk than Mandy."

I let that slide and grab a towel from the rack to cover his body. Even in a quick panicked minute, I can see how perfectly he's shaped, all toned and tanned, tight lines and tattooed skin.

Rhett is on his side, curled in the fetal position with his right leg stuck straight out. I gently roll him toward his back, sliding my hands under his knee and thigh. "I'm gonna try to manipulate the joint." Applying the slightest pressure, I urge his knee to bend, but stop when Rhett cries out.

"Holy fuck, that hurts."

"You should go for an x-ray. Maybe an MRI."

"No," he breathes, eyes widening in panic. "Nononono. Just get me to bed."

"Ignoring the problem won't fix it."

"I didn't bang it when I fell, it just locked up on me. I landed on my ass. Maybe you should check that." He's trying for humor, but his face is drawn too tightly with pain for me to laugh.

"It's probably inflamed from your workout earlier today.

Maybe I pushed you too hard," I murmur, thinking out loud and feeling guilty for pushing him.

"Don't start. This would happen whether you pushed me or not. It's just a fact of my life now," he says miserably.

Worry gnaws at my gut like bitter acid. "We need to apply ice to reduce the swelling. Did you hurt anything else when you fell?"

"Like I said, you'll have to check me over *thoroughly*."

Before I can stop myself, a laugh bubbles up from my throat. It's the most absurd situation to try to flirt with me, but it doesn't stop Rhett.

I have no idea how to get him to the bed besides to pick him up in my arms and carry him. All one hundred and sixty wet, naked pounds of him. As a trained combat medic and physical therapist, I've learned the ins and outs of body mechanics, and how to roll a person's dead weight onto your body to carry them from a seated or prone position.

"What the fuck?" he asks as I maneuver his body. It takes a minute—he's slippery and fucking solid—but I push to my feet with a grunt. Rhett loses his towel in the process, but he's not shy and I don't give a fuck. I'm more concerned about getting him to the bed. It takes great effort to lay him down gently instead of dumping his ass in a heap, and my body goes down with him.

Suddenly, his nakedness is a thing.

The heat of his body sears my skin.

His warm breaths merge with my harsher gasps, becoming one shared breath.

My heart swells with adrenaline, beating as furiously as a hummingbird's wings.

I can feel his eyes on me, searching my face, pleading with me to look at him.

If you look at him, you're going to kiss him.

He *wants* you to kiss him.

Don't fucking do it, Riggs! Don't look.

It's as if the air between us is charged with magnetic electrons, compelling me to look him in the eye. And when I do, when I finally raise my eyes to meet his, I feel like I've been punched in the gut. I can't catch my breath, I can't swallow, and I can't think of anything but how he tastes. I lick my lips, softening them for him, and my head draws closer to his. His throat slides as he struggles to swallow, and his lips part for me.

I can taste his breath and it's so, so sweet.

He touches his mouth to mine, soft, warm lips, and I feel his wet tongue snake out to lick my bottom lip.

And I... I can't. My conscience is screaming at me like a coach with a bullhorn, warning me to pull back, to run.

But it doesn't prepare me for the look of rejection and hurt in his eyes. *Nothing* can prepare me for that devastating blow.

Way to fucking go, Riggs. Like he hasn't been hurt enough already.

"Rhett—"

"Don't, Riggs. Whatever you're gonna say, don't. I get it, you're not interested." His head flops down on the pillow with a sigh. "I don't know what I was thinkin'. Look at me," he laughs derisively. "I can't even pick myself up off the floor without your help. I had to call you to put me to bed—a bed that you bought for me. In fact, you furnished this whole fuckin' place for me. I've got nothing. No life, no future, no hope. Why in the fuck would you want to hitch your wagon to my horse?" He shakes his head. "I don't blame you. I just... I had to try. Didn't realize until just now how far above myself I was reachin'."

"You're wrong, soldier. It's not possible for you to reach too high. Trust me, you're worth it. I just... I can't."

"It's fine, it's... whatever. I'd rather have you as a friend than nothin' at all."

We lay like that for a minute in silence, and I rack my brain trying to think of what to say to make it better, but I've got nothing.

"My leg really fuckin' hurts," he complains.

"Let me get you some ice for your knee." I rise to my feet and throw the edge of the blanket over his body, for his sake and mine.

"Can you grab my pills from the kitchen while you're in there? And maybe an extra handful of ice? I've got a few other spots I need to cool down."

Despite the gravity of the situation, I laugh at his joke, knowing he's serious. He just never quits, even when all seems lost. In the kitchen, I grab a bottle of water from the fridge and randomly open a few cabinets, looking for the one that holds his meds. I find it above the stove. The label says *Percocet*, to be taken with food, may cause drowsiness, and don't operate machinery while under the influence. Ducking into the hall bathroom, I flush them down the toilet. In the kitchen, I reach for the bottle of *Ibuprofen* instead.

These pills are addictive as hell. I've seen it time and again with so many of the veterans who come through the doors at BALLS seeking help. Hell, I saw it with some of the guys I actively served with. It was a damn near daily occurrence at Womack. I'm not gonna let it happen to *my*... not to *my patient*.

He's not your patient.

Like fucking hell he's not.

Closing the cabinet, I search through the drawers for a plastic bag I can fill with ice. Then I grab the water bottle and head back to his room. Rhett is lying exactly where I left him. "Are those *Percocet* all you're taking for the pain?"

"Yeah, the doctor at Womack prescribed them to me."

"Well, you're finished with them. No more." I hand him four ibuprofen and the bottle of water.

"What do you mean, no more? My fuckin' leg hurts."

"As it should, you shattered it. Ibuprofen will do just fine."

"Says who?"

"Says me."

"You're a doctor now?"

In all my years in the medical field, I've never once encountered a situation where a patient acted magnanimously or gratefully when you took away their drugs. "Well, you called me doc when we met," I tease.

"It was a formality. I didn't know your name."

Leaning down over his body, I get right up in his face. "I don't care what the fuck it was, I told you that you're done with the painkillers. Your leg is supposed to hurt; it reminds you to take it easy, but not too easy."

Rhett snorts. "That makes no sense."

"It makes perfect sense. The pain tells you where your limit is, how far you can push yourself."

"So when it starts hurtin', I can stop?"

"That's not what I said. I'm telling you when it hurts, slow down, but don't stop. You can always go a little bit further than you think you can. If it's not hurting, you're not doing it right."

He curses under his breath and then sighs with defeat. "You can be a real prick sometimes."

"Don't I know it," I laugh. Plopping down beside him, I place the bag of ice over his knee.

"I'm drownin', Riggs. It's not supposed to feel like this. I'm doin' everything I'm supposed to, everything you tell me to do, but I'm still drownin'. If it doesn't get better than this, what is even the point of continuing to fight when all I wanna do is give up?"

Genuine fear grips my heart. I want to tell him it gets better, to hang in there, but that would be a lie. Just because it got better for me doesn't mean it's going to for him. "You can't give up, not yet. Just keep fighting, one day at a time. For me. Promise?"

"For you? Yeah. 'Cause I owe you for savin' my life."

I'm not going to debate it with him if that's what gets him to hang on.

"Give me somethin' real, Riggs. Not that motivational bullshit. Tell me you know what it feels like, that you know what I'm going through. Tell me you understand the pain I'm drowning in. The way I feel almost numb from it."

"I know exactly what you're feeling."

"Prove it. What was the name of the person you lost?"

Our voices are nothing but a whisper in the silent room, blanketed by the still of the night. Outside the window, still open to the evening breeze, I can hear the chirping crickets in the trees. With the exception of Brewer, I've never told anyone what I'm about to tell him.

"Most of the time, my mind is solid, like a frozen sheet of ice. But underneath there are soft spots, and if you step in the wrong place, with too much pressure, it splinters apart. Like cracks in the ice. Sometimes I don't even see it coming. It's stupid shit like the other day, I was watching TV and there was a baby food commercial on, and the mom was feeding her kid applesauce."

My voice becomes thick with emotions I haven't identified in a long time. "I cried. The fucking applesauce got me. It took me right back to the mess hall at Bagram. Applesauce was the meat identifier for pork chops. You couldn't tell what the damn meat was without the sauce as the clue. Cranberry sauce meant turkey." My mouth feels thick and dry. "Fucking Bandit, he was crazy about that applesauce. Used to ask us all to scrape our extra sauce onto his plate."

"Is that why they called him Bandit?"

"No," I laugh. "It's because he was always stealing our foot powder. He was a *Gold Bond Powder* thief. Had the nastiest case of athlete's foot I'd ever seen. We used to tease each other and say, '*If you fuck this up, I'm gonna make you wear Bandit's socks.*'" I swipe the tears that unexpectedly fall from my eyes. "You could tell when he got into the powder, because you could see the dust caked under his fingernails."

Rhett shudders, then, in a soft voice, asks, "What happened to Bandit?"

"His name was Mark. Mark Grainger. He took a bullet to the face. It wasn't even nothing, wasn't supposed to happen. A stupid, senseless accident. They opened fire on us as we were driving out of the village. Bandit stuck his head out the window and a bullet ricocheted off the Humvee and went right through his cheek." The tears stream down my cheeks now, pooling on his pillow. Rhett reaches for my hand in the dark, and I squeeze back. "I was sitting beside him. I wore his dried blood on my face for twelve hours straight. They had to hold me down to scrub it off."

I don't have to see his face to know he's crying as silently as I am. I can feel the tremors running through his body.

"I'm sorry." His voice is shredded with grief. "I'm sorry about Bandit. I'm sorry about all the men we've lost."

I clear my throat loudly, hoping it works like a reset button. "The fucking applesauce and the baby made me think of my buddy's face exploding. I'll never ever unsee that shit." Swiping at my eyes, I continue softly, "I don't want to remember him that way. I want to remember Bandit chewing with his mouth open, singing the wrong words to every song, stealing everyone's fucking powder, and always scratching his nasty feet. I don't want to remember his death."

"He doesn't want you to remember him that way, either."

"It feels like a betrayal, like that's what I reduced him to. His whole life is all about his death."

"That's how I feel about Brian sometimes." Rhett's voice breaks when he says his buddy's name.

"You've been through a trauma, and it changed you. It changed the way your mind works. That's not up to you. It's not your fault."

"It's not yours, either," he reminds me. I untangle my hand from his and tuck it under my ass so I'm not tempted to reach for him again. "I miss my mama," he admits sadly.

My heart breaks for him. He's lost so much. If I could just give him back something, *anything*.

"I can't understand why she hasn't come to see me yet. Wild horses couldn't keep my mama away normally, but since I've been back, things feel different. I don't know why."

"I'm sorry. In the meantime, you've got me."

"Do I, Riggs? Do I have you? 'Cause you just got done tellin' me how complicated it is for you, and I gotta say, it don't feel like I have you at all."

The sound of my blood whooshing through my veins is loud in my ears, like a heartbeat. "I'm here, aren't I?"

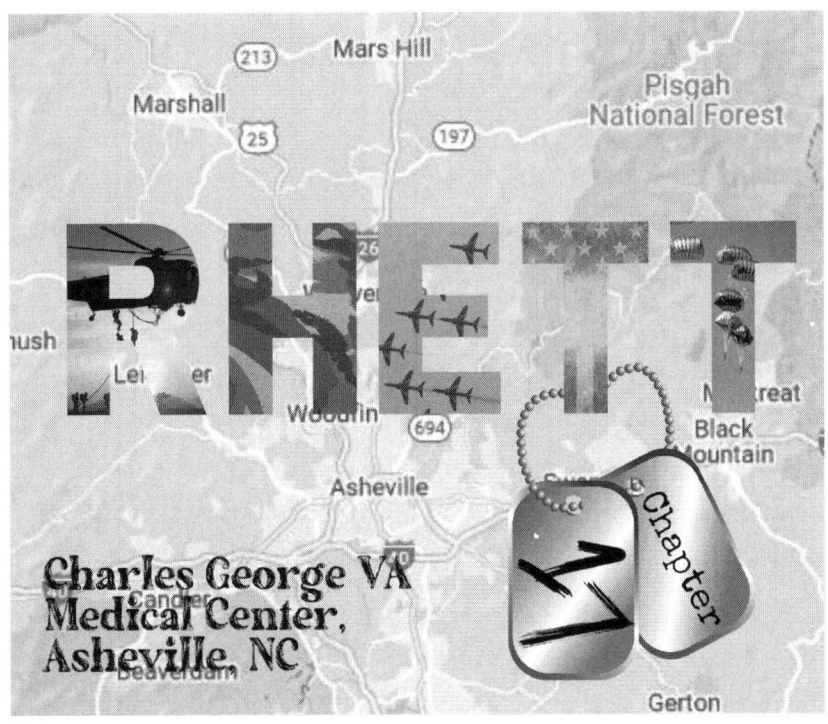

"SO, how often do you have to go through this?"

Mandy sighs heavily. "*Too* often. Feels like every month just about I'm going through some sort of treatment, whether it's dermabrasion or another skin graft. They only do those every quarter, but then there are the checkups in between."

"And West usually comes with you?"

"Usually. I hate going through this shit alone. I hate having to admit that, but I spent so much time in the hospital after it happened, and then alone in that rehab place, and... I don't know. I get so much anxiety, and all this bad shit comes back and haunts me. I just don't handle it well. It helps having someone with me."

"Well, I'm glad it's me today. So, what are they gonna do to you?"

"Dermabrasion for my last skin graft. Basically, they use this sanding tool to grind down the scar tissue and smooth it out."

"Get the fuck out of here. Seriously? That's a thing?"

Mandy laughs. "Yeah, it's a thing. But don't worry, they numb me first."

"Shit, when we leave this place, I'm gonna buy you ice cream."

He laughs again, shaking his head. "That's more than West offers me."

I make the turnoff on the exit for the Charles George VA Medical Center in Asheville, and the ball of nerves in my stomach grows larger with each mile we get closer. Hell, it's not even my face being sandblasted today, and I feel like I'm gonna throw up. How in the hell does he go through this every month?

I park my car in the full lot and before we get out, Mandy folds his hands in his lap and bows his head. *Is he praying?* After a minute of silence, he looks up and gives me a little smile.

"Just something I do every time I come here. I ask for strength and courage, and I ask for acceptance that no matter what the outcome of the procedure, that it's enough for me, that I'm happy with the results." He grabs for the door handle and then stops. "Oh, and I ask that they don't remove the wrong body part by accident."

I smack his shoulder. "Get the fuck outta here."

"I'm serious. You wouldn't believe how many articles I read like that."

"You have no business reading medical journals and articles

about amputating the wrong limbs or organs. Not with your medical anxiety."

He just shrugs and climbs out of the car. Tucked under his arm is a thick-ass manila folder. I'm betting it's his medical records, and judging by the thickness of the file, he knows this place like the back of his hand. I follow him inside to the reception desk, where he checks in, and then we're told to wait. We take a seat in the waiting room that's packed wall-to-wall with other vets. Apparently, waiting is a thing here.

We don't have to wait long before the entertainment arrives.

"Oh good, I'm not too late," West huffs, jogging up to us.

"I thought you couldn't make it," Mandy says, looking up with surprise.

"I was getting fitted for a new prosthetic, but they didn't make me wait long to be seen, unlike this fucking place," he complains, looking around the packed room.

"Oh, but I loved the old one. It had the painted toenails."

West sticks his middle finger right in Mandy's face. "I was due for a pedicure. I think I'll go with purple this time." West stands directly in front of the man sitting to Mandy's left and lifts his pant leg, shamelessly exploiting his prosthetic leg until the man feels honor bound to give up his chair. "Thanks for your service," West says, clapping him on the shoulder. He snatches up his seat in a heartbeat.

I'm a little disappointed he showed up. Not that I'm in the market to make new best friends, but I was enjoying getting to know Mandy a little better. He's actually a great guy, but so is West. He pulls out a *Mad Libs* pad from his backpack and Mandy shakes his head, chuckling.

"What?" West asks. "You love these. Give me a synonym for big."

"Ginormous," Mandy answers.

"Oh, that's a good one." He writes it down. "Rhett, what rhymes with art?"

"Cart, dart, heart, fart, and start."

"That'll work perfectly," he says with a smirk. "A verb that starts with G."

"Grinding," I answer at the same time Mandy says, "Gloating."

"I'll take them both," West says. "All I need is the name of a fruit."

"Avocado," I supply.

"Avocados are fruits?" West asks.

I answer with a shrug. "I read that somewhere."

"Well, aren't you a smarty-pants?" he says sarcastically.

"Just one of my many good qualities," I tease back.

He reaches into his backpack again and pulls out a stack of flyers. "Here," he says to Mandy. "Pass these around while I work on this story."

Mandy passes the stack to me, and I read the flyer on top. '*Squeeze your BALLS for all you can,*'" it reads before listing some of the many services provided by BALLS. These are the ones Margaret Anne hands out at the front desk to new visitors.

"Here, pass these around," I tell the guy next to me.

I think it's great how these guys volunteer to represent BALLS just because the organization has given them so much. I hope I can say the same for myself after I see what they can do for me.

I watch as the stack gets passed around; some people fold it up and put it in their pocket or purse, and some crumble it in their fist and toss it under their chairs. I get it. Not everyone wants the help or feels like they need it, but I bet every single one of these fuckers could use it.

"All right, here's what I've got. Laundry day," West starts.

Mandy groans. "Laundry day? None of those words we gave you have anything to do with laundry."

West grins. "That's the point. The wicker basket overflowed with a ginormous load of dirty clothes. Most were stained by darts and farts." Mandy snickers and West laughs before continuing. "Sometimes, they get downright filthy with the grinding and the gloating. If you toss them in the washing machine with a ginormous helping of laundry soap, you can usually get them sparkling clean and smelling sweet and delicious like avocados."

Mandy smiles. "Not as good as your space alien one, but I laughed, so it worked."

"You do these often?" I ask.

"Yeah, I've always got this pad handy. It passes the time. We spend a lot of time in waiting rooms, don't we, Nutter buddy?"

"Unfortunately," Mandy agrees.

A weight drops into the pit of my stomach. This is what I have to look forward to. When you have a chronic injury, the kind you're going to spend the rest of your life with, like mine, like Mandy's burns, and West's leg, you become very intimate with waiting rooms and doctor's offices. It's an eye-opening glimpse into my future.

"I better get myself a Mad Libs pad."

West rubs his thigh just above his amputation site and

grimaces. "You know, I'm actually thinking of borrowing your origami book. I could use some variety."

"You can borrow it any time. At this point, I don't think Liza expects I'll ever give it back."

"Hey, are you coming over to stay with us after this?" West asks Mandy.

"Yeah, I've got a bag packed in the back of Rhett's car."

"You know, you're welcome to come stay with me."

"Thanks for the offer," Mandy says graciously, "but at his house, I've got my own room. All you've got is the couch."

"It's a nice couch," I insist. "And I don't mind sharing the bed with you; it's plenty big enough."

"If you think I'm sleeping on those kids' sheets, you're nuts," he laughs. "I'm pretty sure I know what you do on those sheets."

West straight-up cackles. "Should I even ask why you have kid sheets on your bed?"

"I didn't buy them," I defend hotly. "Riggs did."

"Oh, this I've got to hear," he insists.

But before I can explain, the nurse calls Mandy's name. "Wish me luck," he says grimly.

"Good luck," West calls.

"Break a leg," I add. West's eyes go wide and he shakes his head.

"Not here," he advises, looking sideways to see if we drew attention. "It doesn't go over well with this crowd. You should stop by our house tomorrow. We always have a movie day when Mandy is recovering. All the Bitches will stop by with a care package and there'll be food."

"Sounds good. Thanks." It seems like these guys are determined to make a friend of me, no matter my reservations.

He grins wickedly. "Now, tell me about those sheets."

Group with the guys is never boring, but I could have skipped today, since it seems to be focused solely on me. Well, me and Riggs.

As usual, he's the last to arrive, taking his seat after everyone's already present and pulling their knitting out of their bags. I haven't even attempted knitting yet, so I pull out my origami instead. Liza sent me an envelope of colorful printed paper in the mail. It sure beats using the BALLS brochures.

There's an undercurrent in the room I'm picking up on, some sort of inside joke, evident by the whispered conversations and covert glances I've witnessed since taking my seat. Of course, I'm not a part of it, but that's my choice. I chose to keep these guys at arm's length, for... reasons, and if they don't include me in their inner circle, then that's on me, not them.

Even yesterday when I stopped by West and Brandt's home to check on Mandy, I felt out of place and on edge throughout the entire movie. I was the only guy who didn't bring a care package, and I was the only guy not complaining about watching *Top Gun*. I also chose to sit in a chair by myself in the corner, instead of trying to dogpile onto the bed with the rest of the guys, mostly to protect my leg from getting kicked accidentally, but it just added to the solitary feeling.

"All right," Riggs addresses us. "We're two men short today.

Mandy is recovering, and Pharo is deployed, so if we finish a few minutes early, it's understandable. Who wants to kick us off?"

West raises his hand. "I'll go first." He shares another look with Brandt, who nods at him before continuing. "I've been training for the Warrior's Walk, and it's kicking my ass. But also, I'm grateful I'm far enough in my recovery that I'm even able to train for it. A couple months ago, that wouldn't even have been a possibility. It got me thinking about when I first started PT, when I met Riggs. I had zero hope that I would ever recover enough to even walk, let alone train for something like that. You promised me," he says to Riggs.

"You promised that someday I could run and jump, and even snowboard if I wanted, and I thought you were fucking high," he laughs. "You never let me down, never stopped believing in me, even when I didn't believe in myself. Neither of you did," West says, placing his hand on Brandt's knee. They share a look full of meaning that gets me right in my heart.

"I had a real lack of motivation when I first started out, and I remember Riggs told me he had a theory that he used sexual desire to motivate his patients. I thought he was coming onto me." He laughs. "It sounds ridiculous, but he was right; it worked like a charm. He asked me if my dick still worked."

"West," Riggs warns. "Is this necessary?"

"Yeah, I've got a point I'm trying to make."

"Then make it," Riggs snaps.

"Anyway, that night in the shower, my buddy here," he slaps Brandt's leg, "helped me figure out if my dick still worked."

McCormick cracks up. "Let me guess, it worked perfectly."

"You bet it did," West winks. "But Riggs was right. Sexual desire is a great motivator for recovery. When Brandt started playing with my dick, I never wanted him to stop, which meant—"

"West," Riggs barks.

"I swear I'm making a point," he laughs. "Which meant that I had to work twice as hard in the gym so I could start fucking again. Anyway, I just want to say thank you for asking about my dick, Riggs."

I laugh along with the rest of the guys, but Riggs isn't laughing.

Nash goes next. "Yeah, this training is kicking my ass, but that's a good thing. I think I was getting complacent with my workout, because now I'm sore *everywhere*. Much like West, I had a real lack of motivation when I first started therapy with Riggs, and he gave me the same advice. If you want to have sex again, you better start working harder. I've busted my ass in that gym every goddamn day because I had a mission, and his name is Brewer. Unfortunately, my dick was broken, but not from an injury. It was because of my head. And just like I worked hard in the gym, I worked even harder in therapy, trying to overcome that roadblock between my head and my dick."

Riggs interrupts. "Listen guys, I'm not *Dr. Ruth* and this isn't sex therapy."

"I've got a point, Riggs, I promise," Nash laughs. Riggs glares at him as he finishes speaking. "My point is, it may sound like crazy advice, but he knows what he's doing. Riggs is the best therapist there is, and when he asks you if your dick is working, just go with it."

McCormick shares a similar story, and by this time he's finished, Riggs is breathing fire. He's pissed, but not as pissed as I am.

How come I never got that speech?

He's never once asked if my dick works.

Maybe because it clearly does, but these guys are right. Sex *is* a great motivator to recover. And Riggs hasn't pushed me like that, not once.

The meeting wraps up early, and the guys high-five each other as they head out. I remain seated as Riggs starts stacking the chairs, banging the metal legs loudly together as he takes out his frustration.

"Is there a reason you're sticking around?" he asks tersely.

I'm angry, but also, I just feel... alone. *Lonely*. I'm so far away from where I want to be with him, I'm just *nowhere*. "Don't you want to know if my dick works?"

"It clearly does because you were rock hard the other night when I helped you to bed."

He caught that? My bad. "So how come I've never heard this speech from you? Or do you only save it for your special patients?"

Riggs loses his tether on his temper and throws the chair. It bounces across the linoleum floor. "By all means, Rhett, if you want to get fucked, then that's what you should do. You should push yourself even harder in the gym. When you're on your knees for some guy and he's slamming into you from behind, I hope you think of me and send me a silent thanks for getting you to where you want to be. Or better yet, when you're with a girl, and she's riding your cock, juicing it up real good, and she asks you to flip her over, you can think of me, and thank me for being able to fuck her the right way."

He picks up the chair he threw and stacks it with the rest. I'm fucking speechless. I can't believe he said that. Definitely not where I thought this conversation would lead, and now I'm even more pissed off.

He's fucking *jealous*. The thought of me on my knees clearly angers him. Is that why he didn't suggest I use sexual desire to motivate my recovery? *It has to be.* So why does he keep fucking denying me?

He storms out before I can ask, and like a fool, I just keep sitting here, replaying his words in my head. Finally, I pack up my paper and head out, but I don't make it far. Riggs is standing just outside the door, leaning against the wall with his head in his hands. He snags my arm as I pass.

"Rhett, I'm sorry. I didn't mean to say those things, and you don't..."

"You know what? I don't need an apology. An explanation, maybe, but not an apology. You do you, and I'll do me." I've nearly crushed the paper eagle in my hand, and I loosen my grip and offer it to him. "I'll see you in the gym. Apparently, I have a lot of work to do and I'm feeling *very* motivated."

I thought Riggs would have adopted a softer attitude toward me after our heart-to-heart the other night, but that shit didn't last two minutes. He's back to ignoring me again, giving me the cold shoulder, and after his temper tantrum after group, I really shouldn't be surprised. It's ridiculous; he's working with another guy right beside me, and his eyes haven't strayed to me once. I can practically feel his icy mood gusting in my direction.

And I look fucking good today. I chose a navy blue sleeveless compression top to show off the progress I've made on my arms.

I change out the weights strapped to my ankles for a heavier set and continue my reps, counting out another twenty leg lifts. I stare straight ahead, pretending like I don't hear Riggs conversing with the guy beside me. He's pleasant but professional, even making the guy laugh at some of the things he says. It makes my blood pressure boil over.

Has he given that guy the sexual desire motivates recovery speech?

The signs on the walls have been taken down and replaced with the original motivational posters. It looks boring as fuck. Our neon signs were much better.

From the corner of my eye, I spy Riggs putting his hands on the guy, grasping his thigh as he leans over his legs.

"You feel tight. Are you cramping?"

"Yeah," the man grunts, sounding wiped.

Riggs positions the man's foot against his chest, still gripping his thigh. "Push against my chest."

I grit my teeth and grab a heavier set of weights. Sweat drips off my forehead as I bend over to strap them on my ankles.

"That's good, push harder. Give me all you've got," he jokes, making the man laugh again.

Fuck me for glancing over, but Riggs is massaging the guy's calf muscle, and all I can see is the color red clouding my vision. Or maybe it's green.

"How does that feel?" he asks, the sound of his voice way too gruff for my liking.

Adrenaline courses through my blood, giving me the strength to lift my leg higher, to increase the speed of my repetitions until... The pop in my knee is loud enough to be heard by everyone in the immediate area. Several of them look at me to make sure I'm okay. Riggs drops the guy's leg and plants his feet in front of my bench. He rips the weights off my ankles and throws them to the floor.

"Are you purposely trying to injure yourself?"

"No," I grit. "Why would I?"

"I don't know," he sneers. "Maybe so that later on, when your leg is so inflamed that it locks up on you, you can call me again to help."

"Seriously?" I'm actually shocked. "Is that what you think I was doing?"

He leans closer so that he can't be overheard, his voice an angry hiss in my ear. "I get it, soldier. Your dick works and you want to use it. You want me to fuck you. But I told you, it's not going to happen. Don't you think that's why I haven't given you that speech?" His lips actually brush the shell of my ear, making me shiver. "I'm not going to stop you if you're hell-bent on getting fucked, but it won't be by me. But I will stop you from damaging your knee further because, despite what you think, soldier, I do care. I care very much."

My heart can't beat any harder without giving out on me. I feel like I can't catch my breath. Without another word, he returns to his patient beside me, and I continue to sit here, staring at my ankle weights on the floor.

"Marsh," a deep voice booms, echoing off the gym walls. "Rhett Marsh! Front and center, soldier." My head snaps up along with many others as four soldiers in full uniform stomp through the doors.

"Holy fuckin' shit," I breathe. Warren, Ormen, Villaro, Mandell—my unit came home. They came for *me*.

I'm on my feet in the blink of an eye, moving as fast as I can one second, and then in the next, my body hits the ground hard, and I'm on my face.

I had to overdo it, didn't I? Just had to fucking push myself past my limit. And now, my knee is locked up again. Tan boots appear in my line of sight, the only thing I can see as I stare at the floor, and I feel their hands on me, helping me to my feet. "Rhett, you all right? You okay?"

But Riggs's deep voice supersedes everyone's. "Don't touch him. Back up."

"Hey man," Warren says. "That's my brother."

"No, that's my patient. Back. The fuck. Up."

"Riggs," I plead, picking my head up off the floor.

"On your feet, soldier," he orders.

"I can't; my leg."

"I said, on your feet, soldier." His voice is harsh and direct, like a drill sergeant.

Swallowing hard, I try to do as he showed me, rolling to my left side and getting my knee up underneath me for leverage. My buddies are glaring at him like they want to bury him six feet under, but I get it—because I know him. Four of my brothers, my former unit, dressed in fatigues and fresh from deployment, are standing on their feet, and here I am, a recovering patient, former Army, critically injured, in workout clothes, lying flat on my face at their feet. The differences between us are wide enough to fit an ocean, whereas we used to be on even footing.

Them helping me off the floor is a bridge too far.

Neither will Riggs help me up.

I've got to do this on my own, to show them I'm strong enough, that I'm still a soldier, still their brother, still a member of their team, even if it's only in my heart.

My body is suffering, but I refuse to let my pride suffer with it, and Riggs is making sure that it doesn't. I owe him for it. He doesn't deserve my anger from earlier. He only deserves my respect and my unending gratitude for this, and for everything he's done for me.

I have to physically manipulate my leg to get it to bend so that I'm kneeling on both knees, lunging with my left into a squat to push myself up. I'm breathing like I ran a marathon, my skin flushed with heat and sweat, red-faced and out of breath.

When I straighten up to my full height, my brothers stand at attention and salute me. Hot tears burn my eyes. "Welcome home," I say in as strong a voice as I can muster.

The tears fall down my cheeks, but I'm not going to wipe them away and draw more attention to them. I'm just grateful that I'm on my feet, and that they're here in front of me in one piece, *all of them*. They all made it back home safely.

That's all that matters to me; not my pride, not my leg.

I nearly fall over again when they crush me in a hug, the four of them at once.

"Come on, brother, show us where we can get something to eat around here."

"I'd give my left nut for some greasy wings or a burger," Ormen adds.

"And some beer," Villaro says.

When I glance back at Riggs, he's gone. He returned to his patient, but he's watching me. He gives me a nod.

"Come on, I know a place," I say, winding my arm around Warren's neck for support.

Ruston, LA

Chapter 18 — RIGGS

PUT THE PHONE DOWN!

It's my twelfth reminder of the day and it's only ten o'clock in the morning. For two days straight, I've held this phone in my hand, waiting for it to ring. *Willing* it to ring. A phone call, a text message, anything. But they were all from someone else, *not Rhett*.

I thought maybe, with his fall the other day and overexertion in the gym, that he would need me that night. He probably had his friends over instead.

How many of them has he slept with?

I hate that my mind goes there, but I can't help it. It's a toxic thought, followed by the sting of jealousy, like poison in my blood.

Has he had a relationship with any of them? A friends-with-benefits arrangement?

Fucking quit, Riggs.

Aren't you gonna ask me if my dick works?

He's got some fucking nerve. I can't believe he asked me that.

Yes, you can. That's who he is. It's one of the things I love about him.

Love? Jesus Christ, I've got to get my mind off him before I combust.

Yesterday, when he didn't show up for therapy, I had to physically restrain myself from going after him. If I don't see him today, I might just...

My phone beeps, and I check the screen so fast I have whiplash. Again, it's not Rhett. Instead, it's the Bitches group chat, which is the last distraction I need right now since it only reminds me of him. The only reason I check the message is to see if he responds.

> West:
>
> He's not good.
>
> Brandt:
>
> Totally depressed.
>
> Mandy:
>
> We gotta do something or he'll lie in bed all day. Again.

. . .

So that's where he was yesterday, hiding under the covers. I can't blame him. His unit came home, and they're back on base and life goes on without him, a stark reminder that he's lost everything.

> **Nash:**
> Let's meet up at his place around two. I'll bring lunch.

I guess I won't be seeing West or Nash in the gym today, either. It's better this way, though. Rhett needs them. I'm still not over being pissed about how they set me up. Rhett hasn't made much of an effort to hide his attraction to me, and I think the guys have finally picked up on it and are trying to push us together because that's what nosy Bitches do.

I have time for two patients before lunch, and at twelve sharp, I head for the cafeteria. Brewer's right on time, coming down the hall at the same time as me from the opposite direction.

"Who's treating today?" he asks. "You or me?"

Smart ass. "I don't care. I just need the distraction."

Today they're serving spaghetti and meatballs, a side salad, garlic bread, and a bowl of minestrone soup. The cafeteria is always packed on spaghetti day, and I wave to Dylan and his dad.

Brewer and I snag our usual table, and as I begin to chew, I can feel the weight of his stare resting on my shoulders. "What?"

"Did I say anything?"

"You didn't have to. I can hear your thoughts like you're screaming."

He continues to shovel forkfuls of spaghetti into his mouth, chewing silently. My agitation mounts until I feel like I have ants crawling beneath my skin.

"Your boyfriend has a big mouth!" I stab my fork in his direction. His smug expression just pisses me off more.

"A long time ago, I learned this handy technique, where all I have to do is sit silently and listen, and a patient will bend over backward to fill that awkward silence with plenty of information. I don't even have to ask any questions, really. I just wait for them to find the answer on their own. Self-guided discovery."

"Is that what you're doing? You're shrinking me?"

"Is that what you want me to do?" he asks calmly, his face a mask of serenity.

Losing my patience, I kick his shin under the table, and he laughs.

I know he knows! And he knows I know he knows.

"The Bitches ratted me out."

He's still chuckling as he says, "As Bitches will do, but only because they care."

"Bullshit. It's revenge, pure and simple. Revenge for all the times I stuck my nose in their business. For all the pain they endured in my gym."

He twirls strands of spaghetti around the tines of his fork. "And was that because you cared?"

Fuck. There's no getting around this. "Obviously, whatever I'm doing isn't working. The situation between us is progressing, and I don't know what to do about it."

"Don't you?"

"If I did, would I be asking you for advice?"

"Oh, I didn't hear you ask." He pops a meatball in his mouth.

Lord in heaven, give me the patience not to choke this man. "Brewer, in your expert opinion," I mock, "what do you think I should do about Rhett's growing attraction toward me?"

"What do you want to do?" he returns frustratingly.

"Come the fuck on, Brewer. That's not advice, you're just turning the tables on me. If I wanted to answer my own questions, I wouldn't be asking you."

"You already have the answer. You don't need to ask me."

"Really? And what's that?"

He glances over his shoulder toward the vending machines. "Sit tight, I'll be right back." Brewer crosses the room and purchases a snack from the machines, and when he returns, he drops a king-sized candy bar on the table.

"Dessert? I haven't even finished lunch yet."

Brewer takes his seat. "Tell me what you see."

"A big-ass candy bar."

"Yes," he laughs. "But look closer. What do you see?"

I don't know what game he's playing with me, and I wish he

would just make his damn point already. Reading from the label, I say aloud, "Dark chocolate, family-sized bar, seventy-seven percent cacao, satisfaction guaranteed."

"Good. What does that mean?"

Blowing out a frustrated sigh, I push my garlic bread through a puddle of spaghetti sauce on my plate. "I don't know, that it's sweet? Just say what you want to say."

"At first glance, it's a huge bar of chocolate. Sweet, decadent, and delicious. You want it. It's hard to resist."

"Is the candy bar supposed to be Rhett in this situation?"

"Do you want it to be?" he asks with a raised brow.

"Jesus Christ, just go on."

Brewer grins, clearly amused by my irritation. "Your second thought is that as much as you want to have it, you know sensibly that if you eat an entire king-size candy bar in one sitting, there will be consequences, correct?"

"Yeah, I'll have a stomachache. I'll feel like shit." *Where is he going with this?*

"Exactly! So, it's a red flag and you pull back. But if you look closer, maybe flip it over and read the ingredients, you can see it says that it's seventy-seven percent cacao, dark chocolate with very little sugar. Many studies show that dark chocolate is actually beneficial to your health. Abundant in antioxidants and minerals, and it supports brain function, a healthy heart, and healthy skin."

"Are you lobbying for *Hershey's*?"

"No," he smirks. "Just pointing out that perhaps your red flags are biased against most chocolate bars, but not this chocolate bar in particular."

"Good God, do you feed this shit to your patients?" I blow out a heavy breath and grab my iced tea. "Okay, so the chocolate bar is sweet and delicious and healthy for me. Now what?"

"Knowing that, would you still grab it and eat the entire thing in one sitting?"

"Probably not. I'm still gonna get a stomachache."

"Exactly, because everything in moderation, correct?"

"Yeah, moderation," I agree.

"So, if you were to approach the candy bar with that attitude, eating small amounts here and there, perhaps two ounces a day, would that make you sick?"

"No, probably not."

"I guess you could say the same about jumping headfirst into a relationship. Moderation is key."

"All that for that? Really?"

Brewer chuckles. Setting down his fork, he leans back in his chair, regarding me thoughtfully. "Let's try a different approach, a non-food related approach. As a therapist, when your patient comes to you with an injury, usually they're in pain and hurting, and probably afraid to start therapy. Correct?"

"Now you're in my wheelhouse. And yes, usually they are afraid. I have to gain their trust before I can see any real progress with them."

He nods. "They have to trust that you're going to protect their vulnerabilities, and that if you push them past what they think they can handle, that it won't turn out badly. Correct?"

"Yeah, that's exactly right."

"Imagine you're the patient, that it's Rhett who you have to trust with your vulnerabilities, and that if you push yourself outside of your comfort zone, it's not going to hurt you and cause further injury."

Christ, I hate it when he's smarter than me. "And if it all blows up in my face?"

Brewer rubs his hands together. "Well, at least your best friend is a therapist."

I hate his smirk.

I hate that he's right.

I hate that I have to push myself out of my comfort zone now and make the first move.

No, Rhett made the first move. He's made it twenty fucking times. The ball is in my court now.

Brewer leans forward, bracing his elbows on the table. "I just want what's best for you."

"And you think this is what's best for me? Honestly?"

"Would I have wasted my lunch hour if I didn't?"

On my way out of the cafeteria, I drop the candy bar on Dylan's table and ruffle the kid's hair. "Not one bite until you finish all your spaghetti."

Knowing what I have to do and wanting to do it are two completely different things.

Searching through my contacts, I find Loretta's name and hit send.

"Hello," she answers.

From what Rhett has told me about his mother, I've imagined Scarlett O'Hara's doppelgänger, and her voice doesn't disappoint. It's pure southern.

"Hello, ma'am. I'm looking for Loretta Marsh?"

"This is she."

"My name is Riggs. Navarro Riggs. I'm Rhett's—"

"Riggs!" she exclaims. "I know exactly who you are. Rhett has told me so much about you. Is my little pecan okay?"

Little pecan? Oh, I can't wait to use that. "Mostly. He's doing well with his recovery, working really hard in the gym and pushing himself a little too hard sometimes. I'm calling because I think he might be feeling down. Really down. He needs a boost, and I think you're just the face he needs to see."

She pauses before asking, "What happened to him?"

"His unit came home from deployment. They visited him and he was so happy to see them, but when they left, well, he's been down ever since." Down is an understatement. He's still hiding under the damn covers.

"What can I do? My poor, sweet boy, he needs his mama. He's been through so much. If only I could just get there, wrap him in my arms, and cheer him up."

"Ma'am? Is there a reason you can't come?"

She sighs tiredly. "I feel just plain tuckered out. I can't fix myself to rights lately. If I piddle around for more than just a minute, I'm completely wiped. I just don't see how I can travel all the way there from Louisiana."

I'm not sure exactly how old Loretta is, but no matter, she shouldn't be feeling that level of exhaustion if she's healthy. "Ma'am, have you gone to a doctor? Maybe you should get checked out."

"Oh, I reckon, but no need to 'cause a fuss over me."

I'm not making any headway like this, so I try a different approach. "Loretta, Rhett needs you. I wouldn't be calling if he didn't need you that bad. Please, for him?" She sniffles, and I can hear the pain in her voice. Knowing her son is hurting is killing her. "Maybe it would be easier for you if I come and get you myself? I'll drive you back home when you're ready."

"Really?" she asks hopefully. "You would come all this way just for my persnickety old ass?"

"Yes, ma'am, for Rhett."

"You must be something real special, Navarro Riggs. I can tell. A mother knows these things."

I chuff, humored by her intuition. "Pack your bags, ma'am. I'm coming for you."

I must've been high when I called her.

I shake myself awake as I pass through my third state and turn the radio up. "Welcome to Louisiana," my GPS informs me.

Loretta lives up north, near Ruston. I don't have much longer to go. My worry for Loretta kept me awake for most of the drive. She shouldn't be that tired. What if something's wrong? The nurse in me won't let it go. Loretta lives alone now that Rhett is gone, and probably thinks she doesn't have to take care of herself because she has no one left relying on her, but she's wrong. Dead wrong. Rhett relies on her. She's all he's got left.

The GPS leads me through an older section of town with

large historic homes immaculately maintained and landscaped. Just as I start to think Rhett hid the fact that he came from money, I realize my ETA still says I'm ten minutes away. Passing through the old neighborhoods, I head back out of town through endless fields of sugarcane. There are fewer homes out here, spaced further apart, and some look like former plantation homes, and others, rundown farmhouses. I turn down a gravel drive that leads to one of those. The two-story home has seen better days. Faded yellow paint is peeling off the wooden siding, and the aluminum gutter on the left side of the house is hanging askew, and that's just the start of the repair list.

I grab my duffel from the backseat and make my way up the broken concrete path. Loretta opens the screen door, waiting to greet me with a huge smile. She's a tiny woman, her bright red hair dyed and pulled into a bun. She's wearing a blue dress and an apron that looks older than she is.

"Riggs! Or is it Navarro?"

"Riggs," I correct, sliding my arm around her tiny waist. I pull her in for a hug and breathe in her sweet perfume.

"Well, you just call me Retta. Come on in, honey. I've got biscuits in the oven. We're havin' crawfish and dumplins."

I don't know what to address first—my joy over having homemade cooking, the fact I just crossed the threshold into a freaking museum that could honestly be the thrift store version of the set of *Gone with the Wind*, or that she switched out the chicken for crawfish.

"Retta? So you're Rhett and Retta?" *How fucking cute.*

"Isn't that just a hoot? I bet my son told you to call me

Loretta. He gets so doggone embarrassed about his name. Did he tell you his middle name?"

A smile touches my lips. "He did, the first night we met," I recall, trying not to get lost in the memories. Every time I think about that night, I get sucked into the past. "He doesn't know I'm here."

Retta wipes her hands on her apron and then places them on her slim hips. "What nonsense are you talkin', boy? Why wouldn't he know you're here?"

"As I explained, he's having a difficult time right now. We haven't exactly talked in the last few days. He's sort of hiding out."

"Is that normal behavior for him? Does he do that often?"

"Not since he moved to Black Mountain, no. Before that, I couldn't say."

"Sit down, Riggs. Can I get you some tea, hun?"

"Yes, please." Beside the fridge, there's a macramé wreath tacked to the wall. Everything in my mother's kitchen is perfectly matched, from the paint on the walls and the fabric of the cushions to the hardware on the cabinets and the finish of the appliances. Retta's kitchen is a mismatched hodgepodge of collected things that feel homey and comfortable. It feels lived in.

"Let me ask you a question, and you better give me God's honest truth. Should I be worried about him?"

"Ma'am, I drove eleven hours to get here, and I'm going to drive eleven hours back, and when you're ready to come back home, I'm going to make the trip all over again. I wouldn't be here if I wasn't worried about him."

I've worked with so many veterans and served with them, and I've seen the consequence of ignoring the warning signs that someone is in trouble. Last year, I watched West struggle terribly, trying repeatedly to take his own life. I witnessed Nash's battle against drugs and alcohol as a way to cope with the insanity in his head. I'd rather suck-start a pistol than watch Rhett suffer through the same hell.

She places a glass of tea before me and retrieves the biscuits from the oven. "My God, they smell delicious."

"Come and wash up at the sink while I make your plate," she instructs me.

"Yes, ma'am."

"I have to say, I'm a bit nervous about this trip. I haven't traveled this far in years."

"You mentioned you weren't feeling well. Are you sure you're up for this trip?"

We take our seats at the table and she serves two steaming plates of dumplings. The fragrant steam wafting in my face makes my stomach growl with hunger.

"Whether I am or not won't stop me from going to see my son. I can't tell you how grateful I am that you came for me. It broke my heart not to be able to see him as soon as he came home, just thinking of him lying in that hospital, hurtin' so bad and all alone."

"He wasn't completely alone."

Retta squeezes my hand. "You're a special man, Navarro Riggs. You'll always have a place at my table."

I have to swallow past the lump forming in my throat. The sudden rush of emotion is unexpected. My mother doesn't inspire the same warmth and generosity as Loretta Marsh, and it's been a long time since I've felt so welcome at someone's table.

She's wrong about me. I'm *not* special, but she *is*.

I see where Rhett gets it from.

"I remember the day he told me he was joinin' the Army to jump out of planes. We were sittin' at this table. I nearly choked on my fried chicken."

I can't help but laugh. "I bet that was a shock for you. Why would anyone want to jump out of a perfectly good plane?"

"It wasn't that so much as him volunteerin' to move thousands of miles away from me. He never talked about college, so I just assumed he would stay right here after he graduated. I didn't know he was itchin' to go off and see the world."

"I think he feels lost, struggling to figure out where he belongs and what comes next."

Retta picks up her fork, loaded with crawfish and a dumpling, and pauses halfway to her mouth. "We'll help him find his place. We'll help Rhett figure out where he belongs."

He belongs with me. I shake my head, erasing the thought.

After dinner, which was decidedly one of the best meals I've ever eaten, Retta directs me up the stairs. "You can bunk in Rhett's room. We'll leave first thing after breakfast in the mornin'."

On the landing, I pause. A huge gilt-framed portrait catches my eye. I recognize Loretta, but the other man... "Is that Clark Gable?"

Retta's laughter floats up the stairs. "Rhett had that painted for me for my fortieth birthday. Isn't it somethin'?"

Oh, it's something, all right.

At the top of the stairs, I turn left, and there's no mistaking which door belongs to him. There's a macaroni heart taped to it he must have made over twenty years ago. Above that is a handwritten sign that says 'Rhett's room: Trespassers will be made to do chores.'

I enter with a smile on my face that grows exponentially wider when I get a load of his bed. The sheets on the twin-sized mattress look decidedly familiar, and very similar to the ones I bought for him recently. Wooden shelves line the walls dotted with baseball and soccer trophies. A *Louisville Slugger* leans against the headboard. Dozens of paratrooper posters are taped to the walls.

After washing up in the bathroom down the hall, I change into a pair of plaid sleep pants and climb under his covers. The old frame squeaks, but the mattress is soft enough that I won't have any trouble falling asleep.

How many nights did he lie here wondering what he would be when he grew up? Unfortunately, he's still trying to figure that out.

I can feel him here, like a dominating presence in the room, as if he crawled under the covers to lie beside me. I may be thousands of miles away from him tonight, but I've never felt so close to him. Except maybe that first night we met, when he refused to let go of my hand. When he cried with me and begged me not to leave him alone.

I bet he feels alone tonight, lying in his bed, wondering why everyone he loved left him.

I haven't left you, Rhett. I'm coming home.

RHETT
Black Mountain, NC
Chapter 19

I FOUGHT IN A WAR.

For nine months, I lived under the constant threat of gunfire and mortars.

I jumped into a hot zone and nearly lost my life.

But none of that compares to the danger I pose to myself right now.

My head is the most dangerous place I've ever been.

I don't know whether it's day or night, nor do I care. It's always dark under the covers.

I'm exhausted, but I haven't done shit. I just feel... empty. Numb. I guess there comes a point when grief stops hurting. I think this hollow feeling might be worse.

I hear a knock at my door. *Shit, I'm not in the mood.* I wish everyone would just go away. Stop texting, stop calling, stop coming around.

I bury myself deeper under the blanket, hoping they'll go away.

A minute later, they knock again.

"Dammit to fuck." Slowly, I lift the covers off my head, like a turtle peeking out of its shell. Another knock, this one louder. I roll out of bed and grab my crutches. "Keep your fuckin' boots on," I grumble as I shuffle down the hall.

When I pull the door open, seven ugly mugs stare back at me. "Great, it's a fuckin' party." Company is the *last* thing I need.

They push past me, not even waiting for an invitation, which is good because they weren't getting one. The guys make themselves comfortable on my couch, some leaning against the breakfast bar, and West rifles through my fridge, tossing bottles of water to each of them.

"Thought you said you were bringing lunch," he accuses Nash.

"I did. Should be here any minute." He's got some ugly, ass-green sling around his shoulders and chest, and I swear to fuck as I'm staring at it a black kitten pokes his head out and stares at me curiously.

Brandt grabs the remote control and flips through the TV channels, settling on an action movie with lots of loud explosions. "Does this trigger anyone?" he asks politely.

It's like I'm not even here. Did they really come to check on me, or did they just want to use my TV and eat my food?

"Yo Rhett," Stiles calls. "Take a seat, man. You can't be standing around on that leg."

He scoots over and pats the space beside him. "The fuck are y'all doin' here? Is this because I missed group?"

McCormick shakes his head. "Group was canceled today. We had a Code Black."

That sounds serious. "What's a Code Black?"

"You know, a blackout day," he answers. "When one of the Bitches can't get out of bed. When their head's not right."

He pulls a skein of black yarn from his knitting bag and points his bamboo needles at the TV screen. "Oh my God, watch this next part. He totally fucks this guy's day up."

I hobble to the couch and lean my crutches against the wall, fitting myself into the tight space between Stiles and McCormick. Concern makes me ask, "Who's having a shit day?"

"You," Stiles snorts.

That one word hits me like a punch to the gut. "You canceled the entire group for me?"

He shrugs like it's no big deal. "We didn't cancel. We just brought the group to you."

They continue with the movie, ignoring me, and I look up and catch West's eyes. "You're part of the group, bonehead. You're one of us," he tells me.

"Yeah," Mandy adds, leaning across McCormick to punch my thigh. "You're a fucking Bitch."

Well, fuck me. There's absolutely no use in trying to keep these guys at arm's length. They're like a bad rash, they just keep coming back.

The right side of Mandy's face is covered in white gauze. I feel like a piece of fucking shit stuck to the bottom of my boot after latrine duty. He texted me several times, even called once or twice, and I ignored every one of them.

"How do you feel?" I ask, knowing it's too little too late.

He rubs the spot where he punched me and then pats my thigh. "About as good as you do," he winks.

At least they get it. I may not have an obvious injury with a bandage, but grief hurts just as badly. It bruises your soul from the inside out.

From outside, a loud, obnoxious horn blares, followed by the sound of a mariachi band. "Lunch is here," Nash calls, jumping up.

Brandt follows, craning his neck out the window. "Is that Nacho?"

"Tacos," they shout, rushing through the door at once like someone rang the dinner bell.

I can't eat a thing. My appetite is nonexistent. While the group is outside, I return to my room and grab the camouflage blanket off my bed, wrapping myself up in a cocoon of safety. It's harder to walk like this, but more comfortable when I'm sitting on the couch surrounded by so many bodies. Before I sit, I peek through the window and see a food truck parked behind my car. Nacho's Cantina, it reads. Suddenly, the mariachi band makes sense. It's blaring through a speaker attached to the truck.

A little blond jumps out carrying bags of food. He's dressed in cut-off denim shorts and cowboy boots. His cropped tank reads, "Do you wanna taste my tacos?" I realize he's coming inside, and when Mandy sees him come through the door, he immediately tries to cover his face, his body going stiff.

"You must be Rhett," he guesses, placing a brown bag in my lap. "I'm Tex."

His light hair has darker strands that offset all the blond. The mussed locks barely kiss his shoulders. He smells like watermelon and I squint, realizing his skin shines like he's wearing body glitter. He takes a seat beside Mandy, placing his hand over Mandy's as he urges him to drop his hands from his bandages.

"Does it hurt?" he asks. Mandy nods. The man sighs sadly, shaking his head. "You don't deserve to hurt. You're the bravest man I know. Are you hungry? I brought you tacos, the mango habanero ones you like best."

"Thanks," Mandy says gruffly. "I'll eat in a minute."

"Don't let them get cold, big guy," the blond says before placing a kiss on Mandy's good cheek. Then he sashays out the door, the heels of his boots clacking against the concrete outside.

Mandy looks at me and I swear he's blushing, which makes me crack a smile for the first time in days. "Was that the guy, the one that works at *Hooters*? Friendzone guy?"

If his face gets any redder, that bandage is going to catch fire and burn away to ash. "That's him," he confirms.

"Oh, man," I cackle. "You're so fucked. How does he look in those little orange shorts?"

"Don't worry about how he looks," Mandy snaps.

I grab the bag of tacos from my lap and place them on the table next to his bag. "You can have my tacos if you want them. I'm not hungry."

This time, he laughs. "You look like a taco, wrapped up in that blanket."

"I feel like one, ground up and deep fried." I pull the blanket tighter around my shoulders and head. "Maybe tomorrow night we can go out for wings," I suggest wickedly, thinking of the little blond with the Texan accent.

"Maybe you can fuck off."

Mandy isn't Brian. In fact, he couldn't be more opposite. Mandy isn't loud or witty, he's not sarcastic, and his jokes are actually funny, unlike Brian's were. He's quieter, more reserved. I guess that's what happens when you suffer as badly as Mandy has, as I have. Tragedy and grief change your brain chemistry. It's something that only someone who's been through it can understand. A shared experience that fills the silence between our words in a way that isn't awkward, just comfortable. Although Mandy and Brian are as different as night and day, they're both good for me, and I guess I can call both my best friends.

But Brian's gone, and that just leaves me with Mandy.

I think that's enough for me, though.

I never moved off the couch after the guys left. Going back to my bedroom felt too far away, and I just don't have the strength or will to get there. If I never move again, it'll be too soon.

An incredibly inconsiderate person knocks on my door. "Fuuuuccckkkk," I moan. "Go away!"

"Rhett, open up. It's Riggs."

I poke my head out of the blanket, sitting up. "Riggs?" I might be able to muster the will to move for him.

Slowly, I hobble without crutches to the door and open it to find him standing there looking tired and irresistible. He's always irresistible looking, though.

"Hey," he greets me with a lopsided half-smile. Then he moves aside and...

"Mama?" I can't believe my lying eyes!

"My sweet Pecan." She wraps me in a bear hug, nearly knocking me off my feet.

"What... How? How are you here, Mama?"

"Riggs came and got me, baby. You gonna invite us in?" she teases.

I stand aside to let them in, and when Riggs brushes past me, I grab his hand and squeeze. "Thank you," I whisper, on the verge of tears.

He squeezes back and winks. "Anytime, soldier."

Fuck me, this man went and got my mama. This man, who I already thought hung the fucking moon, drove all the way to Ruston to bring my mama back, 'cause he knew I needed her.

Yeah, forget holding back the tears. I don't have the strength for that, either.

I follow them to the couch and sit between them. "Let me see your leg, baby."

Obediently, I prop my leg on the coffee table, but Riggs moves it to his lap. He lifts my pajama pants up to expose the ugly maze of scars.

"Here and here are where they inserted rods," he explains. "And this is where the pins were placed." His finger traces the long, jagged scar and raised patch of grafted skin. "This was all torn and hanging, and most of the tissue died, so they grafted fresh skin from his thigh." He raises his dark eyes to mine and smiles softly. "I think it's healing nicely."

My mama has tears in her eyes like me as she reaches out to touch my skin. "Sweet baby, my God, you've suffered!" She swallows her anguished sob and smiles valiantly. "I'm here now and I'll take good care of you while you heal."

Her words are a soothing balm on my ravaged soul. No matter how old I get, or how tough I'm supposed to be, I'm never not gonna want to crawl into her arms when I feel like shit.

Riggs lowers my leg and I regret the loss of his touch. Mama envelops me in her arms and I breathe in her sweet perfume, letting it wash over me until my tears dry up.

"How long you stayin', Mama?" *Forever?*

"As long as you need me, baby."

Thank fuck.

"Show me your place. I need to find a bathroom."

Grabbing my crutches, I hop to my feet, feeling a rush of energy for the first time in days. "Isn't it nice? Riggs picked out everythin'." Mama gives Riggs a knowing look. His expression remains passive. "Down here's the bedroom. I've got my own bathroom. First time I've ever had one all to myself."

"Just one bedroom?" she asks, taking in the full-sized bed.

"Plenty big enough for me." Then I realize what she's saying. "You can have my bed, Mama. I'll sleep on the couch."

"I won't hear of it, you sassafras fool. I'll check into an affordable hotel."

I know for a fact my mama can't afford nothing like that long term.

"I have a guest bedroom, Retta. Rhett can stay with me while I oversee his recovery."

Retta? He's on a first name basis with my mama? Fuck, my heart's melting. But all I can focus on is that I'm apparently bunking with Riggs... *indefinitely.*

Forget my heart. My dick feels all perky and interested in that suggestion.

"There you go, Mama. I'll bunk with Riggs."

"That settles it, then," she grins with satisfaction. "Now shoo. I gotta powder my nose."

While she's using the bathroom, I start packing a bag, seeing how it's already dark and getting later by the minute. They must be exhausted from driving all day.

Riggs's eyes follow me around my room. I catch his gaze and grin. I can't help it. Feels like I just won the lottery. "You really got an extra bed, or you just sayin' that for the sake of propriety?"

He barks out a laugh. "I actually have a second bedroom. And yes, you'll be using it for more than clothing storage."

Killjoy.

"Let's get her settled and we'll leave and come back first thing tomorrow morning."

"Riggs, I can't thank you enough. I needed this."

His throat slides as he stares into my eyes. "I know you did, soldier. I refuse to let you slip away. I've got you."

Fucking tears again! I swallow them back and nod.

When my mama is settled in for the night, we take off in Riggs's truck. "How far out of town do you live?" I ask after passing our third exit on the interstate.

"Just after this next exit. Wait until you see the view in the morning. Kind of hard tonight, with it being dark already."

I take a deep breath and hold it in my chest, waiting for my heartbeat to slow before breathing out. Less than an hour ago, I could barely get the thing to beat for how slow and depressed I felt, and now it's threatening to come out of my chest, pounding away like a jackhammer from excitement and my nerves. I'm not sure how long my mama plans to stay, but I have at least a week with Riggs in his home. A week to convince him I'm a good bet, a solid guy, and serious about my recovery. Yeah, the last couple of days my motivation was slightly derailed, but this is my chance. If I want this man, and I do, I need to make sure he finds me absolutely irresistible.

I've got this. Even with a shattered leg, grief, and depression threatening to swallow me, and no future prospects, I can be charming as fuck.

When I look over, he's watching me, and he looks a bit worried.

"Your mama is really excited to be here, to spend time with you and to take care of you, but maybe you could keep an eye on her and make sure she doesn't push herself too hard."

It's like he's giving voice to the quiet fears in my head, the ones getting louder every time I talk to her, setting off warning bells when I saw her tonight. "You think there's something wrong with my mama? She's got me worried."

"I think maybe you need to talk to her, one-on-one, without me around. See if she'll open up to you." Anything concerning my mama sends me into a panic. Riggs notices, looking over at me when he stops at the red light. "Hey, whatever it is, we'll get through it."

We'll? Does he realize he's including himself in my problems? The same guy that told me it's complicated, that he's not interested in a relationship. But the idea he's all in with me makes me feel less scared to face my future, to face the possibility that something might be wrong with my mama, or that I may never find a better job than tending bar.

The thing is, with Riggs, I really don't have to try to be charming. He seems to like me best when I'm just being myself.

Minutes later, Riggs pulls his truck down a long, gravel drive and parks in front of a small beige house landscaped with short grass and trimmed hedges. The house doesn't have much personality save for the landscaping, but Riggs mentioned the view, and I bet it's spectacular.

I grab my bag and my crutches and follow him inside. Thank God it's one story and I don't have to navigate any stairs.

"The place is small, but I didn't buy it for the layout," Riggs explains. He continues toward the sliding glass doors that lead to the back deck, and I drop my bag and follow him outside.

"You've got a hot tub?" Even though it's dark, the glow from the moon is enough to illuminate a partial view of the valley below. I can make out dark shadows, the sound of rushing water, and the sounds of the nightlife coming alive. An owl hoots in the distance, crickets buzz, and a squirrel runs across the deck. "Can I rent a room here? Hell, I'm not leaving!"

Riggs laughs. "I figured you'd say something like that. I know it's late, but do you want to get in?"

Hope soars. "Is this a trick question? Are you joining me?"

"Yeah, I'll join you for a minute. Did you bring a bathing suit?"

"No. You didn't mention anything about needin' one. Can I just borrow one of yours?"

Riggs looks away and then down at his shoes. "We can do it another night."

"Seriously? You won't let me borrow your bathing suit? Did I miss the part where I have a contagious skin rash?"

"No," he chuckles. "I don't have any. I don't wear one when I soak."

Instant fucking boner. "Well, then, I don't need one either," I say casually, playing it off like it's nothing.

Riggs chuckles harder. "Good night, soldier. Don't stay up too late."

He disappears inside, and after a minute more, I follow. Grabbing my duffel, I search out my room and pull my sleep pants out of my bag. The bed is soft, made up with black sheets and a gray comforter. My head hits the pillow, and I release a tired sigh, letting go of everything—the long day, the excitement of my mama's visit, the sexual tension with Riggs, and the loneliness I feel over saying goodbye to my team, again.

That sexual tension, though. *Fuck*, he's right down the hall. Literally in the next bedroom. Close enough to hear me snore tonight. I could easily slip into his bed while he's sleeping. Maybe sneak into his shower in the morning and surprise him. I could... "Riggs, I'm—"

"Don't even try it, Rhett," he calls.

I get the feeling he expected this. "Night," I say with disappointment.

"Night, soldier."

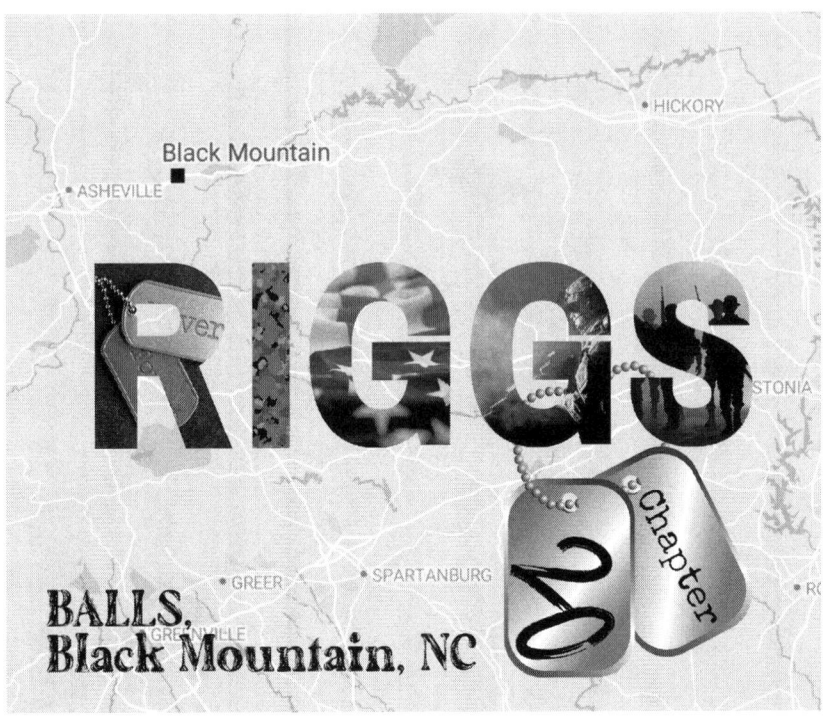

RIGGS
BALLS, Black Mountain, NC
Chapter 20

EVEN FOR A MORNING person like me, having Rhett in my house put some extra pep in my step. I practically jumped out of bed with a smile on my face. I can hear him moving around, shuffling to the bathroom down the hall, and when he limps into the kitchen, dark hair mussed, sleepy eyes, and shirtless with plaid sleep pants slung low on his slim hips, I have to white-knuckle the edge of the counter so I don't jump his ass.

"Morning," he mumbles.

How is he so effortlessly gorgeous? Some people are just born with it, I guess. "Breakfast is served."

Rhett stares at the tall glass with horror. "What the hell is that supposed to be?"

"A green smoothie."

"Yeah, but what's in it?"

"Collagen and vitamin C supplements, kale, carrots, cilantro, collard greens, and romaine lettuce."

His skin turns almost as green as the juice. "Not for all the love and money in Vegas. God himself couldn't get me to drink that shit."

Chuckling, I explain, "You need all of that to aid in healing your bones. It will speed up your recovery. Also," I grab the bottle from the cupboard and retrieve two pills, placing them on the counter. "Teriparatide. It's an anabolic med that increases the rate of bone growth by boosting the concentration of calcium in your blood."

"I don't know what all that means," he says skeptically. "But it sounds like good stuff, even though it looks disgusting."

The grimace on his face amuses me. He has a terrible poker face. "As long as you're staying under my roof, we're going to do things my way. That includes your therapy."

"I'm busting my ass in therapy!"

"It's not enough. We're going to make some changes, starting with these." I grab his crutches leaning against the counter and stow them in the hall closet.

"My crutches? You gotta be kidding me! How am I supposed to get around?"

"With your own two feet. The more you use them to walk, the quicker your leg will strengthen. As long as you're distributing your weight on crutches, you're slowing your recovery."

"Come on! Can't I at least get a walking cane? One of those badass ones with a hidden knife inside!"

His enthusiasm makes me chuckle. "Not a chance. You're

walking from here on out. When you finish that juice, get dressed, and we'll swing by your place and pick up your mother."

I can't help but laugh at the face he makes as he gobbles down the smoothie, chased by a full body shudder. "I'll be ready in ten minutes," he swears.

On the drive to his apartment, he lowers the volume of the radio and turns to face me, his expression serious. "Riggs, I don't know if I'll ever be able to find the right words to thank you for all you've done for me. Not just with savin' my life, but the support and encouragement, kicking my ass in the gym, and now this shit with my mama. Even the supplements this morning. Everything you do is so selfless, and I know sometimes I give you a hard time. I'm angry and depressed, sometimes I just don't feel like I have it in me. But you're always right there to prove me wrong."

For all his wise-ass remarks and fuckboy nature, sometimes Rhett levels me with his sincerity. His gratitude leaves me speechless. I choke down the feelings that are trying to form words and spill out of my mouth. "I just want you to get better. That's all. Just get your life back," I say gruffly.

And when that happens, I pray to God I'm still a part of it.

Retta is dressed and waiting for us in the kitchen. "Dig in, boys. I made pancakes and bacon, and for my little pecan, I made honeyed peaches to top your pancakes."

"Yeah Mama, that's what I'm talkin' 'bout! You can't believe what I had for breakfast earlier."

The urge to touch him is strong. When he mouths off like

this, I find him irresistible, with his dimples popping, framing that lopsided grin. *Fuck.*

I sit beside him, and I don't know if I'm imagining it or not, but I can almost feel the pull between us, like a tangible thing.

"What?" he asks, suddenly looking shy. *He feels it too.*

The voices in my head become loud, coalescing into a deafening roar. I hear my conscience, or maybe just my insecurities, telling me to back off, to push him away. I also hear Brewer telling me to indulge in moderation, and Retta selling me on her son's virtues. I hear my body begging me to touch him. I hear his voice, through the filter of pain and tears, the first night I met him, asking me to hold his hand, to never let go.

Like a moth drawn to a flame, I'm begging to get burned.

There's a spark between us—more like an inferno.

I didn't ask for any of this. I didn't choose him. *My heart did.*

The harder I fall for him, the more I hate myself for being so gullible and careless, but I feel it. It's happening. My heart is getting wrapped up around him. No matter how much I try to fight it, it's inevitable.

This is going to fucking hurt.

"I think about you more often than I should," I admit, surprising myself with my daring.

Rhett's eyes pop wide, and he checks to make sure his mama isn't listening before he whispers, "I think about you constantly."

I've got to get out of here before I give in and kiss him. *Jesus, I'm dying to kiss him.* That first taste is going to be unforgettable.

"I'll see you at BALLS. Don't forget to grab your bathing suit."

When I pull into the parking lot at BALLS, I shut the truck off and sit there for a solid ten minutes, staring at my reflection in the rearview mirror. I can't believe I told him that, and yet, the world didn't end. I didn't spontaneously combust, nor did Rhett. It doesn't mean game on, all in. It just means I won't continue to lie to myself and him. Giving myself that small freedom feels like the greatest thrill, a rush of adrenaline straight to the heart. I'm actually nervous to see him again, which is fucking ridiculous.

Time to go in and face the music. I can just imagine the smug look on Brewer's face when I tell him I've stopped fighting myself. Or the pranks and catcalls from the Bitches. It's all in good fun, I guess. I've given the guys so much shit, I certainly have it coming.

"Good morning, Riggs," Margaret Anne greets cheerfully, offering me a steaming cup of coffee in a paper cup.

"Morning, MA. Don't you look fetching in that pink blouse?"

Of course, she blushes and smiles, which was my goal. "Have a wonderful day."

As I pass down the hall on my way to the gym, I read the posters taped to the walls. "Show off your BALLS at the Veterans Day celebration in Black Mountain!"

I can't hide my laugh thinking of Rhett's reaction to reading the posters. Another ball joke he'll find absolutely ridiculous.

"Hey, Riggs. You gonna show off your balls?" Jax asks, coming up behind me.

Smirking, I answer, "Only if you show yours first."

"Shit, I'll keep them tucked safely away, thank you very much. Actually, I'm riding with the ALR in the parade with Stiles and McCormick. I'll leave all that ball flashing to you Bitches."

The American Legion of Riders is a motorcycle club that does a lot for vets in the way of raising money to cover unpaid medical bills, keeping vets' houses from being foreclosed on, and buying Christmas gifts and school supplies for their kids.

"That's a shame. No one likes to flash their balls more than McCormick."

Jax cracks up and continues down the hall and I duck into the gym. West and Nash are training hard on the step climbing machines, trying to outpace each other. They're both going to complete the Warrior's Walk this quarter; the only question is, who will come in first place? It's never been a competition before, just a personal achievement, but leave it to these two nimrods to change the rules.

"I'll see you both in the pool in an hour," I remind them, making my way to the back of the gym to check on another patient.

Minutes later, I spy Rhett escorting his mama into the gym. He makes a circuit around the room, showing her the equipment and explaining to her his workout routine.

They stand and watch West and Nash compete with each other. "I'll never get there," I overhear him say dejectedly.

"Not with that attitude, you won't." He jumps at the sound of my voice and turns to me, a huge grin working its way over his face.

"Hi," he says in a breathy voice, totally giving himself away. My admission over breakfast turned his brain to mush.

"Did you bring your bathing suit?"

"Yeah, I've got it right here in my bag," he explains, hitching his backpack higher on his shoulder.

"Good, I'll meet you in the pool in an hour."

I try not to laugh at his otherworldly glow and get back to the business of helping people help themselves.

At twelve-thirty, I cut through the locker room to grab some towels on my way to the pool. No matter how many times they clean this place, it always smells like sweaty jockstraps.

When I round a bank of lockers, I see Nash with his head in his locker, searching through his bag. He pops two pills in his mouth and slams the locker shut. Red flags freeze me in my tracks, making goosebumps rise along my skin. I watched Nash struggle through the end of his addiction and the beginning of his recovery, and if he's entertaining the idea of revisiting that hellish nightmare, I might just have something to say about it.

I plant my feet in front of him, arms crossed over my chest. He startles when he turns.

"What?" he asks. The look on my face tells him everything I'm not saying with words. "Oh, that? Ibuprofen, I swear." Nash reaches into his bag and pulls out the bottle to show me.

"It's not that I don't trust you, it's that I'm always going to worry about you." Last year, he was badly tortured in captivity and shot in the leg. After the bullet shattered his femur, he suffered fifteen more days without getting it treated. He walks with a slight limp now, but at least he walks.

"I know. I overdid it earlier in the gym."

"Well, the pool will be the perfect cool down for you. When you get home, ice your leg."

"I will. I promise. So, I heard Rhett's joining us today. Nice to have a new addition to the swim team."

"He's just starting out in his therapy, and though he needs to push himself to stay motivated, don't let him try to keep up with you. He's not there yet."

"I'll keep an eye on the little tyke," Nash teases.

When I walk out into the enclosed pool area, the humidity slaps me in the face and I breathe in the chlorine scented air, letting the steam open up my chest and sinuses. Nash is the first one in the pool, followed by West, and then McCormick. They sit on the edge of the pool, removing their prosthetic legs before jumping in the deep end. Today I have two other vets joining us for the first time, but they're further along in their recovery than Rhett.

When Rhett walks out of the locker room, wearing a very short and very tight pair of black swim trunks, I do a double take, failing to school my expression before he catches me. He's the second one who fails to hide his surprise.

"What's this? I thought you invited me to swim with you."

Nash cracks up and splashes him with water. "I fell for that once, thinking I was meeting Brewer here. Boy, was I wrong."

"This is aquatic therapy. The water acts as a resistant force without any of the impact on your body that the machines in the gym cause. Jump in," I add, eyeing his shorts once more. Jesus, what will they look like when they're sopping wet and stuck to his skin?

"Also known as the *'Bitches' synchronized swim team*,'" McCormick jokes.

"This better not be stupid," he grumbles, gingerly climbing down the ladder.

"For everyone but Rhett, take two full laps back and forth." When I blow my whistle, they take off, kicking and splashing across the pool.

"What about me?" he asks.

"I want you to hold on to the side of the pool and just kick your legs out behind you like you're swimming."

He does as instructed, and the move makes his butt breach the surface, popping out of the water. Because his bathing suit is wet, the thin fabric molds to his cheeks, highlighting the crack between them. My mouth waters for a taste of that crease. If we do this, if we go ahead with this relationship and get naked at some point, the first thing I'm going to do is drag my tongue through his ass and taste his hole.

By the time the rest of them finish their laps, Rhett is almost out of steam. "I'm fuckin' sweating in the pool! That's gotta be a first for me."

West swims up to him and grabs the wall. "It's harder than it looks, isn't it? But that's the point. Riggs says that when you find new ways to use your muscles, you use new muscles. The pool does for our bodies what the gym can't."

You have to love it when your patients start quoting you. It means they're listening. "Are you angling for my job, Wardell?"

"Hell no. I refuse to carry around that stupid clipboard all day."

"Move to the shallow end. Thirty jumping jacks, and then running in place until I blow the whistle."

They grumble and groan as they swim over to the shallow side of the pool. "Rhett, you can join them. But don't try for thirty. Just stop when you feel like you've reached your limit." I know for a fact, he'll push himself past what he thinks his limit is, which is fine with me. It's what he needs to do.

For thirty more minutes, they continue to push their bodies past what they think they can handle at the sound of my whistle. "Nash and Rhett, stick around and do a cooldown before you get out. Everyone else hit the shower." They're both experiencing inflammation today, and the least I can do is encourage them to treat their bodies right. The cooldown exercises followed by a cold shower and some ice packs will do the trick.

"Yo, Riggs! I was told I'd find you in here."

"Randall fucking Mallory, how the hell are you?" My former patient, who I haven't seen in some time, strolls in looking tanned and healthy. Much like Rhett, he broke his leg on a jump gone wrong, and I worked with him for months until he was strong enough again to continue risking life and limb by jumping out of perfectly good airplanes.

"Better than expected," he grins. His dark hair is showing threads of silver around his temples and forehead, and the laugh lines and crow's feet that kiss his skin hint at his sunny, lighthearted demeanor. Randall is an easy-going guy who loves to laugh and lives life to the fullest.

Rhett and Nash finish their cool down and jump out of the pool. "Hey Randall, good to see you again," Nash says on his way to the locker room, shaking the guy's hand.

But Rhett stops beside me, joining the conversation. "Hey, I'm Rhett Marsh. Good to meet you, Randall."

Randall's eyes travel down Rhett's dripping body before returning to his face, and I have to restrain myself from throwing him in the pool.

"Good to meet you, Rhett. How'd you hurt your leg?" he asks, checking out the maze of dark red and purple scars that zigzag across Rhett's leg.

"82nd Airborne. My chute got shot down and I hit the ground too hard. Shattered the right leg and fractured the left." He slides his arm around my shoulders, getting my shirt wet as he pulls me tightly to his side. "Riggs saved my life."

Every time he says that, I have to fight the urge to blush.

Randall squats down and brushes his fingers up Rhett's leg, touching his scars. "You sure made a mess of it, kid."

"You should've seen it before they sewed it up," he teases.

My blood pressure spikes, and I feel the heat rise to my face. My fingertips feel numb. Randall Mallory has exactly half a second to remove his hands from Rhett's leg before I go fucking ballistic.

His survival instinct must kick in because he stands and straightens. "I'm 82nd myself, retired now. I own the flight school out of Asheville Regional Airport. Well, flight and jump school. You should come by, check it out.

Maybe I'll take you up in the air," he offers. "I bet you miss it."

"Hell yeah I do. It's in my blood. Chasing that thrill, it's what I lived for."

"Lived, not live? I'll tell you what. You stop by and I'll take you up in the air, and then maybe we'll grab some lunch, see if we can't get that thrill back."

I'm gonna fucking blow a goddamn blood vessel and have a stroke right here on the pool deck, clutching my clipboard. He's blatantly flirting with Rhett, who either doesn't seem to realize it, or is so desperate to get back up in the air again that he's going along with it.

"That's the best offer I've heard in months," Rhett grins, sticking out his hand. Randall doesn't take it. Instead, he pulls Rhett in tight for a hug, clapping his back.

"It'll be a cold day in hell before he ever jumps out of a plane again," I snap, gritting my teeth.

"You're about as much fun as a wet blanket," Randall jokes.

I swear to God the man has no idea how close he is to death. A violent death.

"Don't let that stop you, kid. Come on by and we'll get you up in the air. You don't have to jump. Maybe I'll teach you how to fly instead."

My legs move on their own accord, and I lunge for him just as Rhett moves to hug him again, blocking me with his body.

"I can't think of anythin' that sounds better than that. I'm gonna take you up on that offer real soon. I gotta get out of these wet clothes, but I'm so glad I met you." Then he turns to me. "I'll see you later. I've gotta work tonight, so don't wait up."

I know my face is red because I can feel the heat warming my skin. Randall laughs lightly. "You're sleeping with him? Your patient?"

My heart beats furiously from the rush of adrenaline coursing through my blood. "I'm not sleeping with him, and technically, he's not my patient. He utilizes the gym here and takes advantage of the services of all the physical therapists on staff, just like the rest of the vets here do. Just like you did."

"Oh, so when he sleeps over, you two just sit up and play cards at night?" He laughs like it's a joke, a joke that I don't find funny.

"Is there a point you're trying to make?"

"Not at all, Riggs. Not at all. It was good running into you again. I'll see you soon."

Chapter 12

RHETT

Black Mountain, NC

THIS TIME, the sky is black instead of light. "Geronimo," I yell just before I throw myself from the plane, executing a perfect swan dive into thin air. The sky is littered with other parachutes, my buddies giving me a thumbs up as they fall around me. It becomes so dark that I can't see them, their bodies fading into blurred shadows. Something crashes into me, a heavy body splattering blood on my face. I can taste it on my tongue, the bitter coppery tang.

The taste of death. If only I could see their face.

Maybe... maybe this time it's not Brian's.

Rain beats down on my shoulders, pelting my face like bullets. It stains my goggles red. But it's not rain, it's blood. It's raining blood.

I know what comes next, and I brace for it, the impact that will crush every bone in my body to dust. Blinding pain that will seize every function except my breathing.

I wish it would take my breath.

Maybe if I die in my dream, I won't wake up and remember that he's gone. Maybe I won't have to dream this again tomorrow night.

I swipe the blood from my goggles and look up into the face of my best friend. His face is frozen in death, staring back at me like the Grim Reaper, like he's coming for *my* soul next.

The piercing scream rips from my throat and the sound of it wakes me from my sleep. Before I can catch my bearings, I flail wildly and roll, banging my head against the nightstand.

"Holy fuck!" That hurts. But it stops me from falling on the floor.

A dark shadow appears, and I can barely make him out, but I'm relieved to see Riggs's face instead of the one from my nightmare.

"Rhett, are you hurt?"

I try to straighten out and roll over, but my legs are tangled in the sheets. "Turn the light on," I rasp, my throat raw and dry.

He reaches for the bedside lamp and a soft glow chases away the dark shadows that haunt me.

"You're sweating and pale. Are you okay?"

"I don't know. I guess, I mean, I didn't hurt myself, but I feel —" anything I might have said dies a quick death on my tongue when I raise my head and realize... Riggs is *naked*. His cock is soft and dangling, and he's uncut.

He follows my gaze and curses. "Shit, I rushed in here without thinking."

"I'm not complaining. You're—" *thick...* "You're—" *trimmed...* "You're—" *perfect.*

"Naked. And leaving."

"No, wait. I—"

"I'm not gonna stand here while you eye fuck me. Let me grab some pants. Christ, what did you think I slept in?" he mumbles.

"Do you wanna see what I sleep in?"

"Do not pull that cover back, Rhett," he warns, choking on his laughter. He runs out of my room and reappears a minute later, wearing an old, worn pair of gray sweats.

How disappointing. I used to love a man in gray sweats, but now that I've seen him naked, sweatpants don't hold a candle to birthday suits.

Riggs surprises me when he spreads out on the bed, occupying the cold, empty space beside me. Unfortunately, he's lying on top of the blanket while I'm underneath it. My heart is still racing as if I ran a marathon, and my stomach feels off like I swallowed sour milk.

"That's not the first time you dreamt that, is it?" He's more stating a fact than asking.

"I wish."

"Tell me what you see."

If anyone would understand, it'd be Riggs, but that doesn't make the words flow any easier. "I see his face. But it's not his face, not really. More like some grim death mask. He bumps into me mid-air, which really happened, and his blood splatters on my face."

Riggs sneaks his hand across the divide between us and takes mine in his grip, softly squeezing. "Did that happen, too?"

I nod, swallowing past the hard lump constricting my throat. "But in my dream, it's night instead of day, and it's raining. After I see him dead, the rain turns to blood, and by the time I crash, I'm soaked and slippery with blood."

"Is it his blood?" He brushes his thumb across the back of my hand, sending a wave of electric heat up my arm.

"I guess so. When I hit the ground, every bone in my body crumbles to dust, but I'm still conscious."

"Jesus Christ, Rhett."

"Pretty much. That's usually when I wake up."

"When are you going to start talking to Brewer?"

I look down at our joined hands before turning my head to face him. "I know I've been puttin' it off. Maybe after my mama leaves."

"It'll help, I promise. You know what else would help?"

I lift my brows, asking silently.

"Talking to the guys, either in group or one-on-one. Nash especially. He suffers terribly from nightmares. Ask him what works for him."

"Smooth, Riggs. Real smooth."

He chuckles. "We didn't create the group because we wanted to learn to knit. It helps, but as Brewer says, it only works if you work it."

Sighing loudly, I breathe out and nod again. "I hear you, Riggs. I do, I swear." He lifts our joined hands, smiling at the sight before he tries to pull away. I tug him back. "Did you mean what you said?"

"I don't know, I say a lot of things," he jokes, evading the question.

"Do you think about me a lot?"

Riggs rolls on his side and stares back. "What do you think?"

I smile devilishly. "I think you can't stop. I think you're dyin' to touch me."

"I am," he admits boldly, his dark gaze dropping to my lips.

My tongue snakes out to lick them. "What are you waitin' for?"

Riggs reaches out to stroke my jaw. "I have no fucking clue."

His head draws nearer and I can feel the heat of his breaths ghost across my lips. Am I still dreaming? Because if I am, I hope I never wake up.

"Riggs," I groan as his mouth brushes mine. He dives right in, swiping his tongue over mine, getting tangled up in it. I feel him everywhere, like wildfire flowing through my veins, igniting my entire body on fire. He loses control, burying his face in my neck, sucking hard on my skin, his fingers bruising my jaw, tugging at my hair. Like me, he can't catch his breath, and I feel like we're falling over the side of a cliff together. Like a jump from the highest altitude with no chute. "Fuck," I breathe, rolling onto him to straddle his hips. His cock strains against the thin cotton. I'm dying to taste him, but I gotta go slow. It took me forever to get this far with him, so I can't risk spooking him now. Maybe if I drive him out of his mind, he won't be able to hit the brakes. I rock my hips into him, grinding my ass over his dick.

"Rhett," he hisses.

"Feels good?"

He answers by digging his fingers into my hips and urging me back and forth. He looks lust drunk as he stares up into my eyes. I can't stop looking at his mouth. He nods and I lower my head to his lips, sucking on them until they're puffy and wet. When I nip his bottom lip, he bucks hard against me, fitting his hard length into the crack of my ass. Riggs glances down at my bare cock bobbing with each thrust of my hips, his eyes going wide. It's not uncut or as thick as his, but he seems to like what he sees. Riggs licks his lips, looking hungry.

"Yeah?" I scoot forward, curling my fingers around the base of my cock, and feed it between his parted wet lips. That first swipe of his velvet tongue feels like religion. "Oh fuck, yes." He slurps on my crown, making my toes curl. My cock throbs, and it feels like the head is going to explode in his mouth. "Oh, God, suck me."

Riggs stares up at me as he sucks and I palm the back of his head, feeding him more of my hard length. Seeing his lips stretched around my cock has me ready to fucking blow.

How many nights have I dreamt of this? *Almost every single one since I met him.*

"Turn around," he rasps, his voice pure gravel.

Oh shit, is he gonna—I straddle his lap in a reverse cowboy position, facing his feet, and stick my ass in his face. His tongue glides between my cheeks and my breath rushes from my lungs like a popped balloon. He swipes over my hole and my entire body clenches before opening for him like... like... I don't fucking know. He melted my brain.

I snap my hips back and forth, shamelessly fucking his tongue. He stabs his tongue through my rim, setting all my nerve endings on fire, and I shout his name. "Riggs!"

He chuckles. "You like that? Been dying to do that to you."

What else has he been dying to do to me? "Do everything. I want it all."

Without warning, he pushes me forward, face first, into the mattress. Riggs raises onto his knees between my thighs, pushing his sweats down his legs, and grabs his cock. Glancing over my shoulder, I watch his face draw up tight in concentration as he rubs his cockhead through my crease. He slaps it against my cheek a few times before dropping a wad of spit between my cheeks. His saliva feels warm and slippery, and my body heats with anticipation, knowing it's about to get so fucking good. He uses his cock to spread it and then braces his arms beside my shoulders and drops his weight onto my back. Like a snake slithering through wet grass, I feel his dick slide through my crease, dragging over my sensitive hole.

"Been dying to do this, too." His voice is nothing but a sinful hiss in my ear, making shivers dance down my spine.

"Have you been dyin' to fuck me?" I ask hopefully, though I'm pretty sure I know the answer.

"Yeah, but I'm not going to. Gotta save something for our second date," he teases, licking the shell of my ear.

The caress of his tongue makes me shudder. "I don't mind if you play fast and loose," I pant.

Riggs chuckles, his hips slowing. "That mouth of yours." He

nips my ear lightly with his teeth. "Every time you shoot it off, I imagine how to shut you up."

Fuck, yeah, he wants me to suck him? Game on! I crawl away from him and flip around, pushing him back against the headboard. "My turn." The wicked gleam in my eyes makes him huff.

God, it's fucking gorgeous. His skin color is slightly darker than mine, and my mouth waters to be filled. I slip my tongue under his foreskin, sliding around his crown. He bucks his hips and gasps. "Get it wetter," he murmurs.

Gathering all the saliva in my mouth, I bathe his sensitive head and lick under his foreskin again, pausing to tease his slit. Riggs palms my head, forcing me to take more.

"That's it, soldier, suck me."

Oh fuck, if he's gonna throw out endearments, I'll choke on his cock until he comes down my throat. Using my lips to slide his skin back, I glide down his shaft until his crown pushes against the back of my throat. His fingers tighten in my hair when I gag loudly.

"Just like that," he encourages.

My knee is screaming at me to straighten my leg, but I'd rather cut it off than stop. I use my free hand to roll his sac as I suck him noisily, and the sounds he makes are pure filth.

"You suck my cock so good." He strokes my cheek, and I pause to look into his eyes. He looks so intense, but when he smiles softly and pulls me in for a wet, sloppy kiss, my heart fucking melts. It's gone, dusted, totally owned by him.

He can fucking have it. I don't want it back. I know he'll take good care of it.

"I'm gonna make you come in my mouth," I vow, breaking the kiss. My head drops to his lap and I resume where I left off, working his length and sac in harmony until he's writhing and bucking down my throat.

"Gonna shoot, Rhett."

I suck harder, forcibly drawing out his load. Riggs grunts, pulling my head down onto his dick, pulsing thick ropes over my tongue that I greedily swallow. When I lift my head, I smile wickedly and lick my lips.

"Give me your cock," he demands, flipping me on my back.

Thank God I can straighten my leg in this position.

Riggs doesn't fuck around; he takes my dick straight to the back of his throat and sucks hard, and he doesn't let up until I come.

"Fuck. Riggs," I pant as I spill, flooding his mouth. I pull him down for a kiss before he can swallow and swipe my tongue through the mess, sharing my flavor with him.

He turns the kiss into a passionate, face-sucking, neck-bruising event that leaves me breathless. I'm addicted to him—to his kisses, his flavor, his cock, his touch, his scent, to the sound of his voice. *Fuck*, I sound like a goddamn greeting card. He looks into my eyes and I see that soft smile again.

I love that smile.

"Despite everything I imagined, I never could have imagined that. You blew my mind, soldier." He follows that up with a quick but soft peck on my lips.

And then he's gone. Just gets up and walks the fuck out without another word, and I lay there trying to remember my damn name, my cock still twitching pathetically, begging for another round.

But he's not gone long. He must have washed up because he returns wearing his sweats again and turns back the covers.

"Scoot over."

Hell, he don't have to tell me twice. Riggs climbs under the blanket and nestles up to me, spooning my body in a bear hug. His body heat feels like an inferno, but I love it.

"If you dream again, I'll be here. I've got you."

Don't ever let me go.

I WAKE with a smile on my face because I can feel Riggs's solid body behind me, his arms still wrapped tight around my waist. The warmth his body creates feels like I'm cocooned in a weighted blanket, cozy and safe. I've got to piss something fierce, but I'd rather hold it for hours than move from his embrace.

His body tenses as he comes awake, causing anxiety to spike in my chest. Is he going to give me the whole *'this-was-a-mistake'* speech? 'Cause if so, I might just kick his ass. I've waited months to get where we are now, and I refuse to go backward.

First, his arms disappear, and then he rolls over to his back, sighing heavily as he rubs the sleep from his eyes.

"Morning," I say, testing the waters.

"What time is it?" he asks.

"Almost eight."

He tosses back the covers like that's it, he's done with me. He's gonna get dressed and head off to work, leaving me to wonder and worry all day about where we stand.

Fuck no.

Lightning quick, I roll over and pin him beneath me. "I said, good morning."

He pats my ass. "Come on, get up. We gotta get going."

"We're not going anywhere until we get somethin' straight."

"Rhett, I really—"

"Look at me, Riggs."

"Rhett," he repeats, sounding exasperated.

"Look. At. Me."

Riggs looks into my eyes. "What?"

"We're not doing this."

"Doing what?"

"*This*. Where you pretend like last night didn't happen."

"Of course it happened," he sputters.

"Well, then, pretending like it was a mistake."

He searches my eyes. "What was it then?"

"*Not* a mistake. It was long overdue. It was absolutely perfect. And it was the first of many more nights together in this bed."

A slow grin spreads across his kissable lips. "In this bed? I was thinking we could move over to mine. It's a little bigger."

Fucker. "Say it. Say it wasn't a mistake."

"Which part?" he teases. "The part where you sucked my

cock like a *Hoover* vacuum or the part where I rimmed your ass until you forgot your name?"

I match his grin. "All of it."

"It wasn't a mistake," he agrees, popping a quick kiss on my smiling lips. "Anything else you want to discuss before we're late?"

"Yeah, I want to know whose bed we're doing this in tonight, yours or mine?"

"I don't know. I've got a really nice couch out there. It's wide and soft. Then there's the hot tub…"

I can't. I'm done with him. Sliding my arms beneath his neck, I get him in a headlock and noogie his head with my knuckles. Riggs wrestles against my hold, wrapping his legs around mine so he can flip our positions and pin me beneath his weight.

He stares down into my face, smiling and breathless, his dark eyes shining. Riggs dips his head, licking my lips before sucking them into his mouth and lavishing each one with his tongue before doing the same to my tongue.

"That's how I should have woken you up. I'm sorry. I'm not used to waking up with company."

"Better not be," I sass, still dizzy from his kiss.

"Let's go pick up your mom and have breakfast together and then we'll all head over to BALLS."

"Mama?" As soon as I walk into my apartment, I know something's wrong. My mother isn't in the kitchen cooking, or sitting on the couch, flipping through the morning news channels. "Mama," I call again, expecting to hear her voice muffled through the bathroom door. But when I walk into my bedroom, it's dark, but not so dark that I can't make out her shape in the bed. Switching on the bedside lamp, I sit on the edge of the mattress and stroke her back through the layers of the covers piled on the bed, many more than I usually have on there. "Mama," I call softly. "Wake up."

She turns, opening her eyes to half-mast. "What is it, baby?"

"Mama, it's almost nine in the mornin'. Are you feelin' all right?"

"I'm tired, pecan. Just let Mama rest."

Her words sound slurred, almost like she's drugged with medication. I press my hand to her forehead, but her skin feels cool. "Can I get you anythin'? A glass of water? Some *Tylenol?*"

"No, sugar, just go do your therapy and leave me be. I'll be fine. Maybe we can have dinner together later."

"I have to work again tonight, Mama. But I'll call and check on you." She pats my hand and turns back over, hiking the covers over her face. A shock of her red hair peeks out, stark against the khaki green pillowcase. Worry gnaws at my gut like an ulcer.

She's asleep again before I even leave the room, and I tiptoe quietly down the hall. "Come on, we'll get breakfast on the way," I tell Riggs.

"Retta's not coming?"

"She's sleepin' in."

———

I count out ten more reps, struggling to keep my breathing even as sweat drips into my eyes. This machine is going to kill me today. My arms are wrapped around a long metal bar hanging by a suspension cable attached to weights. Heavy fucking weights. With each lunge and squat, I have to bear that weight, and it all feels like it's centered on my right leg.

"Ten," I grit, letting go of the bar. The weights settle with a loud clank, which catches Rigg's attention.

He's helping two other patients while keeping an eye on me, and I hate it. Hate that he's not giving me a hundred percent of his attention. I hate that the guys are good-looking and young, and I hate that I'm not his priority.

"Good, now the parallel bars, but with each step, do lunges," he calls out.

Hell. Easier said than done. My fingers white-knuckle the bars as I struggle to stay on my feet. After the last set of lunges, my legs feel like jelly. I'm about a third of the way finished when I stumble and fall. Thank God for the soft mat beneath my ass. I close my eyes and take a deep breath, trying to center myself before I grapple to pull myself up.

"Come on, Rhett," Riggs barks from across the gym.

I swear to God, I'm done with this shit. Riggs claps his patient on the back, smiling and laughing with him over something I can't hear, some inside joke or something I probably wouldn't find funny even if I could hear. He gives that guy one more smile, and I'll fucking kick him. I'll kick them both.

I complete the parallel bars without even feeling proud of myself because I'm so fucking irritated and move onto the arm weights because it's closer to where Riggs is.

He glances at me and nods, but keeps on working with the guys. With each curl, I do a squat, but I can't make it past six reps before I'm plum wore out. I stumble back, knocking a weight from the rack. It falls heavy on my toe, which causes a dull throb that I feel throughout my entire foot.

"Fuck this, I'm done!" Hot, bothered, and done.

Riggs sets down his clipboard and approaches me. He plants his feet right in front of me and calmly says, "Pick it up."

"You fuckin' pick it up. I'm done!"

He crosses his arms over his chest, looking like a drill sergeant. "I said, pick it up." The words are slower, more drawn out with emphasis on each one.

"Fuck. Off." I snap, matching his tone.

Unholy light shines from his dark eyes. He's pissed now. Good, so am I.

"I'm not moving and neither are you until you pick that weight up. I'll stand here all day if I have to," he swears.

Fuck. Reluctantly, I bend and pick the weight up, returning it to the rack with a loud thud. When I straighten, I'm glaring. Riggs gets up in my face and lowers his voice.

"You're the only one of the two of us that sees yourself as less than. Don't taint my image of you."

That's what he thinks this is about? That I'm not strong enough? "Easy for you to say. You didn't shatter your legs. I hit the ground goin' thirty miles an hour, maybe more."

"Our situation could've easily been reversed."

"But they weren't!"

The vein at his temple visibly throbs, yet he remains calm in the face of my anger. "But they could've been, and you wouldn't have let me quit, so don't expect me to give up on you so easily. Ten more reps, soldier. Count them out," he commands.

I glare defiantly, but he stands his ground. "That's insane! You're sadistic."

Riggs shrugs, still maintaining that calm, blank expression. "Welcome to physical therapy."

"No! Look." I point to the posters on the wall. "Those guys look happy; they don't look like they're in pain. This isn't how it's supposed to be done. They're *enjoying* themselves. I'm not enjoying myself."

He taps his pen against his bottom lip and then does that annoying ass clickety thing with it. "I am," he smirks.

I lunge for him because he wanted to see me lunge, right? A pair of strong arms wrap around my waist and pull me back.

"Slow your roll, *Rambo*." It's Nash. I didn't even see him move across the gym. "What do you say we go for a drive, cool down a little, and then I'll drop you back at home?"

Riggs nods at Nash, ignoring me completely, before rejoining his patients. "Yeah, sounds good. I'm ready to get the fuck outta here."

"Where are we headed?" I ask when he passes my exit.

"I need to make a stop. I've got to meet up with someone important."

Great, I just wanna go home. To check on my mama, take a cold shower, and then sit and do nothing for the rest of the afternoon.

"My partner always says you have to talk your way through a problem to get to the other side."

I snort, 'cause I was expecting some sort of therapeutic bullshit talk. After all, the guy's sleeping with a therapist. "Is that right?"

"Not me though," he smirks. "I say, if you can't get over something, try getting under it instead."

This time my laugh is genuine—and unexpected. "Did that work for you and Brewer?"

Nash shrugs. "It's working fine so far." He takes the next exit. "There's no avoiding talking, though, not with the people who matter to you most."

About two miles down the road, Nash pulls through an ornate wrought-iron gate. The sign reads 'Western Carolina State Veterans Cemetery.' I have no idea who he's meeting up with, in a cemetery of all places, but I keep my mouth shut and follow his lead. He gets out of his truck and walks up two rows before coming to a stop in front of what looks to be a newer headstone. Nash runs his fingers over the engraved name.

Victor Gutierrez
Beloved and honored for his heroic
sacrifice and deeds on and off the battlefield.

He kneels in front of the marble stone and makes the sign of the cross before kissing the tips of his fingers and touching the man's name again. I remain silent when he bows his head. This is a private moment between him and the man buried six feet beneath him. I feel like a voyeur just standing here watching.

Maybe fifteen minutes pass before he pulls a small card from the pocket of his cargo shorts and places the blue envelope at the base of the stone. Nash straightens and takes a few steps back.

My curiosity gets the better of me. "Was this who you had to meet up with?"

"It's my best friend's birthday. I couldn't let him celebrate alone."

Fuck. This is his best friend? The man buried here was his brother.

Grief stabs me right in the heart. It's Brian all over again.

"He's been gone just over a year now," Nash says. His voice sounds thick with unshed tears. "He lived a great life, but he died a terrible death."

"What happened?" I ask, afraid to hear the answer. It's too raw, too real. The wound of losing Brian is too fresh.

"We got separated from our unit, kicking down doors, and fell through a trap in the floor. We were held captive for twenty-two days." He laughs harshly. "Just saying that doesn't even begin to summarize the hell we lived through day after day. You can't even imagine—" his voice cracks, and I watch his throat work furiously, trying to hold back the damn of tears. "We both were shot, but G, he didn't make it—sepsis. He died slowly, painfully, his organs shutting down one by one. We were together, though, right till the end. Right until they came for us and put us on the bird to take us home. I never saw him again after that, after I let go of his hand. I was laid up in the hospital recovering when they buried him."

"It was." I clear my throat. "It was the same with me and Brian. I was at Womack with two broken legs. I couldn't go and bury him."

"It's not too late. It's never too late to say goodbye. I think," he starts, pausing to swipe at his eyes and nose, "I think time stands still over there; that time is infinite. They don't know or care if it's one day or ten years, but when you finally make your way to him, he'll know. He'll hear you."

My chest feels heavy, and the pressure clouds my head. Hot tears roll down my cheeks. They blind me until I can't see outward, only inward. Memories of Brian flash before my eyes—laughing and smiling, drinking with me, grocery shopping and playing video games, running beside me during PT. I can hear his voice.

God, what if it fades someday? What if I forget what he sounded like, what he looked like? Remembering hurts, it fucking kills me, but I don't ever want to forget.

"Maybe, when I finish therapy and I'm a little stronger, I'll take a road trip. You ever been to Fort Worth, Texas?"

"No," he smiles, swiping at his eyes again, "but I'm down anytime you're ready. The first tank of gas is on me."

It's late when I come in from work, and Riggs's house is dark and silent. The curtains to the sliding glass door are drawn and billowing in the breeze, and I realize it's open. With a little smile of satisfaction, I strip my clothes off as I head out back. I can hear the hot tub bubbling as I approach. Riggs's dark head rests on the edge of the tub.

He looks momentarily surprised, probably to see me naked, but hides it well behind his usual mask as I climb in. Neither of us says a word, and I follow his lead, resting my head against the edge of the tub to stare up at the many stars above. It looks almost fake, it's so beautiful.

Finally, he reaches over the edge of the tub and grabs a glass from the little table there, and hands it to me.

"You skipped breakfast this morning."

"You made me a green juice? Aw shucks, you shouldn't have, really."

He laughs a little. But I'm touched, the way he takes care of me, always concerned about my health and recovery, even after the way I treated him.

"You want to tell me what that was about today?"

No accusations or pointing fingers, no raised voices and drama. I love that about him. Riggs is a great communicator, better than I am, for sure. It's good that one of us has a cool head most of the time.

I down the juice in three gulps and cringe at the nasty, bitter taste. "That shit is straight up disgustin'." He raises his brows, staring into my eyes. "Oh, you're still waiting for an answer?" I breathe out a heavy sigh and set the glass down on the edge of the tub. "My mom is sick, or somethin', but she won't tell me what. She's keepin' it from me because she thinks my problems are more important than hers."

"I figured as much. You've got to push her though. You've got to get her to open up."

"I can't—" the urge to swallow is so strong I can't resist, "I can't lose her, too. I've already lost so much. But my mama, I can't, Riggs. It'll kill me."

He moves closer, sliding his arm around my shoulders. He feels like a solid presence, like safety, *like home*.

"No, it won't. It won't kill you. Nothing will kill you, except maybe me if you ever blow up at me like that again in my gym." I glance sideways and chuff at his expression. "We'll figure it out, together. I promised you that, and I mean to keep my word."

All I can do is nod and trust in him, 'cause I've got no answers and no bright ideas. "So, about the sleeping arrangements tonight. Have you decided on the couch, your bedroom, or the tub?"

It's his turn to laugh. "You never quit, do you?" he asks fondly. "I guess it was a given the minute you saw me naked last night."

"Hell," I scoff. "It was a given when you asked me to move in."

"I didn't ask you to move in," he laughs incredulously. "This is temporary."

I smile knowingly. "Yeah, we'll see about that." He doesn't move his arm from my shoulders, and I'm in no rush to get up. "I'm sorry about today. I was sick with worry and slightly jealous."

Riggs hums. "Just slightly?"

"I don't like seein' you get handsy and smiley with the other guys."

"It's kind of my job, so you're going to have to work on it."

I slide my leg over his thigh, turn into his side, and cup his cock. "Maybe that's the problem. Maybe I'm not workin' on *it* enough."

"*It?*" he asks, smiling like he finds me funny.

"Mmmhmm. Definitely needs more work. More *practice*. So I have reasons not to worry so much."

"Do you really worry that I'm interested in other men?" Riggs sounds skeptical.

"I don't wanna lose the only thing that's mattered to me for the last six months. Sometimes it feels like you're the only thing keepin' me going."

"Rhett, that's—"

"Shhh." I cut off his protestation with a kiss. I don't wanna hear him spout nonsense about how I have to find a balance, how I have to rely on my peers and start therapy. I only wanna hear more of me and him. "I like it when you call me *soldier*."

I breathe the words over his lips, like a secret, and he swallows them and slides his tongue back into my mouth, wanting more.

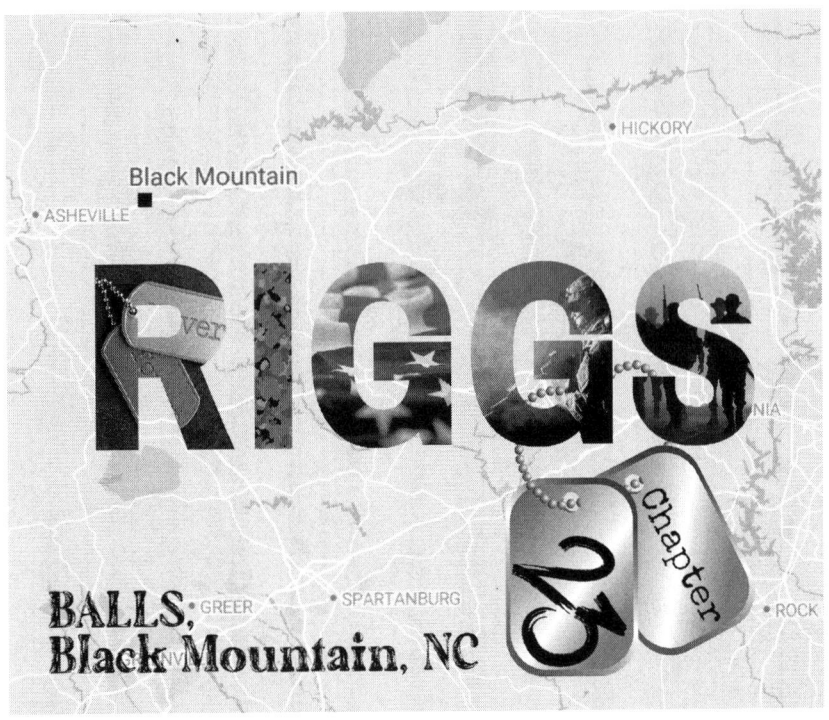

RIGGS
Chapter 23
BALLS, Black Mountain, NC

HIS AMBITION DOESN'T COME as a surprise, not with the way he's been flirting with me. Rhett has made his interest in me known since the beginning. My concern is with how long it will last. Will he still want me after his leg heals? Will he still want me when his confidence returns? What about when he moves on from the Black Mountain Tavern to wherever it is he's going next in life? Will he still want me then?

Would Rhett fight for me?

Could we weather a storm through thick and thin?

I guess we'll find out because I've already decided to take a gamble on him. On *us*.

I love the way he's looking at me right now, with that heat in his eyes that almost turns them emerald. His wet hair appears even darker, almost black, and those dimples. Fuck me, those dimples. "Why don't you sit on my lap, soldier, and practice on me?"

I can see his hand beneath the water, wrapping around his cock as he teases my lips. He's going to leave marks on my neck. Rhett straddles my lap, facing me. He brushes his lips over mine, as soft as a whisper, teasing me with his kissable smile. A dark curl falls over his forehead. God, I could just buck my hips and push right up inside him, grab onto his shoulders and fuck him hard and fast. I want to tear his neck up with my teeth and lips so that when he drops by Randall Mallory's flight school, that fucker doesn't get any ideas.

Rhett slides his thumbs over my nipples, teasing the hard peaks. The playful grin on his face tells me how pleasurable he finds it. He traces over the tat on my shoulder—two snakes intertwined over an M4 assault rifle capped with a white rose, my take on the caduceus, combining the combat medic and Army nursing symbols.

"I love this," he murmurs, dropping his lips to my skin. He sucks hard, leaving a purple bruise over the black ink.

"Embrace the past, engage the present, envision the future," I repeat from memory.

"The Army Nursing Corp motto," he smirks. "I guess you could apply that to anythin'. Is that what we're doin'? Engaging the present?"

"It doesn't take a genius to envision the future," I tease, playing along. "In about ten minutes, we're going to end up in my bedroom."

"You're gonna make me wait ten more minutes?" He

suckles the hollow of my throat, making my cock pulse like it has a heartbeat.

He has a point. Why wait? We both want this. With Rhett straddled across my hips, I stand, sliding my hands beneath his ass to support his weight. It's an awkward struggle to climb out of the tub like this, but I want him in my arms. We trail through the open glass door, leaving a dripping mess in our wake as I head to my bedroom.

I drop Rhett on the bed, taking in his wet, sprawled, naked body. His skin is covered in tattoos and scars that tell the story of his life.

He's beautiful. Gorgeous. Tempting as sin.

His shoulder sports the silhouette of a paratrooper with the double-A Airborne logo and motto, *'All the way.'* It describes Rhett to a T. He's all in with everything in life, all the way. No fear, no reservations, just balls to the wall.

Was I like that at twenty-three? Invincible? Before life kicked me in the ass and taught me to slow the fuck down.

"You gonna draw me, or fuck me?" His smart mouth begs to get stuffed.

"Which would you prefer?"

"I want you to fuck me. Should I turn over?"

"As tempting as that is, I want you just like this."

Rhett fists his cock, stroking it slowly to tempt me, as if I need more convincing. He draws out a clear bead of fluid that pools in his slit before spilling down his cockhead. Rhett gasps as I bend to lick it up. The salty flavor brings my taste buds to life, making my mouth water for more. The tight muscles of his abs ripple beneath the silken skin as I suck him between my lips.

His dick kicks in my mouth, a blatant sign of his arousal.

Nah, I think I'll play with him first, like a cat with a mouse.

Hovering my mouth over his length, my hot breath tickles his sensitive skin until he pushes at my head. My tongue snakes out to lap at his wet slit.

"Fuckin' suck me," Rhett begs, his head raised to watch me.

"Like this?" I ask, taking him to the back of my throat in one quick suck.

"Ah, fuck," he hisses. "More."

Slowing down, I take my time, savoring him, drawing out the glide of my lips over each vein and ridge. My tongue tickles the groove beneath his crown.

"I'm in love with your mouth," he moans, making me smile despite my stuffed mouth. "Does my cock taste good?"

Shit, if he starts talking like that, I'm done with the sucking and moving onto the fucking, real quick.

My answer is to suck hard on his inflamed head until he cries out. "Too much!"

Chuckling, I pop off his cock. "Turn over."

"Hell yeah. You got lube in your nightstand?"

"I didn't say I was going to fuck you, did I?"

"Then what're you—" He gets the idea when I run my tongue through his crease, licking over his hole until he clenches tight. "Oh, shit!"

Rhett's ass tastes fucking amazing. I could eat him for every meal. Looking up, I see the swell of his ass, the perfect bubble. I slow my strokes, lapping at him, driving him out of his mind until he backs his ass up against my face, begging for more.

"You're a dirty fucker," he pants, obviously loving it.

Swallowing his musky flavor, I crawl over his back, planting my knees between his spread thighs. My tongue traces the ridges of his spine, sending shivers throughout his body.

"You gonna fuck me *now*?"

"Eager, aren't you?"

"For your thick, uncut cock? Hell yeah, can you blame me?"

I love hearing that. Rhett makes me feel like the world's hottest stud, the most accomplished physician, the most hardened soldier. He elevates me with his admiration, lending me just a small measure of his invincibility that makes me feel twenty years younger.

I'm still not ready to fuck him. When I get my dick inside his tight ass, it'll be a struggle to hold back, to last long enough to please him. I want to savor this, to draw out the pleasure for both our sakes.

Bucking my hips, I drag my cockhead through his cheeks, rubbing over his hole. My arms are under his, which gives me leverage to grind harder against his ass. The clean scent of him is in my nose, the smell of his evergreen shampoo settling over me until he consumes me—sight, smell, and the feel of him. His broad body is warm and hard beneath mine. Rhett fits perfectly against me. His ass lines up perfectly with my cock while giving my mouth unfettered access to his neck and ear.

"Feels like I've waited a lifetime for this," I whisper.

"God, at least six months," he smarts. My crown catches his rim and I push against his hole. "You're right, feels like a lifetime."

"Grab the lube from my drawer."

"Shit, yes," Rhett breathes with excitement. He crawls out

from under me, reaching for the nightstand, and holds up a foil packet. "Do we need these?"

"Only if you feel we do."

"Fuck, no." He tosses it back in the drawer and grabs the blue bottle. "Don't use too much. I want to feel you."

Chuckling, I reply, "Either way, you're going to feel me."

Rhett spreads his legs wide. His hole is tantalizing—dark and smooth, with just a smattering of dark fuzz creeping near his rim. One more lick before swiping the tip of my finger over it. I'm obsessed with watching him clench at my touch. I dip my finger inside and back out, opening him up slowly. His channel feels like warm velvet. I wish my tongue could delve as deep as my finger. I want to taste him from the inside out. I'd devour him if I could.

Every inch of his toned, scarred body is magnificent perfection.

"Turn over." I stop him when he rolls to his side and prop his injured leg over mine, sliding my thigh between his. Wrapping my arms around his chest, I spoon him against my body and softly push into him.

Rhett gasps, his body going tense.

"Relax for me, soldier. Bear down."

"Been so long," he hisses as I set his rim on fire.

"I fucking hope so." Christ, he's squeezing the blood from my cock.

"Go slow at first," Rhett cautions, beginning to relax.

Softly, I sink balls deep, astonished by the incredible heat of him. "Like this?" He chuckles, turning his head for a kiss.

I take his lips passionately as I slide out of his body before slowly plunging back in. The friction grips my balls in a vise. His body is my favorite place on Earth. I never want to separate from him.

"Oh God, you feel—" he chokes on his next word, swallowing hard. "Make it last, okay?"

"I'll try," I grit, not making any promises.

My dick pulses inside him and he gasps. "Fuck, Riggs." His breathing sounds labored when I'm doing all the work. "I knew it'd be this good," he sighs.

We work up a good pace, falling into a faster rhythm where Rhett pushes back against me, meeting me thrust-for-thrust. The sound of skin slapping against skin fills the room with a debauched symphony. As badly as I want it to last, I can't make myself slow down. I chase my orgasm like it's as vital as my next breath.

Heat sears my gut, and the spasms start in my belly, spreading down my thighs. I clench my ass and slam into him hard, burying my cock deep within him as it begins to pulse; thick ropes coat his inner walls, marking him from the inside.

"Feel that?" I growl. He nods, unable to speak from his ragged breaths. "Come with me." I reach for his cock and jack him quick and hard until his stomach contracts and he shoots with a cry.

"Riggs!" Rhett's seed coats my hand and his chest, making a small mess on the blanket.

I squeeze him tight and breathe his scent in deep, getting my fill of him before I have to let him go. Dropping my forehead between his shoulders, I whisper, "You're worth every lonely night I waited for you and dreamed of you."

Rhett's head drops to the mattress with a blissful sigh. "Yup, every fuckin' one of 'em. You're so worth it." A minute later, he blurts, "Hey, you kept it!"

"Huh?"

"The eagle I folded for you. You kept it." He points to the origami eagle on my nightstand.

"Of course I kept it, soldier." A smile curves my lips. Fuck it, I'm keeping *him,* too.

When I walk into the classroom where we hold group, the guys are already working on their knitting, with the exception of Rhett who's folding colorful paper in accordance with the instructions in the book on his lap.

No one spares me a glance. Brandt and West are working on more green butt plugs, which they swear are Christmas trees... whatever. Jax is knitting a black skullcap, and Mandy is making an owl. I'm curious until I realize it's wearing a cowboy hat. *For Tex.* A Texan Hooters owl. Damn, he's got it bad.

"Hey, are we talking about our feelings and shit, or just knitting?"

It's a rhetorical question that I immediately regret asking when they all answer in unison, "Knitting."

Sighing with defeat, I explain, "BALLS is opening a gift shop in the front lobby. Margret Anne would like you to submit ideas for merchandise you'd like to see featured." The laughter starts up before I'm even done talking. "Can I finish, please?" I huff. "She wants to include things you want, which is sweet of her. Personally, I don't know why she even bothers," I finish, talking over their chatter.

"I want a shirt with the BALLS logo because I like to display my balls proudly," says McCormick, who's wearing a shirt that reads, '*HOW TO KNIT. 1. Stab it 2. Strangle it 3. Scoop out the guts 4. Toss it off a cliff.*'

I know enough about knitting to understand it's a crude set of instructions for the basic technique. The shirt fits his personality to a T.

Stiles swallows his laughter and says with a mostly straight face, "Maybe some mittens with the BALLS logo because I like to hold them in my hand."

I glare, begging him not to continue with his bright ideas. But then Jax adds, "A hat with the BALLS logo." He holds up the skull cap he's working on, and I think, *finally, a real idea.* "Nothing feels better than balls on your head, like being tea bagged."

I should have known.

"You like getting tea-bagged, Jax?" West snarks.

Jax chuffs. "Not as much as you do."

"I wonder if they'll sell tea bags," Pharo asks, smirking at Jax.

Mandy sets down his knitting. "Maybe a stress ball. There's nothing like squeezing your balls."

"I expected better from you," I say disappointedly, pointing at him. He just laughs. "Are you all finished? You know, you used to be a respectable bunch of guys, but lately, it's like KinderCare around here." Explosive laughter erupts.

"Can you imagine the kid's merch?" Nash asks, picking up my daycare joke and running with it.

"A shirt that reads, '*My Daddy is so proud of his BALLS*,'" Rhett muses, snickering so hard he can barely spit the words out.

Shaking my head, I check my watch. Thirty more minutes to go, unfortunately. "I'll let Margaret Anne know you bunch are too infantile to be creative. I'm sure it'll come as no surprise to her. Maybe Brewer's addiction support group can come up with something useful."

Then the fun really begins. The Bitches unleash a torrent of terrible ideas.

Jax snorts. "Oh yeah, ask the recovering addicts. They have great ideas. Maybe a tote bag that reads, '*My BALLS say you can't come unless you're clean.*'"

"Hit your knees and pray to BALLS for the answers," Pharo adds.

West doubles over with laughter. "Your Higher Power is in my BALLS."

Rolling my eyes, I get up and walk out as the chorus of snickers grows louder. *Fucking idiots.*

Black Mountain, NC
Chapter 24

WHEN I COME in the front door, my mama is sitting on the couch in her robe, wrapped up in a pile of blankets like a burrito. She's sipping a cup of hot tea.

"Hey Mama." I plant a big smooch on her cheek, noticing her skin feels slightly warm.

"Baby, where're your crutches?"

"I graduated, don't need 'em no more."

"That's wonderful," she smiles, looking brighter than I've seen her all week.

"What are we watching?" I snuggle beside her, grabbing one of the blankets for myself.

"Would you believe A&E is showing *Gone With The Wind*?"

"Jesus Christ."

Mama smacks me upside the head faster than I can see it coming. She's an old pro. "You watch your mouth, son. That dog won't hunt round here, and don't you dare blaspheme my Scarlett!"

"Sorry, ma'am," I mumble, rubbing my head and trying my damnedest not to laugh. If she heard me around my friends, she'd blow a gasket.

I guess we're watching *Gone With The Wind. Again.* Now I see why the Bitches complain about *Top Gun*. After you watch anything fifty-something times, burning your TV and canceling your cable subscription seems like a great idea.

"Mama, remember them costumes you made for us so we could be Rhett and Scarlett for Halloween?"

"Good Lord," she laughs, her face lighting up with the memory. "You must have been about six or seven."

"You looked so pretty in that dress." My mama blushes, which is something I haven't seen in years.

"Well, I do declare, Rhett Butler, your tongue is as slick as a buttered casserole dish."

She's cute when she puts on her most dramatic southern voice. "Can I get you something to eat or drink?"

"No baby. I'm supposed to be fussin' over you, not the other way around."

"I don't mind at all, Mama. You've fussed over me for twenty-three years."

"Let's just sit and watch this movie together."

Her favorite part is coming up, where Rhett tells Scarlett he doesn't give a damn. I already know she's going to say it out loud. If this was on DVD, she would rewind it three times.

"Mama, have I told you how happy I am you're here?"

"Me too, my little sugared pecan." She leans into my side, and I wrap my arm around her blanket-covered body.

My body reacts physically the closer I get to the airfield. A boost in energy, my mood soars, and I feel excited about something for the first time in… in what seems like forever.

Adrenaline spikes when I walk into the hangar, and my heart feels like it's gonna beat right outta my damn chest.

"Rhett!" Randall Mallory jogs over and gives me a one-armed hug. Damn, he smells amazing. Like pine and leather? I'm not sure, but I love it. "I can't wait to show you what I've got." His words sound innocent enough, but it's the gleam in his gray eyes, and his sexy smirk, that add meaning to the words.

"Show me. I'm all yours."

He laughs wickedly, sliding his arm around my shoulders. Randall guides me to a small room packed with metal racks of equipment and packed parachutes.

"I guess you have some experience with these," he guesses, smiling. "You're out of commission as a jump instructor, but I bet you can pack a tight chute."

Is that a sex reference?

"With my eyes closed, sir."

"Drop the sir and call me Rand."

I spot a bucket of carabiners, rigging and paracord, chutes, and backpacks. I'm in my element, finally. This beats wrapping silverware and refilling condiment bottles at the Tavern by a country mile.

"You can help book appointments, print and file waivers, and schedule plane maintenance. My flight logs are a damn mess, and I've got a pile of updated certifications and regulations sitting on my desk collecting dust. Wanna help me out?"

His enigmatic smile is hard to resist, especially when he's speaking my language. "Hell, yeah. Point me in the right direction."

"Right there." He points through the hangar doors to the sweet little Cessna 172 parked on the landing strip.

"You want me to wash it or somethin'?" I just want to put my hands on her, even if I'm just holding a soapy rag.

"No," he laughs. "We're going for a spin. Climb in."

Holy fucking nitrous! I've never moved so quickly, even with my bum leg. I click the seatbelt and blood whooshes in my ears. My cheeks hurt from smiling. I feel *alive*, and I'm not even in the air yet.

Rand settles into the pilot seat beside me and points out the various gauges and levers, explaining everything as he runs through his preflight checklist. He motions for me to put my headset on, and then his smooth voice flows into my ear like honey.

"Hang on. I'm about to blow your mind. Let's get you back in the air where you belong."

I've never heard sweeter words spoken. *Back in the air.* Yup, that's exactly where I belong.

The roar of the engine is deafening, barely muted by the

headphones. My stomach flips with the increase in altitude, something I haven't felt in a long time. Too long. Goddamn, I've missed this.

"I'm glad I could give it back to you."

Shit, I said that out loud? I give Rand a thumbs up and he smiles beautifully and points out his window. I have to lean over his lap to see. The Blue Ridge Mountains stand tall and proud, spread out like a blue-gray blanket over thousands of miles. Puffs of white smoke billow into the thin air.

His voice tickles my ear. "You should see it from this height in the Fall."

"Can't wait."

By the time we land, my cheeks are rosy and sore, and my perma-grin's gonna last all day, no matter what happens. I'm exactly where I'm meant to be. *I'm home.*

Rand goes on about my PPL license for private pilots, logging flight hours, and how next year I'll be ready for my commercial license and working toward my flight instructor certification. His words rush by like wind at gale force speeds, which is exactly how fast my head is spinning, but I'm totally on board with whatever he has planned.

If I can't jump, I'm gonna fly.

Like he said, I belong in the air.

The Footlocker is exactly how I remember it—nothing about this bar has changed in the time I've been gone. In fact, everything about Fayetteville looks the same. No new construction, nothing went out of business, just the same old, same old, different day. It's bizarre because I feel as if *everything* has changed for me, almost as if I'm becoming a different person.

My priorities have shifted. Whereas I used to live for the moment, the next thrill, taking life day by day, I now see the bigger picture. I never imagined I would fall for a man. Hooking up with them, definitely, but always on the down low, never out in the open. No longer am I a soldier trained to take orders instead of thinking for himself, trained to jump on command. I'm now learning to fly, to soar above the clouds and pilot my own plane, to chart my own destiny.

I feel like the world is wide open and full of possibilities. It's a little scary, but for an adrenaline junkie like me, it's thrilling.

My first thought when I stepped off the plane, still high from the rush, was to drive four hours to Fayetteville and tell my best friends, my brothers. If anyone can understand, it's them. They still have what I lost, and they know how much I loved it, what being in the 82nd meant to me. Airborne was my whole life, and when I lost that, I lost everything. I felt like my life was over. I couldn't imagine there was another path waiting to be discovered.

"Marsh! Get your ass over here," Ormen shouts across the bar when he spots me.

They've already bought the first round and my glass is waiting by the empty chair beside Warren. "You won't believe what I did today."

"Jacked your cock?"

"Stubbed your toe?"

"Joined the Peace Corps?"

"You're all way off base. I flew in a Cessna. I'm getting my pilot's license! In the meantime, I'll be working at the flight school, packing chutes and booking appointments." My face stretches into a perma-grin just talking about it.

Villaro laughs. "A jump instructor who doesn't jump?"

"Fuck off," I snort, showing him my middle finger.

Warren claps my back. "That's awesome, man. Can't wait to go up with you."

The conversation turns back to Army life, to the unit and barracks drama, and I listen with a smile, but I've got nothing to contribute because that's not my life anymore.

Riggs's words come back to haunt me. *'Life will go on without you, and you'll be watching from an outsider's perspective, and every time they mention anything to do with the Army, you'll feel bitter and resentful.'*

Fuck, I hate it when he's right. Except I don't feel bitter, just sort of lonely and sad that this isn't my life anymore, and that they aren't a part of my new life, my new friends, and that I still haven't told them I'm falling for Riggs.

Brian died with his secret, but I don't want to be that guy that dies with regrets. I want to live, I want to love, and I want to do it out loud.

"Hey, listen up. I got somethin' I wanna say." All heads turn to me as the conversation dies. My stomach solidifies into granite. I think I might be sick before I can even spit the words out. "I'm bisexual," I blurt, my heart pulsating in my throat. "I like girls and guys."

"I think we know what it means, genius," Ormen replies.

"Well, what you don't know is that I'm dating a guy. His name is Riggs. Navarro Riggs."

Warren asks, "That therapist from the gym? The one that wouldn't help you on your feet?"

I nod, swallowing hard past the constriction in my throat.

"He's badass! Reminds me of my drill sergeant in basic," Villaro cracks.

I roll my eyes, snorting at his assessment of Riggs. He's not far off. Warren and Ormen are grinning, like they're impressed I kept a secret this long. "Are we good?"

Ormen clasps my hand. "Of course we're good. We're brothers."

Warren straight up cackles. "You dirty dog. He's gonna put a hurting on you, boy. You're gonna need more physical therapy after he's done with you."

All my fears pop like a balloon and I dissolve into laughter with them as they make joke after joke about my sex life. I wish Brian were here, that he could have found the courage to do what I did and come out the other side better for it.

We shoot the shit for another hour, and another round of beer. "Hey, I'm gonna take off. I've got a long drive home."

"Do you want to crash with us? I bet we could sneak you into the barracks."

"No," I laugh. "I got someone waitin' for me at home. I'd rather share a bed with him than you."

As I head out to my car, I feel relieved that it went so well. It feels like shedding a fifty-pound rucksack from my shoulders after carrying it for a fifteen-mile run. If that fifteen-mile run lasted the last four years. I guess they truly are my brothers because they were definitely tested tonight.

The drive flies by quickly as I sing along to the radio. *Peter Gabriel's 'In Your Eyes'* comes on—a classic—and I turn the volume up. The words remind me of Riggs. The light... the heat... I am complete. God, I can't wait to see him. I bet he's in the hot tub, buck-ass naked and waiting for me. The roads are empty at this time of night, and I step on the pedal a little harder, trying to shorten my ETA. At about the halfway mark, I pick up the phone and dial my mama. It's late, but I'm dying to tell her about my day, but the phone just rings and rings before it goes to voicemail.

"Mama, it's me. You won't believe the incredible day I had. I can't wait to tell you about it. Call me tomorrow mornin' first thing. No, never mind. I'll come by and have breakfast with you. Night Mama, love you."

It's almost midnight when I finally make it home. Riggs isn't in the hot tub. He's sitting at the dining table in the dark, his silhouette backlit by moonlight shining through the sliding glass doors.

"You're still up."

"You'd know that if you'd have called." His tone sounds ominous, and I immediately go on the defensive.

I set my keys down on the counter, cautiously moving closer, and gauging his mood. "You're pissed."

"No, Rhett. I'm not pissed."

He says it too calmly, and I can only guess the words on the tip of his tongue that he hasn't spilled. "I guess I got wrapped up in my head and lost track of time when I was drivin' and then, before I knew it, I was here."

Riggs comes to his feet, sliding his hands in his pockets. He just stands there, feet braced wide, waiting for me to spill it.

"I had the most amazin' day. Rand took me up in the air in one of his planes. Riggs, you wouldn't believe how good it felt. I was flyin'! At the mercy of the crosswinds. It rattled the plane every which way but loose, and the vibration of the engine, and the roar, it was deafening. He gave me these headphones to wear, and it muffles it some, but not completely, just enough to make it bearable. But you're still in the moment, you know? Still feelin' and hearin', and experiencing everything, and the thrill of it, fuck, I can't even describe the thrill of it."

I feel myself getting all worked up again just talking about it, yet Riggs is as calm and collected as I've ever seen him. "And then what?" he asks.

"And then... I called up the guys 'cause I had to tell them. Couldn't wait to share it with them. I mean, if anyone knows what I'm missin', and how bad it hurts not to jump anymore, it's them, you know? They were worried about me after they visited and I just wanted to tell them I think it'll be okay. If I can't jump, maybe I can fly. I've never felt so alive, not since..."

My words die off with my next breath. We both know how long it's been since I've felt alive. I don't have to remind either of us.

I wish I could get a read on him. I'm starting to feel like I stepped in deep shit. He moves closer, but even when there's less than three inches separating us, it feels like the widest canyon.

"I'm not pissed at you. I'm just angry with myself for believing this could work. I knew better, but I wanted this so badly, and I convinced myself that we could make this work."

I slide my hands in the pockets of my jeans 'cause I'm so fucking nervous I don't know where else to put them. "We can! Of course we can. I just..." My fingers brush against a slip of paper, and I pull it out of my pocket to see what it is.

Riggs frowns and grabs it from me. "What's this?" I can't see 'cause there's no fucking lights on! "Really, Rhett? Tell me again how you were just out drinking with the guys."

"I don't even know what that is! I've never seen it before." He flicks on the dining room light and holds up the slip of paper so I can see. A phone number written in pink ink.

Fuck. Fucking fuck. Triple fuck.

"The waitress must've slipped it in with the change she handed me. She was makin' eyes at me all night."

Riggs snorts, shaking his head in disbelief. "This is exactly what I'm talking about. You're a wild card, and I just can't keep betting on you and gambling with my heart."

My heart pounds furiously as I work myself into a panic. Ten different scenarios run through my head, and they all end with Riggs dumping my ass. "No, I'm not a wild card, I'm a sure fuckin' bet! You can trust me. I swear it." Adrenaline courses through my blood as my fight-or-flight reflex kicks in 'cause I feel like I'm being threatened. Threatened with losing everything I care about, again, and it's just too much for me to stomach. I place my hands on his hips, but he takes a step back. "Riggs, you've got to listen. Believe me when I tell you I'm all in, I want this. I want *you*. I even told the guys about you tonight."

"I should've been the first person on your mind when you left the airfield. If you were all in like you say you are, I would have been the first person you called. You would have come straight home and told me. I'm thrilled for you, I really am. Thrilled that you found something you love as much as you loved jumping, but if I could just be second, and not tenth behind flying... that's all I'm asking. You couldn't even give me that."

I'm still stuck on the fact that he referred to his home as mine. It is, I feel like it's home, the first one I've had since I left my mama's house, and now he's taking it away from me. Tears burn my eyes, and my panic heightens, making my stomach swirl with nausea.

"Riggs, please. Just listen—" The ringing of my phone cuts off my words. I reach for it, noticing how Riggs glares like he expects me to ignore it. "I'm not puttin' the phone before you, but it's late, and it might be important. I've got to answer this."

He bites off a curse as I pull it from my pocket. "Hello?"

"Rhett, it's Mandy."

"Hey, Mandy. It's late, is everythin' alright?" My eyes are on Riggs, with his hands on his hips. He looks concerned now, or curious.

"It's your mom. They rushed her to the hospital."

"Who? When? Why?" I pull the phone from my ear and hit the speaker so Riggs can listen.

"I was just getting in bed when I heard your smoke alarm go off. It just kept going and going. So I knocked on your door, but she didn't answer. I had to call the paramedics."

All the blood drains from my face, and my mind freezes. My

breath freezes in my lungs. I don't even know what else to say or ask because I'm just... frozen.

Riggs jumps into action, taking the phone from me. "Did you overhear the paramedics say anything?"

"No. They carried her out on a stretcher, though. They took her to Mission Hospital in Asheville."

"We're on our way," he barks. "Come on, Rhett."

Tears stream from my eyes, and I can't see, I can't think, and I damn sure can't move. Riggs steps in close to me, gripping my shoulders. "Listen to me, soldier. I need you to be sharp and strong right now, so you can help me take care of your mama." He tilts my chin up to meet his eyes. "Can you do that for me?"

I shake my head no and he smiles, this sort of sad, half smile, which totally convinces me nothing is going to turn out all right.

"I need you to do it, anyway. Come on. Your mama is waiting on you. She needs you."

And I need you. Promise me I can count on you.

I GRIP the steering wheel with one hand because Rhett has a chokehold on the other. He stares out the window, but I know he's not seeing trees, cars, or mountains; he's lost in his head.

"When we get there, I need you to remain calm. Just let me do the talking. These doctors, they like to speak in medical terms, I think because it lessens the emotional impact of what they're saying. There's also a lot they won't say, but I can read between the lines. I'll break it all down for you."

Finally, Rhett glances over at me. His wounded hazel eyes are wet with unshed tears. "I'm so grateful you're here. I don't know what's going on with my mama, but I don't know if I could handle it alone."

His words hit me right in my heart. He's so young, and he's

got that twenty-four-karat gold heart he told me was something he looked for in others, and he's lost more than anyone deserves to lose. I'm not sure he can handle one more thing. Not without damaging his beautiful soul.

"No matter what happens, you can bet I'll be right here by your side through whatever comes our way. We'll handle it together."

"Really? 'Cause not fifteen minutes ago, you were tryin' to ditch me."

"I... I wasn't trying to ditch you. I was—" *Trying to ditch you.* "I haven't done this before, the relationship thing. We're both new at this, and we knew there was a strong possibility we were going to fuck this up. I was trying to remind myself to be cautious, to guard my heart, instead of handing it to you on a silver platter. Where you're concerned, I tend to forget about boundaries and good sense and I just do what feels right."

He blinks slowly as my words penetrate through the fog he's using to insulate himself from what's coming. "What feels right?"

The words try to stick in my throat, behind the knot forming. I clear it loudly. "I broke all my rules for you. I guess protecting you, loving you, that's what feels right."

His tears start to fall one by one, rolling down his cheeks. "You love me?"

"That's not what I—I meant loving you, the act of being good to someone, caring for someone."

"You're wrong about me, Riggs. I may have a wild streak, but I'm not a wild card. I think you know exactly who I am. I think that's why you're able to love me, even when it scares you."

Of course, he's going to advocate for himself. Rhett is always looking for a loophole, always trying to push his agenda, and ever since I met him, I seem to be his agenda. It's kind of cute, actually. "Is that what you think?"

"You've denied it before, but you're a fuckin' liar. When we were in the desert, the night I got hurt, I felt something when I met you. I don't know what, but something, and I know for a fact you felt it too. Then, at Womack, you fuckin' knew I would be there, that you would see me again when you said goodbye to me in Afghanistan. You were back for two fuckin' weeks, spyin' on me before you made yourself known. Why would you do that if you didn't care? Every time I need somethin', every time I turn around, you're there with a solution. I know you do that for all the guys, but look me in the eye and tell me it's not different with us. I dare you."

There he is, my cocky soldier. There's the fire in his eyes that makes my blood heat. "The truth is, since I met you, no one else has been worth thinking about."

He swipes away his tears and sniffles. "You wanna know how I know you're the one? 'Cause I've never felt this way before about anyone or anything. Just you, Riggs. Loving you, yeah, that feels right, but also, I'm *in love* with you. I know it for a fact. That might scare you, that might make you want to push me away, but you already know by now that I'll just keep coming back. I'll always come back to you, 'cause you're mine."

It's best if I don't say too much right now, or I'll be a blubbering fucking mess like he is. "I'm yours?"

"Hell yeah. I claimed you the night I fuckin' met you. I snotted all over your shirt. You've been mine ever since."

He's right. Absolutely fucking right. I'm his. "Well, now that we've got that settled, let's focus on your mama. We can talk about us later."

By the time we arrive, Retta's already booked into a room in the ICU. Only Rhett is allowed in, and I watch through the observation window. She looks like she's aged twenty years since the last time I saw her just days ago. But what's more heartbreaking is Rhett's face. His whole body is slumped over at her bedside. He's constantly wiping away his tears, and his hair is a disheveled mess from running his fingers through it. If I could see his eyes right now, I'm sure I would see his entire heart in them, broken and suffering.

A nurse wearing blue scrubs walks by, and I flag her, desperately seeking information. "Hi, can you tell me anything about Loretta Marsh?"

"Are you family?"

I know this game, I play it with my patients. Of course, she can't tell me anything if I'm not kin. "Yes ma'am, I'm Retta's nephew."

She checks her chart and then peers through the window at Rhett. "Would you like to wait until her son is finished visiting so I can tell you both together? That'll give me time to get the doctor."

I'd rather hear the news first, so I can tell Rhett privately.

"That's not necessary. I can discuss it with him as soon as we're finished."

She sighs and checks her chart again. "I can't discuss her condition. You'll have to wait for Doctor Anson for that, but I can tell you that, for now, she's stable. Probably not likely to wake up soon because she's drugged to the gills. We had to sedate her to bring down her blood pressure."

"Can you tell me why her blood pressure spiked? Or what caused her to be brought in?"

"She was found unconscious in her home. Dr. Anson will discuss the reasons her blood pressure spiked with you. I'll go page him."

It's bullshit. I know she can tell me; it's right there in her chart and she has permission to discuss her patients' conditions with family. The fact she's deferring to the doctor tells me everything.

It's bad. Real fucking bad.

I look through the window again, and Rhett raises his head as if he can feel my eyes on him. He shakes his head sadly, maybe indicating that it doesn't look good. My throat works, convulsing like it's having a seizure. How do I tell him? How do I find the words to explain to Rhett that he's likely going to lose his mother?

How do I break his heart when I swore to protect it?

Finally, after what seems like hours, but is likely only ten minutes or so, Doctor Anson approaches me. I rap my knuckles on the glass to signal Rhett. He closes the door behind him so his mother can rest peacefully.

"I'm Dr. Anson," he says politely, holding out his hand to

Rhett. "You must be Loretta's son. Which makes you her nephew," he says to me. I don't miss how Rhett's head snaps to me.

"Pleasure to meet you, Dr. Anson. Can you tell us what's going on?"

"Your mother was brought in unconscious. Her blood pressure spiked too high, and she fainted. We've given her medicine to bring it down, and she's taking IV fluids for dehydration. We've also given her medicine to keep her sedated for now so that her blood pressure doesn't rise again. It's easy to become agitated when you're not feeling your best, and pain can make it spike."

"Pain, what pain? Why is my mama in pain?" Rhett sounds panicked, his voice climbing higher and higher.

"Your mother has an inherited condition called polycystic kidney disease."

"What does that mean?"

"PKD causes clusters of cysts to grow throughout the body, mainly around the kidneys. Your mother's kidneys are failing her. When the kidneys fail, the body begins to shut down because it can't filter toxins. This causes high blood pressure and hypertension, which is what your mother suffered tonight."

I'm thinking there's no way Loretta didn't know she was sick. There would be too many signs and symptoms she would have had to ignore. "Is she on the donor list?"

"She's not. But it's not just her kidneys, it's her pancreas as well. And it could be a matter of weeks or even days before it affects the rest of her organs."

"So—so what? What does that mean? You can't fix her? You can't replace all those organs?" Rhett sputters.

My heart clenches painfully. He's desperate, he's bargaining, and it's going to get worse before it gets better.

Dr. Anson looks sympathetic. "Even if we could, which is unlikely, her body will continue to attack new organs, and the cysts will continue to spread."

"So, what are you saying, Doc? What does that mean?" Rhett grips my forearm. "What does that mean, Riggs?"

It means she's going to die.

"For now, all we can do is keep your mother comfortable and keep her sedated. If she becomes agitated, she could be at risk for an aneurysm or stroke." The doctor clears his throat. "I'll let you know more when I have more information."

He walks away, and Rhett is still clinging to my arm desperately. He's looking at me like he wants me to deny everything the doctor just told us.

I fold him in my arms, rubbing my hand up and down his back soothingly. "Come on, let me buy you a cup of coffee. We can talk more about it."

In the cafeteria, we find a table near the window, and Rhett stares, unseeing, out the foggy pane as rain beats against the glass. Clutching my coffee in both hands, I let the warmth seep into my skin, hoping it will thaw the icy pain of watching him suffer.

"They're just gonna let her die." His voice sounds flat, dead. "They're not doin' anything for her. They're just gonna let her die."

"They're doing all they can. You know that."

He turns to me, showing me his red-rimmed eyes. "What if I give her my kidney? Will that help?"

He's killing me. Crushing my heart in his fist. "Rhett, even if you were a match, you heard the doctor. Her body will continue to attack her organs."

"But I could buy her a little more time, right?"

"It wouldn't be much. Not nearly enough. You would likely spend whatever time you bought her recovering from your surgery. You wouldn't even be able to see her."

The damn holding back his emotions cracks under the pressure, and he falls apart, sobbing, his face just sort of crumbling in on itself. "Riggs. Help me. Do something."

Tears sting my eyes, and I drag a deep breath into my heavy chest, willing myself to hold it together, for his sake. "Babe," my voice is thick and warbled with emotions I'm holding back. "I wish there was something I could do. But you know I can't. All I can do is be here to support you and be strong for you. I can listen, I can hold you, and I can watch over your mama while you sleep."

He presses the heels of his hands to his eyes, holding them there while he gets a hold of himself. "Ugh! I don't think I can do this. I'm not strong enough."

"You're the strongest person I know, soldier. I've seen men go through less than you have and suffer way more horribly. You're a fighter, a warrior, you get knocked down, and you bounce right back again."

"Not this time. This time, I think I'm gonna stay down."

He sounds utterly defeated, like a kicked dog. "Do you want

to head home and get some rest? We'll be back first thing in the morning, or would you like to head back to your mother?"

"I can't leave her. What if she wakes up?"

"Rhett, they have her heavily sedated."

"I know, but maybe... maybe she can feel me, ya know? Like, sense me or hear me if I talk to her. Maybe she just needs to know I'm here."

"All right, I'll walk you back."

"Are you gonna go back home?"

"No. I told you, I'll be right by your side, every step of the way."

"So, you're just gonna hang out in the waiting room?"

I shrug, giving him an easy smile. "I think I saw some good magazines."

He pulls his phone out of his pocket. "Poly—cystic," he mumbles, typing away.

"Kidney disease. What are you looking up?"

"Gotta learn all I can about her condition. Maybe... I don't know, maybe I'll find somethin' that will help her. Maybe I'll think of something."

Denial. The first stage of grief.

"Come on, you can look at that while you're sitting with your mama." I refuse to tell him it's pointless to think he's going to make the next medical breakthrough in PKD. Rhett has a lot of things to come to terms with, and he's going to have to do it alone, even if I'm standing right beside him, holding his hand the whole way.

When he stands, I round the table, taking him in my arms.

He's warm and his scent is familiar, and I just want to bury myself in him.

He sighs deeply. "I needed that."

Taking his face in my hands, I bring my mouth to his, softly pressing kisses on his lips. Rhett opens for me and I slide my tongue in his mouth, sharing the same breath. It's not a passionate kiss, more comforting, reaffirming.

"I needed that," I parrot, touching my forehead to his.

In the hall, Rhett turns left to head back to the ICU and I turn right, heading for the waiting room. As soon as I push through the door, I freeze and do a double take, no, a triple take.

The entire room is filled wall-to-wall with Bitches.

Some are reading magazines, others are knitting, and others are scrolling through their phones.

I shouldn't be surprised, though; this is what they do, show up for each other when someone needs it, but it's one o'clock in the morning.

"Riggs, how's Rhett?"

"How's his mom?"

"Is she gonna be all right?"

"Guys, one at a time. He's a mess. He's all over the place. Retta is... not good. There really isn't much they can do for her. It's just a waiting game at this point."

West comes over to me and wraps me in a hug. "We're here for you, for both of you."

"I appreciate it. I do, really, and so will Rhett, even if he doesn't act like it right now."

"Mandy called us and told us the paramedics came. It's just

like with Nash," West recalls. "Man, Liza's friend is gonna be pissed off. That's the second door she's had to replace in six months."

Mandy snorts. "It'll be a cold day in hell before she rents to one of Liza's friends again."

Nash leans over and taps Mandy on the shoulder. "I'm the best damn neighbor you've ever had."

Mandy shakes his head. "Dude, I pulled a shovel out of your wall."

McCormick takes the empty chair between them, talking around a mouthful of honey bun from the vending machine. "I always thought I made a great neighbor. I don't have a lot of people over and I've never had the police called—"

"*Bullshit*," Stiles coughs.

"—Okay, that one time with the ferret, the goose, and the chick from the Piggly Wiggly don't count. That was totally not my fault. But other than that, I idle my bike out of the parking lot, I don't let my mail or trash pile up, and unfortunately, I don't have loud sex that can be heard through the walls." He takes another bite. "The perfect neighbor, really."

He sounds ridiculous, and it breaks the ice, as everyone laughs. "Hey," I tap Mandy. "You got another ball of yarn in there and a set of needles for me? It's gonna be a long night."

"Of course." He digs in his bag and pulls out the brightest orange I've ever seen. "We should all knit something for Retta."

"Maybe an afghan," Stiles suggests.

"Even if she doesn't use it for long," Jax points out sadly. "Rhett will have something of hers to take home."

"Guys, I think that's a great idea. Let's get started." My voice breaks on the last word, overwhelmed with gratitude for these men.

RHETT
Black Mountain, NC
Chapter 2

I'M EXHAUSTED, slurping from the straw of my iced coffee like it's Riggs's cock 'cause I need that extra hit of caffeine. We stayed up talking late into the night and this morning he set his alarm an hour earlier, so he could get to the gym and set up for the Warrior's Walk.

"So you only do these every three months or so?" I ask.

"Yep, stack those weights for me, would you?"

"When do you think I might be ready?"

He looks up and gives me that shit-eating grin that says *'I'm in charge,'* and I love it. "When I say you're ready. You haven't exactly been keeping up with your therapy lately with all that's been going on."

"I know," I blow out of breath. "I can't keep everything

straight. Support group, work, flyin' lessons, therapy, and now with my mama, which supersedes everything. How am I supposed to find a balance?"

"By asking for help. There's no way you can do it all on your own. You have to delegate, ask for help, and be willing to receive it."

He goes back to wiping down the gym equipment with disinfectant wipes, and a smile teases my lips. Watching him is one of my favorite things. The way his sinewy muscles ripple like a big cat as he moves. His arms look hot as fuck stretching the sleeves of that T-shirt. The curve of his bubble ass as he bends over the equipment. Damn, I'm worse than a stage five creeper with a toxic crush.

The gym begins to fill up with vets trying to sneak in a few minutes of warm-up before everything comes to a halt for the competition. Nash and Brewer duck inside, and that damn cat is with them, slung across Brewer's chest in that ugly green sling.

Riggs gives Brewer a hug and tickles the cat between his ears. "Hey Valor, did you come to watch your daddy kick Uncle West's butt?"

"Kick it? I'm going to slaughter it," Nash jokes.

"You talking smack again?" West asks, coming up behind him and taking him by surprise. They laugh as they hug it out, and then I'm laughing when I catch the words written on West's T-shirt. Riggs also notices, doing a double take.

He reads it out loud. '*I walk like a warrior because I have BALLS. Do you have BALLS?*'

"Fucking really?" Riggs asks, shaking his head.

"What? I got it from the gift shop," West swears.

Riggs snorts. "I'm afraid to see what else they sell."

"Did they have that in a double XL?" Nash asks.

"Quit yapping and go get warmed up," Riggs snaps, smacking him lightly in the back of the head. The whole exchange makes me laugh.

West and Nash hit the treadmill to warm up their muscles. I notice Nash has a slight limp, and I wonder if I will too, even after prolonged therapy. To be honest, I don't care either way; it doesn't stop me from flying, which is all that matters. West has his blade leg attached, and he's moving a lot faster than Nash. He's also not shy about letting him know.

"Just wait till I get warmed up, asswipe. I'm gonna leave you in my dust."

As they're trading insults, the rest of the Bitches file in, touching and making a mess of everything Riggs carefully set up.

"Okay, everybody stop touching my shit and find a spot along the wall. Let's get going. Nash and West are competing today, not that this is a competition," he clarifies. "But with them, *everything* is a competition, so go figure. They've been in my care for more than six months and have worked extremely hard through bad days and busy days and days where the pain seemed like it would bring them to a halt. I can't tell you how proud I am of these guys. Especially West. When we met, he was convinced that I was lying when I told him he would be able to do this someday."

Riggs's voice becomes emotional, which is uncharacteristic for him to give away how he's feeling. Listening to him is making me *feel* how proud he is of West. I'm starting to get choked up, which is the last thing I need. I'm sick and tired of crying, dammit. But God, I hope someday I can make him that proud of *me*. I hope I give him a reason to be.

Riggs continues. "I have no doubt these gentlemen will be able to complete the Warrior's Walk today, but the real question is, who will finish first?" All the Bitches cheer, and other vets that have gathered around to watch are clapping. "We're going to start with the mile. Both of these guys are at a point in their recovery where they can blow through this with ease. But can they do it in under seven minutes?"

"Shit, I used to do it in four," West brags.

"Bullshit. You never ran a four-minute mile in your life," Nash argues.

"No, it's true. I've seen it," Brandt swears. "I could never keep up with him."

"Let's see what you've got now, Wardell," Riggs says, and then blows his whistle. The sound of their shoes slapping the conveyor belt is the only sound in the room until they hit the halfway mark, and the crowd begins to cheer them on.

"Move it, West!" Brandt yells. "Pretend like I just put *Top Gun* on, and you're running from the room."

The excitement builds, and I can feel the energy of the crowd as we wait to see who will finish the mile first.

West slaps the stop button when he hits the mile mark. "Booyah, bitches," he yells.

"7.4," Riggs barks.

Grunting, Nash takes the lead out, increasing his pace. He's sweating already, and I can only imagine how hard he's pushing himself to finish what should be a simple mile. When he finally stops the machine, he collapses, bracing his hands on his knees as he tries to catch his breath.

"8.2," Riggs calls.

But there's no more taunting, no in-your-face remarks. West slaps Nash on the back. "You kicked that treadmill's ass!"

"Let's go, warriors. On to the bitch bars. I mean the parallel bars." Riggs smirks as he pretends to correct himself.

The parallel bars run about ten feet and are about three feet off the ground, or just above hip length. "God, you remember how much I hated these?" West asks. "We had some bad days on these bars," he recalls.

"I remember," Riggs says grimly. "Let's see how well you can do now. The challenge is for you to get from start to finish, but I want you to put your weight on your hands and walk the bars using only your upper body strength. Do not let your feet touch the ground."

"Piece of fucking cake," Nash says. He's broader across the chest than West, and he seems to have more muscle mass.

West knows he's been beat before he even begins. "Yeah, well, don't get too cocky. I gotta let you win something so it's an even competition." Nash laughs at him. I laugh at him. These guys are a mess, just like my buddies back home.

Riggs blows his whistle hard, and they start off evenly, until about the halfway mark when West slows considerably as he begins to struggle. Nash makes it across the bars first. West's feet touch down halfway, and he has to catch his breath as he works the kinks out of his biceps before continuing.

"Come on West, you can do it," I yell. By the time he

finishes the full ten feet, his brand-new shirt has sweat stains under the armpits.

Riggs is waiting for him, glowing with pride. "I can't tell you how proud I am of you. You've come so far." He looks like a proud papa.

My heart fills to bursting. God, I love this man. I love the way he loves others, the way he supports them and encourages them, how he's fully invested in their lives and their successes. And the way he won't let them take their failures to heart.

Brandt moves into Riggs's spot, wrapping West in his arms. He claps him on the back. "So proud of you, babe. You've got this. You've got to close your eyes and visualize the finish line, and kicking Nash's ass with your big-booted foot."

"Fuck the boot, I'm giving him the blade," West jokes.

Riggs checks his clipboard and resets his stopwatch. "All right guys, take a water break before the last leg of the competition." I hand out bottles of water and the guys chug them in seconds. "For the last test of endurance, you have to climb the rope and ring the bell at the top."

"Fuck," West groans. Nash chuckles.

Riggs told me he tailors the Warrior's Walk to the individual limitations of the competitors. Sometimes, it's all a patient can do to simply walk on their own two feet from point A to point B.

"When you ring that bell, you're telling everyone, including and most importantly yourselves, that you are a warrior. That you are strong and relentless, and that in the face of opposition, you never gave up."

Unexpectedly, my eyes water, and I swipe them dry before anyone can see. No matter what else I have going on, I'm going to make my therapy the most important thing in my life. I want to see Riggs look at me with that same pride, to say to everyone that I'm strong and relentless and that I never gave up. I want to feel like a warrior, even though I'll never step foot on a battlefield again.

"Who's going first?" Riggs has his stopwatch in hand, ready to begin.

"Go ahead, Nash," West suggests. "Show me what I'm up against."

Nash smirks. He presses a kiss on his cat's nose. "Wish me luck, Valor." Taking hold of the rope with both hands, he looks up, his gaze settling on the brass bell at the top. "I'm coming for you," he tells it. Nash begins to pull himself up, using his feet, thighs, and hands to ascend. About halfway up, he slows and grunts with each inch gained. "I don't remember it being this difficult in gym class," he pants, sounding winded.

"You weren't old back then," Jax snickers.

It takes ten more minutes for Nash to reach the top. He smacks the bell hard and loosens his grip, sliding back down in a rush. Everyone, including me, claps for him, but nobody is clapping louder than Brewer.

"Shit, I was about to let go," he admits, struggling to breathe. "Your turn," he grins at West.

West stands under the rope, looking up at it skeptically. "You going to catch me if I fall?" he asks Brandt.

"Always," Brandt vows.

"You'd flatten him like a pancake," McCormick jokes.

West shoots him a dirty look before grasping the rope. He

spits in his palms and rubs them together before he re-positions his hands again. "Wish me luck."

Unlike Nash, West doesn't start off strong. He struggles the entire way, biting off curses, grunting and sweating as he fights to maintain his grasp. "My hands are fucking burning from this rope," he complains, looking up at the bell to gauge his distance.

"You can do it, Professor. Just keep putting one hand in front of the other," Brandt encourages.

"Don't you quit on me, West Wardell. You get your ass to the top of that rope and ring that bell. That's an order," Riggs barks.

I can feel his struggle. He's fighting with everything he's got to hold on to that rope long enough to ring that bell.

When he's just inches away from his goal, his sweaty hands slip, and he dangles one-handed as he wipes his palm off on his shorts before trying to grab hold again. He must dig down deep and find the last reserve of energy he's got in his body, because he clinches the rope between his thighs and surges upward, barely tapping the bell. West screams a primal war cry as his hands slip from the rope again and he falls ten feet. I rush forward, but Brandt is quicker and catches West safely, although they both fall to the mat.

West laughs and his joy is contagious. He triumphed against the odds, against his limitations, and he won. He fucking did it. Soon everyone is laughing and clapping for him and he struggles to his feet, taking a hand up from Brandt. He hugs his partner hard, but then the Bitches surround him and it's a dogpile before they're back on the mat again.

Fuck it. I'm a Bitch as well, and I want in on this moment. I throw myself on the top of the pile of hard bodies, laughing and rolling with them. *With my brothers.*

"So, who won the bet?" Stiles asks Riggs.

Riggs grins, checking his clipboard for the stats. "Technically, Nash had the quickest time, but West had the harder challenge. I'm gonna call it a draw and let them settle it between themselves."

The guys help West to his feet again, since he was on the bottom of the pile. He rubs at his thighs and I wonder if they're cramping up. He snorts. "A draw, my ass. We've decided we're not exchanging money, we're going to let the rest of you Bitches treat us to lunch instead."

"Black Mountain Tavern for wings and beer, boys," McCormick calls.

"Uh-uh," Riggs says, putting the brakes on. "First, I want West and Nash to do a cool down with stretching. Then you can go and celebrate." He turns to me, clicking his little pen that reads, *'You're only as strong as you think you are.'* "Are you going with them?"

"Yeah, I guess. Then I'll stop by the hospital and—" My phone rings, cutting off my words. The caller ID says Mission Hospital. My heart stalls, the breath in my lungs freezes to ice, and the phone continues to ring as I stare at the screen with dread.

Riggs reads my expression, and his face tightens with concern. "Answer it, Rhett."

"It's... it's the hospital."

Why can't I just answer the fucking phone? *'Cause you know it's bad.*

Riggs grabs it from me. "Hello? He can't come to the phone right now. This is her nephew, Navarro Riggs. Can I pass along a message?" I watch his face for signs that it's as bad as I think it is. His eyes widen and he glances at me. "We'll be right there."

"Riggs?"

His throat slides and I can see the bad news written all over his face. "They're waking your mother up. We need to head over there."

Air rushes into my lungs, filling up my chest, and I can breathe. My heart begins to beat again. "Okay, let's go."

BALLS, Black Mountain, NC
Chapter 2

SHE LOOKS the same as she did yesterday except, maybe smaller. Did she shrink? She's just so frail. Pale skin, hollow cheeks, and sunken eyes. They used to be so vibrant and full of life, the same whiskey green as mine. What I wouldn't give to have her open her eyes so I can see them again.

"We're going to wake her up, but I can't make any promises," Doctor Anson explains gently. "Her blood pressure and oxygen are stable, but that could change when she's awake. We'll keep a close eye on her and take it hour by hour."

More like minute by minute. I'm not leaving her side for a second.

The nurse inserts a needle into the IV port taped to the back of her hand. "Now we just wait," she says.

I trace the dark blue veins bulging beneath the pale skin of my mama's hand, waiting to feel her twitch, even the slightest movement, any sign of life. Riggs's strong hand on my shoulder reminds me of his solid presence. He's been my rock, right by my side through this whole ordeal. Reminding me I'm never alone, even though I feel like I am.

She continues to rest comfortably for another thirty minutes until she begins to stir. "Mama? Can you hear me?" When she finally opens her eyes, I'm the first thing she sees. "Hey, Mama. Been waitin' on you to wake up. You needed your beauty sleep, though." She tries to smile but doesn't succeed.

I scoot aside as the doctor completes an assessment, shining a penlight in her eyes, asking her to turn her head from side to side, and checking her extremities for lack of sensation. The nurse changes out her bag of IV fluids for a fresh one and hands me the call button.

"Let me know if anything changes before I come back to check on her."

I sweep her bangs from her forehead and manage a weak smile. "I'm glad you're back. I missed you."

She can barely squeeze my hand. "You didn't sit here the whole time, did you, baby?"

"You know I did, Mama. I sat here thinkin' about you and me growin' up together. The best times of my life were with you." I swore I wasn't gonna cry in front of her, but I can feel the tears coming and I'm powerless to stop them. "You're in every memory I have, and now—" I can't even finish that sentence. Saying it out loud is admitting defeat, and I'm not done fighting.

"You're gonna have to make some new memories now, pecan. Memories that don't include me." Her speech sounds slow, like she's too exhausted to speak.

"No, Mama. No, I won't!"

"Hush. You spent the last four years on your own. The Army made a man out of you in a way I never could. Broke my heart to see you leave, but I thank God every day you made that decision. You can do this, Rhett."

"No, Mama, we still have so many memories to make together, so many things we were supposed to do."

"Life's under no obligation to give us what we expect. We take what we get and we're thankful it's no worse than it is," she quotes from her favorite movie. I'm pretty sure I've rolled my eyes every single time she's quoted that movie, but now I'd give anything for her to stick around and bug me with that shit. "I wrote down all your favorite recipes and left them in your kitchen. Back home, in my attic, you'll find all the stuff I saved of yours when you were little, and in the closet in the guestroom, you'll find all my picture albums."

"I don't want to talk about that stuff, Mama. I want to talk about—"

"You listen to me, Rhett Butler. You can't put off what's comin' tomorrow or the next day. You have to face it head-on, look it in the eye, and flick it off."

I can't swallow, I can't breathe. My head is swimming with thoughts and memories and feelings, and I feel like I'm drowning under the weight of it. "Tell me what to do, Mama. Tell me what you want. Do you want me to take you back home to Ruston? I can stay with you."

"No, baby. Your life is here. You're needed here. That house, it's always been filled with happiness and love. I don't want to die there. I don't want to taint the memories we made there."

"But Mama," I argue. I look around at the sterile room and the medical equipment. Who wants to die in a hospital?

"Rhett, honey, I won't make it that long." She says it so matter-of-factly, like she's already made peace with her dying.

"How long did you know you were sick? Why didn't you say anythin'?"

"You were on the other side of the world when I found out. I didn't need you worryin' about me. I needed you focused so you could come home safe."

"If... if you don't..." I have to pause and clear my throat. "Do you want to be buried next to your parents? You could wear that pretty costume you made. I bet you still fit in it."

The corner of her mouth pulls up like she's trying to smile. "I loved that dress. But no, don't you dare put me in the ground next to my parents. It's so far away from here, I bet you'll never come to see me. I want to be close to you so I can watch over you, so I don't miss nothin'." She closes her eyes for a moment, and I think she's gonna take a nap, but then she opens them again. "Don't you go plannin' no funeral for me, neither, Rhett. I won't have all that sad cryin' and blusterin'. I want to be celebrated. I've lived a good life, short, but good, and I want you to celebrate all the years we had together."

I nod as tears stream from my eyes, coating my skin with grief.

"That man," she nods at Riggs, who's pretending to be

asleep in the corner. I know he's pretending. "He's a goodun'. You hang onto him and don't let go."

"Mama, he's... I love him."

She lays her hand over our joined hands. "I know, baby. And I'm so proud of you. You're both good men. Don't you ever be ashamed of lovin' a good man."

Her blinks become longer as her eyelids grow heavier. "You tired, Mama?"

"Yes, baby. Let Mama get some rest."

"I'll be right here when you wake up," I assure her.

Riggs clears his throat and I turn to him. In the next instant, his arms are around me, and he's holding me so tight he might just squeeze all the grief out of me.

His voice sounds like sharp gravel. "It's killing me to see you hurting so badly."

"It would kill me worse if you weren't here."

"I'm not going anywhere, soldier."

My mama sleeps for hours. Riggs slips out to grab us both coffee. I didn't realize how tired I was, but he gently shakes me awake. I lift my head from my mama's tray table, littered with glossy brochures and folded origami figurines. My mama loves birds, and I've been trying to make every single one I can think of—flamingos, cranes, another eagle, a hummingbird—I want to surround her with the things she loves.

"Here, babe, drink this." He offers me the steaming cup of coffee, and I take it gratefully, savoring the first rich sip.

"Thank you. I don't know what I would do without you."

"You're never going to have to find out," he swears.

I want to believe him because it's what I want to hear, but

then I remember how we argued before and I can't help but wonder how long forever means to him.

I finish off my coffee and push to my feet. My leg aches, stiff from sitting for hours. "I'm gonna go to the bathroom."

The one in my mama's room is jam-packed with medical equipment not being used, so I make my way down the hall, limping as I clutch the safety railing on the wall for support. I feel like I've stepped into another world. The hustle and bustle of the hospital, nurses laughing and eating lunch behind the desk, patients being transferred to various departments, visitors with children—none of it has anything to do with my mama, which feels foreign to me, bizarre even. My whole world revolves around her and right now, with her being sick, with the threat of losing her too soon, I can't even fathom how life goes on or what people would have to laugh about.

There's no life for me outside of my mama's room.

I finish my business in the bathroom and shuffle back to her room, realizing I missed something while I was gone. Riggs looks devastated. He's chewing his bottom lip to pieces, a frown forming between his eyes.

"What is it? Is it my mama?" I can see his throat working like he's having difficulty swallowing, and he scrubs his face.

"Just got a call from my command."

"And?" My heart's gonna beat right outta my chest, like a horse galloping from its stable.

"You know how, in the reserves, we get called up every month or so for a weekend of training?"

A dead weight drops to the bottom of my stomach. I can feel him slipping away from me. "Did you get called up?"

He nods. "But not for the weekend. It's annual training. Two weeks."

I can't lose him now, not when everything is falling apart. He's my rock. My lifeline. I'll lose my fucking sanity without Riggs keeping me anchored. "When do you leave?"

"0600." *Fourteen hours.* I have fourteen hours left with him. "I'm going to run home and pack. Tie up a few loose ends at work. Mandy is on his way to stay with you. I'll be back in an hour or two."

"Riggs, you can't sleep here tonight. You need to rest."

"I told you, I'm not leaving your side, not until they drag me away."

Fucking tears rush forth again, and I don't even try to swipe them away this time. He pulls me close, and I bury my face in his shirt, soaking it with my misery. "Promise me you're comin' back to me."

"I promise you, soldier. I swear to fucking God I'm coming back."

Over his shoulder, I glance at my mama. She's awake, watching us with a sad face. Great, as if she doesn't already have enough sadness on her rail-thin shoulders.

"Rhett, give me a minute alone with Riggs, please."

Her request surprises me. What's she got to say to him that I can't hear? "Yes, ma'am."

I walk out of the room and shut the door behind me. Minutes later, Mandy, West, Brandt, and Nash approach, and I can hear their booted footsteps from all the way down the hall.

They don't say nothing in the way of a greeting, they just crush me in a group hug. The tears fall harder. It feels good. It feels like a release, although there's no end to my suffering. It just keeps multiplying, like a rash spreading throughout my body until it immobilizes me.

"Do you want to come back home while he's gone? I'm right next door and I can check on you."

I don't ever want to go back there. It was never my home. I don't ever again want to sleep in the bed where my mama was slowly dying or eat in the kitchen where she passed out. I shake my head.

"Then I'll come stay with you at Riggs's place. I hear he's got a hot tub," he jokes.

He lets me go, and I suck a deep, unsteady breath into my lungs. I could try to be strong, to say I don't need him, how it's not necessary, but I'm not even going to lie like that. I do need him. "Sounds good," I croak, sounding like a bullfrog.

Brandt leans his hand on my shoulder. "I know he's leaving, but that doesn't mean you're alone. You're not. You've got more support than you probably want. We're here for you the whole way, and Riggs is coming back. He'll be back before you know it."

Another round of fresh tears hits and the pressure wells up inside of my head, behind my eyes. I lean in to hug him to hide my wet face.

"I love you, brother."

This is the first time I've said anything like that or acknowledged that these men are my friends, my brothers, really. It feels good. It feels right. Riggs opens the door.

"We'll be in the waiting room down the hall if you need us," says West.

I know Riggs is taking off, and I don't want to be alone. "It's all right, y'all can come in. You just gotta keep it down so my mama can rest."

They make their way inside her room, and I'm alone with Riggs. I search his face, trying to commit his features to memory.

Fuck, I'm gonna miss him so bad.

He tilts my chin up, brushing his nose against mine. "Do you know how I knew I was in love with you?" he asks. I just shake my head. I can't imagine what he's gonna say. "You'd say or do the dumbest shit, and instead of getting angry with you, I just wanted to smile. I wanted to kiss you," he breathes over my lips.

My laugh is quick and shallow. The first one in days. "I fell in love with you because you saw me at my worst and still wanted me. You believed in me when I didn't believe in myself. You made me feel like it was all right to be the worst version of myself, and yet, you made me want to be the best version I could be. That's how I knew I loved you."

He crushes his lips to mine. It's a wild, passionate, sloppy kiss. His fingers tighten in my hair like he never wants to let me go. His kiss steals the breath from my lungs. I don't care. I could die happy while kissing him. In fact, I hope it's the last thing I ever do.

"I'm coming back for you, soldier. You're mine, don't forget that."

Like I could ever forget.

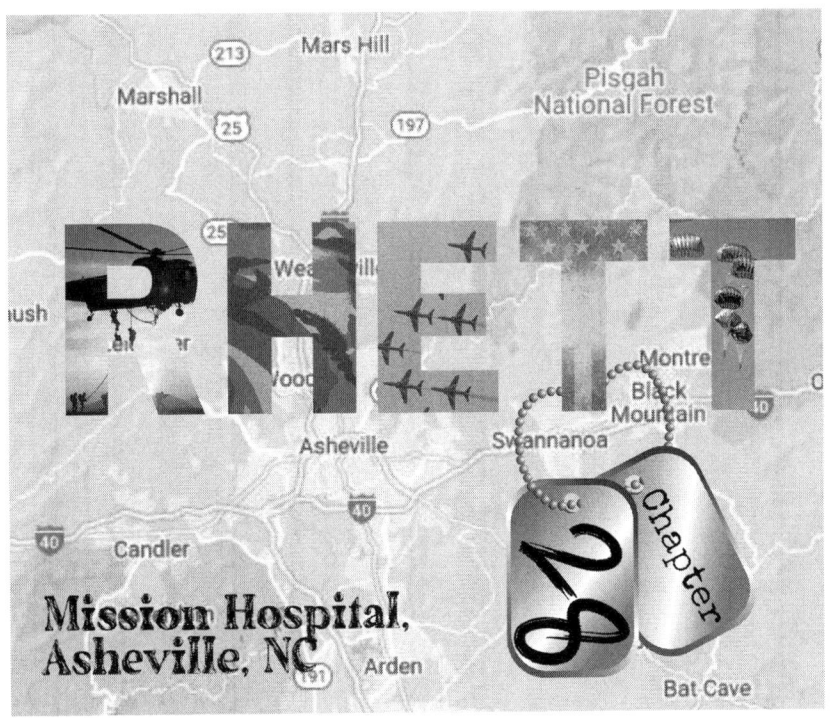

Mission Hospital, Asheville, NC

Chapter 28

RIGGS HAS CALLED TWICE, which is more than I thought I would hear from him. He's miserable. Stuck in a field in Louisiana with nothing but rain for three days straight, getting bitten alive by mosquitoes and sweating his balls off. I know exactly how bad it sucks; I've done it more times than I can count. JRTC at Fort Polk is worse than hell on Earth, worse than basic training, or even deployment. The Joint Readiness Training Center is designed to prepare you for combat situations, but all it prepares you for is the seventh circle of hell.

Because that's exactly what it is.

I read his last text message again for the hundredth time, wishing it made me feel even a little bit closer to him. "Riggs says Fort Polk has convinced him not to renew his contract with the reserves." At least those words bring me some small measure of comfort. I won't have to say goodbye to him again after this.

West snorts. "That fucking place. Don't get me started."

Mandy gags. "The humidity is so thick you could cut it with a knife."

Brandt laughs. "Am I the only one who likes land NAV training?"

"I think something got shaken loose inside your head in that blast," West teases, rapping his knuckles lightly on Brandt's skull. "All right, I need the make and model of a classic car."

West is scribbling in his *Mad Libs* pad. It's the only thing keeping us entertained while my mama sleeps most of the afternoon. Whatever they're giving her through her IV keeps her heavily sedated.

"The 1964 *Country Squire*," Mandy recalls fondly.

"That's not a hot car," West argues.

"You didn't say hot, you said classic. She's a beaut; a real classic."

West rolls his eyes and jots it down. "A kind of tree nut?"

"Pistachio."

"Walnut."

"Pecan," I answer, thinking of my mama's nickname for me. When she's gone, no one's ever gonna call me that again. And out of nowhere, the pain of losing her hits me all over again. Silent tears track down my cheeks and neck, soaking into the collar of my shirt.

Grief is the oddest thing. You're going along just fine one minute, laughing about a classic car, and the next, you fall apart like a rusty station wagon hitting a pothole.

"Put that shit away," Brandt hisses to West, handing me a tissue. "You hungry, Rhett? I can run downstairs and grab you something to eat."

"No, I'm good, thanks. I'll eat when—" Suddenly the monitors start going crazy, blinking and beeping, but my mama looks like she's resting comfortably. Two nurses rush in and silence the alarms. They lift her eyelids and try to get a response from her.

"Loretta? Wake up, Loretta."

"What is it? What's wrong with my mama?"

"She's having a mini-stroke. It's called a Transient Ischemic Attack."

"What do we do? What are you gonna do about it? Is she all right?"

The rapid-fire questions are met with a kind smile.

"There's not much we can do with TIA. I'll administer a blood thinner to make sure there's no clotting, but it's likely to happen again."

She says it like it's no big deal, like it happens all the time. Maybe for her, it does, but not to me. Not to *my* mama. I just feel so... Goddamn impotent and useless, powerless to do anything but watch her suffer and slip away.

"Mama? Wake up, talk to me." I just need to know she's still with me.

She comes back online slowly, and I can't describe the feeling of relief that hits me square in the chest when I see the color of her eyes again.

"Baby, quit yellin' at me." Her words are drawn out, dripping from her lips as slow as molasses dripping off a spoon. "You're louder than a dog in labor."

"You had a stroke, Mama." My voice breaks as tears of relief stream from my eyes.

"I'm still here, ain't I?" She's drooling from the left side of her lips, and I grab a tissue to wipe her mouth. "Introduce me to your friends, pecan."

"Mama, this is West and Brandt, and Mandy. They stopped by to make sure you're okay."

"No, baby, they're here for you. And when I'm gone, you'll have all these friends to look after you."

Her complexion looks sallow and pale, and her skin is clammy with oil and sweat. "Don't talk about bein' gone. Let's just talk about right here, right now." I press my lips to the back of her hand. It's plain now, with no polish and no jewelry. My mama always wore at least four rings. Big shiny ones, fake as a snake, and the brightest nail polish she could buy at Dixon's drug store.

Her hand shakes in mine, and I squeeze her gently to steady it. Her eyes look glassy and red, and I wonder how hard she's fighting to hold back her tears for my sake, like I am for hers.

"Hardships make or break people, baby. After all, tomorrow is another day."

Another one of her favorite lines of Scarlett's. The very last line in the movie. Scarlett's last words. A shiver runs through me and it's soul deep. She closes her eyes to rest and my heart breaks in half and then in half again. There won't be nothing left of it by the time she wakes up.

Eventually, I let the guys talk me into a burger, and I get up and stretch my legs as we head down to the cafeteria. After lunch, Mandy and I are the only ones who return to her room, and we stay until visiting hours are over before he convinces me to go home and get some rest in a real bed for a change. The only reason I agree is 'cause my neck is killing me. My back, my neck, and my leg.

"Spread your thighs and pop that ass out."

Riggs's deep voice is a command I can't ignore. I'm on my hands and knees for him on the mattress like an offering, waiting to be consumed. The rough stubble of his cheeks scratches my ass as he buries his face between them to lap at my hole.

"I missed the way you taste." *I missed his fucking tongue.* "Going to get you nice and wet before I bury my cock in you."

Fuck yeah. He's never deploying again. In fact, fuck life. We're never leaving this room. My chest drops to the mattress, giving him more access, and he rises up on his knees, grasping his cock. He lines it up with my hole and shoves inside without stretching me first.

"Holy mother of..." My words are cut off by the ringing of my phone. "Ignore it. Just keep going," I beg.

But it doesn't quit. It just keeps ringing, louder and louder.

"Holy mother of..." I come awake suddenly, my body jerking, and I'm about to fall off the damn bed before I catch myself and bang my elbow on the nightstand. "Fuck. What?" I yell at my phone.

I was dreaming. The bed is cold beside me. Cold and empty. Riggs is still deployed in Louisiana, and I'm alone with nothing but my dreams to keep me warm.

"All right." I rub the grit from my eyes. "Keep your damn boots on. I'm comin'."

Everything starts to make sense again in a rush, and I scramble for the phone in a panic. It could be the hospital, or Riggs, or even one of the Bitches with an emergency.

"Hello?"

"Am I speaking with Rhett Marsh?"

Cold dread settles over my skin like an icy blanket. "Yes."

"My name is Barbara. I'm calling from Mission Hospital. I'm sorry to have to tell you, but your mother passed away about thirty minutes ago."

I hear her, but the words don't make any sense. They're not penetrating my brain. "What happened? Is she okay?"

"Sir, your mother is gone. She passed away."

"Gone?" I shriek. "Gone where?"

"Sir, she passed away."

Mandy's dark shadow appears in my doorway.

"W-what happened?"

"She had a brain aneurysm. A blood vessel ruptured. She passed away in her sleep. In fact, she never woke again after you left."

I can't process it. Although I've been waiting for this news for days, felt it coming like an unwanted visitor stalking me relentlessly, I refuse to believe what I'm hearing. Not until Mandy comes to sit beside me. Somehow, his presence anchors me back in reality, and her words slam into me like a wrecking ball. From out of nowhere, a flood of emotion breaks me in half, and I shatter apart. It starts with silent tears streaming down my cheeks as my shoulders shake, and then ugly, gut-wrenching sobs break free of my throat, and I drop the phone and cling to Mandy's broad chest.

He picks up the phone from the mattress and wraps his arm around me as he takes over for me.

"What do we need to do now?" he asks. "Thank you." And then he hangs up, tossing the phone to the bed. His other arm comes around me. "We need to call the funeral home and have them pick up her body." *Funeral home? I haven't even made arrangements for her yet. What funeral home?* "But first, we need to have a good cry."

I wasn't there! She died alone. I fucking hate that I thought I needed a good night's sleep when my mother was having her very last night. Why did I leave!?

Mandy's voice cuts through my thoughts. "Whatever you're thinking right now, just stop. You can cry, you can grieve, but you can't beat yourself up. There wasn't a fucking thing you could do to save her. I know you know that, Rhett."

"I could have at least been there to hold her hand."

"It's easy to think that now, but you can't sit there twenty-four seven holding her hand. Your body needs to eat and sleep."

"I bet she knew I wasn't there," I sob. I've made a disgusting snotty mess of his T-shirt.

"Of course she knew, that's why she finally slipped away. She was waiting for you to leave because she didn't want you to see it. Didn't you tell me she didn't want a funeral because she wanted her life to be celebrated? You told me she didn't want to move back home because she didn't want to die in that house and taint the good memories you both made there. She refused to die in front of you because she doesn't want you to remember her that way."

"You think?" I raise my head from his chest, struggling to take a shaky breath.

"Yeah, Rhett. That's exactly what I think."

He's probably right. It's exactly what my mama would do. "I can't..." I lift the hem of my T-shirt to wipe my eyes and nose. "I don't know what I'm supposed to do now. I guess I have to make calls, but...I can't right now."

"Go take a shower and then I'll make you some coffee. While you're in the shower, I'll make some phone calls. You said you wanted to have her cremated?"

All I can do is nod as tears continue to stream down my face.

"Go, I'll take care of everything," he assures me, pulling his snotty shirt over his head.

It's the first glimpse I've ever had of the skin beneath his shirt. His shoulder and part of his back are covered in puckered red scars. It looks painful. It looks like he's suffered ten thousand tragedies. Never once in all the months I've known him have I ever heard him complain, not when his face was sandblasted, not when his skin was grafted, and not when the object of his desire friend-zoned him. Mandy is a true warrior. He fights a battle every single day, and he does it silently, with a smile on his face.

I'm lucky to call him my friend. I'm honored to call him my brother.

In the shower, I don't even bother scrubbing my body with soap. I stand stiff as a statue as the hot water pounds over my face, washing away my tears and opening my clogged sinuses.

Riggs, I need you. I need you so badly right now. Please come home.

When the water runs cold, I step out of the shower and dry my body, dressing in jeans and an old hunter-green Henley. My mama used to say how it would highlight the color of my eyes. Then I laugh, thinking how when I first met Riggs, I was covered in blood, and he told me the red brought out the color of my eyes. God, I miss him. The thought brings fresh tears to my eyes.

I'm so sick of fucking crying I could choke.

Mandy has a steaming cup of coffee waiting for me like he promised. I take a seat at the table across from him and cup the mug with both hands, trying to steal its heat.

"What's going through your head?" Mandy asks.

I take a sip, letting the warm liquid smooth out the lump in my throat. "My body count is piling up. First, Brian, and now my mama. Riggs is gone, and I don't know what I would do without you here."

Mandy winks. "That's what friends are for."

"No, you're more than just my friend. You're my brother, my *best* friend. I fought it for a long time because it hurt to replace Brian, but you're not his replacement. You're just this amazin' guy who wants to be a part of my life, and I'm grateful for it."

Mandy looks skeptical. "I don't know; your best friends

don't have a great track record. I might be better off just being the guy who lives next door."

"Fuck you," I snort, balling up my snotty tissue and chucking it at him. "You can't make dead jokes about my best friend."

"Yeah, I can. I'm *also* your best friend. I have that right."

"I guess you do. So what happens now?"

"I contacted a reputable funeral home here in Black Mountain. They're on their way now to pick up your mama. They're going to cremate her body and call us to pick up her remains when they're ready. In the meantime, we have a celebration to plan."

Fuck it. Fuck decorum and manliness and all that bullshit. I rush to my feet, rounding the table as quickly as my leg allows, and throw my arms around Mandy, bear-hugging him.

"All right, all right," he laughs, squeezing me back.

"It's gotta be epic. Nothing but the best for my mama."

"Of course. Nothing but the best. You're talking to a Bitch, and Bitches know how to throw a party."

RHETT

Black Mountain, NC
Chapter 29

AS I DRIVE THROUGH BRAGG, I feel Brian's ghost haunt me at every turn. Every building I pass brings back a memory of him, good or bad. The DFAC reminds me of Brian and Warren shoving footlongs down their throats in a hotdog eating contest. I pass the PX where we did our grocery shopping together. The field where we did PT every morning, no matter if it was raining, snowing, or sweltering. The softball field where we played on the weekends.

I pull up to the airfield and park. There's only a handful of cars with people waiting to greet their loved ones. This is the field where we took off and landed after jump training, the field where I landed when they brought me home from the desert—with Brian's dead body.

I did the right thing by moving away from the base. I can't keep living in his shadow, bitter that the memories I have of him can't breathe life back into his body. I needed to get away, to walk in the sun and start fresh in a town that isn't trying to suck me back into the past.

About forty-five minutes pass while I sit in my car, listening to the radio, waiting for Riggs to return home. I pass the time browsing the catalog Mandy gave me from the funeral home, trying to choose the best urn to bury my mama in. Most of them look so plain and boring, and I know for a fact my mama would hate them. I need something colorful and pretty like she was. I need something that screams Retta.

The giant 47 Chinook touches down in a thunderous roar, and I shut the car off and make my way to the gate. Riggs is one of the last soldiers off the bird, and my heart flip-flops at the sight of him.

Damn, he looks good. A sight for sore eyes.

I haven't seen him in uniform since the first night we met, and now I'm getting all nostalgic and sappy, remembering the way he cared for me. The spark of heat I felt then has now grown into a raging inferno. Riggs looks so proud and broad and... *ungh*... like a delicious fucking snack, and I'm starving for a taste of him. I should have fucked him before he left, but I'm damn sure gonna do it as soon as we get home.

He texted last night to tell me the details of his return, and I told him about my mama. He's probably going to treat me with kid gloves for the next few weeks, but fuck that... no matter how heartbroken I am, I still want sex.

He spots me and his face lights up, making my stomach

swirl. I love that reaction from him. Riggs picks me up off my feet and swings me in an arc, crushing me in his embrace. I feel high from the thrill of being seen by his entire unit. He doesn't give a fuck if we look gay. Well, we *are* gay... okay, bi/gay, but still, Riggs couldn't care less.

I wish Brian and I had his courage when we were enlisted.

Riggs sets me on my feet. "Damn, I missed you." I breathe the words into his neck, rubbing my lips over his stubble.

"I'm so sorry about Retta, babe." He squeezes me tighter, and I close my eyes and breathe him in.

He smells the same as I remember, if slightly sweatier, and everything settles inside me. The turmoil, anger, and grief settle to a low simmer, taking a backseat to my excitement over seeing him again.

He presses a kiss on my lips. "You're the best thing I've seen in weeks."

With a snort, I tease, "I believe it. I've been to Polk." He grabs his rucksack and we head to the car. "Take me home and fuck me."

Riggs chuckles. "Definitely on my to-do list, but first, we eat. I've been existing on MREs for fourteen days, and I want something greasy."

"Can you believe West eats that shit for fun?"

Riggs smirks. "I can believe anything when it comes to the Bitches. They're... unique."

"Smooth," I laugh. "They really stepped up for me these past weeks. I don't know what I'd have done without them." Shit, I'm getting choked up just thinking about it. Those guys made a home for me here. They welcomed me with open arms and open hearts.

He slides his arm around my shoulder, giving me a squeeze. When we reach the car, Riggs stows his ruck in the backseat and pushes me up against the side of the car. He grabs my shirt and pulls me in for a kiss. His lips crush mine with bruising force, and hummingbirds take flight in my stomach. He rubs his tongue along mine, and it goes on and on. When he finally backs off, I'm breathless and dizzy—and hard as a fucking rock.

"Let's get drive-thru," I suggest, rearranging my junk.

He grins wickedly. "That's a great idea."

We eat as we drive so that our hands are empty when we pull up in his driveway. Riggs kicks the door shut behind us, dropping his ruck on the floor, and backs me up against the wall. My back hits hard, but I barely feel it. The center of my focus is the feel of his mouth claiming mine. He suckles on my tongue, lapping at my mouth in the most seductive, cock-hardening way. His teeth nip my bottom lip, his fingers dig into my scalp. Riggs works his knee between my thighs, widening them, and I can't stop myself from grinding against his thigh.

I can barely pull my mouth away for a second. "We gonna do this on the floor again?"

He grins against my lips. "I want you in my bed this time."

"*Our* bed," I breathe into his mouth.

Riggs pauses and stares into my eyes. "*Our* bed," he agrees.

We strip as we make our way to the bedroom, kissing and handsy the whole way. We fall onto the mattress in a tangle of limbs, laughing. I touch him everywhere, my hands mapping his body, relearning the feel of his skin.

His hot gaze rakes down my body, pausing to take in my hard cock. Riggs's eyes grow wider, and he licks his lips. "You can't imagine the filthy things I dreamed of while I was gone."

"Oh, yeah?" I stroke myself, giving him a show. "What did you do about it?"

"Not much," he laughs. "I shared a tent with five other guys."

"Kinky."

"I'm not *that* kinky," he grins, bending his head down to my lap. His mouth hovers over the head of my cock, breathing warm, moist air over my sensitive skin. A shudder licks down my spine, making my balls draw up tight.

"You gonna suck it, or just think about it?"

His eyes glint with mischief and his tongue snakes out to lick my slit. It tickles, but more than that, it's the sight of it that turns me on. He slathers my cockhead with spit before taking me inside his mouth, using his lips to spread the saliva down my shaft. The easy glide feels like heaven. If he would just touch my...

He swipes the dripping saliva with his finger and rubs over my hole. *Oh yeah, that's it. Touch my ass.*

The tip of his finger breaches my rim, and I bear down, forcing more of it inside of me.

"Christ, you're tight."

The feeling of his finger sliding in and out of my ass, brushing my inner walls, and tickling my gland makes white-hot sparks of desire unfurl in my stomach. I find myself bucking my hips to set a faster pace.

"You want it that bad?" His grin is wicked.

"Dying for it. But not your fingers; I want your cock."

"Let me open you up first," he murmurs, sliding a second finger inside of me.

"Ungh, fuck." He's killing me, bringing me to the edge with each stroke. "Just give me your cock. Don't care if it hurts at first."

He laughs a little, sliding his fingers from my hole. "Gonna make you regret that, soldier." I toss him the bottle of lube from the nightstand, and he drizzles it over his cock, smearing it with his fist. "Lay on your side," he orders, bending my right leg slightly so it doesn't cramp. He grasps my left ankle, spreading my legs wide, and kneels between them. Riggs positions his cock at my entrance, rubbing the slick head back and forth over my hole. He stretches me slowly, taking his time, and the slow burn is the sweetest torture. "Tight and hot," he hisses.

He sinks another inch of his length, and I clench my muscles around his shaft, making him gasp, his eyes going wide. I love watching his hips snap back and forth as he fucks into me, love watching his pleasure play across his face. Riggs doesn't hide a thing from me, and he doesn't hold back, not that I want him to.

His eyes zero in on where our bodies are joined, watching his cock plunge into my ass. I wish I could see it. I'd probably come if I could see it. His face and chest flush with sweat, his breath becoming labored as he picks up the pace, slamming into me. Every nerve ending in my body comes to life, registering pleasure and sensation. I reach for my cock, and he watches as I stroke it for him, my eyes burning with hunger.

"Fuck me harder," I beg, chasing my orgasm.

He drops my ankle, grabbing my thighs instead, so he can thrust harder, deeper. "Come on, soldier, show me how you scream. Let me hear you."

"Riggs, fuck!" He takes me over the edge with him, pulling out of my ass to shoot his load over my stomach. It mixes with my seed, pooling on my skin in a thick white puddle.

Riggs drops my legs and hovers over my body, laughing and breathless. He pops a kiss onto my lips, but I hold him there, deepening the kiss. My tongue swipes inside his mouth, and he opens for me.

"That was…"

I cut him off, supplying the right word he's looking for. "Incredible? Epic? Unforgettable? The best sex you ever had?"

Riggs chuckles. "All of that and more. Let me get you cleaned up, and then you're mine."

"You wanna go another round?" I ask, smacking my ass to entice him.

"Not yet," he grins. "I just want to climb under the covers and cuddle with you all night long."

That sounds even better.

When we're settled under the covers, still naked, wrapped up in each other, Riggs strokes his fingers through my hair. His lips touch my neck, my shoulder.

"I'm so sorry about your mama. I'll never forgive myself for not being here."

"It wasn't your fault. It wasn't like you wanted to leave." His foot rubs up and down my calf. I love the feel of his warm body pressed against mine, his now-soft cock resting against the crease of my sore ass. "Did you mean it when you said you're done with the reserves?"

"My contract expires in three months. I may have one more weekend away, but that would be it. I'm done. No more war. No more fighting. I want to focus on helping and healing the aftermath of destruction instead of contributing to it."

"Is that all you want to focus on?"

He hums against my ear, tickling the shell with the vibration of his voice. "I want to focus on us, on building a life with you."

"I want that too. I missed you so badly when you were gone," I admit, tears threatening to burn my eyes. The grief hits me at the oddest times; when I least expect it. It's like a roller coaster of emotion, hitting me with highs and lows that completely drain me.

He wraps me in his arms tighter. "I wish I could give them back to you—your mama, Brian."

"That's okay. If I had to choose anyone in the world, I would still pick you. As long as I have you, I have everythin' I need."

This is one of the hardest things I've ever had to do. Harder than jump school or basic training, harder than kissing my mama goodbye when I left for boot camp. Brewer's door is open, but I knock on it, anyway.

He looks up with a smile on his face. "Come on in, Rhett." He takes off his glasses and sets them on his desk, coming to his feet. "Did you need to talk?"

"Only if you have time." I almost hope he doesn't.

"I have all the time in the world for you. Why don't you sit down and get comfortable?" He gestures toward his couch, taking the seat across from it. "You look like you have something on your mind, so I'm just going to sit and listen."

"I don't really know where to begin." I can already feel my emotions welling up inside of me, threatening to spill through my eyes.

"Begin wherever you want; we'll circle back around, eventually."

My stomach churns with anxiety. "I was angry when I lost my best friend. So angry, and it was just so unfair. He was young, he was a good man, and he was just doing his job, tryin' to help, fightin' for his country." My voice breaks on the last word, and I swipe my tears. "I thought I'd never get over that, and maybe, maybe I won't. But losin' my mama? I'm not even angry, I'm just... I'm heartbroken. I'm so lonely and sad and lost that I can't even pick myself up off the floor and put the pieces back together long enough to be angry."

I can't see clearly through my waterfall of grief. Brewer hands me a box of tissues, and I blow my nose. "I miss her so much—her stupid movie quotes, the smell of her cookin', the sound of her slippers shufflin' as she moves around the house, tidying up. I thought, you know because I can't jump no more, that she would see me as a failure." I swallow hard, my throat feeling dry and sore. "Like I didn't amount to nothin', but when

I realized I could fly and started workin' toward my pilot's license, I dreamed of taking her up in the air someday and showin' her the world from the angle I love best, above the clouds. I thought maybe she could see what I see when I jump, she could feel that rush, and maybe finally understand why I love it so much. I thought she'd be proud of me and how I amounted to somethin'. I'm never gonna get to show her that now." My sobbing and sniffling are out of control as I go through tissue after tissue, making a dirty pile of them in my lap.

He props one leg over his knee, resting his hands together. Brewer always looks relaxed, like he's never in any rush. He makes you feel as if you're the most important thing he has going on. I guess it's a good quality in a therapist.

"Do you really believe that?"

"No. Maybe. Rationally, no, but if she can't see it, then it's all for nothin', it don't even matter."

"Of course it matters. And I'm not convinced she can't see it, either. What do you think?"

This is what therapists do; they turn shit around on you so that you have to answer your own questions. It's fucking infuriating. If I had all the answers, I wouldn't fucking be here.

"I think... I think she always knew I was capable of doin' my best, and she always believed in me." I'm losing my grip again, and a fresh round of tears rushes forth. My face feels hot and I'm a little dizzy from the pressure in my head. "I think she can see me and she knows."

"I think you're right," Brewer agrees. "I think your mama and your Brian, my Eric, Riggs's Mark, and Nash's Victor, I think they all see us very clearly. I think they're watching over us, and I think we're going to be alright."

All I can do is nod as I blow my nose again. Brewer reaches for the wastebasket beside his chair and hands it to me. I chuck my snotty pile of tissues into it and reach for another.

"Is this normal? Am I supposed to fall apart like this over the littlest thing?"

"Your grief isn't little, nor is your love for your mother. Grief is fluid, and it's immeasurable. One person's grief isn't the same as another's. Whatever you're feeling is completely normal and you have to give yourself time and space to feel your feelings." He gets up and crosses the room to the small fridge next to his desk, grabbing a bottle of water. Brewer hands it to me and I gulp it down gratefully. "The more you talk about it, the more manageable it will feel. Grief is a heavy burden to carry, and it helps to lighten the load by sharing it with others."

He's right. I know he's right. But every time I talk about her, I cry again, and I'm fucking sick to death of crying. Sick of it.

"My door is open to you anytime, or we could schedule a regular visit. Twice a week, maybe?"

Oh, he's good. Real good. "Sounds good, Brewer."

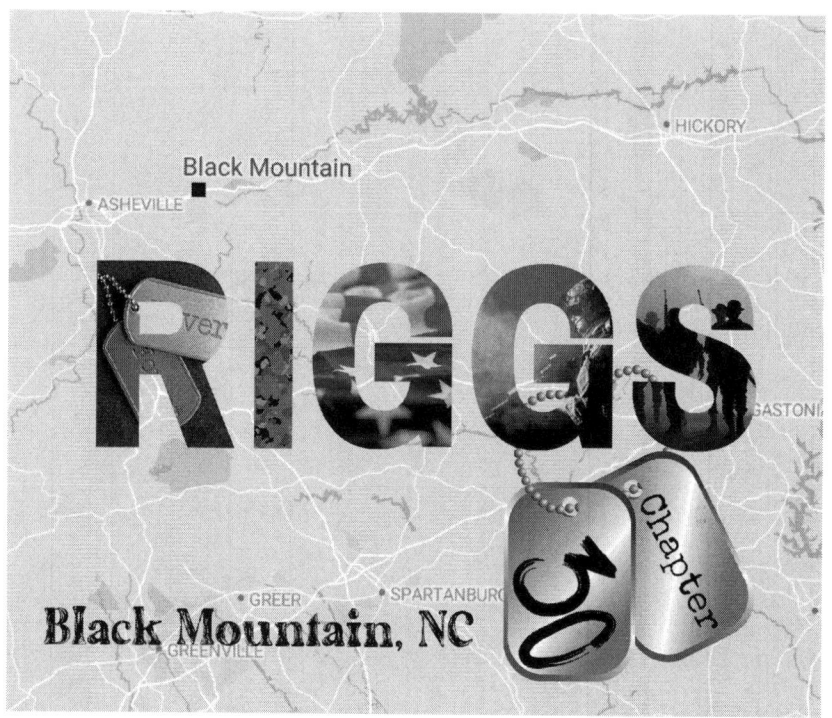

RIGGS

Black Mountain, NC

Chapter 30

RHETT WRAPS his arms around my waist, sliding his hands into my back pockets to squeeze my ass. He smiles up at me, a real one, not the fake ones he pastes on when people ask how he's feeling.

"Thank you for puttin' this together for me. She would have loved it."

I scan the back deck, taking in the brightly colored mylar balloons, the golden velvet cloth that covers the food table, and best of all, the life-size cardboard cutout of Retta and Clark Gable that I photoshopped to look like they were standing side-by-side.

There are fresh-cut flowers on every table, and the *Bluetooth* speaker plays Bruce Springsteen's greatest hits.

"My mama sure did love Bruce. The Boss," he recalls fondly. "She always said he could wear a pair of jeans well. I think that meant she liked his ass," he chuckles.

I can't help but laugh with him. Retta was a piece of work.

I tried to copy her recipe for pecan blondies, but when Rhett took a bite and smiled kindly, chewing cautiously as his face pinched, I knew I'd missed the mark. I'm sure the Bitches will devour them since they have nothing better to compare them to.

It's amazing how large our circle has grown—our family, really. In addition to all the many Bitches and their partners, Liza is here, a whole host of Rhett's buddies from base, and even a few of the guys from Serenity House. Brian, from the Tavern, and Rand. The fucker is staring at me. Great, he's making his way over here.

"Thanks for comin'," Rhett says cordially. "It'll feel good when all this is behind me and we can get back up in the air again."

"Making you feel good is my top priority."

He smirks at me as he says it. This motherfucker knows exactly what he's doing. He waits until Rhett walks away before saying what he's really thinking.

"It's a good thing you finally got your head out of your ass. I thought I would actually have to sleep with him to get your attention." He chuckles, having no idea how close he is to serious bodily injury. I have an urge to put him in an urn right beside Retta.

"You purposely fucked with me?" *Why?*

"Of course. Did you really think I would poach your territory right in front of your nose? Even I'm not that stupid."

"That's debatable," I grunt. "But what was the point?"

His gaze follows Rhett as he poses for a picture with his mama and Clark. "Because he's perfect for you, and I know how much you love to think you always have to do the right thing."

Asshole. He had me figured out all along. "Well, after careful consideration, I realize doing Rhett is the right thing." I smirk and before I walk away to join Rhett, I flick Rand off. The sound of his laughter follows me, and I shake my head. His time will come, and I hope it's messy and humiliating for him.

I hope I get to witness it firsthand, and I'm glad he turned out to be a real friend in the end.

I approach Rhett, West, Brandt, Nash, and Mandy, fixing them with a hard look.

Nash laughs. "Oh, come on. You're not still pissed, are you?"

"You drew dicks all over my clipboard with a hot pink *Sharpie*. I can't get them off!"

West snort-laughs. "Big, hard, hairy dicks with balls."

Brandt laughs as well, and Mandy covers his mouth. Rhett tries to maintain a straight face, but cracks under pressure. "I told them not to, babe, but they wouldn't listen."

"I'll never ask you jerks for another favor, ever." How hard is it to help out in the gym while your buddy is deployed? Fucking fuckers.

"Did you like that thingy I knitted to attach your pen to your clipboard?" Rhett asks. He's incredibly proud of the simple chain stitch, his first attempt at knitting.

"You mean the pink *Hello Kitty* pen? I love it. I also find it hard to believe the only yarn you could find was a sparkly purple."

They crack up harder, doubled over and wheezing, and I shake my head. *Idiots.*

Tex joins our group. "Nice shirt," I tease, trying not to laugh. His red T-shirt says, *'Frankly, my dear, I don't give a damn.'* Why he paired it with blue velvet pants is anybody's guess.

"Thanks, it's one of my favorites. I finally have a place to wear it. Can you take a picture of us?" he asks, sidling up to Loretta. Tex motions for Mandy to stand next to Clark. He pulls a fake mustache from his pocket and sticks it to his upper lip. "Now I look like a proper gentleman," he grins.

"You sure you don't want to stand next to Clark?" I ask. Tex is not only a flirt, but if he wants to look like a gentleman, maybe he wants to stand next to a cardboard one and cop its ass.

"Not at all. Suave and debonair aren't really my type." He eyes Mandy up and down like the big guy is definitely his type. "I prefer more rugged men."

Mandy blushes, but is saved from being laughed at when I prompt, "Say cheese."

"Come on, McCormick," Jax shouts, drawing our attention. He's standing at the buffet table, peeling back the covers on the casserole dishes. "What the fuck is this shit? I thought you said you brought a sausage and noodle casserole."

"I did!" McCormick insists.

"This is hot dogs and ramen! It looks fucking disgusting. Is this mayo?" he asks, bending down to sniff it.

Jax should have known better than to assume McCormick could make a decent casserole. What was he thinking? I recover the dish and point down the table. "There's lasagna and Swedish meatballs over there. Help yourself."

"Riggs saved the day!" he shouts, and everyone cheers.

Stiles butts the line. "I'll eat your meat, McCormick." He digs the serving spoon into the casserole dish and scoops out a heaping portion. My stomach clenches when it makes a wet, squelching sound as it hits his plate. *Better him than me.*

"Hey, listen up!" Rhett calls, stealing the crowd's focus. "I want to tell you about my mama before we all say a last goodbye to her, together."

I check with him, raising my brows questioningly, but he smiles and nods. He's good. He doesn't need me to back him up. *Yet.*

He picks up her urn from the table where it rests with honor beside a gorgeous bouquet of daffodils and lavender, her favorites. The urn he chose looks as if he slathered it in glue and dropped it in a vat of glitter and rhinestones.

It's the gaudiest thing I've ever seen. Retta would love it.

"Can you believe they had this in the discount section?" he asks, smiling and showing off his arresting dimples. "I got lucky! Anyway, I want to start by sayin' thank you to each and every one of you for standin' by my side and supporting me these past weeks. I know for a fact I couldn't have done it without all of you. Now, about Loretta Marsh. My mama was cut from designer cloth, if that cloth was made of beaded sequins. She loved shiny pretty things. Used to say the brighter, the better, makes it easier for God to see it from heaven. She was tacky, but she had class. She liked to eat dinner in her robe in front of the TV, but she had manners. She was loud, but she spoke like a lady. She'd rather burn in hell than let a stranger walk away feelin' unwelcome. She was the kind of mama other kids were jealous of, the kind they wished their mamas were like. I don't remember a single year she didn't bake pecan blondies for the church and school bake sales. She donated our best clothes for the rummage sales. Retta Marsh was a class act. She was one of a kind. The Lord will never make another one like her. If you met her once, you'd never forget her. She was always..."

His voice quavers, and my body tenses, waiting to see if he loses it. Liza hurries to his side, squeezing his hand for strength. "It's okay, Marshmallow, go on."

"I miss you, Mama," he sniffles. I can feel his pain, the tide of emotions about to drown him. He's so damn strong. Tenderhearted, but strong. "We didn't have much, but we had each other, and that was more than we needed. My mama was happy with that. She would fantasize that our little farmhouse was the Tara Plantation. She used to tell me that I was the love child of her and Clark Gable and that any day he would knock on our door and come fetch us and sweep her off her feet. She even told me I looked like him, that I had his hair. I hope she's cozied up in his bed right now in heaven, not missin' me at all."

Rhett's moist eyes find me, and his strong shoulders sag under the weight of his sadness. I rush forth and slide my arm around his shoulders, supporting his weight.

"It's hard to believe I only met Loretta only a few weeks ago. Feels like I've known her for years. That's the kind of woman she was, the kind who just makes you feel welcomed and loved and familiar. Rhett's right, she was cut from designer cloth, and she was one of a kind. It's easy to understand why I fell so hard for her son after seeing what kind of woman she was. She'd have loved this party and been so thrilled to see all of you here today to help us celebrate her life. I left a little book on the table there. If you have a memory of Retta, please be kind enough to share it with us and write it down. Retta might be gone with the wind, but she'll never be forgotten. Thanks for coming out."

As soon as I'm done speaking, Rhett buries his face in my shirt, sniffling softly. I can feel the tremor shake his body and I squeeze him tighter. "Love you, soldier."

"Love you," he mumbles against my chest.

The guys place a large gift box on the table next to the book. I take the urn from him and place it beside the bouquet and the box. "Open it, babe."

"What's this?" Rhett asks, looking over the box curiously.

He lifts the lid and his eyes go wide. "This is what ya'll were workin' on? The super-secret project I wasn't allowed to see?"

Brandt helps him pull it out of the box. "Yup. We all helped."

"Each of us made a square," Mandy adds.

The hand-knit afghan is a colorful hodgepodge of different stitch patterns and types of yarn, yet it all blends together perfectly, a lot like the Bitches.

"Thank you," Rhett says gratefully, wrapping it around his shoulders.

My guy wears his heart on his sleeve, my total opposite. I couldn't love him more.

RIGGS
Chapter 31
Epilogue 1

"WARM UP ON the treadmill before we get started."

Rhett is dressed in black athletic shorts and a black T-shirt that says, '*This is BS! Bitches With Stitches,*' in a circle around a ball of yarn. Straight from the BALLS gift shop. We have trained nonstop for this day.

I'm so fucking proud of you.

Rhett has been relentless in his pursuit of recovery. Swimming, running laps around the lake, hitting the gym almost daily. I'm sure he's worked out a lot of his grief on these machines.

The shorts show off his scars, which have now faded to a dull pink. He's a warrior, he's fucking badass, and he's mine.

As he loosens up, the Bitches crowd in. Their loud voices can be heard from down the hall, joking and bickering.

"Yo, Rhett. You gonna kick ass today?" McCormick asks.

"Maybe he'll kick yours," Jax snickers.

"Everyone wants to touch my ass," McCormick grins.

"I'm good, thanks," Brandt insists, shaking his head.

McCormick shoves him playfully. "Your loss."

I bring the peanut gallery to a close with five words. "Let's go, Rhett. It's time."

Rhett hops off the treadmill and joins me at the parallel bars. He cracks his knuckles, twisting his neck from side-to-side to work out the kinks.

"Listen up!" I say to the crowd. It's not just the Bitches, but Margaret Anne, Brewer, and some of the other vets who regularly work out with Rhett. "This isn't just any Warrior's Walk, this is *THE* Warrior's Walk. This soldier is a fighter. I met him a little over a year ago, on the battlefield. It was one of the worst days of his life." *Aside from losing his mother, and the day they evicted him from Bragg.* "And he braved it like a warrior. I almost lost him that day, but there was something special about him. I saw it immediately." *I looked into his eyes and fell hard for him.* "And I vowed to do anything necessary to make sure he pulled through."

Rhett has this dopey grin on his face that makes his dimples pop and I just want to kiss it off his lips.

"Weeks later, I showed up in his hospital room in Womack and told him he had two choices. He could either do nothing, stay where he was, and rot, or he could get off his ass, move here, and let BALLS put him back on the road to recovery." I grin at him and wink. "I'm glad he made the right choice."

The guys cheer and clap. "My BALLS saved me," Nash laughs. "Can we put that on a shirt, Margaret Anne?"

Shaking my head, I grin and tell him, "Rhett, show us what you've got."

He waits for the whistle before bracing his weight on his arms and using his hands to walk the length of the bars without letting his feet touch the ground. His upper body strength has improved greatly during his training and he traverses the ten feet fairly easily, but slightly winded.

"Next up, the mile. Can you beat your best time of 9.4 minutes?" He once told me his fastest time before his injury was 6.3 minutes, and it was 17.8 when we started training this spring. He's come a long way.

Rhett looks determined. "I'm gonna smoke that time." He winks at me and hops on the treadmill.

He starts off quick almost as if he's sprinting, trying to cover as much distance as he can in a short amount of time. His breathing is labored and besides the slapping of his sneakers hitting the treadmill, it's the only sound in the room.

"8.7," I call out, letting him know it's all or nothing if he wants to beat his time.

Rhett screams a primal cry and pumps his arms, gaining speed as he runs balls-to-the-wall. He slaps the stop button on the machine when it beeps, alerting him that he completed the mile.

I click my stopwatch. "9.2 minutes!"

The crowd goes wild, shouting and clapping. Rhett glows

with positivity. God, he's gorgeous. *I'm so going to fuck him tonight.* Even if he's worn out, I just need him to lie there. I'll gladly do all the work.

"Next up, suicide lunges."

The guys groan, but Rhett rallies. "Nah, I've got this."

He starts at one wall and gets into position, widening his stance. When I blow my whistle, he takes off, falling into a deep lunge with each step.

"My legs are fuckin' burnin' like hellfire," he calls out when he's halfway across the gym. He's crossing the shorter side, not the longer length of the room.

"You got this, soldier. Make me proud." Watching him struggle past the limits of his endurance makes my heart clench tight. This is what I gave it all up for, and Rhett makes it so worthwhile. All my patients do. This is where I belong, helping to heal the aftermath of war after these vets sacrificed everything, and then some. I don't belong on the battlefield, feeding the cycle of war. I belong here in the gym, with these brave wounded warriors. This is my true calling.

Rhett glances back, shooting me a tired grin. "If it doesn't hurt, you're not doing it right," he shouts, gritting his teeth.

Hearing him repeat my motivational sayings is just making me hard. This is *not* the best time to get turned on.

He's nearly to the wall when he falters, his knee buckling, but Rhett catches himself and straightens. "Fuck!" He hisses through the burn of his muscles and pushes on. When he reaches the wall, he lunges forward in a rush and smacks it hard. "Shit, yeah!"

I can't help myself. I hug him hard, crushing his sweaty

body in my arms. "I'm so fucking proud of you." He doesn't care who's watching, Rhett smacks a quick hard kiss on my lips. "Last test of endurance is the pool," I call out.

We cross the hall to the indoor pool. I'm behind Rhett, and I can't help but notice the way his ass sways in those thin nylon shorts from his slight limp. As if he can feel my eyes on him, Rhett glances over his shoulder. "You checking out my ass?"

You bet I am. "I'm not ogling your ass. I'm analyzing your gait. It's my job."

Rhett laughs loudly and Brewer comes up behind me, clapping me on the back. "You were totally checking out his ass."

The crowd gathers around the perimeter of the pool and Rhett wastes no time. He kicks off his shoes and jumps right in, clothes and all. When he surfaces, he shakes his head, sending a spray of water in my direction.

"You're going to swim a half-mile, which is fifteen laps. Touch the wall on each pass. Your fastest time so far is twenty-two minutes."

"You got this, Rhett," Nash calls. Their little synchronized swim team training has really paid off.

Rhett's body is lean and toned from all his running and swimming, and I can't keep my hands or my eyes off it lately. Not that I ever could. I'm addicted to him like a drug. All he has to do is give me that look or show off his dimpled grin, and I pant after him like a dog in heat.

He takes off when he hears my whistle, pushing off from the wall. He cuts through the water with ease, kicking his legs and sluicing his arms. It's almost beautiful to watch.

With less than a minute left on his best time, I call out,

"Twenty-one minutes," to spur him on. He's on his last lap. There's no way he isn't going to make it.

"Ten, nine, eight." I count down the seconds remaining on his best time. "Seven, six..." Everyone loses their shit before I can say five. Rhett touches the wall and jumps halfway out of the water, fist-pumping the air.

West stands at the edge holding a little brass bell. Rhett pushes up and rings it hard, signaling the completion of his long, hard journey in rehab. The guys jump in the pool, fully dressed, and dog pile him.

I'm grinning so hard my cheeks hurt and my eyes grow wet. Why did I ever think he was a wildcard? Rhett Marsh is a sure fucking bet, just like he promised me he was.

He climbs out of the pool and hugs me, sopping wet, and then we're falling into the pool. "My clipboard," I yell in a panic, tossing it over the edge to safety.

"The chlorine is good for it, might make the *Sharpie* dicks fade," West cracks, sending a volley of water in my direction.

I grab Rhett and crush my lips to his. My warrior. My lover. *My whole life.*

"So fucking proud of you," I breathe against his lips. "And that ass is mine tonight." I squeeze his ass and he hops up, wrapping his legs around my waist and deepening the kiss.

"You bet."

RHETT
Epilogue 2

RIGGS REACHES to turn the radio down. "Do you still feel like you made the right decision?"

"Yeah. I could never live in my mama's house again. Not without her there. I have no desire to live in Ruston ever again, really. My family is all gone and buried, my mama was the last of her kin. There's nothin' left for me there anymore. I belong with you, in North Carolina."

"So you allowed Brewer to turn it into another halfway house for vets?"

"It's really the best use of it. He's puttin' Miles in charge of running it. You know, my mama would love that, a house full of good people workin' to make their lives better. She loved a full house."

"Miles is a good guy. Former Marine, he served eight years. He's quiet and closed off, but every time I've met with him, I get the impression he's a really nice guy. A responsible guy. I think he'll make a great house manager."

"What happened to him?"

"I don't know his story, you'll have to ask him."

"Let me ask you a question. It's been eatin' away at me for a long time, and whenever I think to ask, I always get sidetracked."

"You can ask me anything," he offers.

"Last year, when my mama was in the hospital, right before you left for Louisiana, she said she wanted to talk to you, alone. I stood out in the hall with Mandy wonderin' what was so damn important and secretive that she couldn't tell me." Riggs grins at the memory. "What did she say to you?"

"She told me that apples make you constipated, that your grandfather's wedding band was tucked away in a mason jar in the cellar for safekeeping, and that she wanted you to have it someday when I married you."

"What?" My heart skips a beat.

Riggs just chuckles and continues. "And she told me to promise I would always look after you. That I would always keep you safe, and she made me promise to name our first son Clark." He reaches for my hand and rubs the fourth finger where I hope to God my grandfather's ring sits someday.

"And you made a promise to her, even way back then, when we weren't sure about our future?"

"You weren't sure?" he asks with a shit-eating grin. He's fucking with me. "I was sure. Besides, there's no way I wasn't going to keep a promise to your mama. She'd haunt my ass forever." Riggs pulls into the gated parking lot beside the airfield. "You ready, soldier?"

"Hell yeah. I've waited a long time to get you up in the air. The last time we flew together was..." My face tightens with the pain of the memory. *Afghanistan. The day I lost everything.*

"Hey," he reaches out to grip my chin, turning my face toward him. "This is going to go a whole lot smoother. You're the pilot, and I'm the passenger, and we're about to spend two weeks together on an unforgettable adventure."

Swallowing past the dark shadow crawling its way up my throat, I nod and paste a smile on my face. "Right. It's going to be unforgettable."

I climb out of his truck, opening the passenger door to reach for my bag. A small box containing a portion of my mama's ashes is tucked away inside.

"Not so fast." Riggs halts me. He grabs a bag from under his seat and hands it to me.

"What's this?"

"Just a little something every pilot should have."

Curiosity gets the better of me and I peek inside. "Get the fuck out!" Lifting the brown leather bomber jacket from the bag, I turn it over, checking out all of the patches. "Get all the way the fuck out! This is sick."

The Bitches with Stitches logo is sewn onto the right shoulder. The BALLS logo is beneath a bar patch bearing my last name on the breast. The 82nd Airborne patch graces the back of the jacket, and it looks badass. The leather looks vintage, even though it's brand new, and I know without a doubt it will fit perfectly.

"Thank you." I can't stop smiling as I hug him.

"You can thank me tonight by wearing it without anything else on."

"Fuck that, I'm wearing it right now." I hand him the bag and slip into the jacket. The leather feels thick and heavy on my shoulders, which is necessary when I'm up in the air, where the air is thinner and colder.

"You look like a proper fly-boy," he smirks, fingering the lapel. "So, remind me again where we're going?" He grabs his bag from the back and locks the truck. We head to the security gate, hand-in-hand.

"First stop is Marietta, Georgia. We're gonna spread some of my mama's ashes at the *Gone With The Wind* Museum at Brumby Hall. Then we're stoppin' in Ruston to check on the house. I've got to pick up my mama's cookie jar from the kitchen."

"The one that's a replica of Scarlet and Rhett?"

I already put him out by displaying my mama's sparkly urn on the mantle above our fireplace, and I know he's even less excited about the cookie jar. "That's the one," I grin.

"I can't wait," he lies with a smile. "It's going to look lovely next to the coffeemaker."

"Exactly! And then we're headed to Fort Worth to visit Brian's grave."

"Is that the last stop?"

"Wellllll," I hesitate, giving him the side-eye. "We may have one last teeny-weeny stop to make."

"Hopefully something that doesn't involve dead people? A Bed and Breakfast? We could rent a boat and go fishing."

"That sounds great! Unfortunately, it's not quite what I had in mind." I show my security badge to the security guard and he waves us in.

"What did you have in mind?" he asks warily.

"There may be a small *Gone With The Wind* museum about thirty minutes south of Fort Worth."

Riggs stops dead in his tracks. "You're kidding," he says, but from the look on his face, he knows I'm not.

Damn, this would have landed better if I had blown him while he was driving here.

"Is it your mission to visit every single *Gone With The Wind* museum in the United fucking States?"

Maybe I should play the sympathy card. "I only wish I'd taken my mama while she was still alive. She would have loved it."

Reluctantly, his face softens. "Think of it this way. When you spread her ashes there, she'll get to stay forever. She'll never have to leave."

I squeeze his hand. "Thank you for understandin'."

Riggs snorts. "Please, you owe me big time. Now, take me up in your plane and show me what it is about flying that makes your dick so hard."

I cup his cock and pull him close for a teasing kiss. "Not nearly as hard as you make it."

Saying goodbye is so hard... so don't do it! **Grab Hotdoggin', Stiles's and McCormick's story. Hotdoggin'** is the first of three Bitches With Stitches novels.

Grab your very own signed copy from my website, or the book box, along with tons of must-have **Bitches and Scars and Stripes merch!**

Follow me on Patreon for bonus content, giveaways, and early chapters!

ALSO BY RAQUEL RILEY

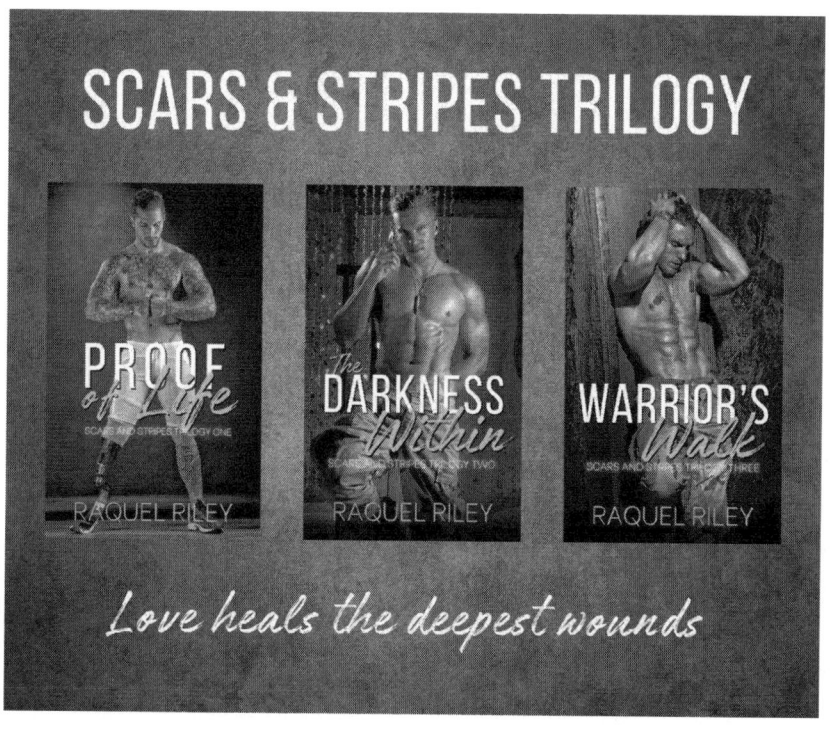

Proof Of Life is available in Ebook, Audiobook, Paperbacks, and Hardcover

The Darkness Within is available in Ebook, Audiobook, Paperbacks, and Hardcover.

Warrior's Walk is available in Ebook, Audiobook, Paperbacks, and Hardcover.

ABOUT THE AUTHOR

Raquel Riley is a native of South Florida but now calls North Carolina home. She is an avid reader and loves to travel. Most often, she writes gay romance stories with an HEA but characters of all types can be found in her books. She weaves pieces of herself, her family, and her travels into every story she writes.

For a complete list of Raquel Riley's releases, please visit her website at **www.raquelriley.com**. You can also follow her on the social media platforms listed below. You can also find all of Raquel's important links in one convenient place at **https://linktr.ee/raquelriley**

ACKNOWLEDGMENTS

Tracy Ann, your feedback is so appreciated! You help me shape these books and characters and give them life. Thank you for your continued praise and support of my stories and for keeping me organized.

Dianna Roman, your sense of humor breathed life into this book. Thank you for the Bitches and the BALLS, and for the inside look at life in the Army.

Also, thank you to my **ARC/street team** for your insightful input and reviews and outstanding promotion.

I can't forget the **Secret Circle!** You four keep me accountable and sane and cheer for every one of my accomplishments, both big and small.

Marsha Adams Salmans I'm so grateful you came into my life. Your dedication to my reader group and promotion of my books is invaluable. Thank you for being irreplaceable and amazing!

Christy Ragle, thank you for the sensitive and valuable insight into mental health, addiction. I love working with you.

THE Emerson Beckett, I can't write anymore without spitballing at lunch or on the phone with you. XOXO

Last, but never least, thanks to my family for being so understanding while I ignore you so I can write.

Made in the USA
Monee, IL
05 November 2024